FLOWERS IN BLOOM

APPLETON VALE BOOK 2

ANNELI LORT

For Henry, Hector, Cora, Juno and Dee who make me laugh every single day.

ACKNOWLEDGMENTS

I've been behind the scenes at some of the biggest sports and entertainment events on the planet, worked closely with A-list celebrities and sports stars, and attended too many VIP parties to count, so it is only right to thank those men and women, the media, agents, managers, and in-the-know Hollywood friends who have helped me out along the way. There are too many of you to name, but I am grateful to each and every one of you for sharing your experiences, insight and gossip. Without you all I would have had to spend many more hours researching my subject matter!

Writing is very much my thing, but editing and proofreading are not, and that's when it's time to call in the professionals.

Once again, I am in awe of the skills of my marvellous editor Alison Bridge. With a simple wave of her magic wand she can turn a good manuscript into a great one.

When it comes to critiquing my work, Freda Jackson is happy to point out the holes and inconsistencies that are always lurking within a first draft. Whilst I get bogged down in the detail, she sees the whole picture and has no compunction in telling me where and how I can improve things. The only annoying thing is that she's usually right!

Cathy Longhurst is THE grammar queen. She is also one of the best people I know and I am thankful for her unconditional friendship, complete confidence in my literary abilities, and her willingness to grammar check five hundred pages.

My beautiful cover was created by the incredibly talented Louise Mizen Ferguson, who is an awe-inspiring artist of the highest calibre. She can take a very sketchy brief and turn it into a reality – one that is better than I could ever have imagined.

Finally, to Hector for keeping me company late into the night as I write. You fill my life with laughter and love.

PROLOGUE

"*B*reathe. Just breathe," she murmured in the split second before the camera went live. The moment was almost upon her and she didn't know if she was terrified or excited. She hadn't seen him in what felt like forever. The producer counted down in her ear, and then it was time.

"Welcome back to the red carpet coverage of the 2018 Academy Awards, live from the Dolby Theatre in downtown LA," she said. "Over the last few hours we've brought you interviews with Hollywood's elite and the ceremony is now just half an hour away. We're waiting for the last big name to arrive - a certain British Oscar nominee who is THE hot favourite for 'Actor in a Leading Role'.

"The atmosphere is electric. Everyone is genuinely excited, and I can tell you from my own perspective that not only is it a privilege to be here, but also jaw-droppingly surreal!" She flashed a dazzling smile at the camera. "Stay with us and we'll be continuing our exclusive coverage right after the wonderful Carole Kirkwood brings you the weather."

"And you're out," the producer announced in her ear.

Everywhere she looked, stars were dressed up in their Oscar finery, their jewels matching the brilliance of the afternoon sunshine. The air was thick with gushy superlatives as the great and good of the movie world greeted each other on the way into the theatre, there to celebrate excellence and to applaud the triumph of the individual. It was a glorious technicolour fantasy that was both intoxicating and bizarre.

She heard a roar from the fans, tightly packed into viewing galleries with a great vantage point of stars rolling up in a never-ending fleet of limousines. She knew it had to be him. He was the only big name left to arrive. She gulped back her nerves and attempted to compose herself.

"You're back in thirty seconds," the producer said into her ear piece.

Suddenly, her skin prickled and the hairs on her arms stood on end. She could feel his eyes on her, burning through to her soul. She swung around and they came face to face.

"Why are you here?" he gasped. He bent down and brushed his lips against hers. She felt her knees buckle and gripped his arm to steady herself.

They were unaware of the commotion they were causing. Every television camera on the red carpet was now fixed firmly on them. Reporters from networks across the globe were commentating on a much-anticipated reunion and speculating on what it was that had driven them apart in the first place. It was complete pandemonium.

Oblivious of their surroundings, their eyes were locked in an unbreakable gaze. They hadn't seen each other for months, but she instantly knew his feelings for her had not diminished in the slightest. In that moment, she realised how cold and painful her heart had been without him.

He whispered something in her ear, kissed her cheek and was quickly ushered towards the theatre.

She watched as he walked away, silently willing him to check his mobile phone before disappearing from view. He fished it out of his pocket at the very last second and stopped dead in his tracks as he read the text. He turned and sprinted back towards her.

"Seriously?" he asked breathlessly.

"Seriously!" she smiled.

CHAPTER 1

"You're live in five, four, three, two, one," Gerry whispered into Georgiana's earpiece.

"Good morning from sunny SW19. I'm here at Wimbledon and it's the big one. Yes, it's mens' final day. I, for one, am incredibly excited. I can hardly contain myself." Georgiana grinned at the camera and millions of men across the United Kingdom swooned in front of their television sets.

"The sun is shining and there's a tangible air of excitement running through the crowds who have poured in to witness what could potentially be one of the best matches in Wimbledon history. The top two seeded players in the world are set to slug it out on the marvellous Centre Court. It's going to be totally awesome."

Gerry Rees, producer of Georgiana's segment, was grinning from ear to ear. Georgiana was gold dust as far as he and the rest of the BBC sport team were concerned. They loved her warm, engaging style of presenting, and she was single-handedly responsible for the ratings going through the roof. In what was already a world-renowned event, with millions of people watching all over the globe, she had boosted the viewing figures by almost twenty per cent.

"I'm now joined on my little perch high above Henman Hill, Murray Mount – call it what you will - by the incredible talented, insanely funny, and downright incorrigible John McEnroe." Georgiana turned to face John and grinned. "So, Johnny boy, what say you?"

For the entire hour of the show Georgiana and John engaged in a tennis match of their own, banter flying back and forth. John's style of presenting complemented Georgiana's perfectly. It was compelling viewing.

"And we're out. Great job you two," said Gerry. The show had gone without a hitch and his bosses were delighted.

Georgiana removed her microphone and earpiece and high-fived McEnroe. "That was so much fun," she grinned. "Gotta go. I'm doing a pre-record with Boris in twenty minutes. Thanks, John."

She grabbed her iPad and flew down the steps in search of former Wimbledon champion and all-round good guy Boris Becker.

Georgiana Bloom had been working for the BBC for almost four months, and she had quickly made her mark with her quirky style and ability to make her interviewees feel at ease. Even the most obnoxious and ego-driven sports stars were putty in her hands. She was honest, funny, genuine, and most importantly, knowledgeable about sport. That's what made her a rising star at the BBC. She was incredibly versatile and could hold her own in any situation.

The younger sister of world number one golfer Sebastian Bloom, Georgiana had not set out to become a star in her own right. In fact, quite the opposite. She had seen what fame had done to her brother, who'd been both darling and demon of the international press since he turned professional. She didn't want to be in the spotlight but it had come around so unexpectedly that she had been swept along by the excitement of it all.

It had started when Georgiana and her sister-in-law, Sebastian's wife Olivia, had accompanied him to the first golf Major event of that year – the US Masters. She had been accosted by the BBC's production team, short of a presenter struck down with food poisoning, to 'get behind the scenes' for the live Facebook feed they wanted to air during the tournament. She knew all the golfers, their caddies, agents, managers, and wives or girlfriends, and effortlessly delivered the requested content. She was an instant hit and had been inundated with work ever since.

She was young, just twenty-three, energetic and stunningly beautiful, and in contrast to her brother at well over six feet tall, she barely nudged five feet two. They shared the same olive-toned skin and defiant expression, as well as the rare condition of heterochromia – different coloured eyes – one a rich dark brown, the other a dazzling green, set under long, thick lashes. Her glossy raven hair tumbled down her back, and she was slim and toned from an athletic, outdoor life.

During her first broadcast, the BBC's Facebook page had gone into overdrive, receiving more 'comments', 'likes' and 'shares' than at any previous sporting event. Georgiana was on her way to becoming a star.

Georgiana sighed with contentment as the village of Appleton Vale appeared in the distance. This was her beloved home, tucked away in a sleepy corner of West Chesterton about thirty miles south of Bath, and a million miles away from the hustle and bustle of London.

She was happiest surrounded by her family, her horses and her devoted whippet, Lady. She cherished the peace and quiet of the countryside, which was in complete contrast to the life she led in London with her burgeoning television career.

She wound her way down the hill, through the rolling fields and meadows of Appleton Vale, and turned into the village. She sighed again. She never tired of the simple beauty of the chocolate-box cottages and pristine green. The moss-covered church of St. Saviour's and its ancient oak tree were at the heart of the village, and the pretty Tearooms, shop and post office, and the Riverside Inn, all backed onto the River Candle that wound its way through the county.

The sight of her friends and neighbours going about their business made her smile, and she waved to Dee Dee and Jane as she passed their Tearooms.

Driving through the electric gates and stone pillars that marked the entrance to the Bloom estate, she made her way down the sweeping, tree-lined driveway with horses grazing in the post and rail paddocks on her left. On the right was manicured parkland studded with ageing trees at their most magnificent in the summer heat.

Her ancestral home, Appleton Manor, was a four-hundred-year-old stone-built mansion. It was vast but not forbidding, impressive but not overwhelming - a tremendous sense of history poured from the building.

She pulled up outside the main entrance to find Hattie overseeing the safe delivery of some unexpected guests. Hattie Banbridge was the family's long-standing housekeeper. She had practically raised Sebastian and Georgiana when their mother died and their father, William, had left them in search of his spirituality.

She was an integral part of the family. Almost sixty years old with greying hair, she was short and plump, warm and charmingly sensible, and also fiercely protective of both Sebastian and Georgiana.

"Did you know about this?" she asked Georgiana.

"Oh yeah. Sorry. Forgot to tell you they were coming today." She grinned cheekily and was instantly forgiven.

The driver nodded his greeting and proceeded to unload a pair of flea-bitten and undernourished donkeys.

"Oh, goodness." Hattie was shocked at their appearance.

"Don't worry. A month or two with me and they'll be back to their best," Georgiana smiled and took their lead ropes from the driver. She rummaged around in her bag for a packet of polos and was pounced upon by her greedy new charges.

"I'll be off then," said the driver as he hopped back into the horsebox.

"Thanks," Georgiana shouted as he drove away.

"So, do they have names?" asked Hattie as she gave one a scratch on his neck.

"This one is Bray Davis Junior," Georgiana grinned and nodded to the brown donkey. "And this is Kong. As in Donkey Kong," she explained when Hattie looked confused.

"Oh. Right, then." Hattie took a lead rope from Georgiana. "Best get them to the yard. I don't know why he had to deliver them to the front door."

"Well, these little darlings are here now so let's get them into a lush paddock and introduce them to everyone else." Georgiana was quite taken with Bray and Kong.

"By everyone else I assume you mean the ones with four legs?" Hattie smiled. "It's always the animals first with you."

After they had settled the new residents in their field and introduced them to the horses either side of the fencing, Georgiana and Hattie linked arms and made their way back across the estate to the house.

"What time's the happy couple back?" Georgiana asked. Sebastian and Olivia were hopelessly in love and expecting their first child together.

"Sebastian said around six o'clock," Hattie replied, looking at her watch. "I hope Liv is ok. What possessed her to get on a plane when she's eight months pregnant is beyond me."

"It's called a babymoon," Georgiana grinned. "Their last hurrah before their lives change forever."

"Well I still say they shouldn't have flown."

"It was only the South of France and they had the jet on standby the whole time. A perk of being loaded," she laughed, and pushed open the door leading to the Manor's kitchen. She was greeted by her Whippet Lady who wound herself around and through Georgiana's legs, delighted that her mistress had returned.

A second later she was ambushed by Ace and Hector – her brother's Great Dane and Olivia's Golden Retriever – who came skidding into the kitchen and almost sent her flying.

"Bloody hell you lot," she cried, steadying herself on the table.

"They've been running around like lunatics all day," Hattie rolled her eyes.

"That's because they know we'll have a full house tonight. All of us under one roof." She bent down and threw her arms around all three dogs and was rewarded with slobbery kisses. "Right, I'm off home to sort a few things out and I'll be back before six to help you with supper."

Georgiana had moved into a cottage on the far side of the estate when Olivia and Sebastian had married. It was her own little piece of heaven and she loved living there.

"Ok darling, see you later," Hattie called as Georgiana swept out of the door with Lady hot on her heels.

Minutes later she was inside her two-up two-down Victorian cottage, renovated by Sebastian the previous year. It had stood empty for over a decade and had needed a complete overhaul. She and Olivia had gone to town on the interior design and furnishings, and both had felt a little guilty about how much of Sebastian's money they had spent.

It had been worth every penny. Georgiana had selected a sleek grey kitchen fitted with all mod cons, and there was under-floor heating installed throughout. Sebastian had added a huge oak framed extension to the back of the cottage, which was where the kitchen was now housed. Tri-fold doors and floor-to-ceiling windows flooded the room with light that warmed the honeyed oak frame and beams.

She kicked off her boots and settled down on the vast leather sofa as Lady snuggled her head into the crook of Georgiana's arm, sighing contentedly.

"Shall we have a little snooze, darling?" she asked Lady who was already half asleep. "I'm shattered. Three weeks away from you is three weeks too many." She kissed her and was asleep in seconds.

CHAPTER 2

"*A*nd CUT. Great job everyone, that's a wrap." The director jumped out of his chair and slapped his assistant on the back. "We're done. See you all at the party tomorrow."

Dan whooped and threw his arms around his co-star. "Thought we'd never get through that last scene."

"I know, right?" Amber grinned and dusted herself down. They were both caked in mud and soaked to the skin. "I'm freezing."

"I know something that'll warm you up," Dan replied with a cheeky grin.

Ten minutes later, they were locked together in the shower of his trailer indulging in one last tryst before Amber had to return to the reality of her husband and children.

Dan Flowers had swapped London for Hollywood ten years' ago after an acclaimed BBC drama television role in which, as a virtually unknown actor, he had dazzled audiences with his emotional and captivating performance.

He had also attracted the attentions of the UK's female population with his looks and charm. Dan was well over six feet tall with a slim, toned body, and smooth, sun-kissed skin. His hair was luscious dark chocolate and his eyes a startling Prussian blue. He wasn't classically good-looking – he had a slightly crooked nose and a scar on his left cheek courtesy of several childhood scrapes – but he resembled a young Paul Newman and women loved him.

Helped financially by his parents, he made the move to LA with the knowledge that he had a little breathing space to get his big break before the money ran out. He attended three or four casting calls every day for two months before he happened to be in the right place at the right time to attract the eye of Hollywood's number one casting agent, Tiffy Boyd.

Tiffy had specifically been looking for a new, young and exciting British actor to take a plum lead role, and Dan fitted the bill exactly. She wanted to offer him the job on the spot but had held back, deferring to the producer and director who were both keen to see more established actors take up the main characters.

She had been right, and after several audition recalls, he was offered the leading role of Orion Powell in a new action series directed by Randy Brewster, the genius behind a score of box office smash hits.

That first film had broken all records for an action movie in its first weekend, and Dan had been in constant work ever since. His first pay cheque paid back his parents and moved him closer to the Hollywood elite, his second bought his dream home where he still lived, high up in the hills overlooking Los Angeles. His neighbours were like a who's who of the movie world, and his circle of friends was mostly made up of British ex-pats, actors, producers and directors he had worked with over the years.

He'd also had a string of lovely companions including Amber, who purred, "I'm sorry it's over," as she lay in his arms one last time, adding, "Remember, what happens on set stays on set."

Dan grinned. "Your secret is safe with me."

"Don't get me wrong," Amber replied quickly. "I love Jack and the kids, but I just couldn't resist you."

Amber Angelo was Dan's senior by fifteen years' and an established actress with a string of hit movies to her name. She was a generous co-star, offering advice and help to her younger leading man. She was kind, funny, and drop dead gorgeous, and had relished the affair with Dan as much as he had.

"Don't you think it's time you found yourself a girlfriend?" she asked as she got dressed. Her driver was waiting outside to take her home. "You're not a kid anymore and there are literally thousands of women waiting to throw themselves at your feet."

"I'm only thirty, you cheeky cow," Dan laughed. "I'm saving myself for the right woman."

"And whilst you wait for her you're screwing me?" Amber stood with her hands on her hips. "I mean it. You're a great guy Dan, don't waste yourself on groupies or married women. Find someone you can love."

"Yeah, yeah." He rolled his eyes and watched as she finished getting dressed.

"I'll miss you," Amber dropped a kiss on his head. "It was fun while it lasted."

"Certainly was," he smirked.

"You're coming to dinner next week, right? It's our tenth wedding anniversary."

"Yeah. If that's not too weird," Dan replied.

"Why would it be?" she laughed, and left the trailer.

When Amber had gone, Dan switched on the television and was immediately faced with a photograph of himself and well-known LA socialite Mariella Tovey. The daughter of one of the most successful producers in Hollywood, she had a reputation for bagging and bedding the hottest actors around.

He laughed out loud when the presenter suggested they were an item. He knew Mariella, but they had never slept together and he had no intention of doing so. He admired her father's work and didn't want to ruin any chance he had of collaborating with him in the future by indulging in a one-night-stand with his daughter. The photograph had actually been taken at a party a few months ago – but the voyeuristic public wouldn't care about that.

He listened as the presenter voiced her opinion on his love life.

"Does this man ever stop? Mariella Tovey is the latest in a very, very long line of Hollywood women to fall under the spell of the charming Mr Flowers. Will this relationship last the distance or do we chalk it up to another notch on the action star's bedpost?"

Dan threw a shoe at the television. He was starting to get fed up with the constant speculation and false rumours about every woman he was photographed with. He had been linked with more than two dozen of his co-stars over the years, as well as suffering plenty of kiss-and-tell stories made up by women he had rejected or never even met.

When he first arrived in Hollywood he hadn't given it a second thought. He was grateful for the publicity and flattered by all the attention he received from the female population of LA. He was twenty years old in a new city and country, and he went a little wild for a short time. He enjoyed sex and the company of women, but the older and more established he became, he found himself less tolerant of the vacuous models and actresses he had slept with in the early days.

"She might be right," he muttered as he got dressed. "Maybe it's time I settled down."

CHAPTER 3

*D*an stepped out of the lift into the swanky, ultra-modern offices of his management company, Walter Moreaux Enterprises – WME. There was a flurry of activity at reception as the female staff jostled for position to be the first to greet him.

"Good afternoon Mr Flowers," one of them purred. "I'll let Mr Manolo know you're here. He asked that you head directly to his office."

"Thank you," Dan smiled and walked down the corridor, chuckling to himself at the commotion he had caused. He reached Vinnie Manolo's office just as he was coming out to meet him.

"Hey man." Vinnie slapped him on the back. "Come on in." He motioned for Dan to take the seat across from his desk.

Vinnie's office was a shrine to his first love – the movies. There were original film posters on the walls, signed photographs from some of the biggest stars in the world, and several dozen pictures of him with his clients.

"You said you had some papers for me to sign?" Dan hated the business side of his profession. He had no interest in investments, stocks and shares, or moving money off-shore, but Vinnie insisted he ran through every minute detail to keep him fully informed.

"Yeah." He slid several documents across the table. "Just a signature on this one, and I need you to read through the small print on the contract from Universal. The lawyers have approved it but you need to know the finer details."

"Can I take it home to read later?" he asked Vinnie. "I'm completely wiped out. I only popped in as I was passing on the way back from the lot."

"Sure thing. But I want your feedback or approval tomorrow morning as they're pushing hard to get it signed." Vinnie shifted in his seat. "Did you read that script I dropped over last week?"

"Give me a bloody chance, Vin. I've literally just finished shooting." Dan glared at him. "I gave it the once-over and it's a load of bollocks. Why did you even put it in front of me?"

"Because I promised Steve Tanner that I would show you. He's super-keen to get you on board." Vinnie sat down opposite Dan. "But now you've read it, you can throw it in the trash and you'll be able to answer him honestly when you see him next week."

Dan laughed. "You think it's awful as well?"

"Sure. And I knew you'd never go for it," he grinned.

Vinnie was a great agent, one of the best in the business. Of Italian descent, he was short, olive-skinned and stocky. He started out in the mail room as an ambitious eighteen-year-old in love with movies. Now, almost three decades later, he was a partner at WME and handled a dozen of the most talented and famous actors in Hollywood.

Dan had popped up on his radar when a British friend raved about his performances in his BBC drama series 'All in at One'. He was a complete unknown, but Vinnie had a gut feeling about him and pushed him hard for his signature on a management contract almost as soon as he moved to LA. Vinnie had been Dan's agent for a decade and they were close friends as much as business partners.

"Are you two done?" Maddie Mitchell, Dan's smart, sassy, well-connected publicist stuck her head around the door. "I need to run through the schedule."

She handled all of his media appearances, interviews and press conferences, and was his last line of defence. She had been in the business of promoting movies and their stars for over twenty years and was known as a real ball-breaker. She was dedicated, loyal, and excellent at her job.

"I told the studio PR guys we'd work around the movie promotional schedule, but there are a few things that have come up I think you'll wanna do." She scrolled through her iPad and turned it around to show Dan.

"Really?" Dan feigned surprise. "Inside the Actors Studio wants me?"

Maddie laughed. "I don't know why you're shocked. You may not believe you're a big shot but the rest of the world thinks you are." She looked at Vinnie. "Tell him, will you?"

"He knows he's hot property," Vinnie smirked. "He's just yanking your chain."

Maddie rolled her eyes. "Of course, it's all down to me. Nothing to do with your acting abilities."

"Ha. You keep telling yourself that." Dan grinned. "What else?"

"The Late Late Show. James Cordon wants you on." Maddie

consulted the diary. "I just don't think we can get it in right now."

"Shame." He shrugged his shoulders. "I like James but the studio is running me ragged and I'd rather pull back on everything else for now. Apart from Actors Studio. I really want to do that."

"I'll confirm with their people," Maddie replied. "There's a few magazine interview requests – GQ, Men's Health – and the usual demands from the British tabloids."

"They can all bugger off." He stood up to leave. "Are we done?"

Maddie nodded. "Yeah, all good with me. I'll email you later."

"Vin?" He asked his manager.

"I want to bring you up to speed on a new project. I think it could be what you've been looking for but the script isn't completed yet," he replied.

"Then let's talk about it when it is." Dan called over his shoulder as he walked out of the room.

He was desperate to get home. He had been surviving on a few snatched hours of sleep a night for almost a month. Now the film had wrapped he could relax for a few weeks before the press junkets to promote the opening of his latest movie, 'Catch me when I fall'. He would be attending premieres in six different countries over a two-week period, with TV and radio appearances in each one.

The traffic was unusually light for downtown LA and he was back home in the Hollywood Hills in no time. The electric gates swung open and he wound up the driveway towards his house. It was a modern, white-washed mansion set in five acres of lush grounds dotted with palm trees and a stunning array of colourful blooms. There was a vast swimming pool, a tennis court, and a movie screening room. The interior was sleek, modern and masculine.

Dan sighed as he walked through the front door. He missed England, and his family and friends, but he had made a good life for himself in LA. Along with Vinnie, his agent, he had a great team around him – Ken Kennedy, his personal manager; Maddie, his publicist; and Coby McBride, his incredibly camp but efficient PA. He had grown close to a few other actors and industry bods, but he still hankered for home.

He grabbed a beer from the fridge in the kitchen, kicked off his shoes and flopped down on the sofa with the television remote control in hand. After a few seconds of channel surfing he found the BBC's coverage of Wimbledon and settled back against the deep-filled cushions to soak up a taste of home. The day's action was being covered in the highlights show and he was struggling to stay awake to watch. As his eyes were closing he caught a glimpse of the presenter and was immediately struck by her luminous on-screen presence.

"Hello, beautiful," he muttered before finally succumbing to his exhaustion.

CHAPTER 4

"You look amazing," Georgiana said as she hugged Olivia. "Did you have a lovely time?"

"It was complete bliss." Olivia had a faraway, dreamy look in her eyes.

Georgiana grinned. "That good, eh?"

"I know the doctor said it wasn't good to fly at this stage of the pregnancy but I'm so glad we did. The villa was in the middle of nowhere and it was so beautiful. We didn't want to come back." She sighed and smiled to herself.

"If it hadn't been for wanting our baby to be born here we would have stayed forever," Sebastian said as he followed Olivia into the Manor. "It was very special."

He dropped the bags, pulled Olivia into his arms and planted a gentle kiss on her lips.

"Oh God," Georgiana groaned, and covered her eyes." You two make me sick."

"Just you wait," Olivia laughed. "When the right man comes along you'll feel the same."

"She's too young to settle down." Sebastian was disapproving. There was a fifteen-year age gap between him and Georgiana. "There's a whole world out there she needs to see before she ties herself down to some unworthy chap."

"Oh, don't you worry," Georgiana grinned. "I have no intention of finding Mr Right. I'm having way too much fun for that."

"I don't want to know." Sebastian shook his head and walked across the hall towards the kitchen.

"He's only being protective," Olivia whispered, making sure Sebastian was out of earshot. "So, what's been going on while we've been away? Any gossip?"

"Dunno." Georgiana shrugged her shoulders. "I've mostly been in London the last three weeks, two of those at Wimbledon."

"Yes, we watched you every night. You were just brilliant. We're both so proud of you darling." Olivia's eyes welled with tears. "Sorry, it's the hormones. I'm crying at everything at the moment."

"Well, we'll have to see if we can get Sebastian a sponsorship deal with Kleenex then, won't we?" Georgiana joked. "Let's go and have supper. Hattie's laid on a feast. I think she's been missing having anyone to cook for, although I had noticed the dogs and horses are looking slightly more rotund than when I left."

"Where is Hattie, anyway?" Olivia asked.

"She muttered something about needing some herb or another and dashed off," Georgiana replied.

Sebastian was opening a bottle of wine when Hattie returned.

"Hello gorgeous," he crossed the room and kissed her on the cheek.

Hattie giggled and swatted him away. "Sorry. Had to get some rosemary from the farm shop, ours has some kind of disease. Well, don't you both look well!" She smiled and gave Olivia a warm hug. "How's the little one?"

"He's fine. Cooking along quite nicely," Olivia grinned and ran her hands over her swollen belly.

"She," Sebastian corrected Olivia. "It's a girl."

"I don't know why you don't want to find out the sex," Georgiana said. "Everyone else does these days. Makes painting the nursery a whole lot easier."

"We don't want to know," Sebastian said. "We want it to be a surprise."

"Well we'll find out soon enough," Olivia rubbed her belly again and was rewarded with a kick from deep within.

During dinner Georgiana quietly took her family in. She loved being with them in her ancestral home - they weren't together enough, she thought. There was so much laughter and joy that echoed throughout the ancient building these days that it was a wonderful place to be.

She was delighted that her brother and Olivia had found each other after experiencing such misery with their previous partners. Looking at them, she knew she wanted to find the same all-consuming love that they had.

CHAPTER 5

"*I*'m sorry Mr Hampton, but we can't reach Camilla right now," a faint voice crackled down the phone line. "Do you want to leave a message? She's due back in a week or so."

"A week? Bloody hell, woman, I could have died and been buried in that time," a slightly deaf Edward Hampton, owner of the ultra-exclusive Riverside Golf and Country Club, shouted down the line. "Yes, all right then. Please ask her to kindly call her father when she has a chance between single-handedly saving the starving population of Africa and negotiating peace in the Congo." He didn't wait for a response.

"Bloody do-gooders," Edward muttered. He struggled out of the chair behind the vast mahogany desk in his office overlooking the first hole of Riverside's championship golf course. He was advancing in years and wanted to get out of the club while he still had some life left. At seventy-six, Edward was a shadow of the man who had once rowed Oxford Blues before taking over the family business, but he could still command a room. He had thick white hair, crinkly sparkling blue eyes, and a tanned, ruddy complexion that told of a lifetime outdoors.

A widower, Edward had been alone since the passing of his beloved wife, Pamela, seventeen years previously from 'surgical complications'. His daughter, Camilla, had dealt with her grief by signing up as an aid worker, disappearing off to Africa almost the moment the funeral had ended. Her brother, David, had joined the army. A month into David's first tour of Iraq his patrol vehicle hit an IED and he was killed instantly. Camilla returned to Appleton Vale for David's funeral and had not been seen there since.

Quite why she had abandoned her father so completely was a mystery to Edward. They hadn't fallen out, and as far as he was aware there simply was no other reason for her turning her back on him. He had been trying to get in touch with her for a month now, and even though he was positive what her response would be, he still felt he needed to tell her about his decision to sell The Riverside and retire gracefully. She wouldn't want the club, it would only be a burden to her, an outrageous example of capitalism gone mad in her eyes.

The Riverside had been in Edward's family for six hundred years. It was a three thousand-acre sporting estate with a magnificent and commanding mansion in the middle of its land. Hidden behind row upon row of trees, bushes and ancient walls, the main entrance was accessed through forbidding wrought-iron gates that shielded the ultra-exclusive club from the rest of the world. The club's crest, a golden eagle, had been fashioned into the gates and there were raised flowerbeds either side studded with immaculate topiary.

As well as the eighteen-hole championship golf course, there was a tennis complex that had been cleverly developed using several ancient outbuildings as indoor courts, with a further six all-weather outdoor courts and a pavilion.

Inside the mansion there were luxurious locker rooms, sumptuous lounges and a billiards room. There was also a

Michelin-starred restaurant, a more relaxed club house lounge, a wood-panelled bar, and a covered terrace that swept the length of the rear of the house overlooking the gardens and the final hole of the golf course.

Edward loved The Riverside but he was ready to move on and he had run out of time. Caleris Global was pushing him for an answer and he was ready to give it. The Riverside Golf and Country Club was indeed for sale.

CHAPTER 6

"We'll be landing in forty minutes, Mr Clayton," the stewardess informed him. "Is there anything I can get for you? Coffee? Breakfast?"

"No. Thank you, Sheila. What are you gonna do with your time in London?" he enquired. Shelia had been looking after Wyatt on his private jet for more than five years along with her husband, Chip, who was the plane's pilot.

"Windsor Castle this time, sir. We never quite seem to get out of town when we're here," she replied.

"That's because we're never here long enough," he smiled. "I'm glad to be so accommodating this time." Sheila smiled warmly and headed back towards the flight deck.

He leaned back in his leather seat and stared out of the window, watching the lush green fields and rolling countryside of England creep into view. Forty-two-year-old Wyatt Clayton was tall, lean and blonde, with a charming dimple right in the middle of his chin. His eyes were cobalt blue and his mouth was set in a permanent, almost mocking grin. He was the epitome of the all-American hero.

Born and raised in a Texan trailer park, he had fought tooth and nail to get away from his abusive father and make something of himself. Almost a quarter of a century later, he was founder and CEO of one of the largest property acquisition companies in the world – Athos.

He had never been married - although he had come close with his most recent ex-girlfriend, Ashley - and had no children. His focus had been on making a ton of money and a success of his life. He had a reputation as a playboy in America but he didn't care. He liked female company and had a voracious appetite in the bedroom.

His money, looks and power made him one of America's most eligible bachelors, but he had a ruthless, mean streak that made him dangerous to get tangled up with - in business or pleasure.

He glanced at his emails one more time, checking to see if his right-hand-man, Bobby Garnett, had sent through the contracts for a huge chunk of land in Montana he had recently purchased.

Bobby had not let him down. The contracts were in order, approved by his legal team, and ready for his signature.

Another email caught his eye. It was from Emily Delevigne at Caleris Global – a company he had recently hired for its expertise in commercial property acquisitions in the UK.

Mr Clayton,

I'm pleased to inform you that I have found several properties that meet with your requirements.
I have attached the particulars for your perusal, and look forward to discussing them with you on Thursday.

Kind regards,
Emily Delevigne

He didn't need to look at them. There was only one property he was interested in and he had hand-picked Caleris, and in particular Emily Delevigne, because of it.

He had purposefully flown through the night to make the most of his time in England - his schedule was tightly packed. As well as his meetings with Caleris Global, he had a handful of investors to woo and a couple of dinners to attend. He had also somehow managed to squeeze in a visit to his tailor on Savile Row - a biannual necessity.

The jet touched down at Farnborough private airport precisely on schedule, and Wyatt's driver was waiting to collect him at the VIP arrivals suite. An hour later, he was in his hotel in London standing under a steaming shower washing the flight off his weary body. He was in fantastic shape, still as fit as he had been in his twenties thanks to a strict regime of running and working out. His appetite for business was unending and he was still as hungry for success as he had been all those years ago. However, it seemed like every new project came with even bigger issues than the last, and it was a constant battle to cross the finish line.

"This is gonna be one hell of a fight," he muttered.

CHAPTER 7

"*M*r Clayton? I'm Emily Delevigne." Emily walked across the lobby with her hand outstretched. "Welcome to Caleris Global. Did you have a good trip over?"

Wyatt shook her hand. "Yeah, it wasn't too bad. Let's get right down to it. Show me what you got." He followed her into the lift that took them to her fifth-floor office.

They sat down and Emily pushed a small pile of documents across the desk. "This is the one you're going to be most interested in, I think," she tapped the top of the pile. "It has everything you asked for. It's an old, impressive building, with an excellent reputation, fantastic facilities, a great deal of privacy, and some very, very rich members. It has been in the same family for many generations."

Wyatt smiled. He knew a whole lot more about The Riverside Golf and Country Club than he was ever going to let on. The property Emily had earmarked was one he and his investors had wanted for a very long time, but it had always been out of his grasp – until now.

Emily continued: "It's not even on the open market yet. It's somewhere I'm already rather familiar with as my closest friend lives in the same area and her husband is a high-profile member of the club."

"And?" Wyatt narrowed his eyes.

"And I think there may be a little local opposition to your plans. But I'm sure that's nothing new for you." Emily had done her research. Wyatt had fought many battles in the cutthroat commercial property market and had a reputation for being one of the most ruthless businessmen in the world. Nothing ever got in his way.

Wyatt studied the brochure for a few minutes, and then flicked through the details of the other properties Emily had matched to his requirements. He returned to the first.

"No. This is the one. Get into it and report directly to me next week when I'm back in the States. I'm flying to China tomorrow afternoon. I've got big plans for this place, so the members can either get on board or find another club." Wyatt stood up to leave. He kept his meetings brief and to the point. "I'll expect a detailed report, I don't want any surprises."

After Wyatt had left her office, Emily picked up the phone and dialled Olivia's number. She answered almost immediately.

"How spooky, I was just about to call you," Olivia laughed.

"How are you feeling?" Emily asked.

"Fat and revolting," Olivia replied with a sigh.

"Don't be ridiculous. You've looked amazing throughout the whole bloody pregnancy." Emily laughed. "Is it ok if I come down for a few days? Is Sebastian home or away?"

"God yes, get yourself down here immediately. He's playing in the Irish Open and he promised Rory he'd go to help with a charity thing. I didn't have the heart to ask him to stick around just to keep me amused, but I'm dying of boredom. You'll be a most welcome guest."

"I'll head straight down after work, so should be with you by supper time. Oh, that's my call waiting. Got to go, see you later." Emily rang off.

In Appleton Vale, Olivia hung up the phone and waddled towards the kitchen. The baby was due in a couple of weeks and she couldn't relax or get comfortable. No-one had been more surprised when she and Sebastian had found out they were expecting a baby. It had most certainly not been in their immediate plans. Delighted as they both were, a tiny part of Olivia wished that they could have had more time to be just the two of them.

Everything had happened so quickly - her life over the past few years had been a whirlwind. She had arrived in Appleton Vale to ghost-write Sebastian's autobiography two years ago and had never left. Sebastian had been at his very lowest and on the verge of self-destruction when they met, having seen his game, his reputation and his personal life torn apart by the tragic loss of his first wife Ellie and her daughter Lizzie. He had fallen in disgrace from the very top of the world golf rankings, and his status as a one-time global sports icon had altered so dramatically that he had become poison to all but a few close friends.

Meeting Olivia had turned things around for him. They had an undeniable attraction from the start, but it took months for either of them to realise that they had fallen in love, and many more to actually admit it. Sebastian had bared his soul in a daring 'Piers Morgan Life Stories' interview in a bid to capture her heart. It worked, and just days later he triumphed in The Open Championship - his fallen star was restored.

Sebastian continued to mine his rich vein of form, fighting his way back to World number one, much to the delight of his fans around the globe. He won a third US Masters title in April, bringing his Majors total to five, and firmly re-established himself as the best in the game.

By contrast, his wedding to Olivia had been a quiet affair, with only a handful of close friends and family invited to Appleton Manor for a beautiful service in the grounds of the estate. It had been an unseasonably warm October morning, with the sun low in the sky and leaves dancing on the trees, when they had promised to love and honour each other for the rest of their days.

And now, as Olivia eased her heavily pregnant body onto one of the chairs around the battered pine kitchen table, the back door opened and Georgiana came bounding in with Lady at her heels.

"Morning, Liv, any movement?" Georgiana asked as she was ambushed by Hector and Ace.

"If one more person asks me that I'm going to explode," Olivia snapped. "Don't you think I'd tell you if it were time?" She rubbed her belly and sighed.

"Ok, no need to bite my head off," Georgiana rolled her eyes and patted the dogs. "Sebastian wants an hourly update, you know what he's like."

"Well he shouldn't have bloody well gone away then." Olivia yelled in frustration.

Georgiana pulled a chair up alongside Olivia and took her hand, "I know it's hard with him being away, but to be fair, you were the one who pushed him to go so you can't really complain."

"God I'm sorry, I'm being a bitch. What the hell is wrong with me? I'm supposed to be all happy and relaxed, and I'm anything but." She sniffed into a tissue.

Georgiana gave Olivia a hug and got up to turn the kettle on.

"There's nothing wrong with you, it's just your hormones. How about a nice cup of tea and some of Hattie's ginger cake?"

"Don't you have better things to do than babysit me?" Olivia smiled weakly.

"No. You're the family priority right now. I have to be at the yard for the farrier in an hour, and then I'm off to London for a production meeting and staying the night. Hattie will be back from Fiddlebury by then to take over."

"Take over? You make it sound like I need a constant nursemaid." Olivia's attempt at a joke sounded hollow.

"Don't be silly. The baby could come any day now, and the last thing you need to be is alone. Sebastian will go nuts if one of us isn't with you if it happens while he's away, and none of us wants to incur that particular wrath." She rolled her eyes.

"Well you don't need to worry, Emily's coming down tonight. She'll be here for supper."

"That's nice, shame I'll miss her," Georgiana replied as she stuffed a large chunk of cake into her mouth. "I'm meeting some friends at The Duke."

"Christopher?" Olivia couldn't keep up with her sister-in-law's prolific dating.

"Nah, dumped him last month," she grinned. "He was way too needy, I just want to have a bit of fun."

Olivia laughed. "Don't let Sebastian hear you say that again. He just can't handle the thought of you dating."

Georgiana shrugged her shoulders and flashed a cheeky smile. "What's he going to do about it?"

"So, who's the new lucky man then?" Olivia was keen to find out more.

"There isn't one, yet!" Georgiana laughed. "Let's just say I'm open to offers for someone to sweep me off my feet."

"That sounds exciting. I doubt Sebastian could even lift me up right now, let alone sweep me off my swollen feet." Olivia looked down at her feet and wrinkled her nose in disgust.

"You've got nothing to worry about, silly," Georgiana said. "He's one hundred per cent in love with you, he worships the ground you walk on. Wait till the baby comes, he'll be showering you with gifts. Ooh, maybe even some enormous diamonds," she grinned.

Olivia laughed. "You mercenary little so-and-so."

"Just saying." Georgiana raised an eyebrow.

"Just saying what?" Hattie asked as she struggled through the kitchen door with a dozen shopping bags.

"Nothing you need to know," Georgiana giggled, and jumped up to help her.

"Oh deary me, that was an effort," Hattie puffed. "I've never seen Fiddlebury so busy for a Tuesday. I got those bits you wanted Olivia, although I'm still failing to understand quite how bananas, caramel syrup, ham and fried onions can blend together to form anything even remotely edible."

"Trust me, it's satisfying every craving I have right now." Olivia began delving in the bags for something else to eat.

"Bloody hell, you've just had two slices of cake. How many are you eating for?" Georgiana instantly regretted her joke when Olivia shot her an evil look.

Olivia sighed. "I look revolting anyway so what's another few pounds? Maybe that's why Sebastian was so keen to get away from me?"

"Now you're just being ridiculous," Georgiana retorted. "He didn't even want to go - you pushed him. If you want him here, just call him. He's got the jet on standby and he'll be here in a flash." Olivia's fluctuating hormones were starting to jar. "Now, stop being so bloody obtuse and go and relax. Read a book, take the dogs for a stroll, do something, anything," she urged.

Hattie backed her up. "Yes, why don't you go and relax in the study and I'll bring you some more tea."

"I'm pregnant, not a bloody invalid," Olivia snapped and waddled out of the room. leaving Hattie and Georgiana looking at each other and rolling their eyes.

CHAPTER 8

*I*t was nearing midnight in the ultra-exclusive private members club The Duke in Knightsbridge, and Georgiana was thoroughly enjoying herself.

The Duke had been open a year and Georgiana had been a frequent visitor since its launch. She liked the atmosphere. The average age of the membership was thirty-five which created a young and vibrant feel. It was, however, designed and furnished in the style of a traditional gentlemen's club with ornate wood panelling, sweeping staircases and beautiful art-deco lighting and furniture. The basement had been turned into a nightclub, dimly lit with private booths dotted around the edges of the room, and a gleaming mirrored bar running the length of one wall.

The eyes of every red-blooded man in the club were fixed on Georgiana. Oblivious to the attention she was attracting, she whirled around the dance floor, her moves perfectly in time with each pulsating beat. In four-inch Louboutins and an impossibly tight dress that barely skimmed the top of her thighs, her outfit left nothing to the imagination.

"A real little firecracker, isn't she?" JJ Proctor nodded in Georgiana's direction and grinned at Wyatt.

"You don't say." Wyatt had his eye on the raven-haired beauty dancing with utter abandonment. He knew exactly who she was.

"Georgiana Bloom. Baby sister of Sebastian Bloom, the golfer. Christ, she's hot." JJ was almost drooling.

"Yeah," Wyatt watched as she floated off the dance floor towards the bar.

"They both lucked out in the beauty stakes, huh? She's the new darling of BBC Sport." JJ said. "Would you like to meet her?"

"Sure thing," Wyatt replied.

JJ and Georgiana were on first name terms, both having spent more time in The Duke than either would care to admit. He was also Olivia's best friend Emily's boss. He cornered Georgiana at the bar where she was chatting to a group of friends.

"Georgiana, please excuse me, but I have a friend who's interested in making your acquaintance. May I bring him over?"

"Hey, JJ. You and I really have to stop meeting like this, people will talk," she laughed and took a sip of champagne. Glancing over his shoulder she locked eyes with Wyatt and was instantly drawn to him. "Sure, bring him over. The more the merrier." She was attempting to sound nonchalant but her stomach was churning. The way the incredibly attractive stranger was looking at her was unnerving.

JJ beckoned for Wyatt to join them.

"Georgiana Bloom, may I introduce you to Wyatt Clayton."

Wyatt stepped forward and offered her his hand in greeting. "Charmed to meet you, Ms Bloom."

"Oh please, call me Georgiana," The second their hands touched her heart skipped a beat. "And what brings you to our shores, Wyatt?"

"I'm here for business, but I may just stay for you." He amped up the charm, fully aware of her immediate attraction to him.

Georgiana gulped and was lost for words. She fiddled with the hem of her dress, finding it impossible to look at him.

"Let me buy you a drink. I'd like to get to know you better. Come with me." He took her hand in his and led her to a booth away from prying eyes where he knew he would have her full attention.

Once inside the booth he closed the privacy screen, sat down and turned to face her.

"You're the most goddamned beautiful woman I've ever had the fortune to meet," he said, unabashed. "You've stirred up something crazy in me, baby."

Georgiana blushed and hung her head to hide her embarrassment.

"Look at me," Wyatt urged. "Don't be afraid, I'm not gonna hurt you."

"I'm not afraid," she whispered. "I'm just a little shocked."

"Why?" he asked.

"I've never felt like this before. I mean, I don't even know you, yet I'm so drawn to you."

"Me too, sugar." Wyatt was playing with her.

She grinned and took a large gulp of champagne.

"I don't just want your body, but it'll do for starters." He raised her hand to his lips and kissed it.

An hour later they were still locked in conversation, oblivious to the world around them. Georgiana's friends and JJ had called it a night, and now they were alone.

Filling her in on his past, Wyatt told her: "My daddy was a real son of a bitch, but grandpa was a different story." He smiled as he remembered the kindness grandpa Clayton had bestowed on him. "He said he knew I had it in me to be better, do better, and I owe a helluva lot of my success to him. I reckon he was pretty bummed out by his loser son and wanted to set me on a different path. By the time I was sixteen he'd saved every spare dime he had to give me a way outta there, and boy did I take it."

"My father isn't much better," Georgiana stated, taking another large gulp of champagne to steady her nerves. "He did a runner when my mother died and is now the founder of some weird cult masquerading as a yoga retreat in Bali." She rolled her eyes and Wyatt burst out laughing.

"A cult? What's their M.O?' He teased Georgiana and was rewarded with a dazzling smile.

"No idea. Don't want to know either. My brother does but we don't really talk about Dad. What's the point? I've only seen him a few times in the last decade or so and he holds no interest for me." She shrugged her shoulders and changed the subject. "So, tell me Wyatt, do you have some moves or can you only manage a Texan line dance?" She grabbed his hand and pulled him out of the booth towards the dance floor - "I love this song."

He followed, keeping her hand tightly enclosed in his, and pulled her into his arms once they reached the centre of the floor. She was tiny in comparison to his six feet one inch, and her head barely met his shoulders. His hand drifted down her back and came to rest just above the curve of her bottom, where his fingers began to gently stroke across the silky material of her dress.

Georgiana gasped and pressed her body against his, unable to contain the rush of desire that was spiking from her. Wyatt looked down and saw her eyes blazing with a craving that matched his own.

"Wanna get outta here?" he whispered.

Georgiana nodded.

"Let's go," Wyatt growled, unable to hide the desire in his voice. "My driver is waiting outside. "Come.""

"Oh, I intend to," she replied with a cheeky grin.

Wyatt pulled Georgiana swiftly out of the club and into his car, immediately activating the glass that separated them from his driver. Without uttering a word, she straddled him and placed a soft kiss on his lips. He groaned, and she gasped with pleasure as his hands drifted up her thighs lingering at the hem of her tiny dress, eager to explore further.

The journey from the club to his hotel was over in an instant, and he was relieved. He knew he was teetering on the edge of ripping her clothes off and taking her right there on the back seat of the car.

"You have no idea how much I wanna make love to you," Wyatt purred in her ear, holding her close as they made their way across the hotel lobby and into the waiting elevator.

Once they were in the lift that led directly to his suite, Georgiana pressed her hand against his groin and started to undo his zip. "I think I do, judging by what's going on in your pants right now," she giggled.

When the doors opened into the cavernous hallway of the Royal Suite he paused. "Are you sure about this? One step further and I won't be able to hold back. I've never wanted to have anyone more than I want you right now."

Georgiana grinned and pushed past him. "Wow, this is

gorgeous," she walked across the marble floor to investigate and Wyatt followed.

"I'd suggest a drink, but I can't wait. Come here," he scooped her up in his arms and carried her to the master bedroom, depositing her on a sumptuous four poster bed. "Take it off," he nodded at her dress.

She giggled again, "You're going to have to help me out of it, it's bloody tight."

He moved to undo the zip and slowly peeled the dress off her petite frame.

"Final chance to say no to an old man," he grinned as he stepped out of his clothes and knelt down in front of her.

She leant forward and wrapped her arms around his neck. "Shut up and make love to me, you old fool!"

CHAPTER 9

*E*mily arrived at Appleton Manor an hour before Sebastian hot-footed it back from Ireland at his emotional wife's behest. The three of them were sitting in the glorious, oak-panelled dining room Olivia insisted they used whenever they had guests. Antique lamps were dimly lit, casting fascinating shadows over exquisite portraits of Sebastian's ancestors, and candles simmered in their gleaming silver sticks from the centre of the table.

"Spit it out, Em," Olivia knew her friend too well. "You've been nervous since you got here. What's wrong?"

Emily picked up her napkin and began fiddling with it. She looked across the table and took a deep breath. "There's every chance you'll be seeing a lot more of me over the next few months."

"What? Why?" Olivia was grinning from ear to ear.

"Christ, that's all I need," Sebastian laughed. "You're a bad influence on my wife." He reached out and took Olivia's hand, raising it to his lips. "And you, my darling, you happily let her lead you astray. What's a man to do?"

Olivia grinned and placed his hand on her swollen belly. "You needn't worry, I'll be too busy with this one to get up to any mischief, and you never know, she may end up staying for good."

"So?" Sebastian urged Emily to continue.

"To cut a long story short, we were approached a few months ago by an American consortium looking to buy up an exclusive leisure property so they can break into the European market," Emily explained.

"What's that got to do with Appleton Vale?' Olivia asked.

"Well, I found a property locally that fits the bill, and I'll be working with the Americans and the current owner over the coming months to secure the deal," Emily replied.

Sebastian's interest had suddenly piqued. "What property? There's nothing for sale locally, I'd have known about it." He was slightly miffed that he was hearing this news from an outsider, albeit a friendly one.

Emily paused and took a large gulp of wine. "It's your club Sebastian."

"Don't be ridiculous," he exploded. "It's not for sale."

"It wasn't, but it is now, and Mr Hampton has agreed to talk to my client," Emily told him.

"Edward wouldn't do that. He loves the club, it's his life, his family has owned the land for generations, back to something ridiculous like the thirteenth century. There's just no way he'd sell." Sebastian was adamant that Emily had got it wrong.

"Calm down darling," Olivia begged. She turned to Emily. "Surely there must be some mistake?"

"I knew this was going to be a problem," Emily sighed. "I'm sorry, it's just business, I'm only doing my job."

"Well you should've done your fucking job far away from here," Sebastian pushed his chair back, threw his napkin on the table and stalked out of the room.

Emily shook her head and turned back to Olivia.

"Why here?" Olivia asked in a small voice. "This is our home, our village."

Emily bristled. "It's not personal, Liv. The deal's all but done anyway, and if it hadn't been my client, it would've been someone else."

"That may be so, but no-one around here is going to like it. We're happy the way we are."

"For fuck's sake Olivia, you've lived here for all of about five minutes," Emily sneered. "I thought you, of all people, would be on my side."

Olivia shifted uncomfortably in her chair and considered her response. Finally, she looked at Emily and replied: "Me of all people? Just because you're my best friend it doesn't mean I have to agree with everything you do. This will impact on my life, not yours."

Emily sighed and leaned over the table, reaching for Olivia's hand. "Please don't let this come between us."

Olivia snatched her hand away, "I should think that's entirely dependent on what you decide to do." She eased herself out of her chair and headed towards the door. "I'm going to find Sebastian and see if I can calm him down."

"That went well," Emily muttered as Olivia left the room. She poured another glass of wine and waited for her to return.

A few minutes later Hattie appeared in the doorway. "Ah, there you are. Olivia asked me to tell you she's gone to bed and that she'll see you in the morning."

Seeing Emily was upset, Hattie walked across the room and sat down beside her.

"Well, that was a bit of a bombshell, eh?" she smiled weakly. "Olivia isn't angry with you, she's just upset for Sebastian, and for the village. But I suppose we can't make assumptions until we know all the details."

"I don't even know all the details," Emily sniffed. "I shouldn't have said anything. Where's Sebastian anyway?"

"He went out. He'll calm down, don't worry." She patted Emily's hand and stood up to leave. "Why don't I make you a nice hot chocolate to take up to your room?"

Emily smiled and shook her head, "Thanks Hattie, but I'd rather take this." She reached out and grabbed a three-quarters full bottle of Chateau Margaux. "Ah, 2009, a vintage year," she laughed. "He's got more money than sense if this is what you're drinking on a regular basis."

"He's earned it," Hattie said sharply. She was fiercely protective of Sebastian.

Emily let out an exasperated sigh. "I was joking. I'm upsetting everyone tonight, perhaps I should go to bed. I don't want to be here when Sebastian gets back anyway."

"I'm sure things will look a lot better come the morning," Hattie patted her hand. "And don't worry about Olivia, she's just overly-sensitive right now."

"We've never fought in all these years," Emily sighed. "I wish I'd never said anything, but it's too late now. The damage is done."

CHAPTER 10

"*Y*ou did what?" Olivia shouted in disbelief.

"Take it easy, darling," Sebastian urged.

"Don't you dare tell me to calm down." She threw a tea towel at him from across the kitchen. "You went out last night without saying a word. You crawled into bed at three o'clock in the morning, and now you're telling me this?"

Sebastian chuckled. He loved it when Olivia was feisty, but he was concerned that her blood pressure would go through the roof if she got too upset at this late stage in her pregnancy.

"A tea towel? Is that all you've got in your arsenal?" He laughed and walked over to her. He lifted her chin with his thumb and gently kissed her lips. Olivia smiled. She could never stay angry with him for very long.

"Emily's going to be furious. You can tell her. I'm keeping out of it." Olivia poured Sebastian a mug of coffee and waddled over to the table with a glass of freshly squeezed orange juice for herself. "And don't gloat, you always have that look of triumph on your face when you've won an argument."

"Ok, fine," he smirked. "I'll be nice and business-like when I tell her. Please, just sit down and relax."

"Tell who what?" Emily was at the doorway of the kitchen, desperately seeking coffee to counter the Chateau Margaux.

"Hi," Olivia said awkwardly.

"Hey," Emily replied with a gentle smile. "And how are you this morning Sebastian?" She poured herself a coffee and sat down at the table in front of her friends.

"Rather good, as it happens," Sebastian flashed Emily his most enchanting smile.

Olivia glared at him and muttered, "You promised."

"I went to see Edward last night," Sebastian paused and looked at Emily. Her face had turned white. "We talked for quite a long time. He's Georgiana's godfather and a close friend of the entire family, actually. We had a lot to discuss."

"Oh my God, what have you done?" she rounded on Sebastian.

"You're now looking at the new owner of The Riverside, paperwork pending of course, but Edward won't back out of a deal with me. He's an honourable man."

Emily jumped up from the table, knocking her coffee cup on to the floor where it shattered into tiny pieces. "You fucking arsehole. How could you?" she shrieked.

"As you said last night, it's just business," Sebastian replied.

"Don't give me that shit. You did this on purpose. My boss is going to fucking kill me." Emily's voice was getting louder as she directed her venomous attack at Sebastian. "You really are a piece of work, you know? What Olivia sees in you is beyond me."

Sebastian smirked. "You'll never win that argument darling. I

49

guarantee that she'll side with me over you, any day of the week."

Olivia was dumbstruck. She wanted to intervene but just sat motionless, watching the argument unfold in front of her. Her beloved husband and her best friend were falling out in the most dramatic fashion, and she couldn't bear to listen to their hateful jibes any longer. She stood up and quietly backed out of the room, unnoticed by either Sebastian or Emily, and took refuge in the study.

The argument raged for a further five minutes before Sebastian realised Olivia had disappeared, and it stopped him in his tracks. He looked at Emily and said, "This is no good for Liv. If you can't be civil then I suggest you go back to London. It's not like there's anything to stay for now, anyway."

He walked out of the room in search of Olivia, leaving Emily reeling.

"Fucking arsehole." She muttered over and over.

"I thought we were going to calm things down this morning," Hattie said as she walked into the kitchen. "But from what I just overheard, you've done anything but that."

"It wasn't all me," Emily snapped. "I knew she'd take his side."

"What did you expect?" Hattie shook her head. "I know you two have been best friends forever, but Sebastian is her husband. Olivia would walk over hot coals for you, just don't ask her to choose between you and him as you'll be sorely disappointed by her decision."

"Well I know that now, don't I?" Emily sneered. "I won't stay where I'm not wanted." She pushed past Hattie, grabbed her overnight bag, and was in her car speeding down the driveway within minutes.

Olivia watched through the window as Emily drove away, and her heart sank. "I can't believe she just walked out," she said as Sebastian entered the room. "And why did you have to goad her like that?"

"Because she bloody deserved it," Sebastian replied. "But I'm sorry that you're upset. That's the last thing I wanted." He pulled her into his arms.

"What's done is done," Olivia sighed. "I'm angry too, believe me. I just don't want to argue about it."

Sebastian placed his hands on her belly. "We've got more important things to concentrate on right now. Let's get this baby born, and then you two can kiss and make up."

"And what about you?" Olivia raised an eyebrow. "Are you going to hold a grudge against her forever?"

"It was just an argument. It'll blow over," he replied. "Besides, we've got the club so there's really nothing to fight about anymore."

"That remains to be seen," Olivia said. "She'll get into so much trouble for letting this deal slip through her fingers."

Sebastian silenced her with a kiss. "Let it go darling. It will be fine, trust me."

CHAPTER 11

*D*an arrived in New York and was taken straight to Pace University's city campus where Inside the Actors Studio was filmed. He stood in the green room listening to his host's introduction and readied himself for the interview. It was a big deal being invited to discuss his career with the Actors Studio drama students – all the Hollywood greats had done it. James Lipton, the host, was an industry institution whose somewhat paused and clipped delivery of his trademark index card questions made him unique. He had captured some of the most intimate and in-depth interviews ever recorded, and was famous for the ten-question quiz he posed to each guest.

"Welcome to Inside the Actors Studio. I'm James Lipton. He's a British actor who, at the age of seventeen, won 'rising star' at the BAFTA Television Awards for his powerful performance in the BBC drama 'All in at One'. Since then there have been Blockbuster and MTV movie awards, and he's even been featured in the top ten 'Most beautiful people in the world' likened to Paul Newman, who, incidentally, was our guest on the very first episode of this show.

"In his recurring role as Orion Powell in the movie franchise of the same name, he has been wowing audiences worldwide with his daring stunts and high-speed car chases. 'One Day Too Many', 'The Chronicles of Fox Bentley', 'Space', 'The Empire' and 'Changing Lives' are just some of his movies we all know and love. We thank him for so generously, so kindly and so selflessly giving us his time today. The Actor's Studio is proud to welcome Dan Flowers."

The audience of worshipful students burst into applause as Dan walked onto the set that had a gritty backstage feel to it – a plain black backdrop with an exposed wooden frame, behind a raised black platform. He waved and smiled at the packed auditorium and strode towards James with his hand extended in greeting. James motioned for him to sit in the brown leather chair opposite his own. Dan knew that the pace of the show would be much slower than a typical celebrity interview, and that they expected to record at least a couple of hours of conversation to be later edited. He was ready to talk in depth about his career, and excited to pass on some of his experience to the students in an interview that was billed as a masterclass.

"Well, that was a special welcome." Dan grinned at the students. "Thank you for having me today."

"The pleasure is ours," James replied graciously. "As always, we're going to launch straight in." The lights dimmed and the room fell silent. "Where did you grow up?"

"West London. Chelsea. The posh bit." Dan laughed and the audience joined in. "In fact, my parents are still in the same house. My teenage bedroom is exactly the same as the day I left."

"And who are your parents?" James continued.

Dan talked about his family with warmth. "My Dad is called Francis and he's a renowned plastic surgeon. But this," he pointed at his face, "is all natural." Laughter rang out around the room.

Dan chuckled and carried on. "My Mum, Claudia, is a tenured professor at the London School of Economics. Very high-brow," he grinned. He leaned back in his seat and relaxed into the interview. The students were attentive, and hanging on his every word.

James glanced at his index cards and continued. "And how would you describe their influence on you?"

"I think it's safe to say they envisaged me as some sort of scholar – lawyer, doctor, historian." He rolled his eyes. There was a collective giggle from the students, incredulous at the notion of Dan Flowers as an academic.

"But seriously," he continued. "They both worked throughout my childhood and were incredibly dedicated to their professions. Their dedication and work ethic directly influenced me in my career, right from the beginning. If you're going to do something, do it properly."

James nodded his agreement and moved swiftly on to the next question. "And how do they feel about your profession now?"

Dan shot a mega-watt smile around the auditorium. "I think we're all in agreement that it worked out pretty well. They'd be more impressed if I was saving lives on a daily basis, but they're proud of me. Or so they say!"

Keen to keep pace with the format of the show, James kept firing questions at Dan. "What made you want to be an actor?"

"That's an easy one. Michael J Fox in Back to the Future." Dan grinned as a ripple of laughter flowed across the room, followed by a round of applause. "I know, right? He's an incredible actor and he made it look so much fun. Seriously, who wouldn't want to give that a go?"

"He is indeed a wonderful actor," James agreed. "And he's been in that chair, so you have a lot to live up to."

"No pressure then," Dan laughed.

"None whatsoever," James smiled. "Let's get back to you. What was your first acting role?"

"Are we including my stint as a sheep in the Nativity play at kindergarten?" Dan reached for a sip of water. He looked out into the audience and saw a sea of adoring faces staring back at him. He rewarded them with a dazzling smile.

"We can if you like," James laughed.

Dan leaned forward and recalled his first time on stage. "I was thirteen when they cast me as Edmund in The Lion, The Witch and The Wardrobe at school. I only went to the audition because our school – all boys – and the very exclusive girls school next door joined forces that year, and I thought I might get an opportunity to chat up some of the girls. I didn't take it seriously until Jenny Clark – a year my senior and totally gorgeous - was given the role of Susan, and I fell head over heels in love. When I fluffed my lines, she would shoot me a look of pure evil when all I wanted to do was win her approval. Her constant mockery of my non-existent acting abilities spurred me on to actually commit to the play. I learned the lines, read the book – the whole series actually – and gave a pretty solid performance, or so the local newspaper critic would have you believe."

James raised an eyebrow and winked at his students. "And did you get the girl?"

"No. She took a fancy to Mr Beaver." Dan feigned hurt as the audience doubled over with laughter.

"And then what happened?" James asked.

Dan squinted through the glare of the lights and spoke directly to the students. "I don't know what it was like for you guys – what made you all want to get into this crazy business – but I fell in love with acting pretty quickly after that first play. Just being on a stage gave me a rush of adrenalin like I'd never felt before. It was like a drug. I wanted more. Don't tell me you haven't felt that!"

There was a spontaneous burst of applause from the audience.

"Yeah," he grinned. "You guys get it. So, I started going to auditions for TV roles when I was fifteen and was as shocked as everyone else when I was chosen to play Paul O'Brien in 'All in at One'. That was a baptism of fire I can tell you." He paused for another sip of water.

"I learned so much on that show. We ran for four seasons with some seriously heavyweight actors in the leading roles. It was terrifying and glorious at the same time, and when I won the rising star award at the BAFTA's it was incredible."

"Let's see what all the fuss was about, shall we?" James turned his chair to face the giant television just to the right of the stage. Dan appeared on screen and the students clapped enthusiastically. The video was a compilation of powerful scenes selected from across all four series of the show.

When it was over, Dan laughed, "That takes me back. God, I look so young!"

"I think the years have been kind to you," James smiled, and the students whispered their agreement to each other. "And it was the BAFTA that led you to move to LA?" James continued.

Dan nodded. "My dear old granny always told me to strike while the iron is hot – one of our quaint British sayings – so that's what I did. It was right to capitalise on my rising star and I had to do it quickly. I was only just twenty when I moved out here and I thought I knew it all when in actual fact I knew nothing." He took another sip of water and continued. "I was lucky. My folks loaned me some cash, which was enough to give me a roof over my head and a few months to focus on auditions before it ran out."

"But you got the part of Orion Powell overnight, right?" James asked knowingly.

"Not overnight, but not far off," Dan nodded. "Look, I know how lucky I am. Some of the very best acting talent in LA is still waiting tables. I just happened to have the right credentials for the role. Randy had a very fixed idea of who Orion should be and what he looked like, and it turned out that it was me."

"Shall we have a look at some of Orion Powell's finest moments?" James asked the students. There was a unanimous roar of approval as the VT started rolling, and for the next minute they watched a series of high-speed car chases, incredible daredevil stunts, fight scenes, and romantic interludes that were the DNA of an Orion Powell movie.

When the tape came to an end there was clapping and cheering ringing out across the auditorium. It took James a moment to quieten things down, and once he had refocused his students he asked Dan his next question. "So, you scooped a leading role in a Randy Brewster action film and you proved yourself with the box office takings. What next?"

Dan grinned. "Once the first film was a hit, I was signed up for another two immediately, and a ton of new scripts landed on my doormat. The rest is history, as they say."

For the next thirty minutes, James showed clips from several of Dan's other movie hits and asked him to explain his methodology and the thought process behind each character he had played. Dan talked in-depth about his approach to each role, and answered questions from the students after each scene.

"Now, moving from your career to more personal things," James said to Dan. "What or who is NYM?"

Dan snorted. "They told me you would know stuff about me that was staggering and they weren't wrong. NYM. New York Minute." There was another burst of applause from the students – any mention of their beloved city was enough to raise a cheer.

James probed further. "Which is what to you?"

Dan laughed. "It sounds a bit weird when I say it out loud."

"We've heard some strange things on this show over the years," James told him with a wry smile. "Do continue."

"Well, apart from the fact that I love the Don Henley song, my first visit here was magical. It was Christmas, it was snowing, and I loved the energy vibrating from every square inch of the city. I stepped on to Broadway – naturally – and stood for a full minute taking it all in, breathing in the excitement, wanting to remember that moment forever. You guys know that feeling, right?" he asked the audience, receiving another round of applause. "It's something I always do when I come to New York now. I take a minute to soak it all up. That's my New York minute."

"That doesn't sound strange at all," James told him. "Moving on to your TV and movie influences? What was good and what was bad?"

"There were a lot of indie-cinema breakout movies when I was a kid, and those were the films that I really loved. True Romance, Pulp Fiction, Goodfellas. De Niro and Scorsese were an incredible combination, still are. I'm also not ashamed to say I loved Forest Gump. Total Recall made me want to be in action movies – the original, not the remake!" Dan laughed as many of the students vocalised their agreement.

"And the bad?" James asked.

Dan laughed. "Godzilla. Who the hell thought Matthew

Broderick should be in an action movie. I mean, the guy is comedy genius, he's a great actor. But Godzilla?"

"And horror movies," he continued. "What is it with wanting to scare yourself half to death? I watched Nightmare on Elm Street when I was about eight and it terrified me. It's the reason I only take showers."

The students laughed again. Dan was relaxed and having fun, and his answers were open and honest.

There were several more questions before James turned the floor over to the students, who were clamouring to quiz Dan.

Dan turned towards the audience and raised an eyebrow. "Well? Who's first?"

"What's the part you'd kill to play?" A clipped English voice came from the crowd.

Dan squinted against the glare of the lights and turned to face her. "Ah, another Brit abroad. How nice." The audience was lapping up his charm.

"That's an easy one," he continued. "Eddie Felson."

The students roared their approval.

"Why?" the same girl asked.

"The Colour of Money. What a fantastic film. What's so special is the complexity Newman gives to Eddie. He's incredibly likeable and completely charming, even when he's being all Machiavellian. If any other actor were playing Eddie he would come across as a snake, but as a viewer you end up rooting for him. That's talent."

Dan fielded a dozen more questions before James launched into his famous ten.

He sat back in his chair and looked at Dan. "We end our class with the questionnaire that was made famous by my hero, the great Bernard Pivot. Dan, what is your favourite word?"

"Seriously. It can be used in so many ways." Dan laughed.

James smiled and continued with the quick-fire questions. "What is your least favourite word?"

"Squirt." Dan shuddered.

James laughed, along with his students. "And what turns you on creatively, spiritually or emotionally?" he asked.

Dan paused to think, and then replied, "Talent, creatively speaking. Honesty from an emotional point of view. I'm not spiritual I'm afraid."

James nodded and continued, "What turns you off?"

"Bad grammar, bad table manners and rudeness." Dan mock shuddered again.

"What is your favourite curse word?" asked James.

"I'm pretty sure I can't say it here," Dan laughed.

"What sound or noise do you love?" James was speeding through the quiz now, but Dan was ready with his responses. The questions were the same for every guest.

"Rain against the windows," Dan smiled his reply. "We get a lot of that in England. Just saying it makes me yearn for home."

James didn't stop for breath. "What sound or noise do you hate?"

"White noise," Dan grimaced. "That fuzz on the radio kills me."

"I couldn't agree more," James told him. "What profession other than your own would you like to attempt?"

"Formula One driver," Dan grinned. "Now that's a high-speed car chase!"

"I should have seen that one coming," James laughed. "What profession would you not like to do?"

"Teaching," Dan replied. "I don't have the patience!"

"And finally," James had reached the last question. "If heaven exists, what would you like to hear God say when you arrive at the pearly gates?"

"I guess I'd like him to tell me I'd done some good with my time here on Earth. Oh, and that he was a big fan of Orion Powell!" Dan shrugged his shoulders and laughed.

The students had remained respectfully quiet during the quiz, the speed of the questions and answers meant they had little time to react before James moved on. The interview was at an end. Dan had been grilled for almost two hours and had enjoyed every moment of it.

"Thank you for being here with us today," James concluded. "Students, please show your appreciation for Dan Flowers."

The room erupted and Dan sat back to soak up the adulation. He didn't really care that he was famous, but on occasions like this, when he was with an intimate audience, it was nice to feel the love for his work from a group of students that has acting at its core.

CHAPTER 12

*G*eorgiana was walking on air. That first night with Texan powerhouse Wyatt had been a real eye opener. Before him she had only been out with boys who were still finding their feet in the bedroom and unable to match the experience and prowess of a real man.

The way Wyatt had utterly convinced her that she was the woman of his dreams was intoxicating. His confidence was only surpassed by his determination to possess her.

His touch, his soft, manicured hands running the length of her body exploring every inch of her – everything about him made her skin tingle. She was completely taken by him. They had stayed awake all night, talking and making love over and over again.

When Bobby's latest email told him that Sebastian had stolen the club from under his nose, Wyatt postponed his trip to China to spend more time reeling in his latest and most important catch. He knew Georgiana was already falling under his spell, and in a few more days she would give herself over to him completely.

That's when she would be prepared to do anything for him. Even go against her brother.

The morning came when Wyatt had to finally leave for China. He looked at Georgiana who was still asleep and fleetingly felt an unfamiliar pang of guilt. He had come to genuinely like her and loved the way she responded to his touch, but he wouldn't let that get in the way of a business deal. She was a pawn in a game, and he didn't ever let his emotions get the better of him.

"I don't want you to go." Georgiana opened her eyes and gave him a lazy smile.

"I don't wanna go but I have to." Wyatt stroked her cheek. "I want you waiting for me when I get back though."

Georgiana giggled and threw the covers off the bed, her naked body in full view. "Waiting like this?"

Wyatt stopped in his tracks. "Wow. You really are beautiful. I just wanna eat you up."

"What's stopping you?" She arched her back, enticing him to rejoin her in bed.

"What the hell are you doing to me?" he groaned.

She grinned and reached out for him. In an instant, he had removed his clothes, pulled her down to the edge of the bed and buried his head between her thighs. Georgiana cried out as she climaxed so deeply that her body shuddered. Wyatt couldn't hold back. Quickly manouvering her into position, he thrust into her and slowly rocked back and forth, her legs tightly wrapped around his waist, until he was close to his own orgasm.

"I can't wait," he whispered in her ear.

"Then don't," Georgiana urged.

An hour later he was on his way to China and she was destined for Appleton Vale.

Four days after he'd gone she started to believe she had imagined the passion between them, such was the intensity of her feelings. He consumed her every waking thought and she was drifting around in a daze. It was the late-night Skype calls that kept her going – he reassured her that he felt the same and couldn't wait to get back to her.

Georgiana was grateful that Sebastian was away. He would have questioned her behaviour and pressurised her for information that she was not willing to divulge. She knew he wouldn't approve of Wyatt, he was almost twice her age and older than Sebastian.

Olivia was so wrapped up in preparing for the baby's arrival that Georgiana's mood had gone unnoticed, and she had actively avoided spending any time alone with Hattie – she knew her better than anyone. It was her delicious secret and for now she wanted to keep it that way.

After checking on Olivia the morning Wyatt was due to return, she hot-footed it back to her cottage and jumped in the shower. He was flying back into London and she wanted to be waiting for him, looking fabulous.

Her mobile bleeped with a text.

Landing in four hours baby. Can't wait to see you.
Wear something beautiful. W x

She had enlisted her friend Holly - stylist to the stars - to update her wardrobe, giving her carte blanche and a platinum credit card. Holly had not disappointed. She sent a car to Appleton Vale packed to the roof with beautiful clothes, shoes and matching bags, and accessories. She had even included a vast array of exquisite, delicate lace underwear. Georgiana knew Wyatt would love her in it.

She was planning to take the train up to London, but just as she was leaving the house a chauffeur-driven Bentley arrived.

"Mr Clayton insisted that you travel in style, Miss Bloom." The driver opened the door for her and she climbed in, settling back against the luxurious leather seat. She closed her eyes and tried to relax, but every nerve in her body was on red alert as if it knew what pleasures were to come.

When they pulled up outside Wyatt's hotel the manager personally greeted her on the steps.

"Welcome to the Mandarin Oriental, Miss Bloom. Mr Clayton hopes you had a smooth and uneventful journey and is looking forward to seeing you soon." He beamed at her. "He also wanted you to have these." He handed her an exquisite bouquet of blood red roses and a small, square box. Georgiana gasped when she saw the name engraved into the lid – Graff – purveyors of the most fabulous diamonds and rare gems in the world.

She was ushered into the lobby and escorted to the private lift that serviced the Royal Suite. The butler was waiting when the lift reached the top floor and took her overnight bag.

"Miss Bloom, how delightful it is to see you again."

Georgiana blushed, remembering they had rarely left the bedroom on their last visit.

"May I offer you a glass of wine? Mr Clayton specifically requested a bottle of 1990 Romanée-Conti for your arrival."

Georgiana was overwhelmed. The car, the flowers, the little black box from Graff, and now one of the most expensive bottles of wine in the world – it was too much. She gratefully received the proffered glass and took an unsteady and rather unladylike gulp of the velvety red wine.

"I'll go now. Please just pick up the phone if you need anything at all. I am here to serve you and Mr Clayton." He backed out of the room leaving her alone to compose herself.

Her mobile bleeped again.

Landed at City. Be there in thirty.
Enjoy the Romanée-Conti, you're worth every cent. W x

"Breathe, just breathe," she muttered and headed for the master bathroom. She opened her bag and pulled out the blue Jenny Packham cocktail dress that she knew he would love. She matched it with a delicate cream lacy bra and panties that she hoped wouldn't stay on for too long after Wyatt's arrival.

She changed into the new lingerie and was touching up her make-up in the mirror when she suddenly had a crisis of confidence.

"Who am I kidding? What am I doing? This isn't me," she muttered. Slumping to the bathroom floor she picked up the Romanée-Conti and took a swig from the bottle.

She was unable to comprehend why a man like Wyatt would want with a girl who was happiest knee-deep in horse manure and who practically lived in jeans or breeches.

"I'm pretty sure wine of that quality is supposed to be drunk from a glass." Wyatt was standing in the doorway.

Georgiana scrambled to her feet, still clutching the bottle of wine.

"Shit. You're here," she squeaked.

"I am," Wyatt pulled her into his arms. "Any reason you were sitting on the floor?"

"I was a little overwhelmed. And terrified when you saw me again you wouldn't want me." She buried her head in his chest and wrapped her arms around him.

"Are you kidding?" He looked her up and down. "Now that's some fancy underwear you've got on there. Let me see you properly." Georgiana stepped back and granted him his wish.

"I've got a dress," she said, still riddled with nerves.

"Fuck the dress. We're getting room service. I wanna be alone with you and your sexy panties."

Georgiana gasped. Just the way he looked at her made her go weak at the knees.

"Can you kiss me, please?" she needed reassurance. Wyatt stepped forward, placed his hands on either side of her face and gently pressed his lips against hers. She melted into his arms as their kiss further stoked the inferno inside her that had been raging since the moment they met.

"Feel better?" Wyatt smiled.

"Much." Georgiana sighed with contentment. "Can we go to bed now?"

"Patience baby," Wyatt slapped her bottom playfully. "I wanna get a shower, it was a long flight." Seeing the disappointment in her face he added, "You could always join me?"

Georgiana grinned and reached behind her back to undo the clasp on her bra. Her full breasts tumbled out and Wyatt seized upon them immediately. Taking one in each hand he kissed them in turn, gently teasing her nipples, making her cry out with desire. She arched her back and pressed her body against his, writhing with pleasure at his touch.

"Aren't you going to take these off?" Georgiana asked, pointing to her lacy panties.

Wyatt's eyes flashed with desire. He hooked his thumbs through the delicate material and slowly removed them. "Oh baby, you're so beautiful," he groaned. "Get in that shower, NOW." His voice was thick with desire.

He quickly discarded his clothes, pulled her towards him and lifted her up so she could wrap her legs around his waist. Stepping into the shower, the hot water cascaded over their entwined bodies and they were lost.

"I'm famished," Georgiana jumped out of bed and began to raid the mini bar.

"Come home with me." Wyatt was moving into phase two of his plan.

"What?" Georgiana almost choked on the luxury nuts she had just stuffed in her mouth.

"You heard me. Come back to New York with me."

Georgiana was floored. Her immediate response was to scream 'yes' from the rooftops but then she remembered the baby and the job she had grown to love.

"I want to but I can't, I'm sorry." She was crestfallen.

"What? Why?" Wyatt's face registered baffled disappointment. He was used to getting his own way.

"The baby. I promised Olivia I would be there. I can't let her down. And then there's work of course."

"That's not the answer I was hoping for." He was miffed. "But it will have to do."

She ran over to the bed and launched herself into his arms.

"Thank you for understanding." She smothered him with kisses. "And anyway, it won't be long. She looks like she's about to pop." Georgiana snuggled into his chest and sighed. "The thought of not being with you kills me, but I promise I'll come as soon as I can."

"Yes, you will," Wyatt smirked. "You're mine now."

CHAPTER 13

"*C*oo-ee!" Thelma was frantically waving her hands in the air in an attempt to attract the attention of The Riverside's Lady Captain, Lucinda Walton-Smythe. "Coo-ee, Lucinda," she shouted.

She could swear that Lucinda had heard her. She even glanced in her direction over the top of her Versace sunglasses before rushing towards the clubhouse and disappearing through the heavy wooden doors.

"Bitch," Thelma muttered. She reached in to the car and pulled out her tennis racquet. Catching a quick glimpse of her reflection in the rear-view mirror, she smoothed her hair back from her face and applied another layer of the shocking pink lipstick that perfectly matched her manicured nails.

Thelma Graystock was a member at The Riverside and lived on the outskirts of Fiddlebury, along with her barrister husband, Larry. In her early fifties, she kept a trim figure by virtue of her twice-weekly tennis lessons with the club's hunky professional, Will Abinger. On the days' she wasn't swooning over Will, she attended Pilates classes, lunched with the girls and frequented the state-of-the-art gymnasium, where she flirted outrageously with its manager, Brendan.

Her marriage was not a happy one. Larry spent most of his time in London, fighting legal battles and imposing super-injunctions on behalf of his wayward celebrity clientele, whilst she floated around the countryside spending his money on whatever took her fancy and glossing over how desperately lonely she was. On the weekends when he returned to the family home they were reminded of how little they actually had in common, other than their three children who had long since flown the nest. They rarely made love, and when they did it was strictly missionary and over in an instant. She was lonely and unhappy, but she would never let anyone know that.

Thelma walked across the car park and headed in the direction of the tennis centre, where the delicious Will would be waiting for her lesson.

"Thelma! Don't you look super-sexy today?" Will bounced over and kissed her on both cheeks. He was wearing impossibly tight, gleaming white tennis shorts with a short-sleeved fitted polo shirt that emphasized his six-pack and bulging biceps.

Thelma giggled and her face flushed red. "Good morning, William," she grinned. "You don't look too bad yourself." She glanced at his outfit and felt her stomach flip. He really was incredibly good-looking. "Lovely day, isn't it?"

"I'm torn between the beauty of the day and the beauty I see standing here before me," Will replied with a grin.

"Oh stop," Thelma giggled again. "I'm old enough to be your mother."

"And?" Will raised his eyebrow and grinned at Thelma.

"Well," she spluttered. "You know."

"No, I don't know. Tell me," Will urged. "I think you're a stunning-looking woman who's crying out for some hot loving."

"Will!" Thelma was shocked. "I know you're only joking, but please keep your voice down. What will people think? What will Larry think?"

"Tell me I'm wrong." He was standing fast.

Thelma looked around furtively and whispered, "No, you're right. Larry is never here and when he is he's such a bore."

"Ha! I knew it," Will smirked. "Don't you think we should do something about it?"

Thelma's heart was racing and she couldn't look him in the eye. "Don't be ridiculous," she muttered half-heartedly. "Stop teasing and start teaching, I want my full lesson." She quickly turned away and ran to the other side of the court.

"I'll give you more than that if you'll let me," Will shouted across court as he started the warm-up.

Forty-five minutes later Will had put her through her paces, and Thelma was exhausted.

"That was great darling, your backhand is really coming along nicely." Will slung an arm around her shoulder and steered her towards the clubhouse. "I'll see you on Friday at ten, yes?"

"Yes, great. Thanks, Will."

"And I meant what I said about the other thing," he shouted as he walked away.

"Oh," Thelma squeaked and was rooted to the spot for a full minute before her mobile sprang into action and dragged her back into the real world. It was a text from Larry.

Won't be home this weekend. Client needs me in Berlin. L.

She sighed and put the phone back in her pocket without replying. It was the club's monthly dinner-dance this weekend and Larry had let her down once again. She hated turning up to those sorts of events without him.

"Sod him," she muttered. "I'm going to buy a new bloody dress and go anyway."

Entering the plush ladies' locker room, she caught a glance of herself in the mirror and wrinkled her nose in distaste. Her carefully applied make-up had been displaced by sweat and her hair had come free from the band holding it back and now resembled a bird's nest. She splashed some cooling water on her face and hastily reapplied some mascara and lipstick before smoothing her hair back into place.

"That'll have to do," she muttered and exited through the door that led to the club lounge where the ladies were meeting for lunch. The lounge did not impose a strict dress code, unlike the rest of the club where jackets and ties were compulsory for the men and the ladies were encouraged to be glamorous.

She made her way over to the central table where her friends were sitting in relative silence, every one of them transfixed by their smartphones.

"Lucinda, didn't you see me across the car park earlier?" Thelma asked as she pulled out a chair.

"Oh, was that you?" Lucinda narrowed her eyes and looked Thelma up and down. "You really could have changed into something more suitable, darling. No one wants to see mutton on the table when they're expecting to eat beef fillet, now do they?"

Thelma gulped and was stuck for a response. Her face flushed with embarrassment, and her mortification increased even further when Marcia Loft and Samantha Connor snorted with laughter and pointed at her cellulite, which was on full view thanks to her short tennis skirt.

"Ignore them," whispered Mary-Jane Lavenham, putting her hand on Thelma's arm. "They're just being bitchy, you know they'd do anything to please Lucinda."

Thelma gave her friend a weak smile and picked up the menu, pretending to read it as she composed herself.

"Did you see Sebastian this morning?" Marcia asked her friends. "He's so dreamy."

"It's a pointless fantasy Marcia," Lucinda said pointedly. "He wouldn't look at you in a million years, and he's madly in love with Olivia for reasons I can't even begin to fathom. It's not like she's the best-looking woman in the world, is it?"

"What?" cried Mary-Jane. "She's drop dead gorgeous and a real sweetie. Stop being a bitch Lucinda, just because you couldn't get your claws into him."

Lucinda bristled and shot Mary-Jane an evil glance across the table. "Oh, don't be so ridiculous. I'm perfectly happy with Godfrey, and Sebastian isn't my type anyway."

"He's everyone's type," Thelma retorted, delighted that Mary-Jane had given Lucinda a dressing down. Feeling brave, she added, "He could've had anyone but he chose Olivia, and I can see why. She's lovely and has made him very happy, there's no need for jealousy."

"Well, there's no accounting for taste I suppose," Lucinda pouted. "Let's order." She raised her hand to attract the attention of a waiter.

"How's your game coming along?" Mary-Jane asked Thelma. "I really must get back into it when the boys go back to school."

"I'm having so much fun," Thelma grinned.

"So, we've heard," Lucinda sneered at her. "It's just embarrassing, Thelma. I mean really, going after a man half your age. Have you looked in the mirror lately?"

Thelma turned crimson. "Don't be ridiculous," she spluttered. "William is just a friend and a fine tennis player."

"For God's sake Lucinda, stop picking on her," Mary-Jane had heard enough. "Call yourself a friend? Come on Thelma, let's move."

Thelma gave Mary-Jane a grateful look and scuttled off after her to a table in the window.

"You really have to stand up for yourself," Mary-Jane told her when they were seated. "She's a bully, but she can't hurt you."

"She could spread all sorts of rumours about me and Will. Then Larry would hear and it would all be dreadful," Thelma whispered across the table.

"Well, if there's no truth to it then you've got nothing to worry about." Mary-Jane smiled reassuringly. "And is there?"

Thelma shook her head. "But that's not to say I wouldn't mind," she giggled and looked around furtively, checking she had not been overheard.

"You're a scream," Mary-Jane laughed. "All butter wouldn't melt, and given the chance you'd be bonking Will in the halfway house!"

Thelma giggled again. "Well a girl can dream."

Across the room Lucinda was shooting Thelma and Mary-Jane evil looks. It was a well-known fact that she considered herself to be the queen of the club. She was the Lady Captain, the head of the events committee, and the chief WAG. No one wanted to fall out of favour with her, she could make life very difficult indeed.

"Bitches," she muttered under her breath. "You just wait. You'll regret walking away from me."

Marcia and Samantha gulped.

CHAPTER 14

"*P*ORG!" Will called as Georgiana arrived at the tennis club. "How are you, gorgeous?"

"Billy balls," she greeted him cheerfully. "Less of the Porg, please."

"But it's what you are," he laughed. "Person of restricted growth."

"I'm five feet two!" She drew herself up to her full height. Will still towered over her.

Georgiana and Will were best friends. They had attended the same exclusive school since they were infants and trusted one another implicitly. Their friendship was unbreakable.

While she had aced her 'A' Levels, Will had completely flunked his and escaped to Spain for a year to qualify as a tennis coach. Instead of taking up one of her well-earned university places, Georgiana spent the next two years drifting from one glamorous holiday destination to another, attending exclusive events in London and generally keeping out of her brother's way. Sebastian had plunged into deep depression after the loss of his first wife and she had been in danger of being dragged down with him. The trips to St Tropez, Paris, New York and Monaco, and sparkly new nightclub openings were a welcome distraction from the dense fog that had descended on Appleton Manor.

Once Sebastian met Olivia things became easier for Georgiana. Free from the burden of trying to keep her brother in check, she finally decided to settle into work and opened the ancient stables at the manor as a five-star livery business. She took on a yard manager from nearby Fiddlebury and had just begun advertising for clients when the BBC and a new career in television beckoned. But she still treasured her old friends.

"Christ, those shorts are tight," she rolled her eyes at Will. "Don't leave much to the imagination, do they?"

"And you should know," Will shot back with a grin. "I seem to remember there was a time when you'd have happily jumped on board."

Georgiana laughed and swatted him with her tennis racquet. "Friends with benefits! That was a long time ago. I'm surprised you still remember shagging little old me with all the women you've had in the past few years."

"Oh, believe me, darling, I could never forget the image of your beautiful little body bouncing up and down on me. Are you sure you don't want to give me another seeing to?" teased Will.

"No, I bloody well don't. God knows where you've been!" Georgiana giggled. "And besides, I've met someone." She was grinning from ear to ear.

"Another poor soul you'll so easily discard into the night when you get bored," joked Will.

"No! This is different," Georgiana insisted. "He's amazing," she smiled dreamily.

"Uh-oh. Have we met our match, Miss Bloom? Are you seriously telling me that you're in love?" Will was surprised.

"Well, not yet, well at least I don't think so. Although I'm not sure I know what that feels like really."

"Me neither," Will laughed. "I'm just enjoying myself whilst I wait for true love to knock on my door."

"True love? You?" Georgiana spluttered. "I heard you got caught the other day shagging one of the waitresses in the sauna. Remind me not to go in there again."

"Ah, Marta," Will grinned. "She's got this whole domination thing going on. I quite like it."

"Oh God, stop!" Georgiana laughed and covered her ears. "I don't want to know."

"You love hearing about my exploits, don't deny it!" Will winked. "So, who's this guy then?"

"No-one you know." Georgiana wasn't ready to share. "I met him in London. But don't say anything to anyone, I just want to keep it private till I know if it's going anywhere. Sebastian won't like it."

"Sebastian doesn't like anyone you hang with, including me. But since when has that stopped you?" Will knew Sebastian well, and had been on the receiving end of his wrath when he had caught him and Georgiana in a clinch on the billiards table at the manor when they were just sixteen.

"Good point," she grinned. "Shall we play? I'm not paying you to stand here and chat you know!"

"You're not bloody paying me at all, you cheeky cow!" Will grinned. "I think you'll find I do this out of the goodness of my heart for my gorgeous friend."

"And the goodness of my brother's membership," she laughed. "And not to mention the fact that Edward is my godfather of course." She skipped across the court to face Will at the net.

"And for that I'm going to work you like a bitch," Will picked up some balls and began pounding them at Georgiana. An hour later, both dripping in sweat, they stepped off the court and headed in to the clubhouse.

"Not bad, darling." Will grinned. "And I wasn't even taking it that easy on you. Are you sure McEnroe isn't giving you secret lessons?"

"I wish. Perhaps I should ask him?" she giggled. "Want some lunch? It's on Sebastian."

"Well, if he's paying, then I'm in." Will was never one to turn down a freebie.

"I'll just go and make myself look a bit more respectable, see you in there." Georgiana skipped into the locker room and joined Will in the lounge five minutes later.

Her hair now free from the bunches she had employed on the tennis court tumbled down her back in silky waves, and her cheeks were naturally flushed from their invigorating session. She had applied some lip-gloss and a squirt of her favourite perfume, and deemed herself adequate to face the Riverside bitches – as she and Olivia called the ladies of the club who lunched and bitched on a daily basis.

Georgiana and Will sat at a table in the window overlooking the magnificent eighteenth green of the championship golf course and mulled over Chef Bernard's specials of the day.

"I'm famished." Georgiana licked her lips as she studied the menu. "It's going to have to be the Wagyu Beef Burger."

"Pig!" Will teased as he ordered a Greek salad. "Where the hell do you put it all?"

Georgiana pulled a face and replied with a grin, "I'm very active you know!"

"I do indeed know. It's just a shame I couldn't win your heart," he joked. "So, are you going to tell me about lover boy or not?"

"Not," she said and stuck her tongue out.

"Do you want to hear more about me and Marta then?" Will joked.

When Georgiana didn't come back with her usual witty retort he looked up and saw her staring at the doorway where a tall, blonde man was standing talking with Edward Hampton and Olivia's best friend, Emily.

She gasped as their eyes met.

"What's up? Who's he?" Will probed.

"That's him. That's the man I told you about. Wyatt." Georgiana whispered. "He said he was in America." She didn't understand why he hadn't told her he was coming to see her.

"Maybe he wanted to surprise you?" Will was ever positive. "I bet he went to the house first and Hattie said you'd be here. He's much older than I'd imagined, and there was you having a dig about me shagging the oldies." His laugh received an elbow in his ribs. "Ouch. I was only kidding."

"Well, don't," Georgiana hissed. She sensed something wasn't quite right about Wyatt being at The Riverside. He was still staring at her across the lounge and she was rooted to her chair.

He briefly took his eyes off her to confer with Edward and Emily and then strode purposefully towards Georgiana and Will's table.

"Hey, babe," he drawled. "Cute outfit." He appraised her tiny tennis dress and his eyes darkened with desire.

Georgiana jumped up and threw herself into his arms, not caring who saw.

"Oh my God," she shrieked. "Why didn't you tell me you were coming? When did you get here? I've missed you so much."

Wyatt pulled her closer to him and bent to kiss her. She melted into his arms and sighed with deep satisfaction.

Will interrupted, "Manners, young lady! Aren't you going to introduce me to your friend?"

"Oh yes, sorry." Georgiana looked a little dazed. "Will, this is Wyatt Clayton."

Will offered his hand in greeting. "Will Abinger. I've heard so incredibly little about you," he joked.

Wyatt eyed up his perceived competition warily. "Teaching Georgiana to play tennis, huh?"

"Err, well yes, but we go way back. Best friends and all that." Will replied, miffed that he had been relegated from best friend to tennis coach.

"And all that?" Wyatt asked, raising an eyebrow at them both.

Will grinned and Georgiana flushed with embarrassment.

"It was nothing," she spluttered. "Just a couple of kids messing around." She didn't want Wyatt to think she was still involved with Will. She was so pleased to see him.

"How do you know Emily and Edward?" she asked.

"Just a bit of business," he replied. "Nothing for you to worry your beautiful little head about."

Georgiana's heart sank. "What kind of business?" She suddenly felt uncomfortable, as if she knew what was coming.

"I'm buying the club, or at least I'm trying to." Wyatt replied.

"What?" Georgiana whispered as her blood ran cold. "You're the American consortium?" She was disbelieving.

"I am. But your brother has kinda screwed with my plans, which is why I had to come myself." He shrugged his shoulders in a gesture that said 'if you want something doing properly, do it yourself'.

"You're really here for this, not for me?" The realisation was suddenly dawning on her. "Did you know who I was when you met me?'

"Sure I did," he told her. "Though I didn't know you'd be here today."

Georgiana's hand flew to her mouth in disbelief. "You used me? None of this was real?" Her eyes brimmed with tears and she steadied herself on the edge of the table.

"Yeah, but I kinda like you." Wyatt shrugged his shoulders. "We had fun, didn't we? You know you enjoyed it, and you've made your feelings for me very clear. Don't let a bit of business get in the way."

Georgina gasped at her own stupidity. She glanced at Will who was standing steadfast. She knew he wouldn't leave until she asked him to and she was grateful for his support. "I should have known it was too good to be true," she muttered before addressing Wyatt.

"Well, Mr Clayton," she was dismissive. "You backed the wrong horse. I don't have any influence or information that would help you, and even if I did, I wouldn't give it to you. Edward and Sebastian have made a deal so I don't know why you bothered coming. It's not like you're going to change the minds of two honourable men now, is it?"

"I thought you'd be happy, honey. It gives me a legitimate reason to spend more time here, with you."

"Don't you 'honey' me," Georgiana hissed. "And I didn't realise you needed a legitimate reason to spend time with me. Up until about five minutes ago I believed your feelings for me were real. Now I know you were just using me." She held her breath in a bid to halt her tears.

"Let's go talk somewhere," Wyatt said. "I want you. You gotta know that?"

"I don't 'gotta' anything." Georgiana crinkled her nose at the Americanism. "The mere fact that you had plans for me before we even met makes me sick to my stomach. Please, just go."

"I'm going nowhere till we sort this out," Wyatt didn't like being dismissed by anyone, let alone the woman he had decided would be his.

"There's nothing to sort out." Georgiana remained calm. "Did you think I'd be an easy target? That I'd fallen so hard for you I'd be prepared to go against everyone I love, just for you? You totally underestimated me if that's what you actually thought."

Wyatt shrugged his shoulders. "Guess I should have done a bit more research, huh?"

"You don't know me at all. You're revolting. GO." She pointed towards the exit.

Wyatt didn't move.

"She asked you to go." Will stepped between Wyatt and Georgiana and drew himself up to his full height, just nudging Wyatt's frame by an inch.

Wyatt bristled. "Who the fuck do you think you are? This is between me and her. Back off."

Georgiana, momentarily regaining her composure, placed her hand calmly on Will's arm, motioning him to stop. She stepped forward and addressed Wyatt.

"I'll tell you who he is," she snarled. "Will is my best friend and he's earned the right to say what he likes. You don't know me. We fucked a few times, so what?

Wyatt said nothing. Georgiana's face told him there was no point in pursuing the conversation - she wouldn't listen to him, not right now anyway. She had been putty in his hands. Just the way she had reacted to his touch betrayed her feelings for him. He was sure she would come crawling back to him once he owned the club. He said no more and backed away from the table to re-join Edward and Emily, who had been watching their exchange with interest.

Behind her Mary-Jane and Thelma's mouths were open in shock, they didn't know where to look.

Across the room Lucinda smirked. She had enjoyed the exchange between the gorgeous American and Georgiana. "She had that coming," she sneered. "As stuck-up as her brother and his wife."

Marcia and Samantha giggled and nodded in agreement.

Will grabbed Georgiana and pulled her into his arms. "I'm so sorry Porg. What a wanker!"

She sniffed and wiped her nose on his shirt. "I can't believe it. How did I get it so wrong? I truly believed he cared about me, but it was all about the club and beating Sebastian."

"Did you see the way he was looking at you? It was a bit creepy. Like he wanted to own you." Will shuddered.

"Yeah, I'm a great shag," she said miserably. "It was never anything else, not on his part anyway. Can we get out of here?"

"Sure. Where to?" Will took her hand.

"The pub." Georgiana replied.

Will grinned. "Ah. An excellent choice, madam. Please follow me." He hooked her arm through his and escorted her through the lounge, away from the glaring eyes and gossiping mouths of the other members who had been thoroughly enjoying the impromptu lunchtime entertainment.

"Don't you have lessons this afternoon?" Georgiana asked as they walked towards her car.

"Fuck 'em. You're more important darling. I'll get Carl to cover me." He referred to his assistant coach. "Let's go and get hammered."

Wyatt watched from a window as Georgiana and Will drove away from the club. He could have kicked himself for handling things with her so badly. In his determination to buy The Riverside he had thought she would be an asset.

"Are you ok Mr Clayton?" Emily asked gently. "I didn't realise you knew Georgiana that well," she probed.

"I don't." Wyatt was dismissive. "Shall we continue?"

"Look old boy," Edward puffed. "I've agreed to sell to Sebastian. That's all I have to say on the matter. Always wanted to keep it in the family and he and Georgiana are as close as it gets."

"I can outbid him many times over," Wyatt said with renewed determination. This was one battle he was not prepared to lose at any price. He had promised his shareholders and investors - one in particular - that this deal would be delivered to them on a platter.

"It was never about the money Mr Clayton. I have plenty of that." Edward was unmoved. "Georgiana is my goddaughter, and that display you just put on has left a nasty taste in my mouth. This club will never be yours."

Wyatt snapped. Nothing had gone the way he had planned today. "So you say, Mr Hampton. But in my experience money talks, and I have a ton of it." He turned to Emily. "Let me know when he changes his mind."

He strode out of the doors and jumped into his waiting car without a backwards glance.

CHAPTER 15

*T*he Riverside Inn was the hub of the village. Housed in a crooked sixteenth century building, it was filled with oak beams and uneven creaking floorboards. An immaculate mahogany bar and huge inglenook fireplace were in the main room, and a cosy restaurant in the back. The pretty garden backed onto the River Candle and had a willow tree to one side with a stunning array of flowering shrubs around the fringes of the lawn.

It was eight o'clock and Georgiana was wasted. She and Will had been in the pub garden since lunchtime and had drunk enough vodka between them to sink a ship.

She had raged her way through the first two drinks, bemoaning her misfortune to be taken in so easily by someone so utterly deceiving. She'd then spent the next few hours lurching between tears and frustration, interspersed with bouts of singing and raucous behaviour.

"Juss one more," she pleaded with landlord, Tom, when he gently suggested that they call it a night. "I'm a victim of fraud don't you know?"

Tom looked quizzically at Will, who shrugged his shoulders and downed the remnants of his glass. "Long story, don't ask."

"Right, one for the road then I'm cutting you both off." Tom poured two more vodka and tonics and brought them out to the garden. "Just remember to keep it down a bit, I've already had a complaint about the noise."

"Yes sir." They mock saluted him and fell about laughing.

When he returned to the bar, his wife Susie was concerned. "Do you think I should call Olivia?" she asked.

"If you're going to call anyone it'd better be Hattie. Sebastian will blow a gasket if you worry Olivia." Tom hugged his wife. "You're so caring darling, just another thing I love about you."

"I don't know what's happened, but poor old Georgiana is desperately unhappy. I think I will call Hattie, she'll know what to do." Susie picked up her mobile and disappeared into the kitchen.

Hattie answered on the third ring and arrived at the pub just five minutes later, worry etched across her face.

"Hatts," Georgiana shrieked with joy and jumped up, knocking over her glass. "Come and have a drink."

"No darling, I don't think so." She walked over and enveloped her in a motherly hug. "I think it's time we went home and had a little chat, don't you?"

"Don't wanna go home," Georgiana muttered before her tears overwhelmed her. She sobbed into Hattie's chest for a full minute and was then helped into the car by Tom and Will.

"Thanks, Will," she slurred from the passenger seat. "Why couldn't I fall in love with you instead?"

"Been saying that for years, gorgeous." Will stroked her hair affectionately. "Now go and sleep it off and we'll chat tomorrow. Love you."

"Love you more," she mumbled as Hattie started the car.

A few minutes later they pulled up outside Georgiana's cottage and Hattie helped her inside.

"Let's have a nice cup of tea and you can tell me all about it." She bustled into the kitchen and switched on the kettle. "Sit down there, darling. Can I get you a glass of water as well?"

"Yes, please." Georgiana was starting to sober up and the reality of what had happened hit her like a wrecking ball. The floodgates opened, she couldn't hold it back any longer.

Hattie rushed over and pulled her close. "Oh, my darling girl. That's it. Let it out. You'll feel better when you have."

She rocked Georgiana in her arms just as she had when she was a little girl, whispering soothing words until her tears subsided.

"I'm sorry. I didn't mean to get that drunk," Georgiana sniffed.

"Don't be silly darling. We've all had a little too much from time to time. Now would you like to tell me what's making you so unhappy?"

"I met a man a couple of weeks ago," she replied in a quiet voice. "He made me feel things I've never felt before but it wasn't real, none of it was. He was just using me for a business deal."

"A business deal?" Hattie was confused.

"He's the one who wanted to buy the club before Sebastian did the deal with Edward. But I didn't know that at the time we met, only found out today. I feel so stupid, and ashamed that I fell for it." She gulped back her tears.

"Oh, I see. And are you absolutely sure his feelings aren't true?" Hattie asked gently.

"Of course I'm sure," Georgiana snapped. "Why else would he want someone like me?"

"Any man would be incredibly lucky to have you. You're one of the best people I know, and I'm not just saying that because I raised you. I'm saying it because it's true. You're beautiful on the inside as well as the outside." Hattie smiled and wiped away Georgiana's tears. "Why don't I run you a nice hot bath, and while you're in there I'll rustle up something for supper."

Georgiana nodded gratefully. "That would be nice, thank you."

By ten o'clock Georgiana was bathed, fed and tucked up in bed with Lady pressed up against her, sensing that her mistress needed her more than ever.

Hattie leaned down and stroked her head. "Now get some sleep, it will all seem a lot clearer in the morning."

"Thanks Hattie. Love you."

"I love you too, so very much. Now sleep." Hattie turned off the light, closed the door and left Georgiana alone for the first time since Wyatt had dropped his bombshell. She was miserable, drunk and exhausted – a wretched combination, but one that offered solace in sleep.

CHAPTER 16

*H*attie and Olivia were enjoying a leisurely breakfast when Sebastian came crashing in through the kitchen door. He had been at the club since six o'clock that morning with his coach, Hugh, preparing for his defence of The Open Championship that he had won so spectacularly the previous year.

"What the hell happened with Georgiana yesterday?" He rounded on Hattie. "Why didn't you tell me what a state she was in last night?"

"I didn't feel it was appropriate given your temper, and I'm glad I didn't, judging by the foul mood you're in now." Hattie stood firm. Sebastian's temper didn't scare her. "Susie called me. I didn't want to worry Olivia so I dealt with it."

Olivia was confused. "What's happened? Is she ok?"

"No, she bloody isn't. She made a complete fool of herself at the club yesterday, and by all accounts she carried on in the pub all afternoon." Sebastian was fuming. He turned back to face Hattie. "Are you going to tell me or not?"

Hattie sighed. "I've never betrayed your trust Sebastian, so don't ask me to do that to Georgiana, she's been through enough."

"Oh, poor Georgiana. What's she been through?" Olivia was concerned.

Sebastian bashed his fists on the table, making Olivia jump. "Right, I'm going over there to get some answers."

"Sebastian, don't," Olivia pleaded. "Let me."

"I don't want her upsetting you, darling," Sebastian softened when he saw how worried Olivia was. "At least let me or Hattie drive you over there."

"I'll take her," Hattie said. "You need to stay here and calm down."

Sebastian looked at them and rolled his eyes. "I'm not going to argue with the two of you. I can't win." He smiled and pulled Olivia towards him, kissed her and turned her to face the door. "No time like the present."

They arrived at Georgiana's cottage a few minutes later and saw all the curtains were still drawn. Hattie dropped Olivia off and went back to the Manor. She walked up the pathway and knocked on the door, waiting a full minute for an answer that never came before fishing the spare keys out of her bag.

"Georgie?" she called out. "Where are you, sweetie?"

When she didn't get a response, she climbed the stairs and opened the bedroom door. She found Georgiana face down on the bed, sobbing into her pillow.

"Oh, darling." Olivia sat down on the bed and stroked her hair. "What's happened?"

It took Olivia a few minutes to calm her down enough to find out the full story, and as she sat patiently listening to the devastated words of a heartbroken woman her emotions got the better of her.

"What the hell are you crying for?" Georgiana looked at Olivia and began to laugh.

"I can't help it. I'm so sorry." Olivia sniffed. "Why didn't you tell me about him?"

"Because you'd have told Sebastian and he'd have gone mad. Wyatt is a few years older than him. Not really suitable boyfriend material." Georgiana shrugged her shoulders. "Doesn't matter now anyway. It's over."

"I don't tell your brother everything you know," Olivia smiled. "Us girls can have some secrets, and besides it's none of his business. Please don't feel like you can't talk to me again, I hate the thought of you bottling it all up and being here on your own."

"I'm better alone," Georgiana whispered. She started to cry again.

"I thought that once, and then I met Sebastian," Olivia replied. "You'll get over it, darling. That's one thing I can absolutely promise. It may take a little time to heal, but I'm living proof that a broken heart can mend and love again."

"It's ridiculous really. I hardly knew Wyatt, and we only spent a few days together, but I really believed it was real. I'm so embarrassed. How did I not know?"

"Well he's clearly a fool." Olivia smiled and stood up. "Come on. Let's get you some breakfast and then you can tell me all about the sex. I'm assuming it was good?"

Georgiana laughed through her tears. "Only you would ask me that at such an inappropriate time."

"Well? Was it?" Olivia grinned.

"Yes. It was amazing." Georgiana remembered his hands on her skin and the passionate love-making, and shuddered. "But now I just feel sick when I think of him touching me."

"Promise me you won't lock yourself away," said Olivia. "Go out. Be happy. You're young and beautiful and should be having fun."

"I'll be fine. He lied. He's a bastard. And that's that." Georgiana was suddenly determined to forget about Wyatt and the incredible hurt he had caused her.

"That's the spirit." Olivia grinned. "And don't worry, I'll only give Sebastian the abridged version."

Georgiana smiled. "Thanks. I really don't need him on my back."

"He's leaving today anyway, so you can wallow in your misery with me and Hattie and he'll never know." Olivia winked.

"I'm so glad I'm not working this week." Georgiana sighed and stood up. "I need coffee. I feel like utter crap."

"Well I didn't want to say, but you smell like a brewery." Olivia wrinkled her nose. "How much did you drink?"

"Too much," Georgiana grimaced. "Way too much. I won't be doing that again in a hurry. Did I do anything stupid? It's all a bit hazy."

"Nothing more than a bit of singing and table dancing, according to Hattie," Olivia laughed. "And we've all been guilty of that."

Georgiana put her head in her hands. "I'll never live that down. Not if Will has anything to do with it."

"Shame really," Olivia mused.

"What?"

"That you don't have feelings for him. He's a lovely man and he's crazy about you." Olivia smiled encouragingly.

"That ship has long since sailed. I adore him and he's my best friend, but that's it." Georgiana was resolute. "I can even think about another man right now anyway."

"Fair enough," Olivia replied. "Now get the coffee on and find me some juice. I'm bursting for a wee. Your niece or nephew is playing football with my bladder."

Georgiana went into the kitchen and flicked the coffee machine on. She knew Olivia was right. She would get over him, and in the mean-time she would take every job the BBC threw at her. She needed to keep busy.

CHAPTER 17

"And it's another beautiful day here at Royal Liverpool. Welcome to day two of the 147th Open Championship." The dulcet tones of Eddie Franklin, the BBC's golf commentator, boomed out of the television set in the Manor's sitting room where Olivia and Georgiana were waiting to watch Sebastian tee off.

Georgiana had filled her work diary with sporting events, starting from the end of July. She had promised Olivia she would be at home when the baby came. She had also given Sebastian her word that she would stay while he played in The Open. Her bosses at the BBC hadn't been pleased, given her popularity with the golfing audience, but she had put her foot down and remained in Appleton Vale.

"I'm pleased to say that we still have world number one Sebastian Bloom with us, and he's about to arrive at the first tee," Eddie continued. "He's here to defend the title he won so brilliantly last year and is topping the leaderboard after the first round, but it's anyone's guess as to how long he'll last. Sebastian has made no bones about walking off the course should he get that all-important call telling him the baby is on the way."

Sebastian appeared on the first tee and was greeted with rapturous applause and a cheering crowd. They loved him and were delighted when he had snatched victory from his arch-rival, Troy McLoud, last year to turn his fortunes around. His game was in great shape and he was the favourite going into the most important Major of the year.

He was drawn to play with his best friend and fellow professional, the Brazilian José de Silva, and he couldn't be happier.

"Have you got the phone?" he asked his caddy, Aiden, for the umpteenth time.

"Yes, boss." Aiden grinned and patted his pocket. "You concentrate on playing and I'll keep an eye on things."

José arrived on the tee and hugged Sebastian. "So, my friend. Any news?" He smiled and patted Sebastian on the back.

"Do you think I'd be standing here if Liv was in labour?" Sebastian laughed and pulled his driver out of his bag for a practice swing.

"A part of me wants your phone to ring. It's the only way anyone else has got a chance of winning, my friend." José was joking, but Sebastian knew that he wanted to win a Major more than anything. José was long overdue the fame and fortune that a Major title afforded. He was the only man Sebastian wouldn't begrudge a win.

The starter cleared his throat and addressed the crowd.

"Ladies and gentlemen. On the tee from England, Sebastian Bloom."

The spectators erupted and Sebastian smiled and waved enthusiastically. He teed up the ball and smashed it down the middle of the fairway.

José stepped forward as he was introduced and received a warm welcome from the largely partisan crowd. He was a popular player on Tour and with the British public. He hit an almost identical shot to Sebastian's, and they were off.

Back in Appleton Vale Olivia was feeling decidedly uncomfortable. She had hardly slept a wink for three days and was, according to her, the size of an elephant.

"Ouch!" She took a sharp breath.

"Oh my God," Georgiana gasped.

"What?" Olivia replied.

"Why didn't you say you were having contractions?" Georgiana's eyes were on stalks.

"I'm not. It's just a bit of Braxton Hicks according to Dr Khan." Olivia attempted to look nonchalant, determined to keep the baby from coming before Sunday night. She desperately wanted Sebastian to have a shot at successfully defending his title, and he was equally adamant that he wanted to be present at the birth.

"You sure?" Georgiana asked, concern etched on her face.

"Yes, positive." Olivia smiled and eased herself up from the sofa. "Need the loo."

No sooner had she stood up, she looked at the wet floor beneath her and then at Georgiana. "Oh, no!"

"Shit!" Georgiana jumped up and ran across the room. She helped Olivia sit down and then darted out of the room to find Hattie.

She was back in an instant with Hattie puffing behind her.

"Right, then. Let's take this nice and easy. You're doing

brilliantly." Hattie smiled encouragingly at Olivia, who had a momentary look of panic on her face.

"I need Sebastian," Olivia whispered. "Please call him."

"Already on it," Georgiana grinned. She had the phone to her ear and Aiden answered on the second ring. "Baby," she shouted.

"I didn't know you felt that way," Aiden joked at the other end.

"Stop being a dick," she laughed. She loved Aiden, he was like a brother to her. "Tell Sebastian it's time."

"You bet," Aiden replied. He hung up on her and she turned back to the television to see him approach Sebastian on the fairway and whisper in his ear. Sebastian shook his head as if in disbelief and then ran over to José to break the news. Thirty seconds later he was on the back of a buggy heading towards the clubhouse.

Eddie Franklin screamed out of the television. "Well that's it folks. That's the last we're going to see of Sebastian Bloom this week. Something tells me a baby is about to make an appearance. Will he get home in time?"

"He bloody well better had," Olivia growled through gritted teeth.

"Shut up, you stupid idiot." Georgiana threw a cushion at the television and turned back to Olivia. "Right. What do you want to do? Hospital?"

Olivia grimaced as another contraction took her. She nodded her agreement and Georgiana flew into action. She picked up Olivia's 'go' bag from the hallway and ran outside to start the car while Hattie helped Olivia through the house.

Georgiana drove her to the clinic where she was met by the maternity team, alerted to her impending arrival by Hattie.

Over in Merseyside, Sebastian's courtesy car had been given a police escort to get him through the build-up of tournament traffic. They arrived at the private airfield in fifteen minutes, he jumped onto the waiting jet and was in the air before he even had time to do up his seatbelt.

As soon as they were at cruising altitude he switched on his phone and called Georgiana.

"Well?" he said when she answered.

"She's fine. It's all under control," she replied. "I'm here and Hattie's at home holding the fort."

"Ok, good. Can I talk to her?" Sebastian was desperate to speak to Olivia. He heard her moans in the background.

"Now might not be the best time." Georgiana gulped as another contraction tore through Olivia.

"Tell her to hold on and that I love her. Please don't leave her on her own."

"I have no intention of leaving her side until you get here. How long will you be?" She looked at her watch and then over at Olivia again.

"An hour and a half tops," Sebastian replied.

"Ok. Be safe and I'll see you soon." Georgiana ended the call and rushed over to hold Olivia's hand.

"Sebastian will be here in an hour or so. He said to tell you he loves you, but you know that," she grinned.

She turned to Dr Khan. "How long do you think it will be?"

"A few hours at least," he replied. "You're doing brilliantly Olivia. Just breathe and relax."

Sebastian arrived at the clinic just over an hour later and

sprinted up to their room on the third floor. He burst through the door to find Dr Khan examining Olivia with a worried look on his face.

"I shouldn't have gone," he grabbed Olivia's hand. "I should have been here. Are you ok, darling?"

"Something's wrong," she panicked.

Sebastian addressed Dr Khan. "What's going on? Is the baby ok?"

Dr Khan looked at Sebastian and then spoke to Olivia. "Baby isn't doing too well Olivia, so we're going to get him out right now." He signalled for the porters to move Olivia towards the lift. "Let's go. NOW."

"What do you mean 'not doing too well'?" Sebastian barked.

"The heart rate is a little low for my liking. I'm not taking any risks. I need you to sign the consent papers." Dr Khan nodded towards the nurse who was holding a form for Sebastian to sign to confirm his wife's emergency caesarean section.

Sebastian scrawled his signature on the papers and held onto Olivia's hand as they moved quickly towards the lifts.

"I'm scared," Olivia whispered.

Sebastian bent down and kissed her forehead. "It's going to be ok. Don't worry. Dr Khan is one of the best." He was calm, but his eyes betrayed his fear.

"I'll wait here," Georgiana called. "I'll ring Hattie too."

Sebastian turned to Georgiana. "Thank you for getting her here safely and staying with her."

Georgiana watched the doors to the lift close and went back into the suite to begin the anxious wait for news of Olivia and the baby.

Seeing how distraught Olivia was and the terrified look in Sebastian's eyes put her problems into perspective. She had been tremendously hurt by Wyatt and was mortified that she had fallen for him and his lies so dramatically. Her pain had turned to anger and she was determined to fight him every step of the way when it came to The Riverside.

Pushing all thoughts of Wyatt out of her mind, she picked up her phone to call Hattie.

CHAPTER 18

"*I* should fire your arse," JJ yelled at Emily as she stood in front of his desk in Caleris Global's London office.

Emily went pale. "Please JJ, don't," she begged. "I know I screwed up but I'll find a way to sort it out. I'll find another property better than The Riverside."

"Wyatt wants The Riverside. His heart is set on it and he's a man who always gets what he wants. I suggest you get down there and talk to Old man Hampton, and throw money at him. Whatever it takes." JJ was furious.

"Mr Hampton isn't interested in money. If he were I wouldn't be standing here now." Emily was exasperated. She had worked so hard to bring The Riverside to the table and she alone was responsible for messing things up.

"Damn Sebastian," she muttered.

"You're the one who'll be damned if you don't deliver for Athos," JJ replied. "And don't think I don't mean it. You may be the best closer I have, but you'll be gone if this goes tits up."

"I'm on it." Emily walked out of his office with as much pride as she could muster. She should have known better than to tell anyone before the deal for the exclusive country club was signed, but she hadn't reckoned on Sebastian and his ego getting in the way.

She hadn't spoken to Olivia since she had run away from Appleton Vale after her argument with Sebastian. Not talking to her best friend was killing her, but she couldn't see a way back - not right now, anyway.

When she returned to her desk there was an email from Wyatt marked urgent. She took a deep breath before opening it.

> Ms Delevigne,
>
> I'm disappointed that there have been complications in tying up The Riverside deal. I have authorized JJ to secure the property, no matter how much it costs.
> Please see to it.
>
> Regards,
> W.Clayton.

"Please see to it," she muttered. "Yeah, like it's that easy."

Emily picked up the phone and dialled the number of The Riverside. She needed to talk to Edward, make him see that he had made a mistake and that Athos was the best option, but deep down she knew it was a waste of time. There was no way in hell that Sebastian would back down, and he easily had the funds to secure the club at the price Edward had set.

She hung up just as the call was answered. "What's the point?" she said aloud. She'd had enough of work for the day. She grabbed her bag and walked out of the office without a backwards glance.

She arrived at her house the same time as JJ turned up in a taxi.

"What are you doing here?" She was shattered and wanted to be alone.

"For God's sake Em, you can't just walk out. Everyone already thinks I favour you and you're not making it any easier to dispel that."

"I don't give a toss what anyone thinks," she replied wearily.

"You care what I think." JJ stepped towards her and pulled her into his arms. "Don't you?" He pushed her up against the front door and kissed her forcefully.

"Not here," she hissed and pushed him away. "I don't want the neighbours gossiping."

"Well, let me in then. A really good shag will make us both feel better." His eyes glinted with lust.

Emily sighed. It had been a truly rotten day so far. Maybe it would make her feel better.

No sooner had she shut the door than JJ had unzipped her dress and let it drop to the floor. He licked his lips as he cast his eyes over her body, deliciously curvy in a Marilyn Monroe kind of way.

"Let's take this upstairs," he growled in her ear.

Later that evening, not long after JJ had scuttled back to his wife, Emily sat in her lounge staring at the television. She had just watched the ten o'clock news, learning that Sebastian had left The Open to be with Olivia for the birth of their first child. It killed her that she had been frozen out of her best friend's life.

"What the hell am I going to do to fix this?" she muttered. "There has to be a way."

CHAPTER 19

"It's ok darling. You'll be fine." Sebastian had hastily changed into a gown and mask and was holding Olivia's hand whilst Dr Khan and his team quickly prepared her for the caesarean.

"We need to move quickly," Dr Khan told them. "I'm going to put you under, Olivia."

"No," Olivia cried. "I want to be awake."

Sebastian stroked her head and muttered soothing words to her. He looked at Dr Khan and nodded. "Do whatever you need to do to keep them both safe."

The anaesthesiologist wasted no time in knocking Olivia out and Dr Khan immediately got to work. Less than two minutes later he delivered the baby and quickly cut the umbilical cord that was wrapped around his neck. He handed him to the specialist paediatric consultant who had been called into the operating theatre to assist, and turned his attentions back to Olivia.

"A beautiful baby boy." Doctor Khan glanced at Sebastian. "Congratulations."

"Is he ok?" Sebastian was choked with emotion.

"We got him out in the nick of time but he needs to go to ICU," Dr Khan replied. "I'm a little worried about Olivia. I think you should wait outside."

"I'm not leaving her," Sebastian growled.

"Go with your baby Sebastian." Dr Khan was forceful. "Now."

Sebastian glanced at Olivia. Her face was drained of all colour and she looked incredibly fragile. He was in a blind panic. "What's wrong with her?" he whispered.

"Haemorrhage. Go with your son," Dr Khan ordered. He turned back to Olivia and immediately got to work.

Sebastian allowed himself to be led out of the operating theatre and stumbled after the team whisking his new son to the infant intensive care unit. He had been deprived of oxygen for just a few moments but they weren't taking any chances. Sebastian stood over him as he was placed into an incubator and attached to several machines to monitor his heart rate and breathing.

He jumped when the nurse touched his arm. "He's going to be just fine Mr Bloom," she reassured him. "All the signs are very good, this is just a precaution."

"I have to get back to my wife." He was in a blind panic. If anything happened to her his life would be over. She was his heart and soul. "Can my sister come and sit with him?"

"Of course," the nurse replied. "Is she here already? We'll get someone to bring her over."

"Yes." Sebastian was already texting her.

A few minutes later Georgiana was ushered in to intensive care where she found Sebastian pacing up and down.

"They wouldn't tell me anything," she cried. "What's happened? Where's Liv?"

"They're working on her now," he replied. He was in shock.

"Working on her?" Georgiana was confused.

"She suffered a great deal of blood loss," the nurse informed her. "But Dr Khan is one of the best, try not to worry."

"Stay with the baby," Sebastian told Georgiana before he ran out of the room to be with Olivia.

Georgiana was stunned. Everything had gone so smoothly throughout Olivia's pregnancy, but in the last hour it had all changed.

"Come and meet your nephew," the nurse smiled. "He's doing very well. A real little fighter."

"A boy," Georgiana gasped. "Olivia will be so pleased. She wanted a boy." She pushed her hand into the hole that allowed her to touch the baby in his incubator. "He's beautiful."

"Isn't he?" the nurse agreed. "Going to be a real heartbreaker."

"Just like his Daddy," Georgiana smiled. She sat next to the baby for what seemed like an eternity before she got a call from Sebastian. She stepped outside the unit to take it.

"She's still in surgery. Massive blood loss." He croaked. "How's my boy?"

"He's beautiful and the nurse says he's fine. No need to worry about him," Georgiana reassured him. "Is Liv going to be ok?"

"I don't know," Sebastian replied grimly. "She has to be. We need her."

Georgiana didn't know what to say to him. She couldn't promise him that Olivia would pull through or tell him that he shouldn't worry. All she could do was stay with the baby and wait for news.

After an agonising wait Sebastian appeared at Georgiana's side and the look of relief on his face was immense.

"She's ok," he croaked, then broke down in tears. Georgiana put her arms around him and he sobbed into her hair.

"I thought we'd lost her," he whispered. "She's in recovery now and Dr Khan said she should be fine."

Georgiana breathed a sigh of relief. "Well this little one is pretty bloody perfect." She grinned at Sebastian. "Trust you two to produce the best-looking baby ever."

Sebastian laughed and wiped away his tears. "Can I hold him?" he asked the nurse.

She consulted the chart and nodded. "I don't see why not. We have to keep the monitors on, but a minute or two with Daddy will do him the world of good." She motioned for Sebastian to sit down in the armchair next to the incubator and gently placed his son in his arms.

He was speechless. He gazed at him in awe and stroked his cheek. "Well didn't you just give us a little scare?" he murmured. "Mummy is sleeping but you'll meet her as soon as she wakes up. She's an amazing woman, you're a very lucky boy."

Georgiana smiled as she watched Sebastian with his new son. She was so relieved that they were both going to be fine. She backed out of the room quietly to call Hattie with the good news.

CHAPTER 20

*D*an arrived in London at lunchtime on Friday for the premiere of 'Catch me when I Fall' the next evening. In the last ten days he had visited five other countries and done more than thirty television appearances and interviews. He was exhausted.

He loved his co-stars, but was fed up to the back teeth of repeating the same narrative over and over again in joint interviews - the jokes were wearing thin.

He jumped into a waiting car as soon as he stepped off the jet and made his way through the traffic to Chelsea. He called his mother to let her know he was on his way.

"Hey Mum," he said wearily.

"Darling. You are coming, aren't you?" she asked. It was his grandmother's eightieth birthday the next day and Dan had faithfully promised he would be there.

"For God's sake mum, of course I'm coming. I'm in a car right now," he exclaimed. "Should be there in under the hour."

"Granny is so looking forward to seeing you," she told him. "We all are."

After an excruciatingly slow crawl through London's ever-present traffic Dan arrived at his childhood home on one of the most exclusive streets in Chelsea. His car pulled up outside the imposing, mid-terrace Victorian house and he climbed the steps that led to the front door.

The house was stretched over five floors and had a fabulous view of the river Thames across Battersea Park. It had enormous rooms with huge sash windows and high ceilings, and all of the original features were still intact. It was beautifully decorated in soft brown and green tones, and Dan had recently paid for a swanky new kitchen that now took up the entire basement level, backing onto the garden.

"You're here!" Claudia exclaimed as she opened the door. "Let me look at you."

Dan laughed and kissed her on the cheek. "Hi, Mum. You look beautiful."

"Come in darling, but watch your step. There's party chaos at every turn. The caterers have taken over my kitchen and God only knows what's going on in the garden with that marquee." She stroked his cheek and guided him inside. "It's lovely to have you home."

"Where's Dad?" Dan dropped his bag on the floor and closed the door behind him.

"He got called out to an emergency but he shouldn't be too long now. Come and see Granny, she's already stuck into the gin, God help us."

"I'll just go and dump my stuff." He climbed three flights of stairs to his old room at the top of the house. He pushed open the door and breathed in the memories. It was like a time warp –

nothing had changed since he left a decade ago. There were still Girls Aloud posters on the walls and his double bed looked tiny in comparison to his oversized one in LA. The desk where he had done his homework was still sitting under the window that looked out over the park. He had spent many hours dreaming about becoming an actor in that very spot when he should have been studying.

He looked around the room and grinned at the stack of vinyl records piled up on the floor – he had once fancied himself as a top DJ – and smiled at the giant teddy bear in the corner that he had had all of his life. It was the room of a child who had long since grown up and flown the nest.

He put his bag on the bed, unzipped it and rummaged around for the gift he had specially commissioned for his grandmother's birthday – a heart-shaped locket containing a tiny, scaled down photograph of her and his grandfather on their wedding day.

A message came through on his mobile just as he was heading back downstairs. It was from his agent, Vinnie.

Montreal moved up a few weeks. Be there by Monday.

Dan sighed. He was supposed to be going back to LA on Monday and taking the next three weeks to relax and recharge his batteries.

He quickly called his PA, Coby McBride. "The jet is out for maintenance. Can you book me on the morning flight to Montreal on Monday please?"

"I'm still in Wisconsin," Coby replied. "But yeah, I'll do it now. When do you think you'll be home?"

"They said a week, but you know how these things run on." Dan checked his calendar. "Can you also cancel my lunch with Johnny and get him to send the script to my hotel? Oh, and can you get a gift for Randy's son? It's his eighteenth and I promised I'd go to the party, but I'm definitely not going to be able to now."

He issued a few additional instructions to Coby and then trotted downstairs to find his mother and grandmother in the kitchen toasting each other's good health whilst the party preparation carried on around them.

"Hello, gorgeous." He bent down and kissed his grandmother on the cheek. "Happy birthday. Bit early for the hard stuff, isn't it?"

"Never too early Daniel," she clucked. "Now stand back and let me look at you."

Dan did as he was told.

"Handsome, as always," she hiccoughed and clinked her glass with Claudia's. "But still no girlfriend?"

"Plenty of time for that," he grinned. "Besides, I'm not settling for anything less than what you and grandpops have." His grandparents on his father's side had been married for fifty-five years and were still as in love as the day they met. "You're my benchmark."

"It would be nice to have some grandchildren before I'm too old to enjoy them." Claudia looked at him pointedly. "Just tell me everything we read isn't true. It gives your father a heart attack every time he opens the paper and sees you in a clinch with some starlet or other."

Dan snorted and reached for a glass. "We've been through this a hundred times. Don't read that rubbish, most of it is completely fabricated."

"Most?" Claudia raised an eyebrow.

"Yes, most," Dan chuckled. He picked up the bottle of gin and poured a slug into the glass. "I might as well join you two drunken lushes."

An hour later his father, Francis, arrived home to find the three of them roaring with laughter and tucking into the canapés that were meant for the party the next day.

"Good to see you, old boy." Francis slapped his back and hugged him. "No girlfriend with you?"

"Will you lot stop this bloody girlfriend nonsense. You'll be the first to know when I do meet someone special. Right now, I'm working my arse off and there's no time to invest in a proper relationship."

"Work hard, play hard, eh?" A voice boomed from behind him. "That's my boy."

Dan turned around to greet his grandfather. "Hey dude!" He hugged him and then laughed as he caught sight of his outfit - some very old-fashioned plus-fours and a Pringle jumper. "Been on the golf course?"

"Bastards took all my cash," he guffawed. "Hello, my darling." He kissed his wife and sat down at the table. "Get me a drink please, Daniel."

Dan poured a scotch and passed it to his grandfather, who took a sip and then raised his glass to the room. "To my beautiful wife. Eighty, eh? Who'd have thought we'd ever get here? Seems like only yesterday when I met a dazzling young girl outside the cinema and now here we are."

Dan spent the rest of the afternoon in the bosom of his family and felt more relaxed and happy than he had in ages. Later that evening after dinner, he sat back and quietly watched his parents and grandparents laughing and chatting, recounting stories from before he was born and from the early days of marriage. He knew he was blessed to come from such a loving and tight-knit family unit, and his only regret about moving to LA was the distance between them.

His grandfather held onto his grandmother's hand all night, gently stroking it with his thumb and listening intently to every word that came out of her mouth. Dan suddenly felt a yearning from deep inside. He wanted to find someone to share his life. If he could be even half as happy as they still were then it would be plenty good enough for him.

CHAPTER 21

"*Y*our wife is awake Mr Bloom, if you'd like to see her?" The nurse bent down to pluck the baby from Sebastian's arms.

He kissed his son and sprinted out of the unit. He met Dr Khan outside Olivia's room.

"She's going to make a full recovery," he smiled. "She's very weak and needs rest, but you can go in for a few minutes. She's been asking for you."

Sebastian shook his hand. "Thank you so much. I don't know what I would have done had I lost her."

"Well, you don't need to worry about that now. Go on, in you go." He pushed Sebastian towards the door.

"Hi," Olivia whispered. She looked dreadful.

Sebastian rushed to her side and kissed her. "Don't ever do that to me again," he said, shaking his head. "You frightened me to death."

"Where's the baby?" asked Olivia.

Sebastian smiled reassuringly. "He's having a few more hours under observation, but he's absolutely fine. Perfect in fact. And Georgiana is with him, he hasn't been left alone for even a second."

Olivia looked relieved. "I'm so glad it's a boy."

"He's beautiful, just like his Mummy." Sebastian kissed her forehead and stroked her hair. He could see she was exhausted. "Get some sleep darling. When you wake up you can meet him."

He stayed with her for half an hour as she slept, listening to her breathing in time with the bleeps of the machines that were attached to her body. He thanked his lucky stars that she had made it through.

He took the opportunity to send a text to the list of friends and family who were eagerly awaiting news.

It's a boy! Arrived at seven-thirty-two pm weighing in at seven pounds exactly. There were a few complications but Liv and the baby are doing well now.

He pressed send and almost immediately replies started to flood in.

The first was from José and the next from José's wife, Angelica. She and Olivia were close, and both had been earmarked as godparents since the start of the pregnancy.

There was one from his long-time manager Richie Rogers, who was out in America tying up a huge new endorsement contract for Sebastian, and another from his caddie, Aiden. Olivia's father, Nicolas, replied saying how excited he and her mother Constance were, and that they would come to meet their grandson whenever they were ready to receive visitors. They were terribly worried about Olivia but Sebastian reassured them enough to stop them rushing to the hospital. He knew Olivia would not want her mother fussing around her – they didn't have the easiest of relationships.

He looked at a few more messages, kissed Olivia and headed back to see the baby. He was exhausted. It had been an emotional and terrifying experience, one that he never wished to repeat. He eased himself into the armchair next to the incubator, leaned back and watched his son sleep. Within moments he was fast asleep, too.

He woke in a start almost an hour later to find Georgiana rocking the baby in her arms.

"Everything's fine," she whispered. "Liv's still asleep and I popped home when you passed out to get a few things for you. I'm guessing you'll be staying here as long as you need to, so there's a change of clothes and some other bits."

"Hand him over." Sebastian reached for the baby. "Do you think it's ok for him to meet mummy now?" Sebastian asked the nurse.

She smiled and nodded. "The doctor is very happy with his progress, but as a precaution we'll bring mum up here. I'll call down and arrange it. She's just been through a difficult surgery, so no over-exertion or any heroics."

"Don't worry," Sebastian replied. "I'll be watching her like a hawk."

Olivia was wheeled into the room twenty minutes later and Sebastian placed the baby in her arms. "Here's mummy," he whispered. "She's pretty great, I think you'll like her."

"Oh, he's beautiful. He looks like you." She gazed at her olive-skinned, dark-haired son. "He's got your eyes. One brown, one green."

"What a relief," he grinned. "At least there's no doubt who the daddy is this time." He was talking about his late daughter, Lizzie, who had died in a car crash along with her mother, Sebastian's first wife. It had almost broken him when he found out that he wasn't Lizzie's biological father, and it had taken a long time for him to come to terms with it.

"Shall we call him Alexander?" Olivia broke into his moment of sadness with a hopeful question.

Sebastian smiled. "I knew that was the frontrunner." He looked at his son and whispered, "Alexander Bloom, welcome to our family. Be brave and strong my boy."

Olivia sighed with contentment. "I'm so happy, even if I do feel like crap."

They sat quietly and companionably for a short while before Alexander fell asleep again in her arms. Sebastian reached for his mobile and sifted through the hundreds of congratulatory messages he had received since he had broken the news. He responded to the ones from José and Angelica – she was desperate for a photo – and from Richie who had sent another text asking if they would be open to a photocall with the media on leaving the hospital. He tapped his reply one-handed.

No. This is private.

A few minutes later Dr Khan appeared.

"Just wanted to check on you before I leave." He smiled at the sight of Olivia with the baby cradled tightly in her arms. "You need some rest Olivia. Don't overdo it."

Sebastian went to shake Dr Khan's hand, but at the last moment pulled him into an embrace. "Thank you. For everything."

"Entirely my pleasure. To be present at the birth of a new life is all the thanks I need." He turned back to Olivia. "You can go back to your suite now and baby can join you in a few hours. Does he have a name yet?"

"Alexander." Sebastian puffed his chest out with pride.

Sebastian walked with Olivia as she was wheeled back to their rooms and settled in bed. The nurse noted her vital signs on the chart. "All good here, Mrs Bloom. Press the buzzer if you need me."

"Thank you," Sebastian told the nurse before turning back to Olivia.

"Come and lie with me?" Olivia held her arms out and motioned for him to join her on the bed.

"That's not an unreasonable request from a woman who's just given me the most amazing gift I'll ever have," Sebastian laughed. "Budge over."

Olivia moved gingerly to make room for Sebastian. She settled back in his arms and they lay in comfortable silence until Sebastian whispered: "That was a close call. Don't you dare leave me."

"Never," Olivia mumbled into his chest as she drifted off to sleep.

After another sleepless night, Georgiana was exhausted. She had come home in the early hours once she was sure Olivia and Alexander were stable. Wyatt was on her mind all of the time. She had never experienced anything like the kind of passion he had stirred up in her, but it was tainted with his lies. She could not abide liars. It was the one thing she asked of everyone in her life - to be truthful, no matter what. She also hated herself for falling so hard for him.

She picked up the phone and sent Hattie a text.

Two hours and counting. Sebastian said we can go at ten o'clock. I'll pick you up at nine thirty. G x

She had received countless messages from Wyatt demanding that she listen to him, and had ignored each and every one of them. She assumed he was back in New York by now and she was glad of the distance. Hattie replied to her text almost immediately.

Terribly excited, haven't slept a wink. Come over for breakfast darling x

Georgiana sighed. She might as well go and pretend to eat something, it would mean she had less time on her own to reflect on her misfortune and wallow in her misery. She looked dreadful. She had lost weight, her insomnia had left her with dark shadows under her eyes, and her face looked drawn and hollow. Sebastian and Olivia had not noticed her rapid decline - they were in a baby bubble and she had purposefully kept out of their way. Only Hattie knew the full extent of her misery and she was doing her best to comfort Georgiana in her time of need.

She quickly got dressed and attempted to make herself presentable, applying more make-up than she would normally wear. She pulled her hair into a ponytail and stared into the mirror. "That'll have to do," she muttered, grimacing at her reflection. She went downstairs, grabbed her bag and keys, and left the house with Lady hot on her heels. A few minutes later she pulled up outside the lodge and was greeted by Hattie who was beside herself with excitement.

"Darling! Come inside." She enveloped Georgiana into a comforting motherly embrace and led her into the house. "You look tired."

Georgiana shook her head. "I know. I look like crap." Her eyes welled up and she fought to hold back the tears.

"I can't imagine what it was like at the hospital. I wish you had let me come." Hattie kissed the top of her head.

"There was no point in all of us being there. I'm bloody knackered, but I bet Liv is feeling a whole lot worse. Poor thing." Georgiana recalled the moment when things started to go wrong. "It was awful. I was so scared for her. You should have seen the panic in her eyes."

"Good job Sebastian got there when he did," Hattie sighed.

"I thought he was going to fall apart at one point. You've never seen anyone look as desolate as he did when they rushed her into theatre." Georgiana shivered at the memory. "I really think he thought she was going to die. Can you imagine?"

"It doesn't bear thinking about." Hattie dismissed the notion. "I'm so happy for them both. Now, what would you like for breakfast? I'm going to sit here and make you eat up every last bit. Coffee?"

Georgiana slumped into a chair at the kitchen table and gratefully accepted the coffee Hattie placed in front of her. "I need to start mainlining caffeine if I'm going to stay awake. I'll just have some fruit, please."

"How about some scrambled eggs?" Hattie suggested hopefully.

"No, thanks. But I'll try to force down a yoghurt if you have one?" She knew she had to get some food inside her, but everything tasted bland and she just wasn't hungry.

"Yes of course, there's some of that raspberry one you like in the fridge." Hattie poured herself coffee and sat down at the table with Georgiana. "Eat up. You're wasting away."

"You're not eating." Georgiana glared at Hattie.

"I had some porridge before you got here. And besides, I'm

hardly in need of sustenance." Hattie had given up dieting years ago.

"You're lovely and you always look beautiful to me," Georgiana smiled. "Thank you for listening to me and for trying to make me feel better. I love you."

An hour later they were in the car and on their way to the hospital. The paparazzi was already camped outside the gates of the clinic when they arrived, desperate to get the first shot of baby Bloom. Sebastian was one of the most recognisable sportsmen in the world and anything to do with him was big news, especially a baby, given what had happened in the past. His life had been played out in the world's media and the public's appetite for him was unwavering.

"Bloody hell, news travels fast." Georgiana was shocked. "How did they find out so quickly?"

"It wasn't exactly a secret darling." Hattie patted her hand. "I think Sebastian walking off the golf course in the middle of a Major championship might have given it away."

"He'll be pissed off," Georgiana said as she turned her face away from the cameras. The gates finally swung open and she and continued down the tree-lined driveway towards the mansion that housed the clinic.

They had to check in with the receptionist on arrival and she called up to the suite to announce their presence. "You can go up now."

The door to the suite was open ajar in expectation of visitors and Georgiana rushed through it, Hattie right behind her. She stopped dead when she saw her brother standing by the window with Alexander cradled in his arms, whispering a private conversation with him, oblivious to anyone else in the room.

"Oh," she gasped. "We didn't mean to interrupt."

"Don't be silly. We were expecting you. Come and meet your grandson, Hattie."

"Grandson?" Hattie exclaimed.

"Of course," Sebastian replied. "You're going to have a huge part to play in his life and you'll be a fantastic grandmother."

Hattie lifted Alexander out of Sebastian's arms and drew him close to her chest.

"Well? What do you think? Isn't he perfect?" Sebastian's voice was brimming with pride.

Hattie was crying. "Oh Sebastian. He looks exactly like you as a baby. It's uncanny."

"And he has my eyes," he grinned.

"Sebastian," Olivia called from the bedroom. "Let them come in."

Hattie and Georgiana gasped when they saw how pale and fragile Olivia looked.

"Stop it," she said. "I'm feeling much better now."

"You'll be back to yourself in no time." Hattie touched her cheek fondly. "How is he feeding?" She rocked the baby back and forth in her arms.

"Not great," Olivia sighed. "They said it would be difficult after the blood transfusion. It's frustrating both of us."

"I've got a little something for you, darling." Sebastian fished a small box out of his pocket and handed it to Olivia.

"See! I told you," Georgiana laughed.

"Told her what exactly?" Sebastian wanted to know his secret gift had not been compromised.

125

"Told her you'd buy her something nice. It's what any decent and fabulously wealthy husband would do." Georgiana grinned. "Open it then," she said to Olivia.

Olivia lifted the lid and gasped. "Oh Sebastian. This must have cost the earth. It's beautiful."

"You're worth every penny. Try it on." He held her hand and slipped the ring onto her finger. "Fits like a glove."

Georgiana shrieked. "That must be at least five carats. Oh my God, it's gorgeous." The flawless, square-cut diamond shimmered in the morning sunlight as Olivia showed it off.

"I don't know what to say." Olivia was emotional. "Thank you, I love it."

Georgiana held Alexander for another ten minutes before Sebastian indicated that Olivia needed to rest. "I can cuddle you as much as I want when you get home, little man," she whispered to the baby. "I'm really happy for you both." She kissed Olivia and squeezed Sebastian's hand before leaving.

She was quiet on the short journey back to the manor. Hattie reached across and patted her hand. "That will be you one day, darling. But for now, just enjoy Alexander."

Georgiana gulped back her tears and focused on the road ahead.

CHAPTER 22

The air was thick with excitement as Dan stepped out of the limo into Leicester Square for the premiere of 'Catch me if I Fall'. He waved to the fans and turned to help his mother out of the car.

"Oh!" she exclaimed. "This is exciting, isn't it?" She linked her arm through his and started the walk down the red carpet with a beaming smile on her face.

Dan's name was being screamed from both sides of the red carpet where fans had been camped out overnight to bag the best vantage point. Both of his main co-stars were ahead of him and already being interviewed by the waiting media, but Dan wanted to mingle with the crowd and thank his fans for their support.

"I'm just going to sign some autographs, mum. Why don't you go on in? Maddie will take you." Dan waved at his publicist, who was at his side in a flash.

"Can you take mum in and get her settled? And don't forget the champagne!" He kissed Claudia on the cheek and headed towards the fans.

For the next twenty minutes, he signed all manner of items from T-shirts to bare breasts, and posed for selfies until Maddie signalled it was time for him to go inside. He slipped into his seat just as the lights were dimming and the credits began to roll.

In the early days', he had relished attending his premieres and watching the audience reaction to his work. But in recent years he had taken to walking the red carpet and showing his face in the cinema, then quietly escaping until the after-show party. Claudia had insisted she accompany him to this latest one, which meant he had to sit through the entire film when all he wanted to do was go home and sleep.

Like many of his peers, he didn't enjoy watching himself on screen and spent the majority of the film mentally criticising his performance. As the final credits rolled, the audience – many invited guests from film, television and music – burst into applause. He stood up alongside his co-stars and acknowledged the praise that was being lavished on them, then spent a few minutes chatting to guests in his immediate vicinity. Maddie appeared and tapped her watch.

"We have to go," she said. "You've got to be at the party in fifteen minutes and we're cutting it fine."

"Are you ready, Mum?" Dan passed Claudia her jacket and guided her out of the cinema and into a waiting car. They were whisked over to Knightsbridge where the party was taking place in private members' club, The Duke.

For the next two hours Dan accepted congratulations for his performance from his movie industry peers, friends and family who had been invited to the party. He was just winding up to disappear off home when a shrill voice called out across the room.

"Darling!"

Dan groaned. Suddenly, he was engulfed in a fog of overpowering perfume and Daphne Stallwort-Hoskins appeared in front of him. Known as the number one 'it' girl in London, they'd enjoyed a brief relationship a few years ago before he realised how completely dreary she was. Undeniably beautiful and rich as Croesus, she was also incredibly dim and tiresomely dull.

Daphne threw her arms around Dan and clung on to him for dear life until she was sure the photographers had captured the moment.

He forced a smile and kissed her on both cheeks. "Daphne. You look beautiful, as always."

"So do you," she purred. "I've missed you Danny."

"Err, yeah." Dan took a step backwards, just out of her grasp. "I'm not over all that much at the moment. Movie commitments."

"I'll be in LA next month," Daphne breathed. "Let's get together then and relive old times." She winked and stroked his arm.

"I'm filming back-to-back movies for the next few months, so I doubt I'll be around." Dan tried to let her down gently. "But let me know when you're over and we'll see how the land lies."

"Ooh," Daphne squeaked. "Think of how much fun we'll have."

Dan glared at Maddie who was standing nearby and she immediately rushed to his side.

"I need you," she said. "Interview."

Dan breathed a sigh of relief. Maddie could read the signs when he needed rescuing.

"Sadly Daphne, I'm needed elsewhere." He kissed her on the cheek and turned away.

"See you in LA baby," she called as he walked off.

Dan shuddered. "Thank you," he said to Maddie. "She's a nightmare. Do not under any circumstances let her anywhere near me when she comes to LA. I'll make sure Coby knows as well."

Maddie grinned. "You can handle her. She's way too dumb and thick-skinned to realise when she's being given the brush off."

"That may be so," he laughed. "But you're my last line of defence when Coby isn't around, so I'm relying on you to keep lunatics away from me."

"Have you heard from him?" Maddie asked. His PA, Coby, was back in Wisconsin for a family funeral.

"I spoke to him yesterday and he sent a text earlier to wish me luck. He said he was going mad being stuck in the back of beyond with a raft of distant relations. Oh, and that he's had to turn down the gay a notch or two."

Maddie snorted. "Poor Coby. He'll be back in all his technicolour glory soon."

"I think we're going to go. I'm knackered and Mum is pretty drunk." He looked across the room and saw Claudia engaged in animated conversation with his director and a handful of hangers-on.

"I'll slip out quietly. Can you grab Mum and meet me at the car?" Dan turned towards the exit with his head down and managed to sneak out largely unnoticed.

Twenty minutes later they were back home and he helped Claudia into the house.

"I think you overdid it a bit," he laughed as she almost tripped up the steps.

"Nonsense," she giggled. "I need to go to bed."

"You do." Dan held her elbow, guided her up the stairs and deposited her in the care of his father, who'd been working while they were at the premiere.

"She's all yours," he grinned.

"Well done son." Francis slapped him on the back. "By all accounts you were a triumph."

"Thanks," he beamed. "Night, Dad."

As he lay in his old bed that night, he realised how quickly the last decade had gone yet how much he had achieved in that time. He was proud of his efforts, loved acting and had every intention of carrying on, but he felt like something was missing now. He wanted someone to share it all with.

CHAPTER 23

Olivia and baby Alexander remained in hospital for three days before they were allowed to go home. Olivia's parents had arrived at the clinic the day after the birth, desperately concerned about her wellbeing. They stayed overnight at the manor and visited again the next morning before returning to their home in Hertfordshire, satisfied that their daughter was on the road to recovery.

Georgiana spent the rest of her time off getting to know her new nephew and helping Sebastian with him while Olivia was recovering. All too soon she was on her way to Montreal for the tennis, but she was actually looking forward to getting back to work.

Seeing how incredibly happy her brother and Olivia were spurred her on to stop moping over a man she barely knew and get on with her life.

She boarded the flight and was ushered into her first-class seat by an effusive stewardess who couldn't do enough for her. She glanced across the aisle and found herself staring at Dan

Flowers. She knew he was a serious Hollywood mega-star, his fame achieved through a series of hugely popular action movies. Not quite Indiana Jones, but big box office nonetheless.

"Hi." He flashed her a dazzling smile. "I'm Dan Flowers."

"Georgiana Bloom," she held out her hand and smiled. She was struck by how manly and attractive he was. The not-so-perfect nose and scar on his cheek gave his face character, adding to his masculinity.

"What takes you to Montreal, Dan?" she asked.

"Off on location for my next film. And you?" He was keen to find out more about her.

"Coupe Rogers. Not playing, of course," she laughed.

"That's where I've seen you before," he exclaimed. "You and McEnroe at Wimbledon. I remember thinking how beautiful you were." He was unabashed.

Georgiana blushed. "Thank you."

"Have a drink with me?" Dan urged.

She nodded. "Why not? We've got a few hours to kill and it may be fun to do it together."

As soon as they were airborne he moved across to join Georgiana, and asked the stewardess to bring over a bottle of champagne.

"And can I assume that Sebastian Bloom is your brother?" Dan said as he sat down with Georgiana.

"Yep," she grinned. "And I usually get asked if I'm his sister so that makes a nice change, thank you."

"I think someone like you deserves their own top billing, don't you?" Dan stared into her eyes and held her gaze. Georgiana looked away first. He was unnerving her. It was like he could see inside her soul.

She quickly changed the subject. "So, tell me about the film."

"It's Orion Powell's latest outing. 'Custodian of War'," Dan said. "We don't go into full production for a few weeks yet, but there are some scenes the director wants to get in the can early. Something to do with access to the location being limited."

"I'm afraid to say I haven't seen any of your Orion Powell movies, but I loved 'Changing Lives' and I watched 'All in at One' last year when Netflix had the box set. It was brilliant." She clinked her glass against his. "Well done you."

Dan laughed and raised his glass to her. "And I'm mortified to say that I've seen absolutely none of your work other than a brief glance at you on screen, but I'm utterly convinced you're wonderful, as well as being totally adorable."

Georgiana blushed again and squirmed in her seat. He was completely charming and clearly well-practised when it came to chatting up women. She thought it strange that there were no alarm bells going off in her head, and given her recent experience with Wyatt she was surprised at how relaxed she was in Dan's company.

They talked for the entire flight and Georgiana found him both witty and engaging. He had her laughing like a drain by the time they were half-way across the Atlantic, and she realised she hadn't felt this happy in ages.

They arrived in Montreal a little worse for wear and exited the plane arm in arm. As they walked through arrivals, cameras began to flash and Georgiana suddenly realised just how big a star Dan Flowers was. She had read all the gossip magazines, she knew he was a serial player, but she didn't really care. He was fun.

She tried to duck out of the way of the photographers, but he held her hand tightly and carried on walking through the airport as if he was oblivious to the unending burst of flash bulbs in his face.

Eventually they made it out to the concourse.

"Where can I take you?" Dan asked as his driver pulled up to the VIP area. "Please, please say my hotel!" He was completely serious.

"That all depends on where you're staying," she grinned.

Dan opened the door and waited for her to climb in. "Ritz-Carlton," he smiled. "Only the best, and I'm assuming that it's your hotel of choice as well."

"How did you guess?" she smirked. "Yes, you can give me a lift. Thank you." She hopped into the back of the limousine.

The journey to the hotel went by in an instant as Dan continued to make Georgiana laugh, regaling her with tales of sordid affairs on location and pranks that he'd played on his co-stars over the years.

"Have dinner with me tonight," Dan insisted when they were checking in to the hotel.

"Love to," Georgiana grinned. She really liked Dan and was having fun. "What time?"

"Meet in the bar at eight?" Dan was hopeful. He was completely bewitched by her.

"Yep, that works for me. See you later." She turned to follow the bellboy to her suite when Dan grabbed her hand and pulled her back.

"You are a delight, Georgiana Bloom." He brushed her lips with his and smiled. "Until tonight."

"Until tonight," she repeated and skipped across the lobby beaming from ear to ear. Maybe Dan was just the tonic she needed to get back on track.

CHAPTER 24

"Are you even listening to me?" Bobby Garnett asked his boss as they sat catching up on several property deals that had been done in Wyatt's absence. Bobby was his number two and Wyatt trusted him implicitly.

Wyatt was staring out of the window of his impressive corner office on the twenty-sixth floor of Athos Towers. Georgiana was consuming his thoughts. He should have told her the truth but that wasn't the way he did business, and he really believed he would be able to use her and move on as he had done with so many women over the years.

His ego would not accept that she didn't want him. Every single woman he had ever wanted, and many he had not, had always fallen at his feet. He had sent Georgiana texts and emails, he even resorted to an old-fashioned letter, but each remained unanswered.

"Have you considered kidnapping and holding her against her will?" Bobby was not being helpful.

"What?" Wyatt broke from his trance and looked quizzically at Bobby.

Bobby grinned. "You heard me."

"I'm pretty sure that's a felony in England as well, but that's not to say I haven't thought about it." Wyatt's laugh was hollow.

"I gotta say I've never seen you like this. Should I be worried?" Bobby was concerned.

"No," Wyatt snapped. "I'm fine. Let's get this done."

Bobby raised his eyebrows at Wyatt's response but knew better than to push him further.

An hour later, Wyatt was relieved when Bobby finished up and left his office. He sat in quiet contemplation. He was a winner - one of the best in the business - yet he had no idea how to close the deal with Georgiana. He had never wanted any woman so badly. He had underestimated her strength and resolution and he was furious with himself. Had he played it better he could have had both The Riverside and Georgiana. His investors were going to be seriously disappointed.

He switched on the enormous flat screen television that was directly opposite his desk and surfed the sports channels, desperate to find something to distract him. He paused when he reached the coverage of the Coupe Rogers tennis from Montreal. Georgiana's face filled the screen.

"Well John, here we are again, just like Peaches and Herb, 'Reunited and it feels so good'". Georgiana grinned at the camera as McEnroe fell about laughing.

"I was starting my professional career when that song was in the charts," John replied.

"Man, that must have been a long time ago." Georgiana winked and set the tone for the rest of the broadcast.

"Feisty as ever," Wyatt muttered.

He couldn't watch any longer. It angered him that she had rejected his advances and just seeing her hurt his ego. He picked up the phone and sent a text to his main investor on The Riverside project. They had met at charity event a decade ago when Wyatt had been in desperate need of a cash injection, and they had enjoyed business success in many deals in the years since.

You free for lunch? My club. W.

A few minutes later the reply came through.

Sure. Wrapping up some business, give me an hour.

An hour later, Wyatt's car rolled up outside the ultra-exclusive members' club, The Metropolitan. He liked the privacy the club afforded him. He could relax, safe in the knowledge that he was keeping company with New York's elite businessmen who valued their confidentiality.

He stepped out of the elevator on the top floor and walked into the club restaurant.

"Welcome, Mr Clayton. Your usual table?" The manager, a diminutive, pretty and beautifully-dressed Asian-American lady greeted him.

"Please," he nodded. "I have a guest joining me."

She led Wyatt to his regular table in the window overlooking Central Park. It was a spectacular view and one he never tired of. He loved Manhattan, how it made him feel alive. His penthouse apartment on the Upper East Side was one of the most expensive and envied properties in the city.

"Hey man." His investor slipped into the seat opposite Wyatt. "You look like crap."

"Tell me something I don't know," Wyatt replied. "Drink?"

"Sure. So, what's the latest on the club?" he asked Wyatt.

Wyatt sighed. "Your old friend Sebastian has screwed us, thanks to that stupid girl shooting her mouth off to him."

"Fuck!" He banged his fists on the table. "I fucking warned you. He's a sneaky son of a bitch. How's it going with the sister?"

"I kinda screwed that one up myself," Wyatt grimaced. "Totally underestimated her. She's nowhere near as weak as you made her out to be."

"I didn't agree to invest this kind of cash into this particular project just for you to fuck it up. I want this place. There's no compromise. I wanna crush Bloom once and for all."

"This vendetta of yours is gonna get us both in trouble, man," Wyatt shook his head.

"You owe me," he replied.

"And I made you even more wealthy, didn't I?" Wyatt sighed, "I'm just pissed about Georgiana. I've never had any woman reject me."

"If you can't get to her, then you gotta find someone else there who's willing to feed us vital information. You gonna be able to do that?"

"Already working on it," Wyatt grinned. "Had an interesting talk with one of the members when I was there. I think she'll be willing to help. She was almost begging for it by the time I'd finished with her."

"Good," he replied. "And forget about the sister for now. I wanna take that bastard down."

Wyatt picked up his drink and drained the contents. "I hear ya.

Right now, I just wanna forget about everything. Let's eat and then I can drink myself stupid."

His guest left the club three hours later and Wyatt was alone. He had been steadily working his way through a bottle of vodka and had finally reached the point where he was numb enough blot out his bruised ego. The more he drank, the less he felt, and it served as the temporary respite he desired.

He didn't remember getting home or even going to bed. When he stirred the next morning, both his head and his penis were throbbing. It took him a moment to wake and was appalled to find that the reason for his raging desire was Ashley, his ex-girlfriend, caressing him with her perfectly-manicured hands. Before he could say anything, she took his penis in her mouth and began sucking, slowly at first and then with some urgency.

"What the fuck do you think you're doing?" Wyatt growled as he fought to regain full consciousness.

"I didn't hear you complaining last night," she purred and carried on with her mission.

Wyatt was stunned. His mind was engaged in a brutal battle with his body. He couldn't let this happen but he needed the release. He groaned as she straddled him and gently lowered herself on top of him, rocking back and forth, taking him in deeper and deeper.

"I can't do this." He struggled to get the words out.

"You don't have to do anything baby. Lie back and enjoy the ride." Ashley was taking full advantage of a much-weakened Wyatt and the fight suddenly left him.

He groaned again as the she began to grind her hips against his. He couldn't hold back any longer. He was now fully awake. "Tell me what you want," she whispered into his ear.

Wyatt grabbed her at the waist and quickly flipped her over so he was now on top. He nudged her legs apart and plunged deep into her slippery warmth. He moaned as he came and shuddered at the height of his climax. "Georgiana," he groaned.

"Who the hell is Georgiana?" Ashley was miffed and pushed Wyatt off her.

"No-one," he grunted. "I'll have my driver take you home." He got out of bed, pulled on a pair of jeans and T-shirt and walked out of the bedroom.

Five minutes later he heard her approaching the kitchen. "You're a real bastard, you know?" Ashley shook her head.

"I've been told that once or twice. In fact, I believe you said that when we broke up." he replied. "My driver is downstairs. You can go."

Mortified, Ashley scuttled off across the lobby without a backwards glance.

"Fucking moron," he muttered. "How could you let that happen?" He hit the news app on his phone and started scrolling down, scanning the day's headlines from around the world.

He went cold when he came across a tabloid photograph of Georgiana and Dan in a clinch in Montreal. He read the caption:

'Flowers and Bloom Get Tangled'

Wyatt snapped. Seeing the woman he was determined to possess draped over another man was more than he could handle. He threw his phone across the kitchen, smashing it to pieces as it hit the floor. If he couldn't have her, then he was damn sure no one else would.

CHAPTER 25

"So, what do you want to know?" Dan leaned back in his chair and picked up his glass of wine.

"Everything," Georgiana laughed.

They were the last two people left in the softly-lit TOCA restaurant on the mezzanine floor of their hotel, and were far too engrossed in conversation to notice the waiting staff silently willing them to hurry up and leave.

"Born and raised in London – Chelsea – and went to St Paul's school." He stopped when Georgiana snorted. "What?"

"Very swanky indeed," she laughed.

"I hardly think you're in a position to judge, Miss Bloom," he grinned. "I'm not the one with a country pile that's been in the family for generations."

Georgiana smirked, "Fair point Mr Flowers. Do continue."

"I'm an only child. Dad – Francis – is a globally renowned plastic surgeon, and before you ask, my stunningly gorgeous features are one hundred percent natural and inherited from my Mum –

Claudia. She's a tenured professor at London School of Economics."

Georgiana raised an eyebrow. "Acting not in the blood then?"

"Yeah, it was a bit of a shock when I told them I wanted to act, but they supported my choice right from the off. Not once did they try to push me down the academic route and they were amazing when I first went out to the States. They gave me some cash to see me through the first few months, and encouraged me to keep pursuing my dream, no matter what." Dan talked about his parents with real warmth. "We're really close, even though I don't see them as much as I'd like. You'll love Mum, you have a very similar sense of humour."

Georgiana gulped. "I'm not sure we're at the meet the parents stage just yet."

Dan reached for her hand across the table. "I'm crazy about you already and I've known you less than twenty-four hours."

She gulped again. She didn't know what to say. Dan had completely caught her off guard. He was warm and funny, and genuinely interested in learning everything about her. It was unnerving. She was still stinging from the Wyatt wobble – as Olivia called it – and was determined to protect herself from any more hurt.

She quickly changed the subject. "How did you get your big break? Casting couch?"

Dan laughed. "No! I guess I was lucky, that's all. Right place, right time. So many great actors are still waiting tables between auditions and remain undiscovered. It could so easily have happened to me."

"But it didn't," Georgiana grinned. "And now you're a superstar heart-throb with girls throwing themselves at your feet everywhere you go."

In the brief time they had spent together, Georgiana had noticed the way women reacted to Dan. From the air stewardesses to the hotel receptionist and everyone in between – they all melted in his presence.

She regarded him as he recounted his first audition and how terrified he had been. She suddenly realised how much she liked him already. He was honest and self-deprecating, well brought-up, educated and informed, and she could sense he had a good heart.

"Why don't you have a girlfriend?" Georgiana stared at him intently.

"I could ask you the same question." Dan smirked.

"I'm not that way inclined," she giggled.

"Boyfriend! You know what I meant," he laughed. "So?"

"I asked you first!" Georgiana exclaimed. "Why is it that an incredibly handsome and charming chap such as yourself is still on the market?"

Dan fell silent for a few moments and then looked at Georgiana. "Because I haven't met the right woman. Until now."

"Oh!" Georgiana squeaked and looked away.

"Look at me," Dan told her.

Georgiana raised her head and locked eyes with him. What she saw was a heady combination of lust and longing, tinged with a touch of concern for her. In an instant, any reservations she may have had about him melted away.

He was quick to register her response as her breathing quickened and her eyes flashed with a desire that matched his own.

"Let's get out of here." He pushed back his chair, grabbed her hand and guided her towards the elevator. He pressed the call button and the metal doors slid open in front of them.

"Your room or mine?" he asked gruffly.

"Yours," she whispered.

They stood in silence for the thirty seconds it took to get to the penthouse suite, and once inside they were both still lost for words.

Dan eventually broke the silence. "Are you sure?" He was desperate to be with Georgiana but had no intention of pushing her to do something she wasn't comfortable with.

She nodded and reached up to put her arms around his neck. He pulled her towards him and kissed her, gently at first and then with a passion so forceful it almost knocked her off her feet.

Dan groaned as he felt Georgiana melt in his arms. He guided her towards the oversized sofa that dominated the suite's living space and greedily peeled her clothes off as they moved across the room.

"You're beautiful," he gasped when she was naked. "Wow."

Overcome with shyness she blushed and looked away from him.

"I mean it," he said. "And I'm going to devour every inch of you if you're willing."

"Definitely willing," she giggled. "I'm sorry, I get a bit giddy when I'm nervous."

Dan kissed her lightly on the lips. "You've got nothing to be nervous about. I'll take very good care of you." He kissed her again, more forcefully, and felt her relax under his touch.

"That's it," he whispered. "Let it go. Don't fight it."

Georgiana had no fight in her. The depth of feeling that Dan had ignited in her was so strong it was impossible to ignore.

"Definitely not fighting it," she laughed and then gasped as Dan's hands travelled across her skin, making it tingle under his touch.

"Good," he replied gruffly and kissed her neck.

Georgiana closed her eyes and allowed herself to get lost in Dan.

CHAPTER 26

*I*n Georgiana, Dan had finally met his match. She made him laugh, and could render him powerless with one bat of her eyelashes. She debated with him on subjects ranging from politics to prison reform, and her knowledge and intelligence shone through their heated exchanges. He loved the way she argued her point and how she refused to back down when she absolutely knew she was right.

He was completely captivated by her, but painfully aware of her reluctance to fully let him in to her life. It had only been a few days, but he had known immediately that she was The One, and there was no way he was letting her get away.

The second night they spent together in bed, eating room service and indulging in each other.

"I'm going to lay it all out for you. No surprises, no secrets." Dan pulled her towards him and kissed her. "Are you sure you want to know everything?"

Georgiana nodded. "That way we start with a clean slate."

He took a deep breath. "Right then. I had a few girlfriends when

I was at school. You know, the usual teenage drill. I lost my virginity at sixteen to a girl named Cressida Wainwright-Thompson who was a few years older than I was." Dan smiled at the memory. "It wasn't too bad as it happens," he laughed. "When I first moved to LA it was a bit frantic. I was alone in a new place and trying to make it as an actor. I was one of a thousand new arrivals filled with hope and expectation. With each rejection came a new disappointment, and I slept with a lot of women to ease my pain, so to speak."

Georgiana didn't say a word. Her eyes urged him to continue.

"I've made eleven films and actually only slept with three of my co-stars, contrary to the rumours. And in the spirit of full disclosure, my most recent was Amber Angelo – and yes, she's married before you say anything."

Georgiana held up her hands. "I wasn't going to say anything!"

"I'm a friendly guy," he continued. "I like the company of women and I appreciate everything you have to offer, I won't deny that. But the extent of my sexual exploits has been greatly exaggerated. You must know that from all the problems with your brother?"

Georgiana sighed. "That's true. There were so many women that claimed they had slept with him when it simply wasn't the case. Most of the time he was home with me when the media had him out shagging half of London."

"Exactly," Dan grinned. "You know better than most how these things can quickly get out of hand." He brushed a tendril of hair away from Georgiana's face. "There's never been anyone special enough for me to commit to, not in the way I want anyway."

"Which is?" Georgiana asked.

"My grandparents are still madly in love after fifty-five years of marriage. My parents are still crazy about each other after thirty-two years together. I want that." Dan smiled at her.

"Sebastian and Olivia are mad about each other too," Georgiana said wistfully. "Is that it? No sordid sex tapes, gang bangs, or anything else I haven't thought of yet?"

"Yep, that's it. I'm no angel but I'm definitely not the guy you read about in the gossip magazines." He leaned forward and kissed her. "Your turn."

"Really?" she squeaked. "Nothing to tell."

"I don't believe that for a minute. Spill it." Dan plumped up the pillows behind his head and readied himself for the wave of jealousy he knew would wash over him the moment he envisioned Georgiana with another man.

"I'm not anywhere near your league," she laughed nervously. She knew she was going to have to talk about Wyatt. "But if you really must know, my first time was with a boy – and he was a boy – called Crispin Fairbanks."

Dan snorted at the name. "And you think I'm posh?"

"Don't interrupt me." She poked him in the ribs. "It was horrible and painful, and not a memory to cherish – but then again most of my friends said the same thing. Must be different for us, I guess." She reached over and took a sip of champagne. "Then there was Will. He's still my best friend in the whole world and is very important to me."

Dan grimaced as he imagined Georgiana being pawed by a spotty teenager, and he hated the fact they were still friends.

"Don't look like that," she laughed. "It's purely platonic. We were just a couple of kids messing around. I was a prolific dater until recently, but I didn't sleep with most of them. Christopher was sweet but boring, and Mike was more interested in his own pleasure than giving me any."

"And?" Dan sensed there was more.

"And then there was Wyatt Clayton." She shuddered at the mere thought of him.

"The property billionaire?" Dan was shocked.

"The very same. And I'm ashamed to say I fell for his somewhat dubious charms, only to find he used me. It's a long story and one I will tell you some time, but for now all you need to know is that he hurt me very badly and I'm still recovering. And you needn't worry. I came to my senses pretty quickly and haven't seen or spoken to him since, and have no intention of doing so either."

Dan swallowed back a wave of jealousy. "Clean slate, right?"

"Definitely," she smiled, relieved that he hadn't pushed her for more of the Wyatt story. "Now we've got that out of the way..." She slid her hand underneath the sheets and grinned at Dan.

He smiled lazily and put his hands behind his head. "I like the way you think Miss Bloom."

CHAPTER 27

*M*ontreal was a blast. During the days, Georgiana performed her presenting duties with aplomb, winning rave reviews from the watching public and her bosses at the BBC. Every night she joyfully fell into Dan's arms in the privacy of their hotel.

He introduced her to his co-stars and crew as his girlfriend and she didn't correct him. She was content to let him take charge, decide what they would be doing each evening, and go along with whatever crazy plan he had concocted while waiting in his trailer to be called for a scene.

"There's a party tonight at a new club in town. We're going," he shouted from the bathroom.

"Sounds like fun," Georgiana replied. She had the next day off and could really let her hair down.

She was sitting up in bed reading through some production notes for that day's filming when she looked up and saw Dan languishing in the bathroom doorway.

"You really are gorgeous," he grinned. "Boy, did I luck out sitting next to you on that plane."

Georgiana laughed. "You're not so bad yourself. Come here and kiss me."

Dan lunged across the room and threw himself onto the bed. He was still dripping wet from his shower, and smelled divine.

"You're getting me all wet," Georgiana squealed.

"In all the right places, I hope." Dan kissed her passionately. "Right, you little minx. You've made me late." He flashed her a dazzling smile and pulled the covers up over her. "I can't leave if you're still tantalising me with your sexy bod."

She smiled lazily and lay back on the pillows watching him dress.

Dan was ready in a flash and ran towards the door, turning to blow her a kiss. "See you later."

Picking up her laptop, she put a video call in to Olivia and laughed when baby Alexander appeared in front of her, propped up against a golf bag.

"Hi, gorgeous." She touched the screen.

"Hi!" Olivia popped into view. "Are you still in bed?"

"Err, yes." She had forgotten that she was naked underneath the covers and must be looking somewhat dishevelled. "But to be fair, it's early here."

"You've been up to something," Olivia laughed. "Is it Dan Flowers? I saw the photos of you with him at the airport."

"Yes," Georgiana grinned. "He's fun, you'll really like him."

"He's gorgeous, but he's got a terrible reputation," Olivia said. "Just be careful."

"I'm fine. Really. Don't worry about me," Georgiana said. "You were the one who told me to go out and enjoy myself."

"Well, I didn't quite mean for you to do it with one of the hottest movie stars in the world," Olivia laughed. "Now tell me all the juicy gossip, and don't leave anything out."

"He's going to come to the village when he's finished shooting so you'll meet him then."

"Oh. Is it that serious already?" Olivia was surprised.

"Well, I really like him. He makes me laugh and he seems to feel the same way about me. He does love to party though, I'm exhausted."

"Take it slowly," Olivia urged. "I'd hate to see you get hurt again."

"Don't worry. I know what I'm doing." Georgiana attempted to reassure Olivia but deep down she doubted her own words. "Now let me talk to my nephew before he forgets who I am."

"He's only two weeks old!" Olivia laughed and spun the laptop round so Alexander came back into view. He was fast asleep.

Georgiana giggled. "So much for that then. What else is going on there?"

"My parents arrived last night. They're besotted with Alexander, of course, but they're already moaning about how much we've spent on the nursery. I swear they walk around the house pricing everything up and shaking their heads at our lack of economising."

"It's probably still a shock that you're married to a multi-millionaire," Georgiana laughed. "Oh my God, is that the time? I'm going to be late. I'll call you in a few days. Give Alexander a kiss from me." She ended the call, jumped out of bed and ran towards the shower.

CHAPTER 28

Georgiana had been away for almost three weeks. Instead of going home after her stint in Montreal, she had stayed while Dan's film completed shooting in the city, and then gone with him to Los Angeles.

When they were out in the evenings, going to the best clubs or joining his famous friends at the city's finest restaurants, they were draped all over each other. The paparazzi was having a field day with them. Everywhere they went they were followed and photographed.

She only rang home when she knew Sebastian wasn't around, and ignored his calls and texts to her mobile. They were always along the same lines:

> *You're plastered all over the newspapers.*
> *Stop making a bloody fool of yourself and come home.*

Georgiana had no intention of going home just yet. She was having way too much fun. Spending all her time with Dan, keeping busy and meeting new people meant she had been able to push Wyatt out of her mind completely.

"Don't go," Dan begged her when she was packing to fly the next day to North Carolina for the US PGA golf championship - the final Major of the year.

"I have to. It's work." She was glum. She didn't want to leave Dan. He had drawn her into his world - they were living in a bubble where no-one and nothing could get to her and she didn't want it to burst.

"Ok, but I'm coming to get you as soon as it's over and we'll go to the South of France. Leo has invited us to his yacht and I don't want to let him down." Dan grinned.

"Leo?" Georgiana squeaked. "As in DiCaprio?"

"The very same," Dan laughed. "He's a great guy, you'll like him."

"Well, I'm not going to turn that down. I always fancied him." Georgiana stuck her tongue out and giggled.

The next morning, she was on her way to Quail Hollow in Charlotte and missing Dan like crazy. She sent Sebastian a text from the plane.

I'm going to France next week and will come home after that. I promise. Give my love to Liv and Alexander xx

Sebastian replied immediately.

I'm just worried about you. We miss you. Lady is pining for you. X

"Well, at least he's not mad at me," she muttered. She leaned back and tried to relax. This was the first time she had been alone since leaving London and it felt strange.

She picked up a magazine from the seat pocket and flicked

through the pages, pausing when Dan's face appeared in front of her. It was a story about him and Daphne Stallwort-Hoskins, and a photograph of them looking intimate at his London premiere.

"He can do what he likes," she muttered. "It's just a bit of fun." She tried to convince herself that she didn't care but a tiny part of her flared with jealousy. Dan was getting under her skin and she couldn't let that happen. She had to protect herself from further heartbreak.

CHAPTER 29

The sun was coming up in Appleton Vale when the phone in the Manor started to ring. Olivia rushed out of the nursery and lunged across the landing to silence it. She had only just managed to get Alexander to sleep.

"Hello," she whispered.

"Is Sebastian there? It's Mary."

"Mary?" Olivia asked.

"Edward's housekeeper," she replied.

"Oh, sorry Mary, we've had a bit of a night of it with Alexander. Is everything ok?"

"Is Sebastian there," Mary repeated.

"Yes. I'll go and wake him up. Hang on." Olivia walked towards their bedroom.

"Darling," she gently shook Sebastian. "Wake up."

Sebastian opened one eye and stared at Olivia. "What's up? Is Alexander ok?"

"Yes, he's fine. Mary is on the phone, I think something's wrong." She passed him the handset.

"Mary? Is everything ok?" He was groggy.

"Oh, Sebastian. Thank God, you're there. I've got some terrible news," she cried. "Edward is dead."

"What?" Sebastian sat bolt upright, his face paled. "How? When?"

"Sometime in the night. The paramedics think it was a heart attack." Mary stuttered. "I can't get hold of Camilla, I don't know what to do."

"I'll be there in ten minutes." Sebastian ended the call and looked at Olivia, tears in his eyes.

"Edward is dead. I've got to go over there."

"Oh my God. I'm so sorry. I know how much he meant to you." Olivia stroked his face. "Go. Do you want me to let Georgie know?"

"Yes please. Call her and keep calling her until she bloody answers. Edward was her godfather, she needs to be here." He leapt off the bed and pulled on his jeans and a t-shirt. "I'll call you as soon as I can." He kissed Olivia and ran out of the bedroom.

He arrived at Edward's just as the ambulance was pulling out of the driveway. When he got to the house he found Mary in the kitchen, sobbing into a tea towel.

"Oh, Sebastian. Thank you for coming." She smiled weakly. "I can't believe he's gone."

"Neither can I," he replied grimly. "Are they sure it was a heart attack?"

"The paramedic said there would need to be an autopsy, but

159

that's the most likely cause." Mary moved across the kitchen and switched on the kettle. "Drink?"

"Coffee, please." Sebastian replied. "Where's Camilla right now?"

"Somewhere in The Congo. I've only got a number for the Mission and they said it would be a couple of days before they could get a message to her."

"A couple of days?" Sebastian was surprised. "Have they never heard of satellite phones?"

Mary shrugged her shoulders and sniffed. "Edward had been trying to get hold of her for weeks to tell her about selling the club and she never called him back. I can't bear to think that he died knowing she didn't care."

Sebastian switched into business mode. "Right. Leave it with me. I'll get onto the Embassy to see if they can help." He walked over to Mary and put his arms around her. "Don't worry. We'll find her."

He went into the hallway and fished his mobile out of his pocket to text Olivia.

Going to be here for a while. Have you managed to get hold of Georgiana? x

Olivia replied immediately.

Not yet. Still trying x

Sebastian tapped his reply.

Let me know when you do x

He then called his manager, Richie Rogers. "Edward Hampton is dead. Who do we know at the Foreign Office?"

"Christ. Sorry Sebastian," Richie replied. "Barnaby Farrington is number two in Washington but I think he's on holiday. What about Bryan Banks? Isn't he from the village?"

"Of course. Old Mrs Banks' son. I forgot about him. Can you get hold of him and ask for a contact at the Kinshasa embassy?"

"Congo? Why?" Richie was bemused.

"Edward's daughter is there and we need to find her. The Mission said she was quite far off the beaten track."

"Ok," Richie said. "Let me make some calls and I'll come back to you." He rang off.

Georgiana was sunning herself on the deck of Leo DiCaprio's luxury yacht in Monaco, watching Dan and a couple of other guests skimming the waves on jet skis. She had worked like a dog for the week in North Carolina, and had as usual dazzled on screen.

True to his word, Dan had flown into Charlotte on Sunday, whisked her away from the golf course and onto his private jet where they had a joyful reunion, taking out membership of the mile-high club. She felt fantastic being back in his arms and he was equally enthralled.

They landed in Nice early the next morning, and were driven to Monaco where they met up with Leo who was sailing around the Mediterranean for the summer. A party was in full swing when they boarded the yacht and Georgiana was bursting to let loose. She was handed a glass of champagne and the rest of the day became a bit of a blur.

Now she had a raging hangover and was just dozing off when

her phone rang. She looked at the caller ID and sent it to voicemail. She didn't want to talk to Olivia.

A moment later she received a text.

Call me. NOW x

A second text came through.

It's urgent x

She immediately dialled Olivia's number. "What's wrong?" Georgiana was worried.

"I'm so sorry, darling. There's no easy way to say this. Edward died last night. You need to come home," Olivia said.

Georgiana went cold. "What? How?"

"They think it was a heart attack. Mary found him early this morning. Sebastian wants you here. How quickly can you get home?"

"Of course I'll be there," Georgiana snapped. She was annoyed that Sebastian thought he had to order her back to the village. "He was my godfather." Tears began to trickle down her cheeks.

"I know, sweetie. I know you loved him," Olivia replied. "I have to go. Alexander's just woken up. Text me when you know what time you'll be back. Love you."

Georgiana ended the call and burst into tears. She was still sobbing when Dan joined her on the deck ten minutes later.

He rushed to her side. "Shit. What's happened?"

"My godfather has died," she sniffed. "I need to go home."

"I'm so sorry." Dan held her close and kissed the top of her head. "We can go now."

"We?" Georgiana squeaked.

"I'm coming with you. I'll sort the jet." Dan picked up his phone and walked inside to tell Leo they had to leave.

He had their bags packed in ten minutes, and an hour later they were soaring high above the Riviera on their way to Appleton Vale.

CHAPTER 30

*B*ryan Banks put down the phone and sprang into action. His call with Richie Rogers had been brief, and now he was tasked with finding and bringing home Camilla Hampton at Sebastian's request.

He pressed the intercom button on his desk. "Bess. Can you place a call to Ambassador Jackson in Kinshasa, please?"

"Of course, sir," his assistant replied.

A moment later she patched him through on the secure line.

"Harry. Bryan Banks," he said. "Need a favour, old boy."

He talked with his counterpart for a few minutes and was satisfied that Harry would move heaven and earth to track Camilla down.

Bryan rang Richie. "I've spoken to our man in Kinshasa and he's confident that they'll find her. The Mission knows where she is but communications are down so we'll send a chopper out there straight away."

Richie was relieved. "Much appreciated Bryan. Can you keep me in the loop?"

"Of course. I'll get a message to you as soon as she's on a plane back to London. We'll arrange everything."

Richie called Sebastian. "Bryan is sorting it out. She'll be home tomorrow night if they can get her on the plane in time."

Sebastian sighed with relief. "Thanks Rich, appreciate it."

"I hate to be the one to bring up business right now, but did Edward sign the contract before he died?" Richie asked.

"Shit," Sebastian groaned. "Not as far as I know. Speak to the lawyers later and find out. Dealing with Camilla may not be so easy. We never got on all that well."

"Leave it with me. I'll be in touch later," Richie replied.

The news of Edward's death spread quickly around the village. Tom had been overseeing a delivery from a local brewery when the ambulance trundled past the pub on its way to the hospital morgue. He ran inside to tell Susie.

Dee Dee had been standing at the window of her flat above the tearoom when Sebastian's car sped past at dawn. She had wondered where he was going in such a hurry. She ran to wake Jane.

Marjorie Rose, the postmistress, broke the news. She had heard it from the postman who had delivered mail to Edward's house that morning.

They gathered outside the post office.

"I can't believe it," Dee Dee sniffed. "He was such a dear man."

"I'm shocked," Jane said. "He didn't even get to enjoy his retirement. How sad."

Susie was upset. "Poor Georgiana, she was more of a daughter to him than Camilla ever was."

"Talking of Camilla," Tom raised his eyebrow. "Do we think she'll even bother coming home to bury him?"

"She can't be that much of a cold-hearted bitch, can she?" Devon Murphy, the local vet, chipped in. He didn't know Camilla. He and husband Patrick had moved to the village after she had left for Africa.

"She is." Dee Dee and Jane said in union.

"She hasn't been back in years. Edward never stopped trying to figure in her life but it wasn't to be," Jane sighed.

"Then we'll give him the send-off that she won't," said Patrick. "He was such a big part of the community. What a loss."

CHAPTER 31

*A*s Georgiana and Dan touched down at the private airfield near Bath, Camilla received the news of her father's death from the embassy aide sent to bring her home.

Just as Camilla was boarding the plane to London, Sebastian received the call from Richie he had been waiting for.

"He didn't sign the contracts," Richie said.

"Fuck," Sebastian growled. "That's opened the door for Athos now. Camilla won't care about sentiment or Edward's wishes. She'll go with the highest bidder."

"Nothing we can do about it now. It'll have to go through probate before any sale can happen," Richie replied.

"Stupid old fool," Sebastian muttered. "He never did anything quickly."

An hour later Georgiana burst into the Manor with Dan following closely behind. She looked dreadful.

Sebastian hugged her. "Welcome home."

Hector and Ace, clearly delighted to see her, came crashing

through the hall and skidded to a halt by her feet. Lady held back. Georgiana crouched down and called her over. She was in her arms in a flash, licking her face and squealing with delight. "I missed you too." Georgiana hugged her.

Dan stepped forward. "Hi, I'm Dan."

Sebastian smiled and extended his hand in greeting. "Thanks for bringing her back."

Olivia appeared from the kitchen and walked slowly towards them. She was still recovering from the operation and taking it easy, but she had regained some of her strength and colour since Georgiana had last seen her.

"You're back," she smiled. "And you must be Dan?" She kissed him on the cheek and hugged Georgiana. "Are you ok?" she asked.

Georgiana sniffed. "I will be when you give me my nephew to cuddle. Where is he?"

"Sleeping, but he'll be awake soon. Do you want coffee?" Olivia asked. "I've just put some on."

Dan nodded and followed Olivia into the kitchen.

"We really appreciate you bringing her home," she said, as she reached for the china mugs.

"Let me do that," Dan offered. "There's no way I'd have let her come on her own. She's very special to me."

Olivia grinned. "Well, that's very good to hear. Milk and sugar?"

"Just milk, please," Dan said. "Nice place you've got here."

"I'm sure your place in Hollywood is pretty swanky," Olivia laughed.

"Yeah, but it's not home. I miss England," he sighed.

"Where is she?" Hattie came running in through the back door. She was out of breath.

"With Sebastian." Olivia pointed to the hallway. "Hattie, this is Dan Flowers. Georgiana's friend."

Hattie giggled like a girl when Dan bent to give her a kiss. She had a soft spot for action heroes.

"Georgiana has told me how important you are to her," he smiled at Hattie. "I'm very happy to meet you."

Hattie giggled again.

"Oh, there you are." She threw her arms around Georgiana as she walked into the kitchen. "I'm so sorry, darling."

"Hi." Georgiana hugged Hattie. "I wish I'd seen him. I didn't spend enough time with him."

"You weren't to know this was going to happen. I don't want any recriminations. He loved you and he knew you loved him too," Hattie said gently.

"So, what's the plan?" Georgiana looked at Sebastian.

"We can't arrange anything without Camilla's agreement. She'll be back tonight. I've sent a car to pick her up and bring her home," he replied.

"Let's have a drink and then you two can go home and sort yourselves out," Olivia said.

Georgiana was feeling better by the time they got to her cottage. Being with her family was restorative and she was glad they liked Dan. Grateful for his support, she threw her arms around his neck and kissed him passionately.

"Be careful," he whispered in her ear. "You know I can't get enough of you."

She grinned and kissed him again. "Take me to bed."

[I can't get rid of these lines – not supposed to be here]

She led Dan up the stairs and into her bedroom. He groaned when she undid the straps on her summer dress and let it fall to the floor. "Are you sure? Aren't you too upset about Edward?"

"I'm sure. Love me. Please." She stepped forward and took his hands.

"I do love you." Dan smiled.

"What?" Georgiana spluttered.

Dan laughed. "I love you, Georgiana Bloom. Of course I do. What's not to love about you?"

"Oh," she was stunned. He was only ever supposed to be a distraction from Wyatt.

He tilted her chin so she was looking into his eyes. "I love you," he repeated. "I can't help it. I'm sorry if it's too soon."

"Oh," she whispered again.

"Don't be scared." Dan scooped her up into his arms. "I won't hurt you, I promise." He threw her on the bed and straddled her. "How about I just make love to you and we can talk about the rest when you're ready?"

Georgiana nodded. She closed her eyes and banished any thoughts of her terrible mistake with Wyatt.

CHAPTER 32

*B*obby Garnett flew into Wyatt's office with the news.

"Guess what?" he shouted.

Wyatt raised his eyebrows. He seldom saw Bobby so animated. "What?"

"Edward Hampton is dead and he hadn't gotten around to signing the contract with Sebastian Bloom." He rubbed his hands together. "Time to swoop in. The daughter's in charge now, so we can renegotiate, throw money at it. You do still want the place, don't you?"

Wyatt smiled. "Couldn't have happened at a better time. Do it," he said to Bobby. "Make it happen. I don't care how much it costs."

The intercom on his desk interrupted them. "Yes?"

"Ms Winton is demanding to see you," Gloria, his PA, informed him.

"Send her in," he told Gloria.

Bobby rolled his eyes as Ashley brushed past him on his way out.

She sashayed into Wyatt's office and perched on the chair in front of his desk.

"Hello Wyatt," she purred.

"Being with you again was a mistake." He was stone-faced.

"I'm pregnant," she smirked.

"What?" Wyatt turned green. "The way you behaved, I'd be surprised if I was the only man you screwed last month."

"How dare you," Ashley spat. "I never cheated on you the whole time we were together and I'm not a slut."

"Could have fooled me. Did you do this on purpose?" Wyatt was floored. How could he have been so careless?

"I took the opportunity when it came up," she sneered. "You broke up with me for no good reason."

"I didn't love you," Wyatt told her.

He stood up and walked around the desk. He grabbed her arm and forced her to her feet. "Get out," he snarled. "You can talk to me through my lawyers."

Ashley laughed and turned to leave. "I checked out that Georgiana chick you were moaning about. I doubt she'll be running back when this news breaks."

"Out!" he bellowed and pointed to the door. Gloria came running in when she heard him shouting.

"Gloria. Please escort Ms Winton out. Call security if necessary." Wyatt turned his back on Ashley and waited until she had left the room before he punched the wall in anger.

CHAPTER 33

*A*s Sebastian had predicted, Camilla had been difficult from the moment she arrived in Appleton Vale. She was enraged at being dragged away from her beloved Mission and her hatred for Sebastian was as clear as day.

"What did you do for her to hate you so much?" Olivia asked after the initial meeting with Camilla at Edward's house, where Sebastian had gone with Georgiana to discuss the funeral arrangements.

"I was close to her brother and when he died she blamed me for encouraging him to join up," Sebastian replied. "She never forgave me when he didn't come back from Iraq, and then she went to Africa."

"What does this mean for the club?" Georgiana asked, dreading Sebastian's response.

"We can hope that she'll honour Edward's contract, but we need to be prepared for Athos to come back in with a higher bid."

Georgiana cringed. The thought of Wyatt in Appleton Vale filled her with loathing. She was happy with Dan and could not bear to be around if Wyatt forced the deal through. He would be on her doorstep, visiting his latest acquisition and forcing his way back into her life. She hated him.

"I can't stay if he buys it," she said.

"What?" Olivia cried. "Don't be ridiculous. This is your home and besides, how much is he going to be here, really?"

"It doesn't matter how much or how little he's here. I don't want him in my life in any way, shape or form. He's a hateful man."

Two days later, they joined the rest of the village and the entire staff of The Riverside at St Saviour's church to say goodbye to a man they had all liked and respected.

The self-styled Kev the Rev gave a beautiful eulogy and Georgiana read a passage from the Bible that had been chosen by Edward himself. He had laid out his wishes for his funeral alongside his will, and Sebastian had made sure they were followed to the letter. He and Camilla had fought over it and relations between the two of them were at an all-time low.

They gathered in the drawing room at Edward's house to hear the reading of his will. Camilla had been shocked to hear that Sebastian and Georgiana had been included, but there was little she could do about it.

"Thank you for coming," Edward's lawyer, Simon Scott, addressed the group that included housekeeper, Mary.

"I'll get straight to it." He shuffled some papers in front of him and cleared his throat.

"I, Edward Hampton, leave the bulk of my estate to my daughter Camilla. Knowing her as I do she will either reject it or use the money to fund her mission for a further decade." Mr Scott looked up and spoke directly to Camilla.

"The estate entails eighty-five percent of The Riverside, eight London properties that are rented out, and the majority of the contents of this house. It also includes most of your mother's jewellery."

"Most? And what about the actual house?" Camilla asked.

"I'm getting to that, Miss Hampton," Scott replied.

He then looked at Georgiana and continued: "To my goddaughter, Georgiana Bloom, I leave Avalon House. She grew up running through the grounds and I wish for her to enjoy it for many years to come. I also leave her the Diadora diamonds, and fifteen percent of The Riverside. She has been a joy from the moment she was born and made me a very happy old man. I attach two conditions to these gifts. She must not sell her share in the club for five years and she must wear the diamonds on her wedding day. I'm just disappointed I won't get the chance to give her away."

Georgiana gasped and Camilla shot her a look of pure evil. "The Diadora diamonds? They were my mother's," she spat. "She can't have them or the house. This is my childhood home."

Mr Scott addressed Camilla again. "These are Edward's wishes and it is my job to ensure his instructions are followed."

He cleared his throat once more. "To Sebastian Bloom I leave my Aston Martin DB4/GT. I know he has coveted her since he was a boy and he's the only man I trust to look after her properly."

Sebastian drew a sharp breath and Camilla shrieked: "That car has to be worth millions. It's one of the rarest cars in the world."

"Again, Miss Hampton, may I remind you that this will is watertight. You must respect Edward's wishes."

"To my wonderful Mary," Mr Scott looked across the room at Mary and smiled. "I leave five hundred thousand pounds with strict instructions for you to take an early retirement, spend time with your family, and see some of the world. Thank you for looking after me so well all these years."

Mr Scott paused as Mary wept in the corner. Camilla was set to lodge another objection when Sebastian glared at her.

There were some charitable donations, bonuses for each and every staff member at The Riverside, and a few small personal items gifted to distant family members before Mr Scott concluded his business.

Camilla stormed out of the drawing room leaving Sebastian, Georgiana and Mary to digest what the lawyer had told them.

"Oh my God," Georgiana whispered. "Those diamonds are enormous. They must be incredibly valuable."

"He often talked of you wearing them," Mary smiled. "He thought they would sit well on your neck and said that even the brightest diamond could never outshine you."

Georgiana gulped and hugged Mary. "I miss him."

"Me too," she sniffed.

"Fifteen percent," Sebastian whistled. "That's worth a hell of a lot of money."

"And the house," she said. Suddenly the enormity of Edward's gift hit her. "What if Camilla sells her share to Athos? I can't sell mine."

"Let's cross that bridge if and when we come to it, ok?" Sebastian smiled encouragingly. "Hopefully it'll be the family business you own fifteen percent of so you won't need to worry about anything."

"Don't you think you've taken enough from my father?" Camilla sneered from the doorway where she had been listening to their conversation. "Let's be certain of one thing that has come from today. I will never, as long as I live, sell this club to you for any amount of money." She glared at Sebastian, turned and walked out of the room.

True to her word, Camilla refused to conduct business with Sebastian. She opened up the bidding to Athos and watched with some satisfaction as they and another three companies fought over her father's precious club, knowing that she would sell to anyone but Sebastian at the end of the day.

Wyatt had instructed Bobby to go all out and his counter-offer was twice what Sebastian could afford, even when some of the other members and close friends offered to chip in with substantial donations.

Five days' after Edward's will was read, Camilla agreed to sell to Athos at a ridiculously inflated price. Bobby was jubilant and called Wyatt with the news.

"We got it," he shouted down the phone. "And I have even better news."

Wyatt was delighted. At last something had gone his way. "What's the better news?"

"The old man left fifteen percent of The Riverside to the one and only Georgiana Bloom with a condition that she can't sell for five years."

"What? Are you serious?" Wyatt replied.

"Yeah. Looks like the two of you are gonna be business partners," Bobby replied. "Do you wanna sign the contracts in person, seeing as it's her?"

"What?" Wyatt wasn't concentrating.

"Do you want to go and sign the contracts with her or shall we do it electronically?" Bobby repeated.

"I'll go," Wyatt said. "Meet me there."

She would have to see him. There was no way she could avoid it. He was determined to claim her as his own.

CHAPTER 34

"So, he's coming then?" Dan said to Georgiana. They were getting ready to go to dinner with Sebastian and Olivia at the pub.

"Who?" Georgiana asked as she finished applying her mascara.

"You know full well who I'm talking about." Dan was edgy. Georgiana had told him the full Wyatt story recently and he felt threatened.

"Yes. He's coming. I only have to be in a room with him for five minutes, don't worry." She smiled and reached up to kiss him.

"Want to show me how much I don't need to worry?" Dan grinned and started to unbutton her shirt.

Georgiana laughed. "You're insatiable."

"I'm insanely in love with you," he replied. "Now come here," he growled and dragged her into the bedroom.

They were half an hour late for dinner and ran into the pub hand-in-hand, laughing.

"I don't need to ask what you two have been up to." Sebastian rolled his eyes.

Georgiana grinned. "Budge over," she said to Olivia, who slid along the banquette to make room for them.

"What are we celebrating?" Dan asked when he saw champagne on the table.

"Life. Love. Happiness and classic Aston Martins," Sebastian replied.

"Well I'll definitely drink to the life, love and happiness bit," Dan replied, looking into Georgiana's eyes. "As for the car, I can only hope you'll let me take her out for a spin."

"Not a chance," Sebastian laughed. "No one is touching that car. I'm saving her for Alexander."

"And what can I get you lovely people?" Susie appeared, ready to take their order.

"Hi," Olivia stood up and hugged her. "How's Rosie?"

"Upstairs, sleeping finally. Now she's toddling around I'm finding it more exhausting than ever," Susie said. "I can't believe you're out."

"Don't say that," Sebastian interrupted. "You have no idea how hard it was to get her away from Alexander."

"He's so tiny," Olivia cried.

"And he's with the best surrogate mother we know. Hattie will call immediately if she needs us and we're literally in spitting distance," Sebastian reassured her.

Susie turned to Dan. "Oh how rude of me. I'm Susie. Tom over there is my husband."

"Georgiana said she had a misspent youth in here," he grinned. "Pleased to meet you."

Susie giggled and turned pink.

"I suppose you have this effect on all the ladies." Sebastian snorted.

"It's the film star thing." Georgiana shrugged her shoulders. "If you really knew him you'd hate him."

Dan elbowed her in the ribs. "Rude!"

"Ouch," she laughed.

Susie took their order and rushed off to serve Devon and Patrick at a table across the restaurant. Both were straining to see Dan and desperately trying to catch Georgiana's eye to engineer an introduction.

Sebastian raised his glass. "To Edward."

"Edward," they said in union and clinked their glasses.

Chef Bernard outdid himself and produced a feast that was worthy of his Michelin star.

"Wow. That was seriously amazing." Dan patted his belly. "I could get used to this."

"You'd go mad here," Georgiana said. "It's the complete opposite of Hollywood."

"You're here," he replied. "That's good enough for me."

"Well I won't be next week. US Open." She was due to fly to New York on Monday, after signing the contracts with Athos.

Dan sighed. "And I've got to get back. We start shooting soon. You'll come to LA after?" He couldn't bear to be away from Georgiana for too long, especially with Wyatt on the horizon both in Appleton Vale and New York.

Georgiana nodded. "Of course. I'll miss you."

"You'll have McEnroe to keep you amused," he laughed. "You two really do make a great double act."

"He's cool," Georgiana smiled. "He makes it fun."

Dan grabbed her hand, not caring that Sebastian and Olivia were there. "You're the best thing that ever happened to me." His lips brushed the back of her hand.

Georgiana blushed.

"A Hollywood A-lister and the world's best golfer wrapped around our little fingers," Olivia laughed. "How did we get so lucky?"

"Luck has nothing to do with it." Sebastian dismissed that notion.

"I'm not sure I should let you fly to New York alone," Dan joked. "God only knows who you'll be sitting next to this time."

Georgiana felt a hand on her shoulder and turned around to find Devon and Patrick hovering.

"Sorry to interrupt darling, but I just couldn't help myself," Patrick looked flustered. He turned to Dan. "I've seen every one of your films," he gushed. "I run the local am-dram society. I don't suppose you'd ever consider treading the boards for our little group?"

Devon burst out laughing. "You'll have to excuse my husband," he addressed Dan. "He has a penchant for the dramatic."

"Well I'm planning on spending a lot more time here, so you never know." Dan grinned.

"Stop teasing." Georgiana gave him a playful slap. "Patrick takes acting very seriously indeed."

"Not to your level, of course." Patrick was still gushing. "But we're really rather good."

"That's true." Olivia nodded her agreement and Patrick beamed.

"You don't have to answer now," he said to Dan. "Just think about it."

Dan was trying very hard not to laugh. "Of course, I will."

"And on that note, we'll leave you alone." Devon took Patrick's elbow and steered him away from their table towards the bar.

"See, I'm making friends with the locals already," Dan grinned.

Olivia glanced at her watch and fidgeted in her seat.

"Ok, ok. We'll go." Sebastian said.

"I'm sorry. I don't want to leave Alexander much longer. Do you mind?" she asked Georgiana and Dan.

"Nope. Go. We have stuff to do anyway." Georgiana grinned and leaned back into Dan's arms.

"Again. Don't need to know." Sebastian shook his head and stood up to leave. "I've got the bill. See you tomorrow." He rushed after Olivia who was hell-bent on getting home to their son as quickly as possible.

"Do you want another drink?" Dan got up to make his way to the bar.

"No. I want to go home." Georgiana took his hand, stood on her tiptoes and kissed him passionately. She didn't care who was watching.

CHAPTER 35

*I*t was Sunday morning in Appleton Vale and the village was buzzing with gossip. Standing outside the post office and general stores, Dee Dee and Jane were deep in conversation with Marjorie Rose, the postmistress.

Tom and Susie were standing outside the pub with a bunch of newspapers in hand and their mouths hanging open. Peter and Andrea Jenner had stopped to chat with Devon and Patrick. They were all looking shocked and slightly uncomfortable.

Georgiana had woken early. Leaving Dan to sleep, she decided to go for a ride out across the vale. Galloping through the beautiful countryside of West Chesterton was exhilarating. She had been out almost two hours when she entered the village on her route home and quickly realised something was wrong. There was a hive of activity and everyone was gawping at her as she rode past. She stopped outside the pub where Tom and Susie were standing.

"What's going on? Everyone looks a bit weird."

Susie looked pained and handed Georgiana a newspaper. She gasped as she took in the front page of the tabloid. The headline read 'Cor-bloomy!' with a full-page photograph of Georgiana topless on the deck of the yacht, draped across Dan, his hand was inside her bikini bottoms. It had been taken only a few days ago when they were in Monaco.

"That's not the only one." Tom grimaced as he handed her another paper. The second photograph was even more explicit than the first – she had been 'papped' having champagne licked off her breasts by Dan, whose erection was clearly in view. The headline read 'Beeb's Bloom Busted,' referencing her contract with the BBC for maximum effect.

Other headlines included "Flowers in Bloom', 'Flowers indulges in French fancy' and 'Bloomin' Marvellous'.

She went pale. "Oh my God."

"Are you ok?" Susie was concerned. "Why don't you come inside and take a breath? Wednesday will be fine tied up out here."

"No," Georgiana whispered. "I'm going home." Tears welled in her eyes and Tom stepped forward to comfort her.

"Today's news, tomorrow's chip paper," he said with a forced grin.

Georgiana didn't reply. She bent forward, whispered in Wednesday's ear, and the mare leapt into action, bolting across the village green and up the road towards the manor. Tears were streaming down her cheeks as they made short work of the winding tree-lined driveway to the stable yard. She slid off Wednesday and slumped down on the cobblestones in utter despair.

She was still sitting there when Olivia appeared. Yet to see the morning papers, she had been given a brief rundown of the situation by Susie.

"Oh Georgie." She bent down and put her arms around her.

Georgiana looked at her, eyes wide with fear. "What am I going to do? It's so awful. I'll never be able to face anyone again."

"We'll sort it out, I promise," Olivia said gently. "I'll deal with Wednesday." The little mare had her head stuck in the open door of the feed room and was devouring a bag of carrots.

Olivia quickly removed her tack and turned her out into the paddock nearest to the yard. She walked back towards Georgiana and helped her to her feet.

"Come on. Come back to the house."

"Where's Sebastian?" Georgiana asked warily. She couldn't face his wrath right now.

"At the club, so it's just you, me, Hattie and Alexander," she smiled at Georgiana.

Back at the manor Hattie was waiting for them with a steaming pot of tea and a motherly hug for Georgiana.

"I'm so sorry Hattie," she sniffed, wiping her tears away with the back of her hand. "I'm so ashamed of myself, I've let you all down."

"Don't be silly. We all make mistakes from time to time," Hattie wasn't entirely convincing. "It'll blow over in a day or two."

Georgiana hung her head in shame. "I doubt it." Her voice was barely audible. "It was just a bit of fun, a private holiday. How did I know I'd get papped? That's normally reserved for you and Sebastian." Georgiana gulped as she thought of her brother's reaction to the latest family crisis. "He's going to go ballistic."

Olivia reached across the table and took her hand. "He may have a little rant, but then I'll remind him of all the trouble he got himself into before he met me," Olivia smiled reassuringly. "He owned the tabloid front pages for a while, so he'll understand. He may not like it, but he's hardly in a position to throw stones."

Georgiana smiled weakly. "Yeah, there is that I suppose. I just didn't think it would happen to me."

"You're dating one of the hottest movie stars on the planet, you're on TV all the time, you're Sebastian Bloom's sister, and you're beautiful. You're a paparazzi dream," said Olivia.

Georgiana snorted and rolled her eyes. "Doubt I'll be on TV much longer. They'll have to sack me." She was crestfallen.

"That may be so, but it's not the end of the world, is it?" said Hattie.

Olivia's phone rang and they all jumped. She picked it up and mouthed, "It's Sebastian."

The colour faded from Georgiana's face as she anxiously listened to Olivia's side of the conversation.

"Yes, she's here. No, she's not ok. Stop ranting. She didn't do it on purpose. You're being a dick." She rolled her eyes and Georgiana giggled nervously. "Ok. See you in a few hours. I love you too." Olivia ended the call and looked at Georgiana. "You see. He's fine. He's angry at the photographers, not you."

Georgiana breathed a sigh of relief. "I'd ask him for advice, but the difference between him and me is that he never gave a toss what people wrote about him, whereas I do."

She pushed her chair back from the table and stood up to leave. "I'd better get back to Dan before he finds out from someone else. Do you think he'll be ok about it?"

"Why wouldn't he be? And let's be honest, it wasn't just a fling, he is your boyfriend. You can't be crucified for that," Olivia offered helpfully.

"Why don't we have dinner together tonight, just the family?" Hattie smiled and patted Georgiana's hand. "And Dan, of course."

"Sounds good to me," Olivia smiled. "Let's close ranks, just for the time being. No one can get to you here."

When Georgiana got back to her cottage, Dan was in the kitchen looking at the iPad. "You ok, babe?" He put his arms around her. "This kind of crap happens all the time. I'm just so sorry it happened to you. I should have been more careful."

"It may happen to you all the time, but this is a first for me." She looked wretched. "What am I going to say to my boss? There's no way the BBC will put up with this. How can they?"

"If I've learned anything from my time in Hollywood, it's to front it out. Face it head on." Dan kissed her. "It will go away as quickly as it appeared if you do that."

Her phone started to ring. She gulped. "It's Gerry." She swiped the screen and walked into the sitting room to hear her fate.

Five minutes later she returned, red faced. "He totally bollocked me. Said I had to give a public apology if I wanted to save my job."

"What do you want to do?" Dan asked. "It's not like you need to work."

"But I love my job," Georgiana exclaimed. "What else would I do?"

"Be with me, all the time?" Dan grinned. "You can keep me on the straight and narrow."

She shook her head. "I have to apologise today and then I can go to New York tomorrow."

"Is that what you really want?" Dan asked.

"Yes." She looked at Dan and suddenly felt terrible. "I love being with you too. I just want to keep working for now."

"Right," he smiled. "Get out there and face the music. Say sorry. Go to New York and hurry back to me." It was cut and dried to Dan.

Later that afternoon Georgiana and Dan stepped out in front of the gates of Appleton Manor to address the press that had been camping out on their doorstep most of the day. Dan insisted on supporting her and taking his share of the blame.

She waited for the flash bulbs to stop popping and cleared her throat. "I'd like to apologise for the rather embarrassing situation I have found myself in. I have a duty to act responsibly under the terms of my contract and this incident was anything but. I realise I am somewhat of a role model and am sincerely sorry for conducting myself in this manner." She kept it short and to the point.

Dan stepped forward before the media had the opportunity to ambush Georgiana with questions.

"What was meant to be a private holiday with friends has turned into a media frenzy. I take the blame for this. I'm used to the attention but Georgiana is not, and I am incredibly disappointed that she has been treated this way. It goes without saying that we'll be a lot more discreet in the future."

He held out his hand and Georgiana grabbed it gratefully. He pulled her towards him and put his arm around her waist. "All we ask is that you try to respect our privacy."

They smiled and posed for the cameras for a moment before walking back through the gates of the Manor, turning away from the barrage of questions that were being hurled at them.

"Do you think that was enough?" Georgiana asked him.

"I think it was more than enough. You've done your bit and I'm proud of you for handling it so well." Dan smiled. "I went into hiding for a whole two weeks after my first run in with the paparazzi. You're fronting it out. You're amazing."

Georgiana smiled properly for the first time all day. She was relieved the worst was over and thankful for having such a wonderful man in her life. She knew he would support her, no matter what.

Wyatt had seen the UK newspapers before boarding his plane to fly to Appleton Vale. His first reaction had been blind jealousy. The photographs were quite explicit but had been taken with a long lens – a blatant intrusion on their privacy. His jealousy quickly turned to fury. He could murder Dan Flowers for not being more careful. He should never have put Georgiana in that position. No woman of his would be on view to the public.

He watched her impromptu news conference and thought how fragile she looked, right up until the point where Dan took her hand and put his arm around her. She visibly relaxed on camera and her expression changed from one of fear, to that of a woman who was certain of the love of the man by her side.

Wyatt was covetous and jealous. He wanted her but she wasn't part of the plan anymore.

To make matters worse he still had to deal with his pregnant ex, Ashley. She hadn't gone public yet but there was every chance she would, and soon. He didn't need that kind of bad publicity right now. He had had his lawyers draw up a non-disclosure agreement that provided Ashley with twenty-five million dollars in exchange for her silence. His lawyers were insisting on an in-vitro DNA test that Ashley had flatly refused. She agreed to undergo one when the baby was born. Until then she was a very large thorn in his side.

CHAPTER 36

*G*eorgiana took a deep breath and turned the door handle to The Riverside's executive boardroom. She had dressed conservatively, wanting to look business-like and avoid any further jibes from Camilla, who had already given her a dressing down about 'boob-gate.'

Wyatt and Bobby stood up when she entered the room and she avoided making eye contact with either of them. She knew as soon as she looked at Wyatt she would struggle to contain her temper.

"Hello, everyone." Her voice was slightly unsteady. "Let's get this over with, shall we?"

"Georgiana. How are you?" Wyatt said.

"Fine, thank you." She fiddled with the pen and paper in front of her, and evaded his burning gaze.

"Are you ready to sign the contract, Mr Clayton?" Camilla asked. "I'd like to be on the next plane out of here."

Wyatt ignored Camilla. "Georgiana. Look at me."

"Pass me the contract please." Georgiana was ready to sign and run. Camilla slid the documents across the table, she scribbled her signature and continued to avoid looking at Wyatt.

"You don't need me now." She got up to leave. "Mr Garnett. Please keep me in the loop regarding your plans. I believe I have a say in what will happen, even if it's a small one."

"Sure thing," Bobby replied.

She turned to Camilla. "You sold us out. Just go and don't come back. No one wants you here."

Camilla curled her lip and a satisfied smirk appeared on her face. "Don't worry. I have no intention of ever coming back to this place again. It holds no good memories for me."

Georgiana opened the door and let herself out. It was only when she was on the other side that she realised she was shaking.

"Pull yourself together," she muttered.

She was almost at her car when she heard him call out. "Georgiana. Wait."

Georgiana fumbled through her bag, desperately searching for her keys and hoping to get away before Wyatt reached her.

She was too slow.

"Why won't you look at me?" He was standing inches from her.

"Go away. I have nothing to say to you," she replied, eyes downcast. She turned her back on him and opened the car door.

Wyatt reached out and touched her shoulder and Georgiana jumped out of her skin. It was as if he had scalded her.

"Get off me," she snarled.

"The fact that you can't look at me speaks volumes." Wyatt was calm and in control. "If you hated me you'd be telling me to my face. Look at me," he demanded.

Georgiana turned around and faced him. "I hate you. Is that what you wanted to hear?"

"I don't believe you," Wyatt replied. "No one has ever turned me down before."

She rounded on him and pointed her finger in his face. "I can honestly say that I'm over it. You used me. More fool me. I'm with Dan now."

"Fuck him," Wyatt spat. "You'll come running back to me when he lets you down."

"There's no way he'd ever let me down. He's a decent and kind human being. You're a liar. That's the only thing I truly know about you." She felt sick. "Just leave me alone. I'll deal with Bobby on any business at the club. I don't want to see you again."

Wyatt was standing firm. "You'll deal with me. I'm not prepared to let you go. I'm used to getting what I want."

She turned away and opened the car door. Wyatt grabbed her arm and pulled her towards him until their faces were inches apart. Before she could protest he bent down and kissed her.

"Get off me," she screamed and pushed him away. "Just fuck off and don't come back."

She turned around, jumped in the car and sped away from Wyatt. She was fuming, so much so that she pulled off the road into a lay-by and started to scream at the top of her lungs.

A moment later there was a knock on her window.

"What are you doing?" Will mouthed through the glass.

Georgiana lowered the window. "Just letting off some steam. I'm ok."

'Well, you don't look ok," Will replied.

"What are you doing out here anyway?" she asked. "Why are you walking?"

"Just been at the Whiteside Estate," he grinned. "Easier to avoid the CCTV on foot."

"Lucinda? Eugh, that's gross," Georgiana crinkled her nose.

"She's not all that bad. At least she's grateful," Will laughed. "I think Godfrey must be a really lousy shag. Are you going to tell me what's going on?"

"I just saw Wyatt." Georgiana was seething. "I actually hate him. I don't know what I ever saw in him, he's not a very nice person."

"Forget about that American twat and get on with your life. As far as I can see he's only brought you misery." Will scowled.

"Don't hold back," Georgiana laughed. "Tell me what you really think."

"I love you Porg. I just want you to be happy." He ruffled her hair. "Can you give me a lift into the village? I said I'd meet Freddie at the pub for an early lunch. He's gone all gaga over Old Ma Banks' granddaughter and wants my advice."

Georgiana laughed. "You're the last person your brother should be listening to. Jump in."

She dropped Will outside the pub and turned for home. Dan came running out of the cottage when she pulled up outside.

"Everything ok?" He wrapped his arms around her.

Georgiana melted against his body. "Yes. Contracts signed. Job done."

"And?" he probed.

"I was in the room for less than five minutes. He followed me out to my car, tried to stick his tongue down my throat, and I very firmly told him to fuck off."

"He did what?" Dan growled.

She reached up and put her arms around his neck. "I had to tell you. I will never keep anything from you." She kissed him. "He means absolutely nothing. You've got me Mr Flowers. I'm all yours."

Dan grinned. "Just the way I like it." He scooped her up in his arms and walked back into the cottage.

CHAPTER 37

*W*yatt left Appleton Vale with renewed determination. They were business partners now. Georgiana couldn't avoid him forever and he wasn't about to forgive her latest rejection of him.

His jet landed at La Guardia and he was on his way home in no time. He picked up the phone and called his lawyer from the car.

"Brad. Wyatt Clayton. Has she signed?" He was desperate for Ashley to agree to his terms and disappear into the night.

"Not yet, Mr Clayton," Brad replied. "Her lawyer is playing hard ball. She wants another five million."

"Bitch," Wyatt growled. "Will she definitely sign if she gets it?"

"So I am led to believe," Brad answered.

'Do it. But that's where it stops." Wyatt was exasperated. He was still furious with himself for getting her pregnant. He just wanted her gone. He didn't want a kid, it was never in his plans.

"Thirty million dollars. Can you confirm that please Mr Clayton?

Are you absolutely sure you don't want to wait for a DNA test? It would be the prudent thing to do."

"Yes. I'm sure. Get it done," Wyatt replied. It was a small price to pay to get Ashley out of his life for good.

"I'm going to take you to New York," Dan said as they lay entwined on the bed.

"Finally!" Georgiana grinned. "Thought you'd never ask."

"Why fly commercial when we can be together for another eight hours?" Dan grinned. "I don't want to leave you alone for one minute. I could devour you in one bite."

"I'd rather a lick than a bite," Georgiana laughed, basking in the glow of their recent mutual climax.

"That was awesome. Best sex ever." He sighed. "It was so intense, like we were on a different planet."

Georgiana giggled and reaching up, she stroked his cheek. "You rock my world, Mr Flowers."

Dan flashed his dazzling smile. "You are so beautiful." He kissed her neck.

Georgiana groaned. Dan's touch ignited fires under her, she loved their bountiful sex. It was different from what she had experienced with Wyatt. It was more intimate and loving – they had a real connection.

"You're the right man for me," she whispered, banishing all thoughts of Wyatt from her mind.

"I should bloody well hope so," he laughed. "Now come here." He pulled her across the bed and lowered his mouth to her breast.

They had taken off two hours later than planned and had a

smooth ride across the Atlantic. When they landed in New York, Dan held her in his arms and kissed her tenderly.

"I'm going to miss you like crazy," he groaned.

"Me too," her voice was barely audible.

Dan tilted her chin up so their eyes met. "It's only a week and we'll talk all the time. And remember what I said. Have a New York minute and then you'll see what I was talking about."

Georgiana shed a tear when Dan's flight took off. She needed him for his strength and utter conviction that they were destined to be together. She didn't want to be alone.

She checked into her suite at The Plaza and was surprised to find a dozen red roses sitting on the table in the lounge. She looked at the card.

You've stolen my heart.
Make sure you bring it back on Sunday.
D xx

She smiled and hugged the card to her chest.

CHAPTER 38

"Georgiana? Are you listening to me?" Gerry talked into her earpiece.

"Yes of course I am." Georgiana made a face into the camera.

'You look like you're a million miles away," Gerry replied. "Are you sure you're ok to do this? I don't need a meltdown half-way through the broadcast."

"I'm fine. Where's John?"

"He'll be here in five. I need you at your best, so if all this boob stuff is bothering you, now's the time to tell me," Gerry said.

"All this boob stuff?" Georgiana glared down the lens. "I've apologised. If I can sit here, hold my head high and do my job, then you lot can bloody well stop thinking about my breasts and get on with yours."

Gerry snorted and the rest of the outside broadcast crew fell about laughing. "That's my girl," he smiled. "Now, let's get this show on the road."

John made it into his chair with seconds to spare.

"Welcome to our coverage of the US Open tennis, live from Flushing Meadow, New York." Georgiana smiled into the camera. "It's going to be an incredible tournament, and here to tell us more is the utterly delightful John McEnroe."

"I think YOU'RE the one who's utterly delightful," John grinned and Gerry groaned.

"Don't you dare," he hissed into their ears.

"Well thank you for saying that," Georgiana laughed and beamed into the camera. "I'll try to remain dressed for the whole show."

Gerry put his head in his hands. There was nothing he could do now they were on air.

Georgiana turned to the camera. "Let's get you abreast of the situation," she grinned. "John, tell us more about Kitty Palmer."

"She won her first slam at Wimbledon. She made the semis of the Australian, the final at Roland-Garros and now here she is, in her home town, with the backing of the entire crowd. She's in the form of her life, but we all know she can blow up at any moment. She's a boom or bust kind of player."

Gerry shook his head and groaned again. Georgiana giggled.

"Who's she drawn in the first round John?" she asked.

John looked at his notes and smirked. "Well you're never gonna believe this. She's up against the relatively unknown Sho Sum Titti from South Korea." John struggled to keep a straight face.

"Sho Sum Titti?" Georgiana giggled. "Are we sure of that pronunciation?"

Gerry threw his hands up in the air. "I give up."

Georgiana spent the next twenty minutes grilling John on the rest of the field and then their half hour segment was almost up.

"And there you have it folks," she smiled into the camera. "John's picked his favourites and you'd be foolish not to listen." She turned to John. "You've certainly titillated our taste buds today. I'm looking forward to the action."

"I'll bet you are," John smirked.

"And we're out," Gerry sighed. He was waiting for the inevitable phone call from his boss telling him to keep Georgiana off the air.

"What the fuck are you playing at?" he growled in their ears.

"Sorry." Georgiana grinned into the camera again. "Couldn't help it. I blame John."

John laughed. "She started it."

"And I'm finishing it," Gerry snapped. "Do you think they'll ever put you two together again? Or that you'll even have a job after that display? Didn't you learn your bloody lesson when your tits were splashed across every newspaper in the world?"

Georgiana gulped. "Sorry." She attempted to look contrite.

Gerry's phone rang and he stepped out of the control room to take the call. Five minutes later he walked into the studio looking bemused.

"Seems you can do no wrong," he said to Georgiana. "They didn't like the content but they can't deny the ratings went through the roof again, and on social media too."

Georgiana breathed a sigh of relief. "Sorry. I promise I won't do that again."

"Wanna come to a party tonight?" John asked as he was taking his microphone off.

"Sure, why not?" Georgiana grinned.

Wyatt glanced at his watch as he left home that evening. The party was only a few blocks away, but he hated being late for anything and today he was running late. The gathering was in full swing when he finally arrived and everywhere he looked there were tennis stars past and present, Victoria's Secret models, actresses, musicians and plenty of hangers-on.

He accepted a glass of champagne from a passing waitress and made his way over to the terrace. He stepped out into the late summer evening warmth and froze. A petite, dark-haired woman was standing with her back to him, waiting to collect her coat. He knew immediately that it was Georgiana.

As if sensing his presence, Georgiana turned around and their eyes locked. She gasped. "What are you doing here?"

"I could ask you the same thing," Wyatt replied, never taking his eyes off her.

"I came with John but I'm leaving now," she sneered. "Had I known you'd be here I wouldn't have come within a million miles of it."

"I don't believe you," Wyatt smirked.

"What do I have to do to get it into your thick head. You'll never have me. Not now. Not ever. Get it?" Georgiana turned and walked back away.

"I thought I told you to leave her alone," a voice growled behind Wyatt.

"I got the deal done, didn't I?" Wyatt scowled at his investor.

"Phase one, yes," he replied. "But we gotta get it through that quaint English planning system before we can go ahead and take that place apart piece by piece."

"You think I don't know that?" Wyatt snapped. "Your vendetta against Sebastian is clouding your judgement. Leave it to me."

"I've invested a bunch of money with you over the years, and that's not including the twenty million dollars for The Riverside. I'm your biggest investor, Wyatt. Don't screw with me," he snarled.

"I'm dealing with it. I hope to hell she didn't see you." Wyatt walked away and caught up with Georgiana as she was getting into the lift. He stepped inside just as the doors were closing. They were alone.

"What are you doing?" she squeaked.

"Trying to talk to you," Wyatt replied.

"Well don't," Georgiana replied.

"Just hear me out."

"Why should I?" she snapped. "There's nothing to say. Just fuck off."

Wyatt stepped forward and Georgiana had nowhere to go. She was trapped between him and the wall.

"I can't leave you alone," Wyatt said gruffly. "I want you to be mine."

"Tough. I've no interest in being yours." She pushed him away.

The lift came to a halt at the ground floor and the doors opened. Georgiana rushed out and Wyatt quickly followed. He caught up with her as they reached the outer doors and grabbed her shoulder. "You're coming home with me."

She slapped his hand away and stepped out on to Park Avenue where she was met by an explosion of flashbulbs. Georgiana shrieked and put her hands in front of her face.

"When did you find out you're gonna be a daddy?" A voice from the crowd shouted at Wyatt. He went pale.

"Why the big pay-off?" Another journalist thrust a microphone in his face.

Georgiana turned on her heels and ran back inside the building. She didn't want anything to do with Wyatt, and especially didn't want to be photographed exiting a party with him.

Her phone rang. She looked at the caller display and saw it was Dan. She took a deep breath and answered.

"Hi," she squeaked.

"What the hell is going on?" Dan shouted.

"Nothing. I promise you," she exclaimed.

"Doesn't look like that," Dan replied. "I was watching the news."

"He turned up at the party. I left. He followed me. That's the truth." Georgiana was infuriated that she had been dragged into Wyatt's life again.

Dan was silent. He hated the jealousy that surged through his veins when he pictured Georgiana with another man, especially Wyatt Clayton. He trusted her and knew she would never cheat on him, but seeing them together on television had stirred up his irrational side.

"Are you still there?" Georgiana panicked.

"I'm coming to New York. I'll see you in the morning." He put the phone down before she could reply.

Wyatt pushed through the crowd of journalists and photographers and jumped into a taxi. He had walked to the party but there was no way he could escape the mayhem on foot.

He barked his address at the driver and they sped away from the media. He was home in five minutes and took refuge in his penthouse. When he was alone, the enormity of what had happened hit him.

Ashley had deliberately screwed him over and sold her story to the media. "Bitch," he muttered. Georgiana's latest rejection of his advances had also left him fuming. "Fucking bitch," he yelled. The rage inside him was slowly growing into an inferno, bubbling away under the surface. It was only a matter of time before it exploded.

Reaching for a glass he poured himself a large scotch and turned off his phone. He would deal with Ashley tomorrow, once and for all. For now, oblivion in the bottom of a bottle of whiskey was all he was seeking.

CHAPTER 39

*D*an flew through the night and arrived in New York early the next morning. He went straight to The Plaza, where Georgiana was waiting.

"Hey," he smiled when she opened the door.

She threw herself into his arms. "I told you the truth," she mumbled.

Dan kissed her and held her close for a moment before he spoke.

"I know you did. You hate liars, so you'd hardly be telling me porkies, would you? I just got a touch of the green-eyed monster when I saw you standing next to him and acted a little irrationally."

"A little?" Georgiana giggled. "You jumped on a private jet and flew all night to get to me."

"Yeah, well I love you, and there's no way I'm letting that bastard get anywhere near you ever again. Now where's my proper welcome?"

Georgiana grinned. "It's only been about forty-eight hours."

"That's forty-eight hours of torture for me. Come here." Dan placed his hands either side of Georgiana's face and kissed her gently.

He led her towards the bed and undid the bathrobe, exposing her nakedness. He ran his hands across her breasts and kissed her neck. "Show me how much you want me," he whispered in her ear.

Georgiana responded to his touch. "Take your clothes off," she murmured.

She spent the next hour making love with Dan like it was their first time. She gave herself completely to him, taking them to a level of closeness she had never before experienced.

"Well, that certainly showed me," Dan grinned as they lay entwined on the bed. "That was by far and away the best sex I've ever had. I know I've said it before, several times, but that just eclipsed it."

"Are we ok?" Georgiana gripped his arm. She needed reassurance.

"I'd say so," Dan muttered as he slipped his hand between Georgiana's legs.

"Oh," she gasped and then laughed. "You know what I mean."

"I've got to get as much of you as I can before I go," Dan said gruffly. "But yes, we're ok. I was being a dick – as you would put it."

"I don't want you to go," Georgiana pouted.

"I'm sending the jet for you on Sunday. Do you think you can try to behave yourself until then?" Dan teased. He lowered his mouth to meet hers.

The rest of the week flew by. Georgiana was in demand from her bosses, who had quickly forgotten 'boob-gate' and conveniently ignored her rumoured liaison with Wyatt Clayton. She had assured them that it was fake news and that she was in a committed relationship with Dan.

The television ratings were consistently high whenever she was on air, and her partnership with McEnroe had been allowed to continue, much to the delight of the viewers.

Dan spent five hours with Georgiana before he had to fly back to LA and, in that time, she felt they had grown even closer. Wyatt had not tried to contact her during the rest of her time in New York, and she was thankful that he had stayed away.

She landed in LA in the early hours of Monday morning and Dan was waiting for her on the tarmac as she came off the jet. She ran into his arms and reached up to kiss him.

"I missed you so much," she cried.

Dan kissed her and smiled. Every time Georgiana came back to him he was increasingly confident in her feelings for him. "Let's get out of here."

The next morning their joyful reunion - photographed at the private airfield by a tenacious paparazzi - was plastered across the front page of every newspaper in America, and Wyatt was furious.

He picked up the phone and dialled Bobby. "I wanna get moving on the plans for The Riverside. Where are we at?"

"We're good to go. Just need permission from the local council and we can send in the contractors," Bobby replied. "What about Georgiana? Don't you need to run things past her?"

"Email her the details," Wyatt snapped. "She can't stop it but she needs to know."

"Don't you wanna deal with her direct?" Bobby asked.

"No," Wyatt barked and hung up the call.

CHAPTER 40

"*Y*ou look amazing," Susie exclaimed when she and Olivia met for lunch at the club. "How are you feeling? Are you sleeping?"

"Much better, thanks. I'll be glad when Sebastian stops clucking around me. And I never did need that much sleep," she laughed.

"And how's Sebastian coping with Alexander?" Susie asked.

"Like a bloody duck to water." Olivia rolled her eyes. "He's a natural. I'm the one who's flailing around and feeling like a novice."

"Well, he has done it before," Susie smiled. "And I bet you're doing just fine. You're so good with Rosie."

"She's my goddaughter so I don't have a choice," Olivia joked. "I must say it's nice to get away for a couple of hours. I don't feel like we've had a proper catch-up in ages."

"I know. We're here now, so let's make the most of it. What are you drinking?" Susie consulted the menu.

"Just sparkling water, sadly," Olivia replied. "But I'm going to eat a huge rare steak and have some unpasteurized cheese just because I can."

Susie laughed. "And so you should."

They were ready to order when Lucinda sashayed towards their table, with Samantha and Marcia a few steps behind.

"Olivia. You look exhausted," she smirked. "Still got a little baby weight to lose as well, I see." Samantha and Marcia snorted with laughter.

"Lucinda. How delightful to see you," Olivia replied with a forced smile. "What can we help you with?"

"I want to know if you and Sebastian are still planning on taking a table at the charity ball next month? You haven't responded to the invitation." She wrinkled her nose in distaste. "I thought you would have had the decency to tell me by now. We can sell the table to someone else if you don't want it."

Susie glared at Lucinda. "For God's sake, she's just had a baby and a major operation. I hardly think your invitation is at the top of the priority list."

"We really haven't had time," Olivia said. "We've had our hands full with Alexander, but yes, we're still coming."

"And which man will we be seeing Georgiana with?" Lucinda sneered.

"That's none of your business," Olivia bristled. "You can go now." She dismissed Lucinda.

Lucinda smirked and turned away from the table. "Oh, and Olivia. If you need to get yourself a new outfit to accommodate the extra weight, I'm sure Marcia can give you the benefit of her wisdom," Lucinda walked off, leaving Marcia agog.

"How rude," Susie spluttered.

Olivia was laughing. "Don't let her get to you Marcia. You're lovely just as you are."

Marcia scuttled off after Lucinda.

"She's such a bitch." Susie shook her head. "So, about the ball. Who else is coming?"

"Tom and you, obviously. Georgiana and Dan. Peter and Andrea, and José and Angelica are coming too." Olivia reeled off the names. "With me and Sebastian that's ten."

"Should be a real laugh," Susie grinned. "How is Georgiana anyway? I've not seen her since 'boob-gate'."

"She called last night from LA." Olivia took a sip of water. "I don't think she's planning on coming back before the ball."

"So, it's going well with Dan then?" Susie asked.

Olivia shrugged her shoulders. "She cares deeply for him, I know that much, but Sebastian isn't quite so convinced. He has a certain reputation with his co-stars and the last thing she needs is more heartache."

"She'll be fine. I'm sure she can handle him. I mean, who wouldn't be happy with a drop-dead gorgeous Hollywood A-list boyfriend?" Susie grinned. "He's like a young Paul Newman. Delicious. Even you have to admit it."

Olivia laughed. "Yes, I can certainly see the attraction, but I'm a one-man woman I'm afraid."

"Me too," Susie sighed. "But a girl can fantasise from time to time."

They had just placed their lunch order with the waitress when Will appeared at the table.

"Hey. Have you heard from Porg?" he asked Olivia.

"Spoke to her last night. Why?"

Will sighed. "I've been trying to catch up with her for ages and she's ignoring me."

Olivia grinned. "I'm sorry to have to break it to you, Will, but she's totally loved up and won't be popping up for air any time soon."

"Oh. Ok." Will looked downcast. "I need some advice. That's all."

"Anything we can help with?" Susie butted in, keen to hear some new gossip.

"It's about Lucinda." Will was sheepish.

"Oh God," Olivia laughed and covered her ears. "I don't want to hear this."

Susie grinned at him. "Go on," she urged.

"I think she's in love with me," he whispered, painfully aware of Lucinda's eyes boring a hole into the back of his head.

"And what makes you say that?" Susie was laughing.

"She said she's going to leave Godfrey for me." Will was stricken. "It was only supposed to be a bit of fun."

"What? Olivia choked on her water. "Dear oh dear, you've got yourself into a right pickle, haven't you?"

"Tell me about it," Will replied grimly. "What do I do?"

"Just tell her the truth," Susie advised. "What's the worst she can do?"

"She said she'll get me sacked for sexual harassment if I don't do what she wants." He shook his head in dismay. "I've totally fucked up."

"I'll get Georgiana to call you. She won't let you be fired. She does have a say in what goes on here you know?" Olivia reassured him. "Don't worry. I'll have a strong word with Lucinda. I may just pay a visit to the house when I know Godfrey is there."

"Would you?" Will was relieved. "She'll listen to you."

"I doubt that, but I'll give it a go," Olivia smiled. "You're practically family. We've got your back. Just make better choices next time, please. I feel a bit sick just thinking about it." Olivia and Susie fell about laughing again.

Will skulked across the restaurant with his head down, giving Lucinda a wide berth.

CHAPTER 41

"*W*hat do you think about this one?" Dan threw a script at Georgiana.

"What's it about?" she asked, thumbing through the first few pages.

"Indie film. Vinnie has been banging on about it for ages and I got the final script the other day. Have a read and let me know what you think. Want a drink?" Dan stood up and walked towards the kitchen.

"Juice, please," Georgiana shouted after him. She was lying on the sun lounger on the terrace of Dan's home high in the Hollywood hills, soaking up some rays and relishing their time together.

Dan's rehearsals had been cancelled and the start of filming for his action movie delayed, thanks to his co-star fracturing her leg in a jet-ski accident. The enforced break gave him time to take on another project and he had been looking for something special, a role he could really get his teeth into. Vinnie was convinced he had found exactly the film.

Dan came back out onto the terrace and dropped a kiss on Georgiana's head.

"Here." He handed her some freshly squeezed orange juice.

"Thanks." She took a sip. "Do you want me to read this now?"

"Would you mind? I've got to give them an answer in a couple of days and I really want your opinion. It's a bit of a departure from my usual blockbuster nonsense." Dan sat down next to Georgiana and she wriggled into his arms.

"Do you mind if I do it in a bit?" Georgiana batted her eyelashes.

"Depends on what you're planning on doing beforehand." Dan reached behind and pulled the string fastenings on Georgiana's bikini top.

"You read my mind, Mr Flowers," she murmured and pulled him down on top of her.

"God, you're killing me," Dan laughed. "I'm worn out."

"Shut up and kiss me," Georgiana whispered and wrapped her legs around him.

Later that evening she walked into the lounge and stood with her hands on her hips.

"What?" Dan looked at her quizzically.

"You HAVE to do this film," she smiled encouragingly. "It was made for you."

Dan grinned. "Really? Do you think I can do it justice?"

"Oh my God, like you even have to ask? You'll regret it if you don't, and I'll disown you too." She clapped her hands. "Get on the phone and say yes before someone else does."

CHAPTER 42

*D*an accepted the lead in Jigsaw Kids and immediately got stuck into what he called his vanity project. Georgiana witnessed for the first time how consumed he became in understanding and growing his character, and learning his lines. Dan was determined to give his all to the new role and she had hardly seen him in a week.

She lazed around for a few days and then started to get bored. She had no dog or horse in LA to fill up her spare time and she needed something to do. When the call came from London to get back to work she was delighted. She didn't want to leave Dan but she was itching to be busy again.

Her bosses were taking full advantage of her being Stateside and sent her to cover several different events, including the box-office-busting Floyd Mayweather and Conor McGregor fight in Las Vegas.

It was only a short hop from LA to Vegas in the jet that Dan had arranged for her. She was glad of a change of scenery.

The jet was cutting a swathe through the smattering of clouds high above the Mojave Desert, and it was perfectly silent.

Georgiana closed her eyes and leaned back in her seat, thinking how much she missed home. Living in LA, however temporarily, was not for her. It was somewhere she would happily visit, but in short bursts. Her heart was in the lush green countryside of West Chesterton, and she sighed as she imagined galloping up the Vale and across the meadows with the wind in her hair, and running across the estate with Lady bouncing at her heels.

She landed in the dazzling neon glare of Las Vegas, and was taken straight to the T-Mobile arena where she met her new producer and crew.

"Glad to meet you." Tony Wren held his hand out to greet her. "I'm producing the show. That's Barry," he said pointing to the assistant producer. Barry waved at Georgiana. "I hope you've done your homework. It's a bit of a baptism of fire having this as your first boxing broadcast."

"I'll be fine." Georgiana flashed him a reassuring grin. She had been reading up on the subject for a few days, and felt that her recently-gained knowledge combined with what she already knew would be enough for the British viewers. Tony got her straight to work.

"I want you to get out there ringside and interview the celebrities. I'm sure you already know plenty of them through your boyfriend."

"Err. Well, not really," Georgiana replied. "But I'm ok with it."

"Weren't you just in France with Leonardo DiCaprio?"

"I think everyone knows that I was," Georgiana grinned. She was over the shame of boob-gate.

"Well start with him and take it from there." Tony said. "Production meeting in five minutes," he shouted across the room to the rest of the crew.

Georgiana grabbed her iPad and started to make notes. She Googled a few of the stars in preparation for her interviews - she wanted to be on the ball and keep the conversations relevant.

The production meeting lasted an hour, then Georgiana was ushered into hair and make-up which took another forty-five minutes. By the time they had finished, she was rushing to change and get down on the main floor before the Hollywood elite arrived.

Her outfit was a world away from what she would usually wear at a sports event, but this was Las Vegas and she had to up her game. She had picked out a beautifully-cut Dolce & Gabbana black blazer embroidered with Swarovski crystals on the lapels, and teamed it with a silky black camisole, cropped skinny black jeans, and a towering pair of Louboutins. Her hair was loose, falling in glossy waves down her back, and she wore a diamond-encrusted, heart-shaped necklace that Dan had given her, along with dazzling diamond earrings that had belonged to her mother. She looked stunning.

Cameraman Jimmy and boom operator Ravi were waiting for her at the doors of the BBC studio. They both whistled when they saw her.

Georgiana laughed. "Enough of that. Let's get this show on the road."

The atmosphere in the arena was electrically charged. This was the hottest show in town, with tickets changing hands for upwards of eighty-five thousand dollars. Georgiana immediately felt the energy in the room and soaked it up - the adrenalin would help when it came to being on camera.

As Tony suggested, she made a beeline for Leo, who was only too happy to chat to her. Off-camera, he also apologised for the press intrusion in Monaco, telling her she had handled it 'great'.

Next up were Jamie Foxx, Bruce Willis and Will Smith who were huge boxing fans and impressed Georgiana with their knowledge. She managed to grab a minute with Jennifer Lopez and a mere thirty seconds with Beyoncé and Jay-Z; had a fit of the giggles when Chris and Liam Hemsworth started cracking jokes on camera; bonded with Justin Timberlake over their shared love of golf; talked Martians with Matt Damon; high-fived Ryan Reynolds when they discovered they had both rescued their dogs, and was engulfed in a group hug that lasted a full two minutes by fellow Brits, Sharon and Ozzy Osbourne.

Once the bout started, she scuttled back to the BBC studio to watch Mayweather take out the UFC pretender in ten rounds. It was an exhilarating and entertaining match, only out-glossed by the A-list audience.

She was invited to a star-studded party after the event which she declined – she wanted to get back to Dan. She had promised him she would come straight home as he was set to go off on location the next day for three weeks. Georgiana was dreading the separation.

She mulled over her feelings for Dan on the flight back to LA. She cared for him deeply, but something was holding her back.

"Stop fighting it," she muttered as the plane touched down.

Dan was asleep when she arrived back at his house. She sneaked into the bedroom and got undressed quietly, trying not to wake him as she fumbled her way across the room, willing her eyes to adjust to the darkness. She was almost at the edge of the bed when she tripped over the rug and landed on top of Dan.

"Crap!" she hissed. "Sorry."

Dan was startled and sat bolt upright. He rubbed his eyes and attempted to shake off his grogginess.

"I knew you'd fall for me eventually," he smiled sleepily. "Come here." He pulled back the sheets and Georgiana slipped in beside him and lay her head on his chest.

"I was trying to be quiet," she giggled. "I know how tired you are."

"If my precious sleep is going to be disturbed, then who better to do it than you?" He stroked her hair. "How was it?"

"Fun, actually," she yawned. "I saw Leo, and the producer was happy so I guess it went okay."

"That's great," Dan mumbled. He was falling back to sleep.

Georgiana suddenly sat up and stared at him. "Three weeks is forever," she croaked. "I'll really miss you."

"It'll go in a flash," Dan reassured her. "I'll be in England before you know it." He kissed her head. "Can we go to sleep now?"

"Okay, but don't fall in love with anyone else while we're apart,' she whispered.

"Fat chance of that," he chuckled. "I'm just hoping absence really does make the heart grow fonder. It's high time you fell in love with me."

CHAPTER 43

$\mathcal{T}$he last Saturday in August was Lady Captain's day at The Riverside. It consisted of eighteen holes of golf under tournament rules, followed by a gourmet dinner and fashion show.

Lucinda, in her capacity as Lady Captain, had been planning her day for many months and she was determined it would go off without a hitch. She arrived at the club early in the morning and went in search of Will. He was just the tonic she needed to start her day with, quite literally, a bang.

She found him in his tiny office at the back of the tennis complex and immediately pounced on him.

"We don't have long," she purred and undid the zip on his shorts.

"Maybe we shouldn't do this here." Will's weak attempt to put her off failed.

"It's never stopped you before," she smirked. "Give me a good seeing-to before anyone arrives."

Will had no choice but to comply. He had got himself into this mess and could see no way out, not without the help of Georgiana and Olivia who were yet to take aim at Lucinda.

He sighed and dropped his shorts. Closing his eyes, he attempted to imagine Lucinda was Maria Sharapova – he had a thing about her. When he finally opened them, after a great deal of thrusting, he was staring at Georgiana who was desperately attempting to suppress her laughter.

"What the hell do you think you're doing?" Georgiana feigned outrage.

Lucinda shrieked and ran out of the office, leaving her knickers and bra behind.

"Thank God," Will groaned. "You saved me. I couldn't come no matter what I tried to visualise. Even Maria wasn't doing it for me."

"I feel sick," Georgiana laughed. "Liv told me you were in trouble so here I am to rescue you."

"I've totally fucked up," he sighed.

"You're telling me," she rolled her eyes. "I'm still getting over the shock of seeing you and her bent over your desk."

Will zipped up his shorts and grabbed Georgiana into a hug. "I've missed you Porg."

"Don't touch me," she shrieked and started to laugh. "I know where you've been and it ain't pretty."

Will grinned and pretended to dust himself down. "When did you get back?"

"Late last night. It's so good to be home, and Lady was deliriously happy to see me."

"So am I," Will beamed. "If I ever needed you it's now. Can you sort Lucinda out please? I can't lose my job."

"No one is losing their job," Georgiana replied. "I do have a little sway here you know."

"What are you going to say to her?" Will asked.

"Never you mind," she winked. "I've got her by the balls now."

"How? Tell me," Will demanded.

"With this!" Georgiana flashed a dazzling smile and handed him her iPhone. She had recorded part of Will and Lucinda's illicit encounter.

"You clever, clever girl," Will grinned, unabashed. "You're so much more than just a gorgeous face."

"I have my uses," she laughed. "Now, are you going to buy me breakfast so we can have a proper catch-up?"

"Only if you promise to show the old witch the video while I'm there to enjoy her reaction." He slung his arm around Georgiana's shoulder and they walked towards the clubhouse.

"I think we can save it for a much more public occasion," she smirked. "Don't you think it's time you started shagging someone more suitable?"

"I did once," Will snorted. "And then she ran off with a Hollywood star." He ruffled her hair. "How's it all going with Dan, anyway?"

Georgiana smiled. "I really, really like him."

"Is that it?" Will was surprised. "You've hardly left his side since you met and you 'really, really like him'?" Will pulled a face at her.

"Oh, you know what I mean," she scoffed.

"No, I don't." Will turned her around to face him. "Are you with him because you're in love with him or is it just a rebound thing?"

"No!" she exclaimed. "I do care about him. He's kind and thoughtful and we have amazing sex and he truly loves me."

"But?" urged Will.

"But nothing," she dismissed. "The only question on your lips should be when are we going to bring down Lucinda?"

"Sooner the better. I need to get her out of my hair." Will was hopeful.

"Nah," Georgiana smirked. "It has to have maximum impact. Leave it with me. And don't worry about your job."

"Ooh, I like this new mean streak. It suits you." Will winked. "Just give me fair warning. I'd like to be prepared for the backlash."

"You'll be the first to know." She linked her arm through his. "Now let's eat, I'm famished."

CHAPTER 44

*D*an stepped out of his trailer onto the palm-fringed beach and was immediately hit by the heat of the midday sun. It was sweltering, and the lack of a sea breeze made the heat even more oppressive. A perfect white-sand beach and the crystal-clear waters of the Gulf of Thailand stretched out in front of him. He paused to take it all in.

He was on Koh Tao, a tiny islet with dramatic, jungle-topped hillside views and tropical coral reefs that attracted a vibrant yet respectful dive crowd. The location manager had selected the island for its privacy and stunning scenery. It really was paradise – all that was missing was Georgiana.

Filming for Jigsaw Kids was well underway, and Dan was completely absorbed in the character he was playing - the father of a child whose sudden death whilst on holiday, and subsequent organ donation, are the catalyst for his breakdown and rebirth.

"Did you send the flowers?" Dan asked Coby as they walked towards the set.

"A totally gorgeous bouquet of blush pink roses," Coby replied. "From that new place on Rodeo. The owner is heavenly."

Dan laughed. "He must be if he's caught your eye."

Coby waved his hands at Dan. "Ooh, stop. You know me too well."

Dan had employed Coby almost five years ago to be his personal assistant, on the back of a recommendation from Vinnie. He had worked for several big hitters before landing on Dan's doorstep and was one of the best in the business. He knew all the right people from chauffeurs to studio heads, and had a knack of making friends wherever he went. There was nothing he couldn't get his hands on wherever they were in the world, and he was discreet, loyal and completely trustworthy.

"Isn't it a little extravagant to be sending flowers from LA to England when there are perfectly good florists on her doorstep?" Dan rolled his eyes.

"Not like this one there aren't," Coby grinned. "Trust me, she'll love them. Do you need anything?"

Dan had his script in one hand and a chilled bottle of water in the other. "I'm good, thanks."

He was enjoying Thailand for its freedom from press intrusion. He could walk around without anyone pestering him or even caring who he was. It was refreshing and relaxing.

"Hi, babe." He kissed his on-screen wife, Cara Keating. "Ready?"

"Naturally," she smiled and kissed him back. Cara was tall and willowy, with caramel blonde hair and blue eyes. She was the epitome of an all-American sweetheart, and no one had a bad word to say about her.

"Did you manage to get some sleep?" she asked him.

"Not really. Too much going on in here." Dan tapped the side of his head. Although he was hassle-free and relaxed he was having trouble sleeping. He knew he would have to dig deep to find the emotion required of his character, and he was struggling to switch off when he went to bed. "I miss Georgiana as well," he sighed.

"I love this side of you," Cara laughed. "I finally get to see the real Dan Flowers. The one who's pining for the love of his life. It's too cute."

Dan threw his script at her. "Stop taking the piss," he grinned.

"You're making it too easy for me." She picked up the script from the floor and handed it back to him. "Shall we run through the last bit of the second scene again? I don't think I've nailed it yet."

"Sure," Dan replied. "Shoot."

He sat on the sand with Cara, running through their lines for ten minutes before the director was ready for them. Hair and make-up dashed over for a final touch-up, and then they were on.

"And ACTION," Rollo Baxter, the film's director, shouted.

CHAPTER 45

"What was that?" Georgiana shouted into the phone. All around her engines revved in preparation for the start of the Italian Grand Prix. She couldn't hear herself think.

"I really can't hear you. I'll call you back later." She hung up the phone and walked back up the pit lane. She hadn't spoken to Dan properly in days and it was starting to get to her. He had been on location in Thailand for three weeks, and the time difference in combination with his shooting schedule and her work was making it difficult for them to have any more than a few snatched words each day.

The celebrity gossip magazines were filled with photographs of Dan and Cara looking impossibly in love on exotic Thai beaches. Each one asked if his short-lived relationship with Georgiana was over before it had even really begun, and went on to detail Dan's extensive history with many of his other co-stars.

Georgiana knew the majority of what she read in the press was completely fabricated – God knows she had lived through it with Sebastian – but a small part of her still doubted Dan. Wyatt had done a real number on her confidence. Dan had told her time and time again to ignore it, but it niggled away at her the longer they were separated.

She had not been pleased when her boss asked her to cover the Italian Grand Prix from Monza – it was a last-minute addition to her schedule - but she felt that she owed it to them for not sacking her. She wasn't completely out of the dog-house yet and was keen to keep everyone happy.

She stopped in the pit lane and sent Dan a text.

I miss you so much x

She had an immediate response, and smiled as a photograph popped up of him blowing her a kiss.

I miss you too sweetheart. Only two more sleeps xx

He would be back in Appleton Vale in a few days and she couldn't wait.

"GEORGIANA," Gerry screamed in her ear. "Get off the lane." She looked up just in time to jump out of the way of Lewis Hamilton's Mercedes flashing past her at speed.

"Christ, that was close," she muttered.

"Telling me," Gerry crackled in her ear. "Bloody idiot. Are you trying to get yourself killed?"

"Not intentionally, Gerry,' she spoke into her microphone. "Do you need me back there or can I go?"

"You can go," Gerry sighed. "Anyone else would give their right arm to be in your position and all you want to do is get back to your boyfriend."

"I was never supposed to be here in the first place," she moaned.

"Yeah, I know," Gerry said. "You did a great job as always. Leave the mic pack in the media centre and I'll see you in Toronto."

"What did you do?" she laughed.

"What do you mean?" he asked.

"You keep getting lumbered with me and being sent all over the world. You must have pissed them off somehow."

"I stuck up for you, that's bloody what," Gerry exclaimed. "But I also happen to like working with you, and my wife has just pushed off with the electrician so I'm all yours."

"Oh, sorry," Georgiana replied. "I didn't know about your wife."

"Hated her anyway," Gerry laughed. "Get going before you miss the flight."

"Thanks G. See you in a few weeks."

She sprinted the length of the pit lane, threw her gear into the media centre, and jumped in a courtesy car to head to the airport.

Dan was exhausted. His shooting schedule had been full on, and the harrowing storyline and depth of emotion he had to give on camera had taken it out of him. He was itching to get back to England and was looking forward to having a week off with Georgiana before he had to fly to Paris for another week of shooting. While he was in Paris she would be in Toronto presenting the Invictus Games with HRH Prince Harry. The separation was hard.

"And ACTION."

Dan immediately sprang out of his reverie and burst into life on camera. The final scene they were shooting was particularly traumatic, and Dan found he was crying when Rollo shouted 'Cut'."

"Great job, everyone," Rollo boomed across the set. "Enjoy your week off and I'll see you in Paris."

Dan hugged Cara and wiped away his tears. "Thanks, darling. You made that easy for me. I'm heading straight to England, but the jet can take you home after if you like?"

"Seriously?" she grinned. "I'm actually meeting Tammy in Paris so that works really well. Give me twenty minutes to get my stuff together."

They reached the mainland by speed boat, and Dan had a car waiting to take them to the airport where the jet was ready to whisk him back to Georgiana. Once he, Cara and Coby were on board he sent her a text.

Don't get out of bed. I'll be joining you in a few hours x

He slept the entire flight and was feeling revived when they briefly touched down in Paris to drop Cara off. When they landed in Bath, there was a driver waiting to take Dan to Appleton Vale, and then on to London where Coby would be staying with friends for the week.

Dan crept into the cottage just as the sun was coming up and found Georgiana sleeping peacefully.

He quietly slipped his clothes off, sat on the side of the bed and bent down to kiss her neck. Georgiana stirred and a grin slowly appeared on her face. She peered at him through one eye.

"I was just dreaming about you," she said sleepily.

"Well dream no more." Dan pulled her into his arms and kissed her. Within moments they were lost in each other.

Over breakfast Georgiana checked her emails and saw there was one from Bobby Garnett with Athos' plans for The Riverside. She opened it with trepidation.

"What the fuck?" she screamed.

"What?" Dan looked up from reading his newspaper.

She turned the laptop to face him. He scanned the plans and groaned.

"Two hundred and fifty new homes? That's outrageous. It's going to be one hell of a fight. You up for it, babe?" He put his arms around her.

"Bloody right I am," Georgiana replied. "Edward would turn in his grave if he saw this. Sebastian is going to go nuts."

Dan looked at the plans again and whistled. "As well as the housing, there's a one hundred bed luxury hotel, glamping site, equestrian centre, eco lodges, quad bike trails, spa, conference centre." He shook his head. "They'll never get permission for this."

"Wanna bet?" Georgiana sighed. "Money talks."

Dan rubbed his hands together. "A fight it is, then. Time to talk to your brother and rally the troops." He pushed her mobile across the table. Georgiana picked it up and dialled Sebastian.

"I've just sent you an email," she said when he answered the phone. "Look at it now."

"Hang on a sec," he replied. "What's the rush?"

"You'll see." Georgiana waited impatiently for him to read the email and prepared herself for the explosion.

"What the fuck?" Sebastian exclaimed.

"That's exactly what I said," she replied. "What are we going to do?"

"Bloody well stop it. That's what," Sebastian growled. "Is that all the information you have?"

"Yes, but I can ask for a more detailed plan. I have the right to see that, don't I?"

"You're a shareholder. They have to give it to you. Email him back now and demand it," Sebastian told her.

"Right. Ok. I'll let you know as soon as I get something. Do you really think we can stop it?" She was doubtful. She knew the power that Wyatt possessed, and that he would stop at nothing to get his own way.

"Watch me," Sebastian snarled. "If he wants a fight he can have one."

"Ok," Georgiana squeaked. "Speak to you later."

She put the phone down and looked at Dan. "He's pretty pissed off."

Dan laughed. "I'd say that was a bit of an understatement, knowing your brother."

"It's not bloody funny," she cried.

Dan wrapped his arms around her. "I know. Sorry." He kissed her. "Clayton has already misjudged you once and you showed him just how tough you are. Now he's up against two Blooms so I reckon he'll be quaking in his boots."

Georgiana grinned. "Yeah. If he thinks I'm a hard nut to crack, wait till he gets in front of Sebastian."

"That's my girl," Dan smiled. "You're a fighter. Just another thing I love about you." He stroked her cheek. "My little pocket rocket."

Her mobile bleeped with a text from Sebastian.

Meeting at the barn at two o'clock x

"Bloody hell that was quick," Dan laughed.

"There's no stopping him when he's fired up. You'll see later." Georgiana rolled her eyes.

"Well now that's sorted can we go back to bed?" Dan reached for her hand.

"Only if you can catch me first." She squealed as Dan lunged towards her. She just managed to evade him by throwing a cushion in his face.

He ducked out of the way. "There's nowhere to run to," he laughed. "Get your perfect little bottom up those stairs right now."

She giggled and stuck her tongue out at him. "I'll race you." She hurtled towards the hallway with Dan in hot pursuit.

"Lady, NO," Dan yelled.

Georgiana looked over her shoulder and saw Lady purposely positioning herself between Dan and the doorway. She was growling and baring her teeth at him.

He bent down and gently stroked her head. "I'm not hurting mummy," he whispered. "Good protection skills, though."

Georgiana turned around and kneeled down to hug Lady. "Clever girl." She kissed her. "But you don't have to worry about Dan. He's one of the good guys."

Lady looked at Dan, stuck her tongue out, and trotted back to her bed next to the Aga.

"Did she learn that from you?" he laughed. "She was sticking her tongue out at me, just the way you do."

"She loves you really," Georgiana grinned. "Just the way I do."

Dan picked Georgiana up and swung her over his shoulder. "I should bloody well hope so. "And now I've got you, I'm going to have my wicked way with you."

CHAPTER 46

"Can we not all talk at once," Sebastian roared. "We're going to be finished before we've even started at this rate."

He was standing on a bale of hay in the barn at the Manor's stable yard. Almost the entire population of the village was crammed into the space attending the meeting he had called to discuss The Riverside.

"We have a lot to do in the next four weeks. That's when the planning council next meets and we need to be ready. Armed with every argument, piece of evidence, environmental surveys...the lot," he continued.

"Let's assign teams," Tom shouted. "I've got a bit of experience with planning and I know Peter has as well."

"What about it, Peter?" Sebastian sought him out in the crowd.

"On it," Peter grinned. "I know enough people at the council to get a read on their opinions."

"You three need to use your celebrity to get the word out." Dee

Dee waved at Sebastian, Dan and Georgiana. "Surely some publicity would help our cause?"

"Absolutely, Dee Dee. We're already working on that." Sebastian smiled at her. "We also need someone to run the environmental side of things." He looked around for a volunteer.

Andrea raised her hand. "I don't really have any experience but I'm a fast learner and I think I could co-ordinate it."

"Excellent. Thanks, Andrea. Now, who else can help with that?"

Will's brother Freddie, and his friends the Lavenham twins - Josh and Jem - threw their hands in the air. "We can," they shouted in union.

"If there's a rare bat to be found, we're the ones to do it," Jem grinned. The barn erupted in laughter.

Sebastian chuckled. "Great." He turned to Andrea. "Do you think you can keep that lot in check?"

"I'll do my best," she laughed.

"Can they really do this, Sebastian?" Jane asked. "Two hundred and fifty new homes equates to at least five hundred new people and cars. What about the infrastructure? It will turn us into a small town."

"They can try," he replied grimly.

"It will ruin the village," Marjorie Rose cried. "Imagine how many people and cars will come through our tiny lanes. And then there's the noise, rubbish and pollution."

"Exactly right," Sebastian replied. "This is the last thing we want for our beautiful home. Are we ready for a fight?"

"Too bloody right," Peter shouted.

"Damn straight," Tom bellowed.

The villagers clapped and stomped their feet in agreement. They may not be ready quite yet, but they would meet Athos head on in one month from now and fight them to the bitter end.

Wyatt looked at the email again. After everything that had gone on with Georgiana, he knew there was going to be an almighty fight with the residents of Appleton Vale. He wasn't adverse to playing dirty and now he had a new spy in the camp it made things much easier. If he knew what was going on behind the scenes he would be one step ahead of them at all times. He tapped his reply.

Lucinda,

Appreciate you letting me know about Sebastian's meeting.
Keep the information coming, I'll make it worth your while.

Best,
Wyatt Clayton

He leaned back in his chair and smiled. He may have lost the girl, but there was no way he was going to lose this fight.

CHAPTER 47

*P*eppy Grainger pulled her phone out of her pocket and smiled at the caller ID on the screen.

"Sebastian," she purred. "What can I do for you?"

"I need a favour," he replied.

"Ooh, I like the sound of that," she joked.

Peppy and Sebastian knew each other through work. She had been the executive producer on Sky Sports weekly golf show for many years, but had recently moved across to Sky Sports News to run the team and inject a bit of her own special blend of magic into the broadcast.

Fun and vivacious, she was in her late forties, blonde, tanned and Amazonian in stature. She wore revealing outfits that accentuated her huge breasts and curvy figure, and had a dazzling smile that could melt ice caps.

"Want to come down for the night?" Sebastian asked.

"Finally!" she laughed. "I knew you always wanted me."

"Don't let Olivia hear you say that," he joked. "I'm serious. Can you spare some time? We need you."

"Well, when you put it like that, how can I refuse?" Peppy chuckled. "Sounds fascinating. I can probably come later today. I'll have to move a meeting or two, but that's fine. Would that work?"

"Perfect. See you this evening." He rang off and Peppy immediately sent her assistant a text instructing her to cancel her afternoon. Sebastian's call had been intriguing and her journalistic instincts kicked in. It had to be a big story to invite her to the Manor. No-one from the media had ever set foot inside Sebastian's home. He fiercely guarded the privacy of his family.

Peppy ran out of the office early in the afternoon and jumped into a taxi, instructing the driver to take her home. She lived in a Victorian terraced house in Richmond, just off the park and only a few miles from the Sky HQ in Isleworth.

The driver dropped her off outside and she flew around gathering clothes into her overnight bag. She was in her car heading towards Appleton Vale within twenty minutes.

Olivia greeted her when she arrived at the Manor. They had met many times on Tour and liked each other very much.

"Hi, darling," Peppy hugged Olivia. "Where is he, then?"

"Sebastian?" she asked, returning the hug.

"No silly, Alexander. I'm desperate to see him. Everyone is." Peppy grinned.

"We've been pestered like you wouldn't believe to release a photo. Sebastian is adamant that's not going to happen, so I may have to frisk you," Olivia laughed. "Come in. He shouldn't be too long."

"Wow," Peppy was wide-eyed when she stepped into the hall. "This is stunning."

Olivia grinned. "Everyone says that. It's a beautiful house. I'll give you a tour later if you like? We've put you in one of the guest suites in the east wing so you won't be disturbed by Alexander in the night.'

"The east wing! Oh, how the other half lives," Peppy snorted. "Now where's that baby?"

Olivia took Peppy up to the nursery where Alexander was beginning to stir from his nap. That's where Sebastian found them when he arrived back from the Club.

"I never thought I'd see the day when you went gaga over a baby, Pep," he joked from the doorway. He crossed the room and kissed her. "You're looking well."

"Oh, you know. Lots of sex is good for the complexion," she winked. "Your son is just scrumptious. He's going to be a heartbreaker."

Sebastian beamed. He was besotted with Alexander. "He's a little cutie, isn't he?"

"He's your mini-me," Peppy snorted. "Even the eyes."

"Like I said. A real cutie," he grinned. "Are you hungry? Hattie's made something delicious. I don't know what, but it smells bloody good."

"Starving," she replied. Peppy had a voracious appetite for great food as well as great sex. "Are you going to tell me what's going on?" she asked as they walked downstairs?

Sebastian got right to the point. "The American who bought my club has got some pretty serious plans for the place. We're going to stop him and I need your help. Media attention will be important for the campaign." Sebastian ran his hands through his hair in exasperation. "He's a real bastard."

"And you had to drag me all the way down here to tell me that?" She rolled her eyes.

"We want you to join our merry band of protesters and lead the media side of things. You know everyone who's anyone and you're great on camera. Georgiana, Dan and I will do anything we can to help, we just can't put it together ourselves, that's why we need you."

"Dan Flowers?" Peppy grinned. "Well that puts a whole new spin on things."

"Keep your grubby little hands off him," Sebastian laughed. "He's very happy with my sister."

"I know. Lucky cow!" Peppy exclaimed. "I was only joking. He does give us another angle to work with, although he may get a bit of stick for not actually being from the village."

"He's living with Georgiana when they're here so I think that qualifies, in the loosest sense." Sebastian pleaded with her. "We can make this work if you come on board."

"I'm seriously overdue a break from work so I guess I could try to swing a sabbatical," she replied.

"You're welcome to stay here whenever you need to." Sebastian breathed a sigh of relief. They were desperately in need of someone with Peppy's experience to handle the press.

"Are you sure I'm the right person?" Peppy asked.

"I trust you Pep. That's enough for me," Sebastian smiled. "Let's eat."

Hattie had created a feast of Orkney sea scallop ceviche, pickled cucumber, pink ginger and Bonito flakes to start with, followed by fresh Cornish silver mullet with sweetcorn, confit tomatoes and hazelnuts. For desert, she made a summer berry and almond tart.

"Is this how you eat all the time?" Peppy asked. 'It's delicious."

Olivia laughed. "I think Hattie tends to go to town when we have guests. Trust me, it's a lot less formal normally."

They sat around the dining room table catching up on Tour news, and further discussing Athos' plans for The Riverside.

"Well, the best form of defence is attack and that's where we need to start." Peppy was fired up for the challenge. "It's going to be fun," she grinned.

"I wouldn't quite call it fun," Sebastian grimaced. "What's the next step then?"

"I'll go back to London tomorrow, talk to my boss – he really can't say no, I've been working like a dog all year - pack a bigger bag and head back down tomorrow night," she replied. "Are you sure I can stay here?"

"Or you could stay in my old cottage in the village," Olivia suggested. "Sebastian bought it from the owners a few months ago and we were going to rent it out, but it's free for now. You'll love it there." Olivia beamed. "Lots of happy memories."

Sebastian picked up her hand and kissed it. "Very happy ones," he grinned.

"Stop it," Peppy laughed and threw her napkin at Sebastian. "You two are so in love it's disgusting."

"Jealousy will get you nowhere," Sebastian chuckled. "Who are you shagging these days?"

"Sebastian!" Olivia exclaimed and turned to Peppy. "Sorry, ignore him."

Peppy snorted, "No it's fine. I'm very open about my sex life. It helps when you work in an all-male environment."

"So?" Sebastian urged.

"No one serious," she shrugged her shoulders. "I did have a bit of a fling with my builder – I've just had the house renovated - but that was to satisfy my disgraceful sex addiction. Still waiting for that someone special," she smiled.

"He'll come along when you least expect it," Olivia assured her, glancing at Sebastian as if she was thanking her lucky stars for bringing them together. "I certainly didn't expect to meet anyone and look what happened to us."

Olivia looked at her watch and stood up. "I need to check on Alexander, he's due a feed. Won't be too long."

"Are you positive you want to do this?" Sebastian asked Peppy after Olivia had left the room. "I'll make it worth your while, you won't go short of a bob or two."

"I don't want your money." Peppy shook her head. "I'll do it because it sounds like something I could really get my teeth into and because you asked. Not to mention that you'll owe me a huge favour and one day I'll cash it in when I need you the most."

Sebastian grinned. "I knew you were the right choice." He picked up his glass and clinked it against hers. "Let battle commence."

CHAPTER 48

*P*eppy took up residence in Brook Cottage just three days later. She had cleared her sabbatical with her boss and had returned to Appleton Vale armed with a detailed media strategy that would see Sebastian, Georgiana and Dan fronting a high-profile campaign.

"Peppy?" Tom was at her front door. "I'm Tom Feltham. I own the pub with my wife, Susie. Olivia said you'd be arriving today."

Peppy bounced over and embraced Tom. "Delighted to meet you. I'll be frequenting your establishment," she grinned. "I can't cook, I like a drink, and I hate to be alone so you'll be seeing a lot of me."

"Well, that's just excellent news," Tom beamed. "Sebastian said you're leading the publicity charge?"

"Can't wait to get started," Peppy grinned. "It's a nice change from being stuck in the studio. I used to hate travelling all over the world, but now I kind of miss it."

"We need you badly, so thank you for jumping on board. I'm in charge of dealing with the council and planners," he grimaced.

"Sounds like you drew the short straw," she laughed. "Let me know if there's anything I can do to help."

"Will do. I'll let you get settled in, but do pop in later and meet Susie. Chef Bernard has a new menu this week as well. You won't be able to resist." Tom grinned and turned to walk back to the pub.

Peppy's phone rang. "Steve," she cried. "About bloody time you called me back. Listen. I've got a juicy story for you. What would you say to an American billionaire, a Hollywood A-lister and a famous pair of siblings engaging in a right old ding dong?"

She listened to his reply and grinned. "I thought as much. Give me the air time and you can have the first interview. Do we have a deal?"

No sooner had she ended the call than her mobile rang again. She quickly answered it and launched into her well-practised spiel. Fifteen minutes and five calls later she had secured coverage with the BBC, the Daily Telegraph, the Daily Mail, Sky News and CNN.

Peppy walked back into the lounge and sat at the desk in the bay window that looked out across the village green. She watched as children played and smiled when the villagers' greeted each other fondly. It was peaceful, stunningly beautiful and incredibly relaxing – a world away from her life in London and the high-octane thrill of running a news team. She opened the laptop and started to fire off another dozen emails to press contacts who she knew would help with the campaign.

As dusk fell, she finished the first draft of the press release for Sebastian to approve and pulled together a list of influential friends that would bolster their cause. She looked at her watch and stood up.

"Bloody starving," she muttered. She grabbed the house keys and walked the twenty yards to the pub, conveniently located right next door to the cottage. Peppy pushed open the heavy oak door of the Riverside Inn and breathed in the delicious scents wafting from the restaurant.

"Hi," Susie cried from behind the bar. "I'm Susie."

Peppy walked towards her and held out her hand in greeting. "Peppy," she smiled. "I'm an old pal of Sebastian's here to help with the campaign."

"Tom said he'd met you, and we're all very glad you're here." She smiled warmly. "What can I get you?"

"A large Shiraz please," Peppy replied. "And do you have a bar menu or is it just the restaurant?"

Susie handed her two menus. "Both. Chef Bernard has just changed the specials which are on the board over there. All utterly delicious. So how long have you known Sebastian?"

Peppy grinned. "Oh, we go way back. We started out pretty much at the same time on Tour many moons ago when I was a lowly assistant at Sky. Over the years we worked together quite a bit and have a healthy respect for each other. It's tough on Tour for a woman, especially in my position - running the show - but Sebastian was one of the only guys who recognised I was there to do a job, and also that I knew my stuff. He championed me right from the start, so I owe him a lot."

Susie nodded. "Husband? Kids?"

"Nope. Just me," Peppy laughed. "Olivia told me you'd all be straight in with the personal questions."

Susie blushed. "Sorry. I can't help myself sometimes." She filled the glass and handed it to Peppy.

"Oh God, don't be sorry on my account. Ask me whatever you like." Peppy glanced at the menu. "I'll have the black bean and ginger roasted hake please. Sounds divine."

"You certainly won't go hungry here and you should try the farm shop for day to day stuff. Andrea Jenner runs it, she's lovely, you'll like her." Susie looked up as the door opened.

"Speak of the devil," she grinned. "Andrea, this is Peppy, Sebastian's friend who's come to run the media campaign. I was just telling her about the farm shop."

"Hi," Andrea beamed. "Nice to meet you and welcome to the village."

"Thanks," Peppy smiled. "Would you like a drink?"

"I only popped in with these." She handed two dozen eggs to Susie. "Chef Bernard sent me a mercy text, so here I am. But whilst I'm here, why not?"

Andrea perched on the bar stool next to Peppy. "Gin and tonic please, Susie. So," she said to Peppy. "What's the plan of attack?"

Peppy spent the next hour outlining her media strategy and was on her third glass of wine when her phone rang. She looked at the caller ID and jumped up. "Got to take this." She walked outside and answered the call.

"Thank you for getting back to me so quickly," she said. "Did you read the summary of the plans?"

"We did, and His Royal Highness will be delighted to write a letter of support against the development. He asked me to pass on his good wishes, and to congratulate you on taking the fight to the Americans. The letter will be sent to you tomorrow."

Peppy ended the call and did a little jig on the spot. She had just secured the backing of one of the most high-profile conservationists in the world - HRH The Prince of Wales. It was a major coup and would add authenticity and gravitas to their campaign.

She walked back inside the pub. "Get the bubbly out," she told Susie. "I've just pulled a blinder."

CHAPTER 49

*G*eorgiana scrolled through the latest photos of Dan that were blasted all over social media, and laughed out loud.

After their week off he had flown to Paris to continue filming for Jigsaw Kids, and the scenes he was shooting with Cara were particularly emotional. The press had snapped some long lens action and played it as if he was having an affair with her.

"Seriously! See what I have to put up with?" Dan said.

"How can they get it so wrong?" she snickered. "Don't they know she's a lesbian?"

"Nope. I met her girlfriend Tammy. She's quite butch as it goes," Dan grinned. "They've done a pretty good job of keeping it under wraps, and Cara is quite happy for photos of her and me to be out there. I don't care because I know it's not true, and if it helps her out then I'm fine with it. She's great, you'll love her."

Although she knew that the Cara rumours were nonsense, Georgiana still felt uncertain when she saw photographs of Dan with different women, day after day. The media revelled in turning an innocent snap of him talking to someone into a sordid sex story, but she had no reason to doubt him. It was Wyatt's fault that she was hesitating in her relationship with Dan. She truly hated him for it.

"Am I interrupting?" Gerry stuck his head around the door of the BBC studio.

"No," Georgiana smiled. "Dan was rushing off anyway. What's up?"

"HRH is about to arrive. I know you know him, but try not to be cheeky. If you piss off a prince there's no amount of pouting into a camera that's going to save you."

"Relax G," Georgiana grinned. "Harry and I go way back. Why do you think I got the gig?"

"That may be so," Gerry sighed. "Just behave yourself on camera."

"Yes sir," she mock saluted him. "Shall we go then?"

Gerry led her out of the studio and down the stairs just as Prince Harry's car pulled up.

"Good afternoon, Your Royal Highness," she dipped into an exaggerated curtsey and grinned.

"Georgiana." Prince Harry smiled and kissed her on both cheeks. "Hilarious as always, I see."

"This is Gerry Rees, our excellent producer." She introduced Gerry, who shook the Prince's hand.

"Shall we?" Georgiana gestured towards the studio. "How's Meghan?" she asked as they made their way up the stairs.

"Surely I should be asking you about a certain Dan Flowers?" Harry laughed. "How did that happen?"

Georgiana grinned. "We met on a plane and it kind of went from there. He's a great guy but it's difficult to get enough time together at the moment."

"I know that feeling," Harry replied. "Right. Let's get this show on the road." He switched into professional mode as soon as the microphone pack was attached to his back pocket.

Five minutes later Georgiana addressed the camera.

"Good afternoon and welcome to our coverage of the 2017 Invictus Games, live from Toronto. We're going to be bringing you the very best action from this incredible event all week, and I'm delighted to say that we will be joined in the studio every day by His Royal Highness, Prince Harry." She grinned at the camera and turned to face Harry.

"This is the third instalment of the games. It's your baby. How proud are you?" Georgiana asked Harry.

"Incredibly proud, but not of myself," Harry replied. "I'm proud of the awesome athletes that literally gave their all defending their countries. We've got eleven different sports that they're competing in this year, so we're going to have our work cut out keeping on top of it all."

"If anyone can do it, we can!" Georgiana winked at Prince Harry and grinned at the camera again.

"And run VT," she heard Gerry in her ear directing the crew. They were off camera temporarily while a montage video from the previous games was shown to the audience.

"So that's what they call the swoon effect," Prince Harry laughed as he watched Georgiana ooze every ounce of charm she could muster into the camera lens.

"Whatever works," she smirked.

Their half hour broadcast came to an end and Prince Harry

rushed off to a drinks reception with the ninety-strong team from the United Kingdom. Georgiana headed back to the hotel. She was tired and it was going to be a long week. She needed to be at her best.

Lying down on the bed, she pulled out her phone to check any messages that had come through whilst she was on air. There was one from Dan signing off for the night. It was the early hours of the morning in Paris.

Close your eyes and I'll see you tonight in your sweet dreams. D x

She sighed and hugged her pillow. She missed him more and more each day. "It must be love," she muttered before she fell into a deep sleep.

CHAPTER 50

"*W*ow."

Olivia smiled and looked over her shoulder. Sebastian was leaning against their bedroom door gazing at her.

"What?" she asked as she stood up and smoothed her dress down.

"You know full well what," Sebastian grinned. "You're beautiful."

"I'm fat." Olivia regarded her reflection in the mirror and crinkled her nose. "It's all a bit tight. I'm worried I'm going to pop out of it."

Sebastian laughed. "Looks perfect to me. And besides, if you do burst out it'll be the second boob-gate in one family. I wonder if that's a record?"

"Do I really look ok?" She needed reassurance. "You'd say I look great in a sack."

Sebastian walked over to where she was standing in the dressing

255

room. "That's because it's true. Look." He turned her around to face the mirror and stood behind her.

She was wearing a black vintage Versace dress that was simple and understated, paired with silver Jimmy Choo heels. Her hair was styled into a chignon leaving her neck bare. Sebastian kissed the nape of her neck and produced a velvet box from behind his back.

"Something sparkly for my dazzling wife." He gave her the box.

Olivia gasped when she opened it. It was a sculptural arrangement of glittering marquis and square-cut white diamonds set in platinum that matched the ring he had given her after Alexander's birth.

Sebastian took it out of the box and fastened it around her neck. "I think that completes your outfit."

Olivia turned around and reached up to kiss him. "Thank you!" she exclaimed. "I love it. You have to stop spoiling me."

"Never," Sebastian laughed. "Now let's get going before I peel that dress off you."

"I like the sound of that," she grinned. "Let's ditch the party and get naked. Although I'll keep my necklace on."

"I would expect nothing less." Sebastian kissed her again and she melted into his arms.

"I love you," she whispered. "More than you'll ever know."

It was all Sebastian could do to pull himself away. "You're killing me," he laughed. "I'm going to ravish you when we get back. Just giving you fair warning."

"Can't wait," Olivia beamed. She picked up her evening bag and sashayed out of the bedroom, deliberately wiggling her bottom.

"Be careful," Sebastian growled. "Teasing me like that is a very dangerous move."

"That's what I'm banking on," she grinned. "I'm just going to check on Alexander and then I'm ready."

"I'll go and rally the troops," Sebastian replied. He headed off towards the east wing where José, Angelica, their four children and a nanny were staying in the guest suites. They had arrived earlier in the day to attend the charity ball that evening and, more importantly, Alexander's christening the next day in their role as godparents.

Fifteen minutes later their car turned through the imposing iron gates of The Riverside and wound up the driveway that was lit up with thousands of twinkling tree lights.

They arrived at the main entrance as Peter and Andrea were getting out of their car.

"Evening all," Peter smiled. "Don't you ladies all look a picture?"

"Peter, Andrea. These lovely people are José and Angelica de Silva." Sebastian introduced them.

"Andrea, you look stunning." Olivia said. "I love that dress."

"And I love those diamonds," Andrea pointed to Olivia's necklace, her eyes wide. "That's bloody gorgeous."

"Isn't it?" Olivia giggled. "I'm a very lucky woman."

"Indeed you are, my darling," Sebastian said. "Let's get a drink." He took her hand and led their party inside. "Georgiana and Dan are on their way. Got held up apparently."

"Dinner with a movie star," Andrea giggled. "Whoever would have though little old me would be keeping such esteemed company."

"Don't forget our two internationally-renowned golfers," Olivia laughed. "We don't want them sulking all night."

"I'm happy to be out of the red light for once," José said.

"Limelight darling," Angelica replied. José made a habit of confusing English colloquialisms. It was one of his many endearing qualities. Sebastian called 'a slip of the de Silva tongue'.

Tom and Susie were already seated at their table and jumped up to greet them.

"Surrounded by the most beautiful group of ladies I have ever laid my eyes on," Tom grinned. "Hello, all."

"Tom, Susie. Let me introduce José and Angelica de Silva." Sebastian did the rounds before accosting a passing waiter.

A moment later the waiter returned with two bottles of Kristal. "Only the best for us tonight."

Georgiana and Dan appeared behind Sebastian. "Hi" she kissed him. "Hi everyone," she smiled at her friends.

She was wearing a blue satin Alexander McQueen dress that hugged her body and her hair was loose, tumbling down her back in glossy waves. Dan looked devastatingly handsome and elegant in his dinner suit.

Sebastian thrust a glass of champagne into Dan's hand. "You're cutting it fine," he grinned.

"We got a little delayed on the way back from the airport," Dan laughed. "You know how it is." Georgiana had flown directly from Toronto to Paris for a night with Dan before returning to Appleton Vale to attend the ball.

"I see Lucinda has gone all out this year." Georgiana looked around the atrium at the dazzling display of twinkling lights bouncing off tablecloths embroidered with thousands of tiny crystals. The place settings were exquisite, as were the flower arrangements in the centre of each table. Lucinda had clearly gone for broke with the decorations, and she had also splashed a great deal of the Club's cash on a celebrity chef and a well-known surprise musical guest.

"Whatever anyone says about Lucinda, she sure knows how to throw a party," Georgiana said. "Anyone know who the chef is? I'm famished."

"Chef Bernard's brother, Claude," Susie replied. "You have no idea how upset Bernard is. They hate each other, and Claude is well and truly treading on his toes by taking this gig. No idea why Lucinda had to bring someone else in. Bernard has two Michelin stars for God's sake. How much more could you want?" Susie shook her head and picked up the menu. "Beetroot panna cotta with goat's cheese crumble and pickled walnuts?" she scoffed. "Seriously?" She was fiercely protective of Chef Bernard, who was the executive chef at the pub as well as The Riverside.

"Sounds yummy to me." Andrea reached over and took the menu from Susie. "In fact, looking at this, it all sounds delicious. I think having a Michelin-starred chef on tap might have spoilt us all a little."

"I've travelled far and wide, and dined in most of the best restaurants the world has to offer. No one comes close to Bernard. Don't you dare lose him," Sebastian told Tom and Susie.

"We have no intention of letting him go," Tom laughed.

Whilst Sebastian, Tom and the rest of them were discussing the virtues of Chef Bernard, Olivia leaned over to Georgiana and whispered in her ear. "You're awfully quiet. Is everything ok?"

"Yes, of course,' she replied. "I'm a little nervous that Wyatt is going to turn up. It is the club's biggest event of the year, so you'd kind of expect him to come."

"You're not still stuck on him, are you?" Olivia sighed. "What about that lovely man over there?" she nodded at Dan.

"Oh. No. That's not what I meant at all." Georgiana was quick to correct Olivia. "I adore Dan. He loves me completely and he's amazing. He's so kind and thoughtful. No games, no nonsense, just him and me."

"But do you love him? I mean, truly love him?" Olivia squeezed her hand.

Georgiana nodded. "I'm happy. Isn't that enough?"

Olivia shrugged her shoulders. "It is. As long as you're sure? He's a great guy and clearly insanely in love with you. Sebastian likes him, despite the rumours about his prolific sex life."

"Well if Sebastian likes him, he must be 'the one' then." She reached out her hand to Dan who was standing behind her in animated conversation with Tom and José. His fingers closed around hers and she sighed with contentment.

Olivia smiled. "I'm happy for you. If he loves you even half as much as your brother professes to love me, then you'll last a lifetime."

"Should my ears be burning?" Dan slipped into the chair next to Georgiana and kissed her neck. Georgiana gasped when his lips touched her skin.

"How's the new film coming along?" Peter asked Dan. "It's an indie movie, isn't it?"

"It is indeed," Dan replied. "Low budget, well a lot lower than I'm used to, and a relatively unknown cast, apart from the delightful Cara Keating, but it's going really well."

"Oh, I love her," Andrea exclaimed. "When will it be out?"

"We're looking at January. It was only a six-week shoot and we're already in editing. The studio wants to get it out in time for The Oscars."

"Ooh, how exciting," Andrea squeaked.

"Don't get too excited," Dan grinned. "It probably won't stand a chance in hell, but there's no harm in trying."

"You did some filming in Paris?" Angelica asked. "It's my favourite place in the world."

"That's because you're from there," José laughed. "And you always said your best place is wherever your family is."

"That's true," Angelica stroked his cheek. "But there's nowhere like Paris."

"I've actually really enjoyed being back in England." Dan looked wistful. "Being able to shoot here has been brilliant and it meant I didn't need to be away from this one much." He nodded towards Georgiana.

"You two are so cute," Susie giggled.

"And you bang on about me and Olivia being all lovey-dovey." Sebastian winked at Georgiana.

"Yeah, yeah," she laughed. "You two are always at it. We're a little more discreet."

"I hardly think discretion is a word you're all that familiar with Georgiana." Lucinda was standing behind her.

Georgiana turned around and shot her a look of pure evil. "Oh, go away. We're trying to have a nice evening, please don't ruin it."

"I have no such intention," Lucinda replied. She looked around the table and made a beeline for Dan. "I'm Lucinda Walton-Smythe. Delighted to make your acquaintance. This is my party."

"I was under the impression the club was hosting this for charity. Am I wrong?" Dan feigned innocence.

Lucinda spluttered. "Well yes, of course. I just meant that I organised it."

"Don't you mean the event company you hired organised it?" Andrea muttered.

"What was that?" Lucinda looked at her.

"Nothing." Andrea stifled a giggle in her napkin.

"I see you're making a statement with those jewels, Olivia." Lucinda turned her venom towards Olivia.

"Beautiful, aren't they?" Olivia smiled through gritted teeth.

"They'd probably sit better on a slimmer neck," Lucinda replied.

"That rules yours out then." Sebastian glared at her. "Is there something you particularly wanted Lucinda, or can we get on with enjoying our evening?"

"Oh, you know. I'm just floating around checking everyone is having a good time," she said, miffed at being shot down by Sebastian.

"More like stomping than floating," Georgiana muttered. Andrea and Angelica fell about laughing and Lucinda's cheeks turned red.

"How rude," she spat and flounced across the room.

"She is truly awful," Susie said.

"Miserable cow," Georgiana sneered. "Just wait till she sees the video."

"What video?" Tom asked.

"Oh nothing." Georgiana dismissed it.

"By all accounts, Will is shagging her," Sebastian grimaced. "Why? Why would any self-respecting man want to do that?"

"How do you know that?" Georgiana asked him, glaring at Olivia.

"It wasn't Liv," he laughed. "It's hardly the best kept secret in the village, is it?"

"Eugh," Peter shivered at the thought. "Wouldn't touch her with a barge pole if she was the last woman on earth."

"Agreed," Tom laughed. "We gentlemen have a lot to be thankful for."

"I'll drink to that," Sebastian raised his glass.

They enjoyed dinner, even Susie who was still championing chef Barnard, and then it was time for the main event.

"This is always fun." Georgiana clapped her hands as the lights dimmed and Mick O'Hanagan - the local auctioneer - took to the stage.

CHAPTER 51

"*L*adies and gentlemen. Welcome to The Riverside's annual charity ball. I'm delighted to have been invited back this year and it's my personal goal to beat last year's utterly ridiculous total. What was it, Lucinda?" Mick squinted into the crowd and found Lucinda.

"Two million, six hundred thousand." She stood up to take a bow.

"And that was entirely down to you horribly wealthy people," Mick continued. 'So, in the indomitable words of Cuba Gooding Junior, SHOW ME THE MONEY." The guests roared with laughter.

"Don't get into a bidding war with Sebastian," Georgiana warned Dan. "He hates to lose and won't let you beat him."

"Let's see who has the deepest pockets, shall we?' Dan's eyes glinted. He loved a challenge.

"Oh God," Georgiana laughed. "I wish I'd never said anything."

Mick cleared his voice. "Lot one. A Charles Harkley original painting of this glorious clubhouse. We all know Charles's work has been shooting up in value in recent years, so let's start the bidding at twenty-five thousand."

Andrea gasped. "Peter and I won't be bidding on anything. That's so out of our league." This was the first time she and Peter had been to the charity ball and she was a little in awe of the other incredibly wealthy guests.

"It's just money," Tom whispered. "Doesn't make them any better than us." The pub was doing very well and they made a good living, but he and Susie would never be able to compete with the likes of Sebastian, Dan, Lucinda and many of the other members and their guests.

A hand went up.

"We have twenty-five," Mick beamed. "Do I have thirty?"

"Thirty thousand," shouted Godfrey Walton-Smythe. Lucinda glared at him.

After five minutes, the bidding was between Godfrey and Cecil Rossiter, a grey-haired luminary of the club's new board of directors.

"Going once, at seventy-five thousand pounds." Mick looked around the room for any late bids. "Going twice. For the third and final time, SOLD to the incredibly generous Godfrey Walton-Smythe." The room erupted with applause.

"Lot two." Mick quickly moved on. "Play with our very own superstar golfer Sebastian Bloom – world number one, no less - at the Dunhill Links professional tournament in St Andrews." Mick consulted his notes. "The highest bidder will fly to Scotland in October with Sebastian and be his amateur playing partner in this spectacular Tour event. Want to rub shoulders with some of Hollywood's biggest stars? Well you can if you bid for this. You might just find yourself paired with Samuel L Jackson and José de Silva."

"Aren't we already rubbing shoulders with Hollywood royalty?" Susie shouted, pointing at Dan.

"I don't even know Samuel L Jackson," José spluttered.

"I think he's just using you as an example darling," Angelica patted his hand.

"I do," Dan said. "He's a cool dude. You should play with him if you get the chance."

"Let's start the bidding at ten thousand," Mick boomed into the microphone.

"Ten thousand?" Sebastian shouted. "Is that all I'm worth? That's just the cost of the private jet," he laughed, and urged his friends to start bidding.

Soon the bid was up to one hundred thousand pounds and Sebastian was flashing his mega-watt smile around the room. "That's more like it."

"Sold!" Mick banged the gavel. "To the gentleman at table eleven.

"Cecil Rossiter," the man called out.

"Well congratulations, Cecil. You and Sebastian will have a fine time together." Mick turned to prepare for the next lot.

"Great." Sebastian rolled his eyes. "Spending a week with one of the new board members is my idea of hell."

"That's the risk you take for being so generous," Olivia laughed and stroked his arm.

"Well at least you and Alexander will be there to keep me amused," he grinned.

"Oh, is that what we do? Keep you amused?" Olivia raised an eyebrow.

Sebastian grinned. "You do so much more than that."

Georgiana threw her napkin across the table at Sebastian. "Stop it!"

"Nothing wrong with a public display of affection," Dan put in. He pulled Georgiana out of her seat onto his knee and kissed her passionately. When they finally came up for air, Georgiana was giddy.

"Err. Yeah. Nothing wrong with it." She remained on Dan's knee, enjoying the sensation of his fingers drifting across her back.

Mick moved onto the next item - a week at Mary-Jane and David Lavenham's ski lodge in Jackson Hole, Wyoming. José and Angelica secured it for fifty thousand and the auction continued, gathering a pace. There were several more fabulous prizes up for grabs before the final two lots were announced.

"We're getting to the big ones, boys and girls." Mick was getting excited. His voice had gone up at least two octaves. "Lot fifteen, our penultimate one of the evening. Two nights at Giraffe Manor followed by a five-day big game drive at Sala's Camp in the Maasai Mara." Mick whistled. "Nice, nice, nice. Let's start the bidding at fifty thousand."

"Fifty grand?" Peter spluttered. "You could probably buy that holiday for a fraction of the price."

"It's for charity." Andrea elbowed him. "Let these fools give away their money." She nudged Sebastian. "You should bid for this," she whispered. "Giraffe Manor is on Liv's bucket list."

"Is it?" he was surprised. "I'd have taken her there already had I know that."

"Now's your chance," Andrea replied. "Go on."

"Fifty grand," Sebastian shouted. Olivia swung her head round and stared at him.

"How did you know?" she asked.

"I know everything about you," Sebastian laughed. He nodded his head in Andrea's direction. "She gave me a clue. You never said you wanted to go there."

"I do," she sighed. "Wouldn't it be amazing to feed the giraffes at our breakfast table?"

"One hundred thousand," Sebastian shouted.

"We were only on sixty-five Sebastian," Mick informed him.

"Well, now it's one hundred," Sebastian looked around the room for a challenger to show himself. None did.

"Any more takers for Giraffe Manor, ladies and gentlemen?" Mick addressed the room. "No? Ok. Going once. Going twice. Sold." He pointed at Sebastian's table and Olivia shrieked.

"Thank you," she threw her arms around him. "You have no idea how amazing it's going to be."

"Our final lot," Mick paused for effect. "The new owner, Athos, has very generously put up a five percent share in this glorious club."

Gasps echoed around the room and the noise level rose dramatically.

"Is he fucking kidding?" Sebastian looked at Georgiana.

"That's the first I've heard of it." Georgiana was shocked.

"Can he do that?" Olivia asked.

"He owns eighty-five percent. He can do what he likes." Georgiana shrugged her shoulders.

"Let's not be silly here, folks. This is worth some serious money so I'm starting the bidding at five hundred thousand." Mick took back control of the room and the bidding war began.

It was up to one million by the time Sebastian jumped in. He was soon involved in a two-way race with David Lavenham and he wasn't about to let him win.

"One point two mil," he offered.

"One point three," David shot back immediately.

Sebastian raised his eyebrows and grinned. "One and a half million."

Olivia grabbed his hand. "What are you doing?" she hissed.

"That's a fraction of what I would have spent if I'd bought the club," he replied.

Olivia sighed and resigned herself to watching the drama unfold.

"Do we have one million six hundred thousand?" Mick directed his question at David.

David shook his head. "It's all yours, Sebastian," he shouted across the room.

"I think we all knew this would be the outcome," Mick grinned. "So, going once. Going twice."

"Two million pounds!" Dan jumped up and waved at the stage. Georgiana went pale. "Oh my God," she muttered.

"Didn't you tell him not to get into it with Sebastian?" Olivia hissed.

"Of course I did." She nodded her head. "But maybe that's what spurred him on."

"Two point two." Sebastian shot Dan a wry smile and counter-offered.

"Two and a half million," Dan shouted. He and Sebastian were now engaged in their own quick-fire, winner-takes-all auction.

"Three million," Sebastian grinned and there was another collective gasp in the room.

"What?" Andrea and Susie cried.

"This is mental." Tom's eyes were like saucers.

Georgiana was sitting back in her seat laughing at Dan. She was slightly hysterical. "I have absolutely no control over him. None whatsoever."

"Oh, you do. Just not when I'm having fun spending my ill-gotten gains," Dan chuckled.

"Three million, two hundred and fifty thousand pounds," Dan was on his feet again. He looked at Sebastian and smirked. "Go on then."

"Three and a half." Sebastian smirked right back at Dan.

"Oh God, I can't watch this." Olivia put her head in her hands. "That's a lot of money."

"You're telling me," Peter gasped. "Totally bonkers."

"It's for charity," Andrea repeated. "It's nice, not bonkers."

"And it's not like either of them can't afford it," Angelica said. "My José is much more sensible."

"I have four children and an expensive wife. We have the Holes of Jackson!" José exclaimed.

"Jackson Hole, darling. The kids will love it there." Angelica was satisfied that they had done their bit for charity.

"Well?" Sebastian was goading him to up his bid.

Dan grinned, bent down and kissed Georgiana and then turned towards the stage. "Five million pounds."

Andrea spat her drink out in shock, while Susie grabbed her glass of champagne and downed it in one go.

"Fuck me," Peter and Tom both said.

The atmosphere in the room was electric. There wasn't a whisper of conversation. All the guests and staff were on tenterhooks, staring at Sebastian and waiting for his next move.

Sebastian threw his arms up in the air and laughed. "Who am I to compete with a Hollywood megastar? I'm fairly certain his pockets are deeper than mine."

The room erupted. Cheering and clapping rang around and Dan lapped up the adulation. He stood on the table and bowed to his audience whilst Sebastian popped the corks on two bottles of Dom Perignon 1961.

"That's almost six-and-a-half grand's worth of fizz right there." Tom rolled his eyes and accepted a glass from Sebastian. "If you can't beat 'em," he grinned and took a sip.

Georgiana was stunned. "Five million pounds? Are you crazy?"

"We're business partners now. How cool is that?" He was excited.

Georgiana gulped. "Why?" she asked.

"It's my gift to you. And over time more shares will come up – they always do - and between Sebastian and I we'll wrestle back control." Dan had it all planned out.

"Oh." Georgiana was lost for words.

"Here." Dan thrust a glass of Dom Perignon into her hand. "Let's celebrate."

She looked at Olivia who raised her hands in a gesture that said accept it and move on.

She suddenly started laughing. "You are totally bonkers, Dan Flowers." Georgiana stood on her tiptoes and kissed him. "Totally bonkers," she repeated.

"I'd rather be totally bonking you right now," Dan purred into her ear. "That's how we'll celebrate later."

It was time for the special musical guest. The lights were dimmed again and the first notes of a familiar song echoed around the room. Andrea screamed and pointed at the stage. "Oh. My. God."

> "It's not unusual to be loved by anyone
> It's not unusual to have fun with anyone
> But when I see you hanging about with anyone
> It's not unusual to see me cry, I wanna die."

"Tom Jones," Susie cried. "How the hell did she pull that off?"

"It's for charity," Andrea was almost catatonic. She drifted towards the stage to get a better look.

"Go with her, will you?" Peter said to Susie. "We don't want her throwing her knickers at him."

"He's ancient," Georgiana laughed. "Even older than he looks on The Voice."

"Before your time sweetie," Olivia grinned. "Before mine really, but who cares?" She grabbed Angelica's hand and headed towards the stage.

"Let's crack open the scotch gentlemen." Sebastian had procured a twenty-five-year-old bottle of single malt from a passing waiter.

"Pour me a large one. This music is making my ears bleed," Tom groaned.

When Olivia and Angelica returned to the table, they found their husbands roaring with laughter and Sebastian topping up the scotch into their glasses.

"We leave you alone for five minutes and look at you," Olivia laughed. "Where's Georgie and Dan?"

"Disappeared a while ago," Peter slurred.

"Probably having sex in the toilet." Tom fell about laughing again.

"There's every likelihood they are." Sebastian cracked up.

"I think it's time we got back to our baby." Olivia picked up her evening bag and walked over to Sebastian. "Come on you idiot."

"With pleasure," he draped his arm around her shoulder. "I seem to remember I'm on a promise."

"Depends how drunk you are," she chuckled.

"Never too drunk to ravish my sexy wife." Sebastian grabbed his jacket from the back of the chair and dragged Olivia towards the exit.

"Wait for us," Angelica cried. She pulled José out of his chair and headed after them.

"I'm guessing we'll be here a while longer." Tom pointed at the stage where Susie and Andrea were dancing to another of Sir Tom's smash hits.

Peter grinned and rolled his eyes. "Best tuck into the rest of this then." He picked up the bottle of scotch from the table and poured another two glasses.

"Let's go," Dan whispered to Georgiana half way through the first song.

"Where?" she asked.

"How about a stroll in the gardens?' he suggested.

"What you really mean is a tussle in the bushes," Georgiana laughed.

"Oh, you know me so well Miss Bloom." Dan took her hand, and they wandered out into the beautifully manicured and intoxicatingly fragrant gardens.

"It's lovely here," Georgiana sighed. "It's going to be ruined if Athos gets permission to build."

"Keep fighting the good fight. You'll win," Dan reassured her.

"Fifteen percent can't win," she replied.

"It's twenty percent now. And a village up in arms can win," Dan smiled. "And I'll lend my celebrity to the cause."

"Oh, you will, will you?" she raised an eyebrow. "We surely can't lose with you on our side."

"Cheeky cow," Dan pulled her into his arms. "I'll always be on your side, I'll always have your back and I'll never let you down." He dropped onto one knee.

He fumbled in his inside pocket and pulled out a dazzling square cut diamond and sapphire ring. "We've only known each other a few months but I am one hundred percent certain that you are the one. I will love you truly, madly, deeply for the rest of our lives. Marry me?

Georgiana was speechless. She looked at Dan, his eyes full of hope, and suddenly she knew what she wanted.

"Love to," she croaked, full of emotion. "I love you."

Dan jumped up and whooped. "That's the first time you've told me you love me. Took your bloody time!" He grinned and swung Georgiana around in his arm until she begged him to stop. "I'm getting dizzy," she laughed. "Stop before I'm sick."

Dan put her down and took her hand. He slipped the ring onto her finger - it was a perfect fit.

"Oh," she gasped. "It's beautiful."

"Just like you," he smiled. "Now can we go home and celebrate?"

"Love to," she repeated.

CHAPTER 52

Georgiana and Dan burst into the kitchen at the Manor the next morning to announce their news. Olivia and Angelica screamed and jumped up to kiss them both. Hattie started to cry and was inconsolable for almost ten full minutes.

"Where's Sebastian?" Georgiana asked. She was a little unsure as to what his reaction might be.

"Don't worry," Dan smirked. "He loves me."

"Who loves whom?" Sebastian and José walked into the kitchen, both looking horribly hung over.

"I love your sister," Dan grinned. "And I've asked her to marry me."

"I'm guessing by the rock on your hand that you said yes?" Sebastian smiled at Georgiana.

"Of course I did," she cried. "I'd be mad not to."

He walked over and kissed her. "I'm happy for you sis. He's a great guy."

Sebastian held his hand out to Dan. "Congratulations, mate. You'd better look after her."

"I have every intention of doing just that," Dan agreed.

"So, when are you doing it?" Olivia asked. She was bubbling over with excitement.

"We haven't really talked about it yet," Georgiana replied. "But I want to get married here. That's ok, isn't it?" she looked at Dan.

"As long as you marry me, I don't care where it happens," Dan said. "But as to when – I'd prefer that sooner rather than later."

"How about after the Oscars" Angelica suggested. "Maybe a double celebration?"

"It's good timing for both of us work-wise," Dan replied. "What do you think babe?" he asked Georgiana.

"April in Appleton Vale?" She raised an eyebrow. "Could be a little chilly."

"But beautiful," Olivia replied. "You know how stunning the estate looks when spring is in the air, and its been really warm the past few Aprils."

"We got married in October and it was pretty warm," Sebastian offered.

"That's because the heat you two were giving off was enough to power the national grid," Georgiana snorted.

"Is that decided, then?" Hattie was hopeful.

Georgiana and Dan looked at each other and nodded. "Looks like we're having an April wedding at home." Georgiana clapped her hands and kissed Dan.

"I hate to be the one to break up the party, but don't we have a christening to get ready for?" Hattie asked.

They looked at each other, then scattered in different directions to ready themselves for Alexander's big day.

CHAPTER 53

St Saviour's church was packed to the rafters when the family and friends of Sebastian and Olivia gathered to celebrate Alexander's christening. While neither really believed in God, they had bowed to the wishes of Hattie, and Olivia's parents.

José and Angelica stood proudly holding Alexander, whilst Kev the Rev gave a rambling sermon on the virtues of children. Alexander began to scream at the top of his lungs and Rosie Feltham joined in almost immediately. Five-year-old Teddy Jenner had been given a homemade catapult by his grandfather, and began shooting an undisclosed packet of bon bons at the congregation.

"Virtues of children, eh?" Sebastian whispered.

"Ouch!" Olivia rubbed the back of her leg. She turned and glared at Teddy, who giggled and ducked behind Andrea.

Susie took Rosie out of the church until her screaming subsided, and finally Alexander stopped crying.

Kev the Rev had fought valiantly through the din, and raced to the end of the service before any more children had the chance to create a racket.

When they stepped outside the sun was hanging low in the sky, casting shadows through the branches of the Lovers' Oak tree across the graveyard.

Autumn was setting in and the leaves were beginning to turn, but the tail-end of an Indian summer meant it was still warm enough for the official photographs to be taken outside the church. A handful of paparazzi had invaded the village, desperate to get the first snap of Alexander. To protect him, the photographs were taken in the Church's walled garden.

The news of Georgiana and Dan's engagement had spread through the village like wildfire, and they were overwhelmed with the depth of genuine emotion and good wishes from everyone.

A journalist from the Daily Mail overheard a guest discussing Georgiana's ring and immediately pounced on the story. It was huge news on both sides of the Atlantic.

Georgiana didn't care that the photographers were clamouring to get a close-up of her ring and shots of her and Dan together. She was deliriously happy and nothing could burst her bubble.

She looked radiant, dressed in a smoky grey Jenny Packham dress and matching jacket, with an elegant fascinator perched on her head. Dan was equally as dazzling as his future wife, his beautifully-cut grey suit perfectly complimenting Georgiana's outfit. They held hands and beamed at the cameras.

"There's no escaping them, so we may as well give them what they want," Dan told her. "They might leave us alone then."

"Fat chance of that," Sebastian laughed. "With any luck, they'll leave me and Liv alone and concentrate their efforts on you. We're just a boring old married couple now."

"It comes with the territory I'm afraid," Dan replied. "I learned to accept it a while back, and I can't very well complain when I openly court publicity for my films. They overstepped the mark in Monaco though. I won't forget that."

Georgiana sighed. "I guess I'll just have to get used to it. I won't be able to go out in my pyjamas to get the papers anymore, though."

Olivia laughed. "When did you ever do that?"

"Well, never!" she grinned. "But I might have wanted to at some point."

"You're protected here. They can't get access to the estate and I'm assuming Dan's home is like a fortress," Sebastian reassured her.

"We should perhaps be a little more careful though," Dan grinned. "Long lenses. The bloody paps will do anything for a photo, and I think the world has seen more than enough of my fiancée already this year."

Georgiana laughed. "Then we're going to have to rent a private island for our honeymoon. I'm not taking any chances."

"Exactly what I was thinking," Dan winked.

CHAPTER 54

*T*he engagement announcement in The Times took up an entire page, and included a stunning photograph of the happy couple together taken at a recent film premiere in Los Angeles.

The photographer had captured an intimate moment between them on the red carpet - it was a favourite of Georgiana's. She was wearing a silver Versace dress she had purchased in a shopping frenzy on Rodeo Drive, and the silk fabric ran over her skin in delicious waves. Dan was handsome in his tuxedo, and together they made an impossibly beautiful couple.

It read:

> *The engagement is announced between Daniel, only son of Mr and Mrs Francis Flowers of Chelsea, London, and Georgiana Sabrina Bloom, daughter of Mr William Bloom and the late Mrs Bloom of Appleton Vale, West Chesterton.*

It went on to detail Dan's meteoric rise in Hollywood and Georgiana's burgeoning career with the BBC, and mentioning how and when they met. There was also the obligatory paragraph on Sebastian, Olivia and Alexander.

Georgiana rushed out to the post office early that morning to buy several copies. She was in the kitchen poring over the announcement when Dan came downstairs.

"Morning gorgeous," he yawned and stretched his arms out. "You were up early."

"Look," she squeaked and waved the newspaper in his face.

He rubbed his eyes and took it from Georgiana. His smile broadened as he read the copy. "Well, it's in black and white now. There's no backing out."

"I'm going nowhere," she laughed and showered him with kisses.

"What do the other papers say?" Dan was interested to know the media's reaction to their announcement.

Georgiana went through each one in turn.

"The Sun – 'Flowers and Bloom put down roots' – that's not up to their usual standards," she laughed. "The Express says 'Blooming Nora – Flowers and Bloom to wed after short romance'," she rolled her eyes. "The Daily Mail says 'Hearts and Flowers - Hollywood sex symbol set to marry BBC's Bloom'. Shall I go on?"

Dan grinned. "I think I've got the gist." He nuzzled her neck. "Let's read them later." He picked her up and threw her over his shoulder. "Right now, we're going back to bed."

The first Wyatt heard of Georgiana's engagement was when Bobby popped his head around the door of his office on Monday morning.

"Did you see the news?" he asked Wyatt.

"What news?" Wyatt looked up from his desk.

"Georgiana's engaged to that movie star guy." He cringed when Wyatt's face darkened.

"But she won't be by the time you've finished with him," Bobby continued. "Still want me to green light the plan?"

"Nothing's changed. Do it." Wyatt nodded his head and turned back to his work.

CHAPTER 55

The Indian summer that had the country basking in its grasp finally gave way to autumn, bringing with it a bitter northerly wind and lashings of rain. Even through the gloom, Appleton Vale was breathtakingly beautiful. The hills and valleys surrounding the village were still swathed in lush green grass, littered with remnants of summer blossoms and wildflowers. The woodland in the distance was draped in a spectacular multi-coloured cloak of red, brown, green, gold and orange, creating a dramatic backdrop against which the village nestled.

The first planning meeting was set for that evening in the Town Hall in Fiddlebury, and the entire village would be attending to lend their support to Tom, Peter and Peppy - the designated spokespersons - as all of their big hitters were away. Sebastian and Olivia were in St Andrews for the Dunhill Links golf tournament, Georgiana was in Hawaii presenting the Triathlon World Ironman Championships, and Dan was finally shooting the next Orion Powell film back in LA.

"Feels like they set this meeting knowing they would all be away," Andrea whispered to Susie as they took their seats.

"Is that the representative from Athos?" Susie pointed at Bobby Garnett, who was sitting on the stage in conversation with the head of the planning committee, Keith Williams.

"Yes, I think so. Looks dodgy, doesn't he?" Susie crinkled her nose in disgust.

"Hello, darlings," Patrick stuck his head in between Susie and Andrea as he and Devon slipped into the row behind them. "Are the boys ready?"

"Tom's nervous," Susie replied. "I think he feels a bit out of his depth."

"He isn't!" Andrea exclaimed. "Peter said he's been incredibly knowledgeable so far."

"Peppy seems like she knows what she's doing, thank God," Devon whispered. "She'll have them on the back foot, I'm sure of it."

"Sure of what?" Dee Dee asked as she and Jane squeezed past Andrea and Susie to bag the last two seats in the front row.

"Devon reckons Peppy is a force of nature," Susie grinned. "Here's hoping. She's got the media here already."

"If Sebastian thinks she's the right person for the job, then who are we to question it?" Jane smiled. "He knows about this kind of thing. Just a shame he couldn't be here tonight."

"Shush," Dee Dee hissed. "They're starting."

Peter, Tom and Peppy walked onto the stage to a round of applause from the villagers and took their seats to the right of Bobby Garnett.

Keith Williams stood up, walked towards the microphone and addressed the audience. "Welcome, everyone. This is the monthly planning meeting for the districts of Fiddlebury,

Appleton Vale and Bears Bridge. We've got a lot to get through tonight, so I suggest we get straight to it."

He began to read from a list of recent planning applications, outlining the support and objections attached to each one. Finally, he got to The Riverside.

"Planning application FAB14765/98/2017. The Riverside Golf & Country Club, Appleton Vale." He cleared his throat. "We are fully aware that the plans for this development are generating a lot of ill feeling in the village and that there has been a committee set up to protest against it. We're here to have a preliminary discussion and to hear more from both sides. I'd like to introduce you to Bobby Garnett who is from Athos, the new owners of The Riverside. Please hear him out."

Keith took his seat and Bobby strode towards the microphone amid a chorus of booing. He waited for the jeering to subside before launching into his well-rehearsed speech.

"Firstly, I wanna say that we're not the enemy. We wanna work with you to create a real luxurious destination resort that will bring a ton of money to the village and surrounding area."

"We don't want a destination resort or your dirty money. And what about the housing?" Dee Dee shouted from the front row. Murmurs of agreement rippled across the room.

"People need houses, we're gonna build them. We're gonna put this place on the map so you gotta get on board. You really don't wanna take us on." Bobby scowled at the audience.

"Well I must say, that's a bit rude," Janice Jenner grumbled. "Don't you think it would have been prudent to try to get us on-side before you tell us we have to get on board or else you'll fight us to the death?"

"We're Athos ma'am," Bobby replied.

"And what's that supposed to mean," Devon shouted at the stage. "Is that a threat?"

"Come on now," Keith Williams interrupted. "Let's not let this get ugly."

"No sir, it's not a threat." Bobby addressed Devon. "I'm just sayin' that we're not the kind of property developer you've ever deal with before. We know what we're doin'."

Patrick elbowed Devon. "Let him continue," he hissed.

Bobby took the residents through Athos' plans in detail, stopping to answer any questions that the committee or audience members had. After a twenty-minute grilling he had hardly broken a sweat.

"Look at him," Jane muttered. "He's enjoying this. What a revolting man."

"Now we've heard from the developer, it's time to hear the opposing voice," Keith Williams said. "Peter, would you like to start us off?"

Peter jumped up and adjusted the microphone to his height. "This is an outrageous development that should never be allowed to go ahead."

"Hear, hear," cried the residents.

Peter continued. "Tonight, we are presenting this." He slammed a six-inch thick dossier onto the table under Keith's nose. "Inside you'll find a detailed report on the environmental impact this utterly ridiculous plan will have on our village and the surrounding areas. And that's just for starters. There's no infrastructure for the housing and you can't triple the population of this village overnight. It's utterly contemptible."

"Yeah you tell 'em," Freddie, Josh and Jem chorused from the back of the room. They were particularly proud of their contributions to the environmental report.

Peter went on to highlight the facts. "We are smack bang in the middle of an AONB – fact." Peter banged his fist on the lectern.

"What does that mean?" Dee Dee whispered.

Devon leaned over her shoulder and replied, "Area of Outstanding Natural Beauty."

Peter talked for a further five minutes and then turned to Keith. "We're yet to see your own report Mr Williams."

"Any day now," Keith spluttered.

"We'll look forward to receiving it," Peter replied. "I'm going to hand over to Tom and our new director of communications, Peppy Grainger. They have some questions we'd like answered before we leave tonight."

Tom and Peppy spent the next ten minutes interrogating Bobby Garnett and the rest of the planning committee on the building plans and regulations that Athos would be required to meet. Every question they had was answered in minute detail, much to the disappointment of the villagers.

"Do you think the American briefed the committee beforehand?" Marjorie Rose grumbled.

"Of course," Jane sneered. "They're all in it together. We don't stand a chance."

"Nonsense," Andrea patted her hand. "Look what we've achieved so far. We've got the letter from Prince Charles, and we've got a meeting with the National Trust, Natural England and English Heritage next week. They'll be on-side for sure."

Keith stepped back up to the microphone. "I believe that concludes our business for tonight. We meet again in a month where we will go through all the reports and look at the plans in more detail. Thank you all for coming."

They trundled out one by one into the brisk night air, chatting amongst themselves. The general consensus was that they had presented a good case, but Athos was one step ahead of them. It was going to be an almighty fight, and they needed to find something concrete - and soon.

CHAPTER 56

"*L*ook," Jem whispered. He pointed at the top right-hand corner of the dilapidated barn.

Josh swung his head around and adjusted his night-vision goggles. "What? Can't see anything."

"Mr J," Jem shook James Jenner awake. It was three o'clock in the morning and they were camping out on the Riverside estate for the fifth night in a row.

James woke with a start and sat up, catching his head on the top of the tent. "What now?" he asked groggily.

"We've found something." Jem was excited. He thrust his goggles at James and pointed to the area of the barn where the activity was taking place.

"Oh, goodness," James exclaimed. "Maybe you boys were right after all. I was beginning to think this was a wild goose chase."

"Told you so," Josh grinned. "Now we just have to find out what it is."

"Look!" Jem whispered again. "There's more."

Through their goggles they could make out a small colony of bats ducking in and out of the barn roof.

"Looks like we might have saved the day," Josh was jubilant.

"Let's not get ahead of ourselves." James was the voice of reason. "We need to wait until the morning and call in an expert. It has to be documented properly. We can't afford any mistakes."

"Shall I text Peter?" Jem asked.

"I think we can wait until a more reasonable hour," James chuckled. "I'm impressed by your dedication, both of you. Well done. I'll make sure your parents are informed. It will be very refreshing for them to get some good news about you two for a change."

Josh and Jem beamed. "Thanks Mr J," Josh replied. "We're not really all that bad you know. We just like to have fun, but we're taking this very seriously."

"Hope it's not just a bog-standard bat," Jem said. "We really need this to help our case, don't we?"

James nodded. "We do. Let's keep our fingers crossed and try to get a little sleep. I'm getting far too old to be camping out at night, let alone three of us in a two-man tent."

The next morning, they reported their findings to Peter and Tom who immediately instructed a wildlife expert to investigate. The news of a possible 'find' had spread around the village quickly and everyone had high hopes for the outcome of the inspection.

By two o'clock in the afternoon, the news came through to the pub that the barn's new residents had been identified as the greater horseshoe bat that just happened to be on Natural England's 'rare and endangered' list. The expert said that it was a relatively new roost, but one of significant importance due to the extremely low numbers of the bats in existence – there were known to be only fourteen populations in roosts in south-west England and south Wales.

"Fifteen now," Peter declared. He was jubilant as he burst into the pub after seeing the expert off. "He's going to get the report over to us tomorrow."

"Super!" Marjorie Rose clapped her hands in excitement. "They won't be able to knock that down now."

"It doesn't mean the rest of their plans can't go ahead," Tom sighed. "But it's a small victory nonetheless."

"We're meeting at the Manor again tomorrow night. Sebastian and Olivia are back, and I think Georgiana is as well." Peter said. "Spread the word."

"They've found something," Lucinda hissed down the phone. She was in her kitchen at the Whiteside Estate and didn't want to be overheard by Godfrey who was in the next room.

"Some kind of rare bat. Can you believe it? There's a meeting tomorrow night where we will find out. I'll update you after that." She ended the call, put her phone back in her pocket and smirked with satisfaction.

Sebastian and Olivia had always looked down their noses at her; Georgiana had always been rude to her; Wyatt was sexy as hell and very available. She rubbed her hands together. "This is going to be fun," she muttered.

CHAPTER 57

Georgiana slipped through LAX airport and into a taxi unnoticed. Dark glasses and a baseball cap afforded her some anonymity, and when she wasn't with Dan she usually managed to evade the paparazzi, much to her relief.

She had flown directly from covering the Ironman championships in Hawaii to Austen, Texas, to report on the American leg of the F1 grand prix season, and was desperate to be reunited with Dan.

She let herself into his house and immediately slipped into her bikini and went for a swim. She had been run ragged in the last two weeks and needed a few days of rest and relaxation before her last two events of the year – the ATP World Tennis Finals and the International Horse Show at Olympia, both taking place in London.

Dan was on a tight filming schedule, thanks to his co-star delaying the shoot whilst her leg mended. He was working eighteen-hour days and was due to leave the next morning to fly to Istanbul on location. They were both finding the separation difficult.

By nine o'clock that evening she was restless. She had slept in the sunshine all afternoon and taken a leisurely bath before ordering in dinner, and was now impatiently waiting for Dan to get home. She walked into the kitchen and picked out a bottle of wine from the fridge. She poured a glass, wandered into the lounge and began surfing through the hundreds of television channels that were on offer in America.

She paused when Dan's face flashed up on the screen. She turned up the volume.

"And if rumours are to be believed, it would seem that he's at it again. Another film another co-star," the presenter said before a series of images flashed up on the screen of Dan and his co-star, Kylie Harrison, on the set of their action film. The first photograph was of them emerging from her trailer laughing and looking into each other's eyes. The second and third were of them kissing passionately and the last was of the two of them at dinner in LA taken two nights ago.

Georgiana knew the ones of them kissing and in the trailer were taken on set. It was the one from the restaurant that made her uneasy. She paused the television and looked more closely at the screen. It wasn't so much that they were out alone. It was the intimacy of the photograph that struck her. She shook it from her mind.

"Don't tell me you're bothered by that, babe?" Dan's voice made her jump. He was standing in the doorway watching her.

"As if." She ran across the lounge and leapt into his arms, wrapping her legs around him. "I've missed you so much," she cried.

Dan silenced her with a kiss so deep and passionate that she became giddy and started to giggle.

"You're an idiot," he laughed and put her down. His eyes were drawn to the outline of her breasts that were barely hidden under a skimpy silk vest. Her nipples were budding in anticipation of what was to come, and the way the fabric draped over them made him groan.

"Come here," he growled and reached out to stroke his thumb across one of her nipples.

"Ah," she gasped.

"You have no idea what you do to me." He nuzzled her neck and continued to tease her breasts.

"You could always remind me if you think it's necessary."

Dan groaned again. "I'm being picked up in five hours."

"I'm fairly certain it won't take that long." Georgiana smirked and unzipped his jeans. She slipped her hand inside and wrapped her fingers around him. "And you really, really need to do something about this." She licked her lips.

"Bloody right I do," Dan grunted. "And if you're going to wear a top like that without a bra and only a tiny pair of knickers you're pretty much asking for it!"

Georgiana snickered. "My cunning plan worked."

"Like you ever need a plan," Dan laughed. "You just need to look at me and I get a hard on. I'll never be able to get enough of you."

"Come on then." She grabbed his hand. "The clock's ticking and I intend to make up for lost time."

Afterwards they lay entwined, talking into the early hours. They wouldn't be able to see each other in the next four weeks and they both felt like it was forever. Dan left a few hours later to fly to Istanbul and Georgiana was heading back to Appleton Vale the next day.

"I love you, Daniel Flowers," she said, waving him goodbye as the sun was coming up. "Speak to you later."

Dan flashed a broad smile and jumped into the car. After he had gone Georgiana made coffee and sat down in the kitchen. She switched on the television and was once again faced with speculation about Dan and Kylie – are they, or aren't they? According to the entertainment news presenter, the on-camera chemistry they shared was spilling over in to real life.

She told herself over and over again that it was nonsense and that Sebastian had been through the same thing. Dan was a massive star, so it stood to reason that there would be rumours aplenty. But every time a new story surfaced a tiny bit of her confidence chipped away. She had no reason to doubt him. "Stop being a stupid cow," she muttered just as her phone bleeped. It was a text from Dan.

> *You have ABSOLUTELY NOTHING to worry about.*
> *I love you with all my heart. D x*

She grinned. His timing was impeccable.

The next day she flew home and arrived to complete pandemonium. The barn at the Manor's stable yard had been commandeered as headquarters for the villagers' war with Athos. There was a makeshift sign hanging inside the door that read RFC – Riverside Fight Club – and someone had scrawled 'what happens in fight club stays in fight club' underneath it. It was a hive of activity and it seemed like most of the residents were involved in some way or another.

She dropped her bags at her cottage and walked over to the Manor. Lady spotted her from the window in Sebastian's study long before Georgiana reached the kitchen door, and was howling and scratching against it to be let out to greet her beloved owner. Georgiana scooped her into her arms and kissed her. "Missed you little lady," she whispered into her pricked ear.

"Hello," she shouted. "Anyone home?"

There was no answer. She put Lady down, walked into the hallway and made her way upstairs. She was desperate to see Alexander and assumed they were all in the nursery.

"Where are you?" she called out again.

As she neared the top of the staircase she heard Olivia giggling, "Ouch. That was my toe." They came out of the bedroom looking dishevelled.

Sebastian grinned. "You're back then."

"Were you just having sex?" Georgiana crinkled her nose.

Olivia flushed with embarrassment. "Err. Maybe," she grinned.

"Where's my nephew? I do hope he wasn't within earshot of that," she retorted.

"Hattie's taken him for a walk into the village. Dee Dee and Jane are most likely cooing over him as we speak," Olivia replied.

"You've got to take the opportunities when they arise," Sebastian said. "How was LA?"

"I couldn't live there, that's for sure. It's all too fake." Georgiana rolled her eyes. "I'm so glad Dan's happy here. I never want to leave Appleton Vale full time."

"How is Dan? Everything ok?" Olivia asked.

"Busy. He's got a gruelling filming schedule and he's also got to start promoting his other movie so he's worn out. And we're fine. Better than fine," she smiled. "I just can't wait to get the tennis done and then we can have a full month off together before I do Olympia."

"Are you having Christmas with us?" Olivia was hopeful.

"Of course. Wouldn't want to be anywhere else," Georgiana grinned.

"My parents are threatening to come," she grimaced. "I can understand they want to see Alexander but it'll be painful for the rest of us."

"Your dad's a push-over," Georgiana laughed. "I'll entertain him."

"She'll hold you to that," Sebastian laughed. "This woman does not forget things easily."

"Hey," Olivia exclaimed. "Bloody cheek."

"How's it going with the RFC? I saw the sign in the barn. There were a lot of people coming and going at the yard when I popped over earlier.

"Ok, I think," Sebastian sighed. "We've got a meeting tonight, everyone's coming. We've got the rare bat thing on our side, as well as all the National Trust and Natural England backing. I just have a feeling it's not going to be enough."

"We've been looking at the plans and there's so much land available that they can easily move the buildings that were due to go where the barn is," Olivia replied. "So effectively that makes the bats a moot point as they won't be disturbed. It's so frustrating."

"I'm still convinced there's something else," Sebastian said. "We just need to find it. Something feels off."

"Dan said that too," Georgiana exclaimed. "He thinks there's something a bit fishy about the whole thing."

"Have you spoken to Emily yet?" Sebastian asked Olivia.

"You know I haven't," she bristled. "I don't think I did anything wrong, she was the one who started it."

"You're not in kindergarten," Georgiana sighed. "Do you really think she would know anything?"

"I doubt it. And if she did, I don't think she'd tell me. She's already been in trouble for telling us about the deal in the first place." Olivia shrugged her shoulders. "It's up to her to make the first move."

"And that's my wife digging her heels in," Sebastian chuckled. "We may yet need Emily, but for now how about we let sleeping dogs lie?"

CHAPTER 58

"You ready?" Gerry asked Georgiana. "We're live in five minutes."

"Oh, Gerry," she grinned into the camera. "Don't you know by now that I was born ready?"

"Yeah, yeah," Gerry replied. "Do you think you two can behave today? I know it's the end of the season but there's no need to fall off the wagon now."

"You're such a spoilsport," she laughed. "The viewers love it."

"Love what?" John asked as he sat down next to Georgiana.

"You two and your ridiculous double act," Gerry sighed.

John grinned. "Most fun I've had presenting in years."

"Right, let's go," Gerry said. "And we're live in five, four, three..."

Georgiana faced the camera. "Welcome to the last event on the 2017 ATP schedule, The World Tour Finals, live from the O2 arena in London. We're set for another thrilling final if this season is anything to go by - we've been treated to some seriously dazzling tennis this year." She swivelled in her chair to face John.

"And my little show wouldn't be complete without the dastardly John McEnroe to excite us with his expert analysis and delight us with his wit."

"Well I wouldn't go that far," John laughed.

They spent the next hour looking back on the season and discussing the in-form players before John talked through his expectations for the final. Gerry signalled that they had two minutes remaining and Georgiana took the opportunity to sign off in her own quirky style.

"Mr McEnroe," she addressed John. "I couldn't have asked for a better wingman to take me through my first tennis season. You've been totally awesome and I've had the most fun working with you." She grinned. "Please say you'll be the Sonny to my Cher or the Ike to my Tina when we return in 2018."

"You bet. Its been a blast," John chuckled. "Can't wait for next year. The big question is can we get through a whole season without a scandal?"

"One can only hope," she laughed. "And to you, the viewers," she smouldered down the lens. "Thank you for coming on this wild ride with me. I could kiss every single one of you!"

Gerry groaned. "Don't," he whispered in her ear as he watched her lean towards the camera. "Please, for the love of God, don't do it."

Georgiana winked and put her lips against the lens. "Mwah." She kissed the glass leaving an imprint of her lipstick, and laughed. "That's me signing off until the next time we meet in your living room."

"I give up," Gerry groaned.

Istanbul was sweltering and Dan was suffering. He insisted on performing most of his own stunts, and had sustained at least a dozen minor injuries during the course of shooting his new Orion Powell film.

Everything ached, he was covered in cuts and bruises, and had ended up with seven stitches in his hand where he had caught the sharp edge of a rusting car door during a high-speed chase. His co-star, Kylie, was making his life a misery. Her latest movie release had scored a major box office success and her inner diva had come to the fore.

She flounced on and off set when it suited her, argued with the director, Randy Brewster, and made little effort to be nice to anyone. Dan had worked with some difficult actresses before, but Kylie was taking it to a whole new level. He was nearing the end of his tether.

"For fuck's sake," he shouted as Kylie fluffed her lines for the seventh time in a row. He turned to Randy and shook his head. "I can't work like this."

Randy stood up and walked over to Kylie, who was busy pouting into a mirror and taking selfies to upload to her popular Instagram account. He spoke to her in hushed tones, then threw his hands up in the air when she snapped back at him and started crying. That resulted in another delay whilst her make-up was reapplied.

They were about to begin shooting a particularly intense and intimate love scene and Dan couldn't think of anything worse. He was starting to loathe her and he was sure it was coming through in his acting. Whatever on screen chemistry they had had was all but gone now, and his performance lacked his usual depth and sparkle.

"Let's get on with it, shall we?" Kylie purred in his ear. "Don't get any ideas though," she laughed and let her gown slip open, giving Dan and the rest of the crew a tantalising glimpse of her glorious body.

There was no denying Kylie's beauty and raw sex appeal. She had topped the 'most beautiful woman in the world' list last year and had also recently been named 'rear of the year'.

Dan stripped off his clothes and got into position. Kylie dropped her gown as soon as she walked on set and sashayed towards him. "You can look but you can't touch," she whispered.

"Wouldn't want to," Dan shot back. "You may be beautiful but you're a real bitch."

"Fuck you," she whispered.

"And action," Randy shouted. Kylie pressed her body up against Dan's and worked the scene exactly as it had been planned. Neither of them was pleased when Randy asked them to do it again.

"Dan, you need to look like you're enjoying it man," Randy sighed. "That's why they call it acting."

"Sorry," Dan replied. "Let's go again." He was determined to get this final sex scene in the can and get as far away from Kylie as possible. She was the polar opposite of Georgiana, who he was missing like crazy.

He closed his eyes and conjured up images of Georgiana in his head. It was the only way he could get through the scene. He let Kylie take the lead and threw himself into the role as if his life depended on it. When Randy shouted 'cut' for the final time he whooped in relief. He had the wrap party to attend that night, and then he would be heading back to Appleton Vale into Georgiana's arms. He couldn't wait.

CHAPTER 59

*T*he wind was howling and the rain lashing down as, one by one, the villagers trudged into the barn at Appleton Manor for the latest meeting of the RFC. The second planning meeting was coming up and they needed to be ready.

"Can we do this in the pub next time?" Will shouted from the back of the barn. "It's bloody freezing in here."

"The whole point is that we're supposed to be meeting secretly," Andrea replied. "It's hardly a clandestine meeting if any Tom, Dick or Harry can walk in."

"I managed to sneak in," Tom shouted.

"Me too," Richie Rogers - Sebastian's manager - shouted. He was staying at the Manor for the weekend and attending the meeting out of curiosity. "Do we have a Harry?"

They all fell about laughing. Hattie was going around passing out hot toddies. "We'll have it in the Manor next time," she reassured everyone. "We've got a lot of guests staying this weekend so the house is jam packed."

Sebastian jumped up on a bale of hay and shouted for them all to be quiet.

"Thanks for coming everyone. Sorry I couldn't make the last meeting, but I'm here now and Peppy has told me she's putting Georgiana and me to work with the media."

"That's why I'm here," Peppy laughed.

"Can't wait." Georgiana rolled her eyes.

Sebastian continued. "I'll hand straight over to Peter and Tom to give us an update."

"Thanks, Sebastian." Peter cleared his throat. "I'm not going to beat about the bush," he frowned. "We're losing this thing. Every which way we turn Athos is one step ahead, but we can't give up."

"Fight to the death!" Jem shouted from the back of the barn.

Peter continued. "We have to dig deeper. There has to be a way to stop this. Tom…" He invited Tom to carry on.

"Hey, everyone. As you know, we've all thought that this deal stinks of dirty money changing hands, but we're yet to find any evidence of it. Peter is right, we need to dig deeper so I want the research team to get back on-line, into the library, wherever, and look harder. I want the green warriors – as Andrea has called her little band of helpers – to talk to similar groups that have been in our situation. Find out what worked and what didn't work for them. We've got one last ditch attempt at this before it goes to a committee vote. We have to give them a solid reason to say no."

"Bloody crooks the lot of them," James Jenner grumbled.

"That may be so," Tom grinned. "But they can't refute hard evidence, so that's what we need, and fast."

"We're going to lose, aren't we?" Marjorie Rose squeaked.

"It's a possibility, but we have to keep fighting," Peter replied. "Let's all split into our groups for an update and then we'll confirm the plan of attack."

"Where shall I go?" Lucinda called out.

"Oh," Peter replied. "We didn't know you wanted to be involved. This is the first proper meeting you've been to."

"I want to do something," Lucinda smirked. "This is my home too."

"Why don't you join the green warriors?" Tom suggested.

Lucinda crinkled her nose. "I think my skills are better suited to helping the executive committee."

"Executive committee?" Tom laughed.

"Well you know what I mean," Lucinda bristled. "I can help co-ordinate each group and collate any new information."

Peter and Tom exchanged glances.

"We need all the help we can get," Peter muttered. "Ok," he looked at Lucinda. "We could do with some help pulling it all together. Why don't you go to each group and get a brief update and we can take it from there?"

"What a good idea," Lucinda smiled. "Leave it with me."

Forty minutes later the meeting came to a close and the residents left the barn under instructions to gather information in time for the planning meeting. Lucinda had whizzed around each group and gained valuable insight to the intricacies of the village revolt. She walked out of the barn and took her mobile phone out of her bag. She sent a text to Wyatt.

I've infiltrated the group as promised. I'll email an update of the situation as it stands as soon as I get home. You've got them on the ropes. When do you think you'll be taking me out for that expensive dinner you promised?" Lucinda x

She had done what had been requested of her. Wyatt had all of the information at his fingertips, he just needed to put the final nail in the coffin and she was going to help him do it.

CHAPTER 60

Olivia was in the kitchen when Sebastian, Georgiana, Hattie and Richie returned from the RFC meeting.

"How did it go?" she asked. "Anything new to report?"

"You didn't miss much," Georgiana looked glum. "We're not going to win."

"Nonsense," Hattie patted her arm. "Something will crop up when we least expect it."

"Well whatever that is, it's running out of time," Sebastian replied. "Where is everyone?" he asked Olivia.

"Alexander is asleep, Mum and Dad are in the sitting room, José and Angelica are putting the kids to bed, Paul and Claire are getting ready for supper, Gillian is in the library and Diana is probably holed up in the airing cupboard with a bottle of gin." Olivia reeled off the whereabouts of their weekend guests. "Did you really have to invite them all at once?"

"I didn't know your parents were going to turn up," Sebastian rolled his eyes. "That's twice in a month."

"Tell me about it," Olivia sighed. "To be fair Dad is getting on quite well with Paul and Claire, but then again lawyers always stick together. Diana is a different matter altogether." Olivia's grandmother was terribly eccentric and thoroughly enjoyed a drink.

"I probably should have taken your family's foibles into consideration before I married you," Sebastian joked.

"I did warn you," Olivia laughed. "You just better hope I don't end up like Diana when we're old."

Sebastian leaned forward and kissed Olivia. "Bonkers or not, I'll love you forever Mrs Bloom."

"And thank God for that," a voice boomed from the doorway. "Although with your money you'll be able to afford round the clock care."

"Dad!" Olivia cried. "That's so rude. And I hardly think we need to start discussing that kind of thing just yet."

"Don't worry, Nicolas," Sebastian smiled through gritted teeth. "Every penny I have will go towards making sure your daughter and grandson are kept in the manner to which they have become accustomed when I start to lose my marbles."

"Humph," Nicolas grunted. "What time is supper? Constance is hungry."

"In about half an hour," Hattie replied. "I can get her some nibbles if you like?"

"I'm sure she won't fade away in that time," Nicolas grumbled and walked away to re-join Olivia's mother.

Olivia shook her head. "Remind me not to have another baby. They'll be moving in if that happens."

"Oh, come on," Georgiana replied. "They're not that bad."

"They bloody are," Olivia cried. Sebastian nodded his head in agreement.

"All we need now is for our erstwhile father to turn up unannounced and we'd have the whole circus together," Georgiana grinned. "But there's absolutely no chance of that happening."

"When does Dan get back? I want to talk to him about a deal." Richie was always thinking about business.

"He's got a manager, an agent, and God only knows who else. I don't think you need to be helping him with any sponsorship stuff," Georgiana replied. "What is it anyway?"

"A new aftershave by Dolce and Gabanna," said Richie. "He's exactly what they're looking for."

"He smells just fine," Georgiana grinned. "But you may as well tell him, you never know."

"Right." Hattie stood with her hands on her hips and spoke to them all. "Please can you all get out of my kitchen. Go and have a drink or something. You can't avoid Nicolas and Constance forever, Olivia."

"I can try," she grumbled and followed Sebastian into the hallway.

"I'll shoot upstairs and drop our bags," Richie said. "Where are we?"

"Thalia suite, east wing. Gillian is in the library, so you may want to tell her you're back," Hattie replied. "I've put Paul and Claire next door to you, and the de Silva's are all on the top floor, so it should be relatively quiet."

"Lovely stuff." Richie took their bags and headed towards the library.

Georgiana picked up her glass of wine, took a sip and raised it in the air. "Once more into the breach dear friends," she laughed. "I'm going to go and charm the socks off Nicolas and Constance." She skipped out of the kitchen leaving Hattie to carry on preparing supper.

Her mobile bleeped before she got to the sitting room. It was a text from Dan.

We're done shooting!!!!!!! Just the wrap party and I'll be on my way back to you. I CANNOT WAIT. Desperate for a shag! Love you babe xxx

Georgiana grinned and tapped her reply.

You just want me for my body!! Have fun at the party. Totally can't wait to see you either. Love you more xxx

"I really do love you, Daniel Flowers," she muttered. "With all my heart."

Finally, she had opened her heart again. She was completely in love with Dan and couldn't wait to be his wife.

CHAPTER 61

*D*an was feeling groggy. He had had a few drinks at the wrap party and let his hair down, but that didn't explain why his head was so woozy or why the events of the party were fractured in his memory.

He groaned as he sat up in bed and rubbed his eyes. It was still dark outside, and it took him a few moments to adjust to the bedside light. When he opened them, he was shocked to see Kylie getting dressed in the corner of his hotel room.

"Fuck," he whispered. "What happened?"

"I knew you wouldn't say no if the chance presented itself," Kylie purred. "And when you made it clear last night how much you wanted to screw me I thought I might as well give you a go."

"What?" Dan cried. "There's no fucking way I would have ever have said that, let alone slept with you. You're lying."

"Am I?" Kylie flashed her mobile phone in his face. He grabbed it out of her hand and began to scroll through the dozens of photographs she had taken of them in bed together.

He paled when they began to get more and more explicit and was almost sick when he saw one of Kylie with his penis in her mouth and his face contorted in apparent gratification.

"Who the fuck was in here?" he growled. "Someone else took this picture. You fucking set me up, you bitch." It suddenly dawned on him that she had done this on purpose.

"Of course I did, honey," she laughed. "Do you really think I'd actually fuck you?"

"Why?" Dan was too shocked to react in anger. He was relieved that they had not actually had sex.

"Because a friend asked me to," she smirked. "You were such a push over. A tiny bit of Rohypnol mixed into your drink and that was that."

"You drugged me?" He was incredulous. "And what do you mean 'a friend asked me to'?"

"He asked me to pass on a message to you," she said on her way out of the room. "Tell Sebastian Bloom to back down or your fiancée will be getting evidence of your dirty little rendezvous in the mail."

Kylie slammed the door on her way out and Dan only just made it into the bathroom before he threw up. Georgiana's face floated before his eyes and he held his head in his hands. He knew there was no way out of this. He had to tell her and hope that she believed his version of events. No matter what happened, he could not and would not put her through the agony and heartbreak of opening an envelope that would send her world crashing down around her.

He slumped onto the bathroom floor and cried. He knew she would never forgive him.

CHAPTER 62

*D*an's flight landed at midday, and as he came down the steps of the jet he locked eyes with Georgiana, who was bouncing up and down on the spot in her excitement. He gulped and forced himself to smile. He felt like his world was about to collapse.

Georgiana threw herself into his arms and squealed: "Welcome home!"

Dan held her tightly and kissed her. "You have no idea how good it is to see you" he whispered.

"Let's get out of here," she said and took his hand.

"I didn't know you were coming to meet me," Dan said.

"I couldn't wait another minute, so I commandeered your driver and here I am." She shoved him into the waiting car.

Once inside she told the driver to head to Appleton Vale, and leaned back into Dan's arms. "That feels so good," she sighed.

Dan breathed in her scent. "I've missed you so much, babe."

"You're back now, and we have a whole month to chill together," Georgiana grinned. "A whole month!"

"Sounds lovely," Dan muttered, unconvincingly.

"What's wrong? I thought you'd be more excited to see me." Georgiana pouted.

Dan stroked her cheek. "Of course I'm excited to see you. I'm just exhausted. It was a bloody long and hard shoot. I'm in bits. Covered from head to toe in cuts and bruises too."

"Well you can relax now and let me take care of you. We can just cuddle on the sofa for the rest of the day if you like?" Georgiana replied. She was concerned at the distance she felt. Even though he was sitting right next to her it seemed like he was miles away.

"Sounds good to me," he sighed. "Do you mind if I snooze on the way home?" He needed to collect his thoughts and work out how he was going to tell her. He looked at her face stricken with worry for him, and he was hit with a tidal wave of guilt.

"Oh," Georgiana squeaked, "OK." She started to wriggle away from him, but he pulled her back.

"I'd prefer to sleep with you in my arms," he smiled.

She leaned back again and let his arms envelope her. She sighed with contentment and closed her eyes. Dan sighed with anguish. This was the hardest and most dreadful thing he had ever had to do. He peered at Georgiana and felt a surge of love that he had never experienced before. Selfishly, he had to be with her one more time. "One more night," he muttered. "Just one more."

The car pulled up outside Georgiana's cottage two hours later, and she shook Dan awake. "We're here," she whispered.

He opened one eye and grinned. "You know what that means, don't you?"

316

"Finally!" she exclaimed. "That's the man I know and love. The one who is ALWAYS thinking about sex!"

Dan laughed and climbed out of the back seat. "Get that cute little bottom inside and upstairs." He grabbed her hand and ran into the house. "Don't worry about the bags," he shouted back to the driver. "Just leave them there. Thanks."

He ran up the stairs behind Georgiana, who was giggling uncontrollably. It was infectious, and within seconds he was laughing with her. She jumped onto the bed and started bouncing up and down.

"I love you!" she shouted at the top of her voice. "I love you, I love you, I love you."

Dan couldn't help himself. He couldn't wait any longer. He wanted to bury himself in her and hope that everything would be ok. "Come here," he growled. "Get those clothes off. NOW!"

"Right back at yah," she grinned and stripped naked. Within seconds they were entwined. Georgiana gasped when Dan's hands touched her skin. His flesh pressing against hers sent a thousand volts of electricity surging through her.

Dan felt it too. He groaned as she littered his face with light kisses, murmuring her love for him over and over again. He ran his hands down her body, making her moan and writhe.

In the next hour, Dan made love to Georgiana like it was the last time they would ever be together – because he knew it would be. He took her to dizzy new heights of intensity, and brought her to the edge of climax over and over again until she was begging him to make her come. He kissed and caressed every inch of her body, taking it all in so he wouldn't ever forget what it felt like to be with her.

She fell asleep in his arms, exhausted from their love-making. He watched her as she slept, and cried quietly for the loss they were both about to experience. Everything he knew about her told him she wouldn't forgive him. He had no evidence to the contrary. It was his word against a bunch of seedy photographs, taken by a woman he had been rumoured to be having an affair with the entire time they were on set.

He knew Georgiana was sensitive to the constant speculation about his love life and the way the media twisted things, and he had done nothing to dispel it or ease her worries.

He was still holding her in the same position when she woke a few hours later. He hadn't slept. "Hey gorgeous," he grinned. "Seems I took it out of you."

"That was the most awesome sex I have ever had. EVER," she purred. "You clearly missed me."

"You have no idea," he groaned. "I've thought about you every second of every day."

"Even when you were in the middle of a high-speed car chase?" she laughed.

"Even then," he smiled. "Now let's get some food, I'm starving."

Dan watched Georgiana as she climbed out of bed and slipped on a silk robe. "You are so bloody gorgeous," he said.

"Why thank you," she laughed and dropped into a curtsey. "What do you fancy?"

"Apart from you?" Dan grinned. "Whatever's in the fridge will do. We just need some sustenance to get ready for round two."

He followed her downstairs and watched as she emptied the contents of the fridge onto the table and poured some wine. She was dancing and humming along to the radio, and she looked the happiest he had ever seen her.

In the early hours of the morning, after they had made love again, he stared at her while she slept. She looked so peaceful and content. His heart contracted.

He was about to put an end to that.

CHAPTER 63

"Are you going to tell me what's going on or not?" Georgiana snapped. Dan had been quiet and brooding all morning. He turned to face her, grief-stricken and pale, and motioned for her to sit down.

"Now you're really worrying me," she gulped.

Dan looked wretched. "I need to tell you something, and I know you won't ever want to see me again. But please hear me out before you tell me to leave."

Georgiana was overcome by a feeling of dread. "What have you done?" she whispered.

"Something happened the other night, and I swear to you that it was totally unintentional on my part," he croaked.

Georgiana was rooted to the spot. She was unable to speak.

Dan continued. "I woke up after the wrap party and Kylie was in my room. She had photos of me and her."

"Doing what?" Georgiana stammered.

"You don't need to know the details," Dan replied. "She drugged me."

"Why on earth would she do that" Georgiana was incredulous.

"Because she was told to. She gave me a message, to tell Sebastian to back off." Dan shook his head. "You have to believe me."

Georgiana rose to her feet and walked towards Dan. She raised her hand and slapped his face before her tears began to fall. Dan tried to reach out for her but she pushed him away. "I knew there was something going on with you two. No smoke without fire," she spat.

"Honestly. That's what happened. And we didn't have sex. It was all so hazy." Dan pleaded with Georgiana. "Please believe me. I've never lied to you, I know how much you value the truth."

Georgiana sniffed back her tears. "I don't understand. Why would you do that? I thought we were happy?"

Dan lunged forward and grabbed her hands. "We were happy. We are happy. I love you and only you, and I swear I would never and have never cheated on you."

"If it's all so hazy how do you know you didn't have sex? Why are you telling me? You could have got away with it." Georgiana sneered.

"Because I can't live a lie, and she has photos she said she would send to you. I couldn't let you find out like that. It would break your heart and that's the last thing I want to do."

"Don't touch me," she cried. "You're a total bastard."

"No. Georgiana, please," Dan begged. "I love you."

"If you loved me you wouldn't have done this. You're

321

disgusting. I should have listened to everyone when they talked about your reputation. How many other women have you fucked since we've been together?" she spat. She was reeling and the room started to spin.

"None!" Dan exclaimed. "Since the moment you sat down next to me on that plane there has been no one else. You stole my heart."

"Well, you can have it back," she screamed. She leaned on the kitchen table to steady herself. "Get out."

"What?" Dan cried.

"You heard me," she yelled. "Leave me alone."

He was distraught. He had been hanging onto a tiny hope that she would understand, and love him enough to get through it. "I won't leave you like this," Dan said softly. "I can't bear to see you in pain."

"You should have thought about that before you got pissed and shagged your co-star." Georgiana's voice was ice cold. "I never want to see you again."

Dan knew there was no point in pushing her. She needed time to cool down and digest what he had told her. He picked up his bag, walked out of the front door and slammed it behind him.

She fell to the floor and began to cry. She was completely and utterly heartbroken.

CHAPTER 64

*W*hen Georgiana and Dan didn't turn up for dinner that evening, Hattie voiced her concerns. Something was wrong.

"They're probably just making up for lost time," Sebastian said. "But if it makes you feel better I'll call her." He picked up the phone and rang Georgiana's mobile. She didn't answer, so he tried Dan's instead. His went straight to voicemail.

"I'm sure she's fine," he reassured Hattie.

"I think there's something wrong," Hattie replied. "I can feel it."

"Ok you silly woman," Sebastian kissed her on the head. "I'll pop over there now. Can you delay dinner and let everyone know?" He headed out of the back door and jumped into the ancient Land Rover. He was at Georgiana's door in minutes and found the cottage swathed in darkness.

He knocked on the door, then let himself in when there was no answer. He found Georgiana asleep on the kitchen floor with Lady pressed up against her. He was immediately worried.

He shook her gently. "Wake up sweetheart." Georgiana opened

her eyes and looked at him. He was shocked to see how blank her expression was. "What's happened?" he asked gently. "Where's Dan?"

"He slept with someone else," she whispered.

Sebastian pulled her into his arms and kissed her head. "It's ok, you'll be ok," he said, over and over again. He let her cry into his chest until her tears subsided.

"Can you get Liv?" she mumbled.

"Of course. She's better at this than me anyway," Sebastian smiled, and sent Olivia a text.

Georgie needs you. Can you come over now?

Olivia appeared at the door five minutes later looking anxious. Sebastian quietly briefed her on the situation and then made his way back to the Manor and their guests.

Olivia led Georgiana over to the sofa. "Tell me everything," she urged. "Do you want a drink?"

Georgiana nodded and Olivia went to the fridge and retrieved a bottle of wine and two glasses. She handed Georgiana a full glass and watched as she swallowed half of it in one go. "Slow down. You'll only feel worse later."

"I couldn't possibly feel any worse," Georgiana replied. "At least this will numb the pain."

"Tell me," Olivia leaned back onto the sofa and looked at Georgiana.

"He slept with that awful Kylie," she replied.

"What? No way," Olivia cried. "There's no way he'd cheat on you."

"Well he did," Georgiana sniffed. "He told me himself. And there are photographs to prove it."

"Photos? Why?" Olivia asked. "That sounds a bit fishy to me. I could understand it if it was a groupie, but not his co-star. How could she possibly benefit from that?"

Georgiana shrugged her shoulders. "I didn't stop to ask. I don't believe him. He said she drugged him, and he woke up to her getting dress and sneering about the photos. But that's ridiculous. He's a liar."

"Well I must admit, it does sound a little far-fetched," Olivia agreed. "But Dan's not a liar. At least I don't think he is. He loves you, darling. And he told you straight away. That's got to mean something."

"Yeah, it means he's guilty," she snapped. "He said Kylie passed on a message from her friend for Sebastian."

Olivia was surprised. "Oh. What was the message?"

Georgiana sniffed. "To back off."

"I think there's every possibility that there are other forces at work here," Olivia replied. "I don't know how we find out, though."

"Dan would know," Georgiana sobbed. "I can't forgive him Liv, I just can't. Not after what Wyatt did to me."

"Are you sure?" Olivia asked. "What if he's telling the truth?"

"He isn't." Her heart ached so much that she couldn't see past the pain. She wasn't being rational. "Why does this keep happening to me?"

"Oh, darling," Olivia hugged her again. "You've just been a bit unlucky."

"A bit?" Georgiana smiled weakly.

"Well ok then, a lot," Olivia laughed.

"I'm going to get pissed and forget about everything." Georgiana refilled her glass and took another massive gulp. "Please will you stay with me for a while?"

"Of course." Olivia held her glass out. "Fill me up."

Sebastian was furious. He slammed back into the kitchen at the Manor where Hattie was waiting anxiously.

"Olivia ran out so quickly she didn't tell me what was wrong," she said. "What's happened? Please tell me she's ok?"

"That bastard's done a number on her. She's heartbroken," he snarled.

"Wyatt?" Hattie asked. "I thought that was long over."

"No. Dan," Sebastian replied.

"What?" Hattie exclaimed. "He wouldn't do that."

"Well he has." Sebastian banged his fists on the table. "I'm going to fucking kill him."

"Oh, my poor girl," Hattie gasped.

"Liv's looking after her, so I wouldn't expect her back for supper."

The baby monitor crackled and Alexander began to scream. "I'll go," Sebastian ran upstairs to see to his son. Hattie heard him whispering through the monitor. "Don't worry, little man. Your mummy and I are rock solid. I love you both with all my heart."

Hattie gulped back her tears. Georgiana didn't deserve to be in so much pain.

Ten minutes later, she heard the front door slam. She went into the hallway and found Richie shaking his head in frustration. "Was that Sebastian?" she asked him.

"Yep. And he is seriously pissed off," Richie replied. "Said he was going out and looked pretty mad. Olivia has disappeared as well. What's going on?"

"Dan and Georgiana have split up," Hattie said. "Don't ask me the ins and outs as I don't know everything, but needless to say Sebastian is on the war path."

"He must be looking for Dan," Richie frowned. "I hope he doesn't do anything stupid."

"I don't know what to do," Hattie cried.

"There's nothing you can do," Richie said gently. "I'll go and update everyone on the situation. Let me know if you hear anything from Sebastian."

Sebastian pulled up outside the pub and rushed inside, leaving his engine running.

"Is he here?" he yelled at Tom.

Tom nodded towards the back of the bar. "Over there. Go easy."

Sebastian stormed across the pub and punched Dan without a moment's hesitation. Dan fell backwards and landed on the floor. He lay motionless for a few moments before turning to look at Sebastian.

"I deserved that," he said as he rubbed his face. "But I didn't do it. You've got to believe me."

"Georgie doesn't believe you, so why should I?" Sebastian snarled. "How could you do that to her? I trusted you, we all did."

Dan got up off the floor and sat down at the table. "I'm telling you. Something weird is going on."

"Don't try to make bloody excuses. I should have known you'd hurt her. Your reputation stinks." Sebastian shot him a look of pure evil.

"You're in no position to judge," Dan snapped. "We all know what you were like before you met Olivia. I didn't do it."

Tom walked over and handed Sebastian a glass of scotch. "Sit down and discuss this without resorting to your fists again, or I'll throw you out."

He snatched the drink from Tom and downed it in one gulp. "You'd better refill it."

Sebastian took a deep breath in an attempt to calm down. He sat down opposite Dan and looked at him. "Start talking. I'll hear you out, but that's it."

Tom returned with a bottle of single malt and a glass for Dan. "You may as well have the bottle." Sebastian poured the liquid into the glasses, and sat back waiting for Dan to begin.

Half an hour later, he was almost convinced that Dan had been set up. "What do you need from me?" he asked. "I can't help you with Georgiana. She's as stubborn as I am. You need to give her time."

"I need you to help me find out who's behind this," Dan pleaded. "The only way she will forgive me is if we give her irrefutable proof."

Sebastian sighed. "Ok, I'll help."

CHAPTER 65

"It's done." Bobby Garnett informed Wyatt that the plan to derail Georgiana and Dan had been a success.

"And?"

"He's back in LA. She's at home. It's over. That's good news for you." Bobby grinned.

Wyatt nodded his head. Georgiana was at a low point now. It was time for him to swoop in and play the white knight. His ego was large enough to believe he could reel her in.

Bobby left his office and Wyatt picked up the phone. He dialled his investor. "I don't know what you offered that actress, but it worked. They're on the ropes."

Dan was suffering the pain of heartbreak in LA, and his home felt empty and soulless without Georgiana there. He had taken Sebastian's advice to give her space, and had run back to America to lick his wounds in private.

He was greeted by a frenzied press pack outside the private airfield. Their split had leaked, and the headlines were damning. Flowers and Bloom Wilt; Withering Heights – a lengthy list of women Dan had loved and lost; Flowers sheds Bloom; Absent without Leaf – Flowers arrives in LA alone.

He jumped into the waiting car, and it was only when he was safely inside his Hollywood fortress did he finally allowed his emotions to spill out. He had held it together all the way home and felt like he was going to implode at any moment.

He sat on his terrace in the sunshine with a bottle of beer and pulled out his mobile to send Georgiana a text.

I'm so sorry. I love you. Please forgive me. D x

A reply came back almost immediately. It was swift and brief.

Fuck off.

A ghost of a smile crossed his face. She had engaged with him. Anything from her was better than nothing at all. He tapped his reply.

Not a chance x

He didn't hear from her again, and he spent his days and nights lurching between desperation and hope. It was exhausting. Despite all of his texts, emails and phone calls, Georgiana had remained silent. He refused to see his friends, who were growing more and more concerned about him each day. He was a mess, and when he received the news from Vinnie that his film – Jigsaw Kids – was a hot contender for an Oscar nomination and that he could get a Best Actor nod when the awards were announced in January, he didn't feel anything.

He turned down all media interview requests, refused to do any work for the studio to promote the film to the Academy Awards committee, and sat around wallowing in his misery.

He knew Sebastian was digging around and had promised to help him, but he was yet to hear anything from him. His desperation and frustration grew daily. It was becoming more and more hopeless as the weeks drifted by. Christmas was looming, and Dan was set to spend it alone in his agony.

CHAPTER 66

*D*an was notably absent from the London premiere of Jigsaw Kids. Rumours abounded about his mental health, and no amount of cajoling from Vinnie or Ken had made any difference. He was resolute in his refusal to undertake any promotional work whilst he was coming to terms with losing Georgiana.

When the movie was released nationwide, Georgiana couldn't help herself. She donned a baseball cap and skulked into the back of the cinema in Fiddlebury to watch the man she loved acting in the role of his career.

Halfway through the movie she found herself crying at the sheer depth and passion of his performance. Both Dan and Cara had poured heart and soul into their characters, and it was their incredible acting that made the film what it was – an Oscar contender. The script was beautifully written, delivered with exquisite timing and intense emotion. The last line of the movie was Dan's, and when he looked directly into the camera to deliver it, Georgiana felt as if he were looking right into her soul.

She made a hasty exit as soon as the credits began to roll and just made it back to her car before breaking down again. She sat in a layby on the road back to Appleton Vale and cried until she had no more tears left to shed.

The next day the newspapers were full of praise for both Dan and Cara's performances, touting them as sure Oscar nominees. Georgiana bought copies of each newspaper and cut out Dan's reviews. Even through her pain she was proud of him, and missed him desperately.

"I'm worried about you, darling. We all are." Claudia stared at Dan through the laptop, concern written all over her face. "Why didn't you come home?"

Dan shook his head. "Couldn't face it. Sorry."

"Is it really over between you?" Claudia asked. "Surely, if you still love each other you can find a way?"

"It's over Mum," he grimaced. "There's no point in dragging it up again. I fucked up and deserve what I got."

Claudia tutted. "You did not, as you say, 'fuck it up'. As far as I can see, you've done nothing wrong. You were set up, darling."

Dan had told his mother the whole story when the news had broken about his split with Georgiana. He sighed. "I don't think that matters any more. She hates me, and there's nothing I can do to change that if I can't give her proof."

"Oh darling, I know she doesn't hate you. When you love someone as much as you both love each other it doesn't just go away. Have a little faith."

After the call, Dan sat at the kitchen table with his head in his hands. All of his hopes and dreams for a future with Georgiana had been smashed to pieces, his heart was completely broken.

"I just don't think you're up to it, love." Gerry shrugged his shoulders. "You're having a hard time, and you're all over the news. I think they just want you to take a break and get your head back in the game."

"Keep out of the limelight more like," Georgiana grumbled.

"It's a big live show," Gerry replied. "You need to be on the ball and you're not. Clare carried you at Olympia."

"But it's Sports Personality of the Year," Georgiana cried.

"Precisely," Gerry nodded. "Too big to balls up."

"Fine," she huffed. "If that's what they want then there's nothing I can do about it."

"Why don't you go on holiday? Disappear somewhere and have a proper rest," Gerry suggested. "We want you back at your best in January, and if you play your cards right you'll get to be with your old mucker McEnroe at the Aussie Open."

"Is that supposed to be an incentive?" She smiled weakly.

Gerry put his arm around her. "Look love. You've been shat on, and your heart is broken but you'll be ok. You're a trooper. Don't let the bastard break you."

"I'll be fine. I'd rather be working but if I'm not allowed to, then that's that." She stood up to leave. "No point in me being here, is there?"

Gerry hugged her again. "Have a nice Christmas, and go on bloody holiday."

Georgiana drove back from London to Appleton Vale in a daze. Not only was her heart well and truly broken, but also, she had been effectively suspended from work until she could demonstrate she was back to her best.

Her performance at Olympia had been a disaster, she knew that, but she had needed the distraction. She had pushed to be included in the team to cover the event so that she could surround herself by horses and horsey people where she felt most comfortable, but it hadn't worked. The London International Horse Show was bursting with Christmas cheer, and Georgiana had felt anything but festive.

Luckily, Clare Balding, an old family friend, was leading the presenting team and stepped up when Georgiana was floundering. That was the only thing that saved her from dragging the viewers into her depression.

As soon as she reached the top of the vale and the road into the village, she breathed a sigh of relief. All she wanted to do was hide away with Lady for company, and wait for Christmas to pass.

The Victorian streetlamps cast a warm glow across the icy ground, and smoke from the chimneys of houses dotted around the village green drifted eerily in the darkening skies. Decorations in windows shone brightly, and the sparkle of fairy lights danced through the descending darkness. She knew that behind every door her neighbours were preparing for festive fun, and it made her feel even worse.

Ten minutes later, she was in her pyjamas with the curtains closed and doors locked. She opened a bottle of wine, lit a fire, and lay on the rug with Lady by her side, staring blankly into the flames. There was no getting away from it. She was a mess, and she desperately missed Dan.

CHAPTER 67

Olivia was perched at the top of the ladder, reaching over to place Georgiana's ancient homemade angel on the tip of the towering Christmas tree that stood proudly in the hallway of the Manor.

"What the bloody hell do you think you're doing?" Sebastian bellowed when he arrived back from the club. "Get down before you hurt yourself."

"Nearly got it." She was straining to get close and almost lost her balance.

"I'll do it." Sebastian held the ladder and Olivia slowly negotiated her way down.

"It didn't seem that high when I went up." She handed him the decoration.

"It's about twenty feet. What were you thinking?" He shook his head. "I don't want to come home and find you in a crumpled heap on the floor."

"You do it then," she snapped. She was exhausted. Alexander

wasn't sleeping well, and she had been up most of the night every night for the past three weeks.

Sebastian had been away in America, and had also done a quick flit to Tokyo and back again for an event with his sponsors, so she had been bearing the brunt of it. She really wanted to do it all herself so didn't let on to Hattie or Georgiana that she was having a rough time.

"What's up?" Sebastian frowned.

"Nothing," she mumbled.

"Now I know there's something wrong. Tell me."

"I'm bloody tired, that's what," she replied. "Your son isn't sleeping, at all."

"Why haven't you asked Hattie to help out if you're that exhausted?"

"If I'm that exhausted?" Olivia retorted. "How would you know? You've hardly been here recently."

"That's not fair." Sebastian put down the angel and walked over to the stairs where Olivia was sitting. "I had work commitments, and I'm trying to help Georgie." He sat down next to her. "Why didn't you tell me?"

"I don't know." Olivia began to cry. "I'm shattered. I look terrible, and I'd literally give my right arm for a decent night's sleep." Sebastian put his arms around her and she buried her head in his chest. He stroked her hair and held her until her tears subsided.

"Right Mrs Bloom," he smiled. "You're going to bed this minute, and you'll stay there until I tell you otherwise."

"Can't," she sniffed. "Got too much to do for the party."

"Maybe we should cancel it?" Sebastian suggested.

"Don't be ridiculous," she cried. "We've got half the village and most of our friends coming."

"Then I'll get Hattie to find someone to help out," he replied.

"I feel like such a failure," she said. "I used to be able to juggle everything, and now I'm a pathetic loser."

Sebastian laughed. "Now who's being ridiculous?"

"Don't bloody laugh at me. You have no idea how I feel."

Sebastian sighed. "Nothing I say is going to make any difference. Go to bed. I'll deal with everything."

"Don't tell me what to do." She wriggled free from his arms and stood up. "I will go to bed, but only to get away from you." She turned her back on him and walked up the stairs.

Sebastian gave her a few minutes and then followed her upstairs. She was already asleep on top of the bed, dead to the world. He covered her with a blanket and kissed her head.

Alexander began to stir from his nap and gurgled through the baby monitor. Sebastian quickly switched it off so it didn't wake Olivia and went into the nursery.

"Now is not the time to be making any noise young man," he whispered as he picked him up. "Mummy's very tired so we need to be quiet." He fed Alexander in the kitchen, and decided to take him for a walk around the estate. 'Let's go and see auntie Georgiana."

The curtains were still drawn when he arrived at the cottage. He knocked several times, and then let himself in where he found Georgiana curled up on the sofa with Lady watching television.

"You can't hide in here forever," he said gently.

"Bloody can," she replied without taking her eyes off the screen.

Sebastian took Alexander out of his pram and handed him to Georgiana. "Here, take him."

She reluctantly reached out for her nephew and cradled him in her arms. "Hey, big man," she whispered. She felt better just holding him. "Where's Liv?"

"Bed." Sebastian stared at her accusingly. "Why didn't you tell me she was struggling?"

"Didn't know," Georgiana replied. She looked at Sebastian with wide eyes. "Sorry."

"She's dead on her feet, and snapping at me and probably everyone else she talks to. She said Alexander hasn't been sleeping at all recently"

"Know the feeling," Georgiana muttered.

"Are you coming tomorrow night?" Sebastian sat in the chair opposite Georgiana. "It's Christmas Eve."

"Don't feel like a party," she mumbled as she bounced Alexander up and down absentmindedly.

"Jesus Christ," Sebastian exclaimed. "I take my eye off the ball for five minutes, and both my wife and sister are on the verge of a nervous breakdown."

Georgiana shot him an evil look. "Bugger off. I'm fine."

"You're not fine," he sighed. "What can I do to help you feel better?"

"Nothing," she muttered. "Just leave me alone." She stood up and gave Alexander back to Sebastian. "Will you go now please?"

Sebastian bristled. "Fine. Sit here and wallow in your misery. There are people who love you, who are here for you whenever you're ready to re-enter life. Will is desperate to see you but he's

339

respecting your wishes to be left alone." He placed Alexander back into his pram and walked towards the front door. "At least have the courtesy to tell Liv if you're not coming to the party. She's put a lot of effort into it."

"I will," she muttered.

She lay back down with Lady and flicked through the television channels looking for a black and white film to lose herself in. She loved old movies that harked back to a time when life was much simpler. She paused when she saw Dan's face on the screen and turned up the volume.

"The question that's on everyone's lips is when are we going to see our favourite action hero again? Of course, I'm talking about Hollywood heartthrob Dan Flowers who hasn't been spotted anywhere in weeks. He even missed the London premiere of Jigsaw Kids so can we assume the heartbreaker had the tables turned? Is he now the one with the broken heart? This is one of Hollywood's best-kept secrets. We really have no idea what happened with his ex-fiancée Georgiana Bloom, but it's safe to say to all you single ladies out there that he's definitely back on the market – if he ever shows his face again."

Georgiana threw a cushion at the television. "And you're bloody welcome to him," she shouted.

Olivia opened her eyes and sat bolt upright in bed. She looked at her watch and shook her head in disbelief. She had slept for sixteen hours straight. She pulled on some clothes and ran downstairs to find a team of event planners, decorators and caterers filing through the front door and taking instruction from Hattie.

"Where are they?" she asked.

"In the study. Did you sleep well?" Hattie asked whilst directing the catering staff towards the kitchen.

"I did. I feel much better," she smiled. "I need to apologise to Sebastian. I was a complete bitch yesterday."

"Then you'd best go and tell him that," Hattie urged. "And don't worry about the party. It's under control."

"I can see that," Olivia laughed. "Thank you."

She walked across the hall and down the corridor leading to the east wing and Sebastian's study. He was standing looking out of the window, explaining the rules of golf to his son.

"He's six month's old, you idiot." She walked over to Sebastian and reached up to kiss him. "I'm sorry I was so vile yesterday."

"And here's my sleeping beauty." He kissed her back. "I thought you were never going to wake up."

"I can't believe how long I slept for. Did you come to bed last night? How did I not I wake up when you undressed me?"

"It's not as much of a thrill taking your clothes off you when you're unconscious," he laughed.

"For me too," she smiled. "Has he been ok?" She took Alexander out of his arms.

"Good as gold." He stroked Olivia's cheek. "I'm sorry. I should have known you were having a tough time."

"Don't be silly. I just hit a brick wall yesterday and took it out on you. I'm a complete bitch."

Sebastian snorted. "Rubbish. You're a new mum who's too stubborn to take help when it's offered. And on top of that, you've organised this whole party single-handed."

"I think it was a little ambitious trying to have the party on Christmas Eve when we have a full house tomorrow as well. Thank you for sorting it out. Have you spoken to Georgie?"

"Saw her briefly yesterday afternoon and she told me to bugger off. She wasn't even interested in Alexander." Sebastian looked worried. "Will you talk to her?"

"I'll try, but you know what she's like. She's a Bloom through and through, and we both know what that means," she laughed.

"And exactly what does it mean?" Sebastian raised an eyebrow.

"Stubborn. Idiotic. Prefers to wallow in one's own misery. Bad-tempered. Rude. Shall I go on?"

"Yet you still love us," Sebastian grinned.

"Well you do have some redeeming qualities, so it's not all bad," she joked. "I'll give her a call now and see how the land lies."

"Was I this bad when I was miserable?" Sebastian asked.

"Oh no, darling." Olivia patted his arm. "You were much, much worse."

The first guests began to arrive at eight o'clock and they had a full house by nine thirty, bursting with Christmas cheer and rising noise levels. The decorators had done an exquisite job, and the whole house sparkled in an unending twinkle of fairy lights that bounced off the ceilings and walls and refracted through the crystal chandeliers that hung in the centre of the hallway.

Hattie had overseen the catering, and had also finished decorating the tree that was drawing admiring glances and gasps of delight from some guests. Underneath it was a mountain of beautifully-wrapped gifts, mainly for Alexander, that was being added to with every guest that arrived.

At nine forty-five Georgiana slipped in to the kitchen through the back door and took a glass of champagne off a tray. She downed it in one gulp, picked up another and walked into the hallway where she ran into Peppy.

"Where've you been hiding," Peppy engulfed her in a flurry of kisses. "Love your dress."

Georgiana was wearing a full length, strapless black cocktail dress. It was simple and elegant, and the colour matched her mood. "Licking my wounds," Georgiana replied.

"Are you about done?" Peppy laughed.

"I doubt it, but I'm here so that's a start, I suppose." Georgiana looked around. "Where's Sebastian? I was horrible to him yesterday."

"I think he's in the library." She grabbed Georgiana's arm. "Before you go how about you introduce me to that hottie over there." She pointed across the room to where Will was standing.

"Will?" Georgiana was surprised. "Really? Isn't he a bit young?"

"Not for me he isn't," Peppy grinned. "Come on, then."

"Porg!" Will was delighted to see Georgiana. "About bloody time." He hugged her and whispered, "are you OK?"

"I will be," she whispered back. "Sorry I've been ignoring you." She turned to Peppy. "This is Will Abinger, my best friend in the whole world. Be gentle with him."

"How is it that we haven't met before now?" Peppy leaned forward and gave Will

a glimpse of her breasts tightly squeezed into her evening dress.

"Beats me," Will grinned. "But now we have, how about a dance?" He swept Peppy into the drawing room. Olivia had fallen for Freddie's persuasive charms and agreed that his band could play the party. They were doing a great job. Freddie was on vocals, Josh on bass guitar and Jem on drums, along with a keyboard player and second guitarist – both friends from school.

"Hey!" Georgiana felt a hand on her shoulder and turned

around to see Olivia. "I knew you'd come," she smiled. "You look lovely."

"I look thin and tired and horrible," Georgiana replied.

"No, you don't! That dress is lovely. Is it new?" Olivia asked.

"Dan bought it for me in Monaco. I was supposed to wear it to a party the night Edward died but never did, obviously." She fingered the material. "It's a bit loose now."

"Well that's an improvement," Olivia smiled. "At least you can say his name without crying now."

She shrugged her shoulders. "I'm all cried out."

"Was that Will I just saw being smothered by Peppy?" Olivia asked.

"Yep. They'll be having sex in the lavatory before we know it," said Georgiana.

"Actually, they're quite well suited, aside from the age difference," Olivia grinned.

"He shagged Lucinda. Peppy's a spring chicken compared to her." Georgiana screwed up her face imagining Will with Lucinda. "Where's Sebastian?"

"No idea." Olivia looked across the room. "Oh good. Andrea's just arrived. I need to talk to her." She waved across the room. "Try the library," she called back from across the hall.

Georgiana wandered down through the east wing towards the library and found Sebastian deep in conversation with Richie, Peter, Tom, and James Jenner. He smiled when he saw her in the doorway.

"Hi," she said. "Can I speak to you for a minute?"

"Sure." Sebastian stood up and walked out into the corridor. "What's up?"

"Sorry about yesterday." She was ashamed. "I've been a right cow recently."

"Well, I won't argue with that." He clinked his glass against hers. "But I'm in no position to judge."

"That's true," she agreed. "You were hell to live with."

"Must run in the family. Have you seen Liv?"

"Just now. She's with Andrea in the hall."

Sebastian frowned. "How did she look to you?"

"Fine. Why?" Georgiana saw the concern on his face.

"She's tired all the time and looks a bit pale. It's not like her." He was worried.

"She's exhausted. You said it yourself yesterday," Georgiana reminded him.

"Will you have a chat with her?" Sebastian asked. "She's just keeps saying she's fine, but she's definitely not herself."

Georgiana touched his arm. "Don't worry, I'm sure she's ok. I'm more concerned about you tonight." It was the fourth anniversary of Ellie and Lizzie's death.

"Life goes on." He replied. "I miss Lizzie, and it will always be difficult this time of year, but I've got Liv and Alexander, and it seems there's no getting rid of you."

Georgiana smirked. "Oh, you're so funny. Go back to your boys meeting. I'll see if I can catch Liv later."

For the next hour Georgiana made painful small talk with the guests she didn't know, and avoided the ones she did. She wasn't in the mood for the Spanish Inquisition. She decided to quietly slip away.

She picked up her coat and walked into the kitchen to exit by the back door. Olivia was sitting at the table looking completely washed out.

"Are you ok?" Georgiana asked. "You look like crap."

"I'm fine," Olivia snapped. "Why does everyone keep asking me if I'm ok? I'm just a bit tired."

"No need to chew me out," Georgiana bit back. "Sebastian's worried about you, and I can see why now."

"Like I said, I'm fine." Olivia glared at her.

"Well that's great then." Georgiana scowled. "You're fine. I'm fine. The world is a wonderful place." She grabbed her coat and marched towards the door. "I'm going home. Maybe you'll be in a better mood tomorrow."

"Georgie. Wait." Olivia stood up wearily. "I'm sorry. I didn't mean to snap at you."

Before Georgiana could reply Olivia fainted.

CHAPTER 68

octor James Elliott finished examining Olivia and sat with her for a few moments before she drifted off to sleep. He left the bedroom and quietly shut the door before addressing Sebastian.

"She's ok. Don't panic." He offered a reassuring smile. "She's physically worn out for a couple of reasons. One – you have a six-month-old baby who isn't sleeping well, and consequently neither is Olivia."

"And the second?" Sebastian urged him to continue.

"She's pregnant. Congratulations." James slapped Sebastian on the back.

"What?" Sebastian couldn't take it in.

"I had a test in my bag. It seemed logical to use it." James shrugged his shoulders.

Sebastian shook his head. "Pregnant? Really? So soon?"

James laughed. "Yes. Really."

Sebastian beamed. He was speechless.

"I'm going to get back to my date now. Olivia's sleeping, so leave her be for a while at least. I've told her to come to the surgery after Christmas and we'll make it all official, so you can stop worrying and get on with hosting your party."

"Thanks James." Sebastian shook his hand. "I really appreciate it."

"Don't look so shocked. It's good news," James replied. "She's going to need a bit of TLC, and you must make sure she's getting enough sleep from now on."

"That won't be a problem. I'll tie her to the bed if I have to." Sebastian grinned.

"I don't need to know what you two get up to behind closed doors," James chuckled. "See you later. Great party by the way. My date is suitably impressed coming to a celebrity's house on Christmas Eve."

"All part of the service," Sebastian bowed.

After James returned to the party, Sebastian sat at the top of the stairs and counted his blessings.

"Well?" Georgiana was standing in front of him. "Is she ok?"

"Better than ok." Sebastian got to his feet and hugged Georgiana. "I thought she was really ill and just not telling me. I'm so relieved."

"Just tired then?" Georgiana was thankful.

"Tired. Run down. Pregnant." Sebastian watched her reaction with amusement.

"Pregnant?" she squeaked.

"Yep," he replied. "But don't tell her I told you. I think she's probably in as much shock as I am. James says she needs to rest and get more sleep. Could be time for a nanny."

"She won't like that." Georgiana shook her head. "She was adamant right from the start that she wanted to do it all herself."

"Well things are different now." Sebastian shrugged his shoulders. "I'm going to be away a lot more this year. She'll need help."

"I'll let you two argue that one out. I'm going home." She reached up to kiss him. "See you tomorrow."

When the last of the guests had departed, just after one o'clock, Sebastian went upstairs to find Olivia crying.

"I can't believe it," she sobbed. "Not so quickly after Alexander. We should have been more careful."

He cradled her in his arms. "It's bloody amazing news."

"Easy for you to say," she replied. "I've only just got back to normal and I've got to go through it all again."

"Aren't you happy about it?" Sebastian asked.

"I'm in shock," she sniffed. "And I'm scared."

"Don't be. There's no way Doctor Khan will let you go through anything like that again. Do you think it's time we discussed a nanny?" He broached the subject carefully.

"No!" Olivia cried. "How many times are we going to have this conversation?"

"I think we need to have it one more time, but not now. Let's just enjoy this moment." He placed his hand on her belly. "This one is definitely a girl."

CHAPTER 69

*C*hristmas Day was a struggle for Georgiana, who had expected Dan to be celebrating by her side.

She woke up cold and miserable with Lady pressing up against her for warmth. It was an effort to get out of bed, and as she switched on the bedside light the bulb blew and she was plunged into darkness again.

She stumbled around until she found her mobile phone and turned on the torch. "Bloody fuse box," she muttered. She made her way downstairs, and opened the cupboard at the back of the kitchen to flip the trip switch. She had to move a few things to get to the fuse box, and as she pulled them out of the way she came across a pile of beautifully wrapped presents with her name on. They were from Dan. He had hidden them there in preparation for Christmas.

She started to cry again. She pulled Lady into her arms and rested her head against her. "I miss him so much," she whispered.

Her mobile rang and she knew it was Dan without even looking. No-one else would call this early on Christmas Day. She ignored the ringing and reached up into the fuse box to get the electricity back on. Only when she was sitting down in the kitchen with a strong coffee did she look at her phone. There was a voicemail from him. She was in two minds whether to listen or not but she couldn't help herself, she wanted to hear his voice.

"I just wanted to wish you a Merry Christmas and tell you I miss you. I miss your beautiful face, your smile, your laughter and your unending zest for life. I know you can't forgive me, but seeing as it's Christmas I thought I'd give it one last try. Call me. It would be so good to hear your voice. I love you. Bye."

Tears ran down her cheeks. She played the message over and over again, fighting her desperation to call him back and tell him that she still loved him.

They sat down to eat at the Manor immediately after the Queen's speech. Hattie had outdone herself with the feast she laid on for them all, and her table decorations were exquisite. Everyone was under strict instructions to make sure Olivia didn't lift a finger all day, and for once she didn't protest.

Sebastian was at the head of the table, with Olivia on his right and Georgiana on his left. They had placed Nicolas at the far end with Constance next to him, and Hattie in the seat nearest the door so she could dash in and out to the kitchen easily. Georgiana busied herself helping Hattie – she was glad of the distraction.

Alexander had been spoilt rotten and overloaded with gifts, most of which would pass him by before he was old enough to understand what to do with them. He was more interested in the fairy lights, decorations on the tree and empty boxes.

Richie and Gillian, and Sebastian's coach Hugh and his wife Alison were also with them for the day, and their revelry more than made up for Georgiana's lack of enthusiasm.

She sloped off home not long after they had finished their lunch. She couldn't fake festive cheer any longer and wanted to be alone. She lit a fire as soon as she got in, poured a large glass of red wine and sat on the rug with her mobile phone in hand. She was tempted to call Dan, but instead she satisfied her craving for him by listening to his message over and over again. "I love you," she whispered into the phone.

She switched on the television and was immediately faced with Orion Powell, mid car chase. It was the Christmas Day blockbuster movie on the BBC, and they would be showing the four other films in the series over the next week. Georgiana changed channels. She couldn't bear to watch him, it hurt too much.

She settled on an old Ella Fitzgerald concert on the arts channel and lay back to listen to her favourite singer. When Ella launched into her rendition of 'Every time we say goodbye' Georgiana gulped back her tears again.

"Pull yourself together," she muttered. "Get over it."

Lady looked at her and wagged her tail in agreement.

"Oh, you think so too?" Georgiana smiled through her tears.

Lady wagged her tail again.

"You're right, of course." She tickled Lady's chin. "You always are, my perfect little girl."

Lady sighed and curled up on Georgiana's lap. She flicked the channel back to Orion Powell and willed herself to watch Dan without crying for the rest of the film.

It was torture, but she was compelled to keep watching. Just having him in her living room, large as life on television, made her feel like she still had a part of him. She wasn't ready to let go just yet.

CHAPTER 70

The sound of his mobile phone ringing over and over again eventually woke Dan from his vodka-induced sleep. He fumbled for it on the bedside table and squinted at the screen to find he had had seventeen missed calls, mostly from Vinnie.

"What?" he barked. He was horribly hungover.

"About time," shouted Vinnie.

"What?" Dan was groggy.

"You've done it!" he yelled.

"Done what?" Dan sat up in bed and rubbed his eyes.

"You've got the nomination. Best actor. So fucking proud of you man," Vinnie laughed.

"Seriously?" Dan was surprised. "Are you for real?"

"Never been more serious in my life. This is awesome news."

"Is it?" Dan sighed.

"Man, you gotta get over it. This is the biggest moment of your career. You need to get it together." Vinnie didn't pull any punches.

"Yeah, yeah," Dan mumbled.

"I'm coming over," Vinnie said. "Get showered, get rid of the stupid beard and get dressed. We've got a press conference to do."

"Okay," Dan replied wearily. He hung up the phone and forced himself to get out of bed. His head was thumping and he felt sick. He peered in the mirror and was shocked at his appearance. His tan had faded and he was pale and drawn. His eyes were dull, and he was in desperate need of a hair-cut. He looked frightful.

Since he and Georgiana had split up, he had retreated into himself. He had lost a tremendous amount of weight and his clothes were hanging off him. He rarely went out preferring to be alone in his wretchedness, and the press had continued to speculate on his state of mind.

Kylie had not yet released the photographs, but that was more down to him telling Georgiana and putting an end to the blackmail threat, than her having a change of heart. He knew they would come out eventually, most likely at a crucial moment in RFC's campaign or his career, but he didn't care. He could handle the attention they would bring, but most importantly, Georgiana could breathe easy knowing she wouldn't be tainted by yet another scandal.

"Georgiana," he muttered. He wondered what she was doing every moment of every day, and spent sleepless nights chastising himself over his stupidity. Christmas had been a wash-out. Friends had invited him over but Dan had refused the invitation – there was nothing to celebrate. His parents had wanted him to join them in London – he declined. He was miserable.

He had watched every second of Georgiana presenting the London International Horse Show from Olympia alongside Clare Balding. She appeared grief-stricken and incredibly fragile, and even though she was trying hard to dazzle, her usual sparkle had all but disappeared.

He knew she had been asked to co-present the BBC Sports Personality of the Year awards and was surprised when he tuned in to find she was nowhere to be seen. Rumours abounded on the internet that she was unwell, or that the BBC had had to replace her at the last minute as she clearly wasn't up to the job in her current state.

Dan scoured the press and online for any mention of her, desperate for any snippet of information that would give him even the tiniest glimmer of hope. Her silence was killing him. He had tried to contact her a million times and had hit a brick wall at every turn, even on Christmas Day when he thought she might have been in touch.

Sebastian was away and not returning his messages, and Olivia had replied to a text asking him to give Georgiana some more time and not to get in touch again. He had no-one else to turn to.

He looked in the mirror again and sighed. Vinnie was right. He was a mess, and it was time to sort himself out before his career went the same way as his love life.

"You're a bloody actor," he muttered. "Get your game face on."

An hour later, he was in the Beverly Wiltshire hotel in the middle of a throng of journalists, there to discuss his nomination. The movie had made it onto the Best Film shortlist, and his director was up for the top gong in his category, as well as Cara getting the nod for actress in a leading role. Dan turned on the charm, laughed and joked, and generally gave an air of confidence that put an end to any speculation about his mental health.

He posed for photographs with Cara, who had decided it was high time she came out of the closet and dragged her girlfriend Tammy to the proceedings. The media went crazy for the story and Dan managed to slip away quietly during the pandemonium.

He knew he had television commitments that evening - The Late Late Show with fellow Brit James Cordon – but he wanted to go home and escape the madness that had accompanied his nomination. It was just the beginning of the awards season, and he would have to face the whirlwind of parties, lunches and press interviews on his own – never mind the actual Oscars ceremony. Without Georgiana, it would mean nothing.

CHAPTER 71

*A*ndrea and Peter, Tom and Susie, Georgiana, Peppy, Hattie and Olivia gathered for Sebastian's pow-wow in the drawing room of Appleton Manor at seven o'clock.

"We're here because we've got a mole," he announced. "I have my suspicions, but we should plant some false information and watch where it leads us."

"Are you thinking the same person as I am?" Tom asked Sebastian. "Lucinda?"

"She's horrible enough," Andrea replied. "And she's not the biggest fan of the Bloom family, as we all know."

"We always turn down her dinner invitations," Olivia said. "And Sebastian has embarrassed her on several occasions in public."

"Do you really think she would do that?" Susie asked. "I mean, it's her village too. Why would she want to encourage the development?"

"She's probably got her eye on Wyatt," Georgiana replied. "She's always been very interested in anything to do with him. Wouldn't surprise me if they were in cahoots."

"I've had the team in New York digging for dirt on Clayton, but they can't find much that would be of any use yet," Sebastian replied. "Trust me, these guys are that good. If there's something to find they'll find it."

"What's the plan?" Peter asked.

"Andrea," Sebastian smiled at her. 'You're going to purposely feed Lucinda some duff information tomorrow and we'll see what happens."

"What?" Andrea cried. "Why me? She'll know I'm lying."

"That's precisely why it has to be you," Sebastian replied. "She'll never suspect you in a million years. The rest of us don't stand a chance."

"You'll be fine," Peter reassured his wife.

"Just because the amended plans are pending approved, it doesn't mean we've lost the fight yet," Sebastian continued. "I'm convinced Edward would have put in a back door somewhere. He loved The Riverside more than anything else in the world."

"Do you think it's time to find out what Emily knows?" Georgiana asked Olivia.

"She wouldn't tell me, not now." Olivia shook her head.

"You could try asking," Georgiana replied. "It's for the greater good."

Olivia sighed. "Ok. Fine. I'll get in touch with her tomorrow. But I can't promise anything."

They talked tactics a while longer, and Sebastian briefed Andrea on her important role in outing the mole before he called the meeting to a close.

"Who wants a drink?" he asked. "And there's food in the dining room. Hattie's prepared a casserole, so dig in."

"Not for us thanks," Susie replied. "We've got to get back to the pub. And we left Dee Dee babysitting."

Tom and Susie said their goodbyes, and the rest of the group descended on the dining room and devoured Hattie's delicious stew whilst continuing to debate the issues that faced the RFC.

It was past midnight when Sebastian saw Peter, Andrea and Peppy off. Olivia had gone to bed already, and Georgiana left immediately after supper.

Sebastian walked into his study and sat down in front of his laptop. He sent an email to the head of the investigation team in America.

Donny,

As I suspected, the rest are in agreement that there are greater forces at work. I have attached a list of people you need to look into. Please pay particular attention to Lucinda Walton-Smythe - one of my neighbours - and a chap called Saul Bianchi. He is my wife's ex and a really nasty piece of work. He could be behind this, things didn't end well between them.

I'm now convinced that this is a personal attack, and I need you to get to the bottom of it quickly, no matter what the cost.

Time is running out on The Riverside development. We have to produce solid evidence if we have any hope.

I have wire-transferred your retainer. I expect a daily report on your progress.

Regards,

Sebastian Bloom

He pressed send, closed the laptop and headed up to bed.

CHAPTER 72

*G*eorgiana returned to work in mid-January, flying out to Melbourne for the Australian Open tennis. In her time off she had learned how to put on a brave face and fool everyone around her into believing she was fine. Underneath the surface, she was still heartbroken.

Reunited with John McEnroe, she threw herself into presenting the coverage to the public back home and kept herself busy away from the stadium. She visited old friends from school who had emigrated, and explored the city's shops and markets in her down time. In the evenings, she dined with the BBC team or had room service.

Gerry had refused to allow her to wallow. "I know you better than most love, you can't fool me. But I'm not letting you sit in your room for the next two weeks. At least come to the party tonight?"

The last thing she felt like doing was attending the players' party, but it was easier to agree than to have Gerry pestering her every five minutes. She dressed casually in a shift and sandals, and allowed Gerry to drag her to the event and ply her with champagne.

She was a little tipsy when she was approached by Jackson Jones, an American tennis player who consistently featured in the top five of the ATP world rankings.

"Hey," he drawled. "You look real pretty tonight Georgiana."

"Maybe you should tell your girlfriend that," she hiccoughed.

"Ex-girlfriend," he shrugged his shoulders. "How about you and I have a bit of fun? Can I buy you a drink?"

"Sure. It's free, but why not?" She glanced him up and down. He was incredibly handsome and quite charming.

An hour later she found herself outside her hotel room with Jackson. "Can I come in?" he asked.

"Yep." She walked inside and kicked off her shoes. She bent down to open the mini bar, and as she stood up Jackson pulled her towards him and started to kiss her. She was too weak to stop him and it felt good to be in a man's arms again. He moved from her lips to her neck and started to unzip her dress.

"I've always had a thing for you," he grunted. Her dress fell to the floor and he immediately seized upon her breasts, undoing the clasp of her bra with one hand and caressing her with the other.

She closed her eyes and all she could see was Dan's face. "No," she cried, and pushed him away.

"What?" Jackson exclaimed. "I thought you wanted this?"

"I'm sorry," she croaked. "I didn't mean to lead you on." She reached for her robe and sat on the edge of the bed. "I'm miserable, and I'm still in love with Dan."

Jackson sat down beside her and put a friendly arm around her shoulder. "Don't worry about it. I'm sorry if I pushed you into it."

"No," she spluttered. "You didn't push me at all. Please don't think that. You're lovely. Let's just chalk this up to a drunken mistake and move on. Is that ok?"

"Sure thing." He stood up and bent to kiss her cheek. "He's one hell of a lucky guy. See you tomorrow."

After he had gone, she ran a bath and sat in it for hours, crying and admonishing herself for almost making a huge mistake with Jackson. He was a great guy, but he wasn't Dan. She was lonely and miserable, and having a one-night-stand wasn't going to make her pain go away.

She made more of an effort to be charming and bubbly for the rest of the tournament, and received praise from her boss for being 'back to her best'. She was far from it.

From Australia, she went directly to Bordeaux for the equestrian FEI World Cup show jumping, and found that spending time around her beloved horses and like-minded people made her feel a little better. She enjoyed interviewing the riders, many of whom she knew well, and it was refreshing to be in the company of professional sportsmen and women who were as down to earth as she was.

"Shovelling shit kind of grounds you," one of them told her. She resolved to spend more time riding when she was home.

She had a day at home before heading to PyeongChang for the Winter Olympics. She had never been to South Korea, and was excited to be part of the BBC presenting team for the two and a half weeks they would be there. Once again, Gerry had been sent to babysit her.

"Seriously?" she laughed. "Don't you ever go home?"

"If you'd take a bloody break then I would," he joked. "This is going to be a lot of work but really great fun. Enjoy it. Go and watch some events – the ski-cross is brilliant."

"I've had a break," she smiled. "And I don't cry as soon as I wake up every day now."

"You're looking better, and the camera is loving you again, so you've definitely found your on-screen mojo," Gerry replied.

His words gave her encouragement, and each day she found she was getting back to her old self. She laughed more and even managed to crack a few jokes. She enjoyed working most with Graham Bell and Ed Leigh – the BBC's ski and snowboarding experts. Their love of alpine sports was obvious and their enthusiasm infectious. It lifted her spirits for the entire time they were there.

One day Graham and Ed dragged her out onto the slopes for a bit of fun. She hadn't skied for a few years, but soon found her snow legs and had an exhilarating afternoon bombing down black runs and letting loose. As they thawed out in front of a roaring log fire in a bar drinking glühwein, she realised she hadn't thought about Dan for most of the day.

The next morning, she bounced into the studio to record her segment, full of energy for the first time in months.

"Ah," Gerry raised an eyebrow. "You're back then?"

She grinned. "Yeah. Kind of. It's time I got out of this funk and started living again."

"Thank Christ for that," Gerry sighed. "I've really missed you getting me into trouble with your cheeky quips."

"Well, in that case I'd better up my game," she laughed. "Can't have you disappointed. You might give me a crappy camera angle."

She made the most of the rest of the games, and by the time she landed in England she was back on track. She still missed Dan but she was no longer angry. She had let go of the hurt as she found it just caused her more pain. Her heart was still broken, but she had absolute faith that it would mend - one day.

hilst Georgiana was in South Korea, the final planning meeting took place in Fiddlebury on a bitterly cold and rainy night.

"Full permission granted." Keith Williams announced the decision of the FAB planning committee with a look of complete terror on his face. He stood back and cringed, waiting for the backlash to come at him with both barrels.

"Are you fucking kidding me?" Sebastian yelled. "Bloody crooks, the lot of you."

"I beg your pardon?" Keith Williams scowled at Sebastian. "I don't like what you're alluding to Mr Bloom. Are you saying we've been bought off?"

"If the cap fits," Sebastian growled and stormed out of the council offices.

"You can't do this," Dee Dee shrieked.

"You rotten bastards," Peter bellowed.

"We're doomed," Marjorie Rose squeaked.

Peppy walked towards the stage and waggled her finger in Keith's face. "We'll be appealing. You mark my words. This whole thing stinks of corruption, and I'm not going to stop digging until I find something. Be afraid Mr Williams. Be very afraid."

She strode out after Sebastian and joined the other members of the RFC outside the offices in the freezing cold, all talking at once and bemoaning their misfortune.

"Let's get back to the pub and break the bad news." Peppy took charge. Sebastian was too angry for words, and the rest of them were in complete shock.

Once they were inside the warmth of the pub with a stiff drink in hand, the reality of what had just happened started to sink in.

"Well, that's that then," Devon moaned.

"It's outrageous," James Jenner grumbled. "There must be something we can do?"

"Appeal," Tom sighed. "They have to agree to an appeal, but we're going to need a lawyer. This is all a bit too complicated for Peter and me to handle now."

"I'll sort the lawyer out." Sebastian ran his hands through his hair in exasperation. "We're not beaten yet."

"I just can't believe it. Even after all the publicity we've had so far." Andrea was mystified. "How have they given permission? It's just not right."

"I'll get on to my lawyer in the morning. He'll be able to recommend someone to take us through the appeal process. Nothing we can do till then." Sebastian downed the remnants of his drink and slammed out of the pub.

"There's something not right about this," Tom muttered.

"Oh, you think so?" Peppy sniped.

"Let's not argue amongst ourselves darlings," Patrick interjected. "Kiss and make up."

"Sorry," Peppy was contrite. "Didn't mean to snap. I'm just at a bit of a loss as to what to do."

Tom smiled. "It's okay. We're all pissed off. Like Sebastian said, nothing we can do till tomorrow so let's have another drink, on me."

When Sebastian stormed into the manor Olivia didn't need to ask how the meeting had gone.

"Can we appeal?" she asked as he poured himself a scotch. "Yes, thank God." He slumped into a chair at the kitchen table. "I'll sort it out tomorrow before I go."

"Don't you think you should let someone else take the lead and get back to golf?" Olivia was concerned he was spending too much time fighting Athos, to the detriment of his career.

"I'm playing the next two weeks, aren't I?" he snapped.

"Fine. Be like that." Olivia stomped out of the room and slammed the door behind her.

She went to bed alone after giving Alexander his late feed and waited for Sebastian to come up. Three hours later he crept in beside her and put his arms around her.

"Sorry," he said gruffly.

"You're a dick." She turned around to face him. "But I love you, anyway. Can you just try not to take your bad mood out on me, please?"

"Are you going to be ok when I'm away?" He pulled her closer.

"I'll be fine. I've got Hattie and Alexander to look after me. Just go and play golf, get back in the zone before you miss another Major."

"Fine," he grumbled. "I'll go and earn my keep, but I can't say I'm all that enthused about it right now. Did you get hold of Georgiana, by the way?"

Olivia yawned. "Yeah. Spoke to her briefly. She sounds a lot happier."

"She'll get over him eventually." Sebastian kissed her. "Get some sleep."

"I'd never get over losing you," Olivia muttered as she drifted off.

"You won't have to. I promise." He fell asleep with her in his arms.

CHAPTER 74

*I*t had been a non-stop whirlwind of parties, interviews, luncheons and special events for Dan from the moment he received his nomination. He spent much of February in a tuxedo and insisting on taking Cara as his plus one to most of the events. That way he wouldn't be seen with anyone he could be romantically linked with, and it worked for Cara as Tammy was away in China.

Even though Georgiana still haunted his dreams, he was so busy he found himself getting through the days without being hit with bouts of depression or anger. Cara's insight into Georgiana had been a revelation. She was able to make him see her point of view. When he raged that she should have believed him, Cara pointed out that she had no reason to, only his say-so. She was blunt and a realist, but a good friend who was determined to help him get back to his best.

Hosted by the Academy of Motion Picture Arts and Sciences' governors, the official Oscar nominees luncheon was held in the second week of February at noon in the Beverly Hilton ballroom. A cocktail hour kicked things off where Dan mingled with his fellow nominees, after which the Academy president delivered her welcome and introduced the producers of this year's ceremony.

Bob Tasker and Rob Goldsmith jumped onto the stage to outline the theme of the show and hand out some tips. "Try not to get political, it doesn't go down great with the wider public," Rob said. "And if you win, you've got forty-five seconds before the orchestra starts playing you off the stage. No exceptions."

Bob continued. "We need your help to keep the pacing of the show on track. Get to the stage as fast as you can, and remember the best speeches are the ones that come straight from the heart and not hastily scribbled on the back of a napkin – you're gonna have a billion people in over two hundred and twenty-five countries watching you."

After lunch, the nominees – all one hundred and fifty-five of them – gathered for an official class photo and were handed their much-coveted Oscar nominee sweatshirts.

Dan escaped as quickly as he could and jumped into a waiting car. He was desperate to get home to watch Georgiana host her first show from the Winter Olympics. He flopped down on the sofa, switched on the television and opened a bottle of wine.

His heart skipped a beat when her face popped up on the giant screen. She looked happier and more relaxed than she had when he watched her at the Australian Open.

"I'm thrilled to be part of this awesome team bringing you live coverage from the Winter Olympics in PyeongChang. Tonight, we've got highlights from an incredible first day of ice hockey where our hosts, South Korea, surprised the life out of everyone by beating Canada. CANADA, SERIOUSLY! You'll also be seeing some fabulous figure skating, crazy cross-country, breath taking biathlon and a little luscious luge to whet your appetite. Firstly, let's head over to our dastardly duo who have been hanging with the cool kids at the Halfpipe and Snowboard Cross for a round-up of the day's events."

The coverage cut to Graham Bell and Ed Leigh talking about the highs and lows of the first day on the slopes. Dan pressed rewind and watched Georgiana over and over again until they switched back to her in the studio.

"It gives me great pleasure to introduce my special guest, who really should be out there winning medals, but instead gets to spend his nights with me whilst he recovers from a nasty injury."

The camera panned across the sofa and focused on Hans Zeurling – the world's best skier. He was utterly gorgeous, with the worst reputation.

Dan found himself growling at the television as Hans flirted with Georgiana for the next thirty minutes. They had an on-screen chemistry that made his heart sink - he knew her bosses would play on it, especially if this first night was anything to go by.

The highlights show was coming to a close and Georgiana looked directly into the camera. She paused for a split second and Dan's heart contracted. He felt like she was staring straight at him and it tore him apart.

"That's all from the first day's action here in PyeongChang, but never fear, we'll be back at the same time tomorrow night with a full round-up of day two. Put a reminder in your phones because I don't want to be here alone. It's not polite to stand up a lady." She flashed a dazzling smile into the camera lens.

"You von't be alone," Hans smouldered as he moved into shot and slung an arm around her shoulder. "We're in zis together."

"Fuck off you moron. Get your hands off her." Dan threw a

cushion at the television in anger. Georgiana didn't flinch or try to shrug Hans' hands off her. She smiled at him and signed off.

"It's late back home. Best you get some sleep. Sweet dreams from snowy South Korea."

Dan watched the coverage over and over again, and he just felt worse every time handsome Hans came into shot. He couldn't bear the thought of her with another man.

He switched off the television, picked up the bottle of wine and staggered off to bed to spend another night in hell.

For the next two and a half weeks' he watched Georgiana night after night delivering witty and engaging highlights, and he fell in love with her all over again. She had regained some of her sparkle, looking more and more relaxed every day. There were photographs of her on the internet from nights out with Graham and Ed where she looked almost happy again.

Her broadcasting style had enchanted the nation, and she was winning rave reviews for injecting humour, youth and vitality into the coverage.

Dan drank in every second of her screen time and prayed that she would one day forgive him.

CHAPTER 75

*S*usie was at the Club finalising the new pub menu with Chef Bernard when she spotted Lucinda walking into the lounge. "I'll just be a minute, Chef." She made a bee-line for her table.

"All alone, Lucinda?" Susie asked.

"Yes, just little old me," she replied. "I have a few emails to catch up on and Godfrey is driving me insane. I just had to get out of the house."

"May I?" Susie indicated to a chair.

Lucinda glared at her. "If you must. I'm assuming you have something relevant to say, or at least interesting."

Susie smiled through gritted teeth. "Just a little catch-up to see how you're getting on with the RFC stuff we gave you to do. Haven't seen anything in the way of meeting minutes or collated reports, which is what you said you'd do."

"And that's exactly why I'm here, for some peace and quiet." Lucinda glared at her again. "Was that all?"

"Err, yes," Susie replied. As she got up to leave she caught a glimpse of Lucinda's laptop and was astonished to see Wyatt Clayton's name at the top of an email. She needed to see more.

The only thing she could think of to separate Lucinda from her computer was to send her drink flying. She pretended to trip up as she backed away from the table and knocked the glass directly into Lucinda's lap.

"Oh, for God's sake," she shrieked. "Now look at me." She stood up and stormed off towards the locker room.

Susie looked around furtively and saw she was alone. She clicked on the email Lucinda was writing to Wyatt.

> *Dear Wyatt,*
>
> *You're not going to like this, but there seems to be some kind of important find at the site where the hotel is going. Sebastian has called in the Natural History Museum and there's going to be a dig to see what they can uncover. They're hoping to find something that will stop your development and have applied for a temporary ban on works pending investigation. This isn't general knowledge yet, but as I have infiltrated the core group they trust me to be on their side.*
>
> *Still very much looking forward to spending the night with you.*
>
> *Best wishes,*
> *Lucinda x*

Susie smirked. Lucinda had fallen for Andrea's lie and now they had proof who the mole was. She quickly forwarded the email to herself before deleting any evidence of her tampering with the laptop.

She scuttled away before Lucinda returned and hid in Chef

Bernard's office whilst she sent the email to Sebastian and Peppy.

Got some evidence. Let's take the miserable old cow down!!!

Sebastian was driving Olivia to the clinic for their first scan when the email came through. Olivia clicked it open and read it out to him.

"I bloody told you it was her," he growled.

"And I didn't refute that. I just said we needed to be sure before confronting her, and now we are." Olivia rolled her eyes. "Can we not talk about her please. This is a special day."

"Yep. You're right. Sod her." Sebastian reached across and put his hand on Olivia's belly. "Today is all about this little one."

Doctor Khan met them on arrival. "Well, I didn't think I'd be seeing you again this soon."

"It's his fault." Olivia pointed at Sebastian.

Sebastian chuckled. "Takes two to tango, darling." He shook Doctor Khan's hand. "Let's hope this one's plain sailing, eh?"

"Well let's have a little look at the baby and then we can talk about any concerns you have. There's no denying Alexander's birth was traumatic for you Olivia, but we won't let that happen again." Doctor Khan opened the door and ushered them into the room.

"I'll let you get changed. Back in a jiffy." He closed the door behind him and Olivia slipped into a hospital gown. She hopped up onto the bed and lay back against the pillow.

"Here we are again." She smiled nervously and reached for Sebastian's hand. "Are you happy?"

"You have to ask?" Sebastian squeezed her hand. "I'm bloody

ecstatic. I'd have you barefoot and pregnant all the time if I could."

Olivia raised an eyebrow. "You're doing a pretty good job of that already."

Doctor Khan popped his head around the door. "Are we ready to see your baby?"

Olivia nodded and Sebastian flashed a dazzling smile. "Can't wait."

Doctor Khan began to move the ultrasound slowly across her belly. After a minute, he paused and pointed at the screen. "See that?"

Olivia was wide-eyed. She looked at Sebastian in fear.

"What?" she cried. "What's wrong?"

Doctor Khan laughed. "There's nothing wrong. Perhaps this will enlighten you." He increased the volume on the monitor and there it was, as clear as day – two heartbeats.

"Twins?" Sebastian gasped.

"Indeed," Doctor Khan laughed. "Congratulations."

"Two?" Olivia whispered. "One almost killed me – literally. How the hell am I going to give birth to two?" She grabbed Doctor Khan's arm. "I can't do this." She was panicking.

Doctor Khan sat on the bed next to her and patted her hand. "You can do it Olivia, you're strong. I'm going to be keeping a very close eye on you the whole way through this pregnancy, so you needn't worry."

"Can I have a caesarean?" she asked.

"Absolutely," Doctor Khan smiled. "I would have advised that anyway, given what happened with Alexander."

"Two!" Sebastian whistled in amazement. "This is going to be interesting."

"Shall we get a couple of snaps for the family album?" Doctor Khan wiggled the ultrasound wand again until he was able to take a picture of each baby. "I'd like to see you in a month, unless you feel a need to see me before that."

"Ok," Olivia mumbled. She was stunned by the news, almost numb.

She drifted out of the clinic and into the car without saying a word as Sebastian chattered incessantly. His excitement was overwhelming. She started to cry.

Sebastian's face fell. "Aren't you happy darling?"

"Two babies? You're not the one who has to carry them around and give birth to them." She blew her nose on a tissue.

"You heard what Doctor Khan said. They're going to see you through this every step of the way." He wiped away her tears.

"I'm scared." Olivia finally admitted her fear. "What if it happens again?"

"It's not going to happen again. We'll all make sure of that." He tilted her chin upwards and kissed her lips.

"Two," she shook her head again. "Two."

Sebastian laughed. "I guess we'd better get used to it."

CHAPTER 76

Georgiana looked out of the kitchen window as a car pulled up outside the cottage. She had been home for a few days and was lying low. She was exhausted. She had run herself ragged for six straight weeks and wanted some time alone.

Will climbed out of the car and Georgiana went to the door to let him in.

"Hey," she hugged him. "You're one of the few faces I can bear seeing.

Will returned the hug. "You look knackered, Porg."

"Yeah, thanks for that." Georgiana pulled a face at him. "Do you want a drink?"

"Nah, can't stop. Just came to see if you were still alive and to give you this." He handed Georgiana an envelope. "I was in the post office and Marjorie Rose asked me to give it to you when I said I was popping over. She said it has missed the delivery round, or something to that effect. I wasn't really listening. She chewed my ear off for half an hour before I managed to escape."

"Oh, thanks." Georgiana took the envelope and instantly recognised the handwriting. It was from Dan.

"It is from him?" Will asked gently. "Do you still miss him?"

Georgiana sighed. "Every single day. I miss him like crazy and I don't think I'll ever stop loving him, but what's done is done. I can't hold onto that kind of pain."

"On the plus side, it does leave the door open for me," Will grinned.

"Not a chance Abinger," she scoffed. "I love you dearly, but no thanks."

"I'm kidding," he laughed. "I love you too. And besides, I'm having a lot of fun with a certain Ms Granger right now."

"Really?" Georgiana was surprised. "You kept that quiet."

Will shrugged his shoulders. "My love life doesn't have to be broadcast all over the village all the time, you know?"

"But it usually is," Georgiana smirked. "And you love it."

"Yeah, yeah." Will looked at his watch. "Got to go. When are you off again?"

"Thursday. LA," she replied. "I'll be back next Tuesday so let's have a proper catch up then."

"Perfect. Have fun in La La Land." Will jumped into his car and sped off down the driveway.

Georgiana closed the door and walked into the kitchen. She poured herself a large glass of wine before sitting down on the sofa to read the letter. Her hands were shaking as she ripped open the envelope.

Georgiana,

I know you don't want anything to do with me. I've accepted that, no matter how much it breaks my heart.

I had to put pen to paper to thank you for pushing me to do Jigsaw Kids. In a few days, I could be holding the highest honour in my profession and I wouldn't have had that chance if it weren't for you.
I'm devastated that I won't have you by my side, but at least you'll be in my heart because I love you. Always have, always will. Nothing will change that.
If I thought there was an ounce of hope for us, I would move heaven and earth to make things right, but you've given me no indication of that and I have to assume you no longer feel as I do.

All I want is for you to be happy, and as hard as it is for me to say, for you to fall in love again with someone who won't let you down, someone deserving of a woman as amazing as you.

I love you, Georgiana Bloom. You own my heart.
Dan x

She read and re-read the letter several times, with tears cascading down her cheeks.

"Who am I kidding?" she muttered. "I'm not even remotely close to getting over you, Dan Flowers."

CHAPTER 77

$\mathcal{T}$he limo was waiting outside Dan's Hollywood home to take him to the Academy Awards. His personal manager, Ken, was desperately hurrying him along – he was tasked with making sure Dan met his allotted time slot to arrive at the red carpet.

Dan had tussled with finding a date to attend the ceremony with, or going it alone – he opted for the latter. He didn't want to be linked with any other women. His mother was unable to be his plus one - she was looking after his grandmother after a hip replacement - and Cara was attending with Tammy. He didn't think he stood a chance of winning anyway, despite the buzz that had surrounded his deeply emotional performance in a film that had surprised and wowed audiences across the globe.

"Give me a minute," he shouted to Ken.

"We gotta go dude, NOW." Ken bellowed back.

Dan picked up the silver horseshoe cuff links that Georgiana had given him when they were still together and attached them to his sleeves. He may not have her by his side, but at least he had a little piece of her with him for the most important night of his life.

"About time," Ken said when Dan appeared in the hall. "You ok?"

"Yeah," Dan smiled. "I'd be better if Georgiana was with me, but she's not so I've got to get on with it."

"This is the biggest night of your life. Enjoy it, man." Ken steered him outside and into the limo. He climbed in beside Dan. "How are you feeling?"

Dan shrugged his shoulders. "Excited, nervous, terrified. Not sure which."

"I know you didn't want to do this on your own buddy," Ken replied. "But it's not like you were short of offers."

"I don't want Georgiana to see me with anyone else," Dan stated. "She hates me enough as it is without me parading some vacuous model in her face."

"Ok, I get it," Ken sighed. "Buck up and get your game face on. I'm pretty sure you're gonna win."

Dan snorted. "I'm pretty sure I'm not."

The drive to downtown LA took forever, and was followed by a painstakingly slow-moving procession of celebrities arriving at the theatre at their allotted times.

The sky was turning a dusky pink and the light was fading when he finally stepped out of the car in an explosion of flashbulbs. An enormous cheer went up from the crowd when he smiled and waved. The show's organisers had deliberately given Dan the final 'big name' arrival slot, knowing it would keep the television viewers watching right till the end.

The giant spotlight in the sky fixed Dan under its glare whilst he smiled and posed for the obligatory red carpet photographs in front of the enormous Oscar statuette. He was still a bundle of nerves inside, but he exuded a well-practised air of confidence and excitement that belied his inner turmoil.

Whatever direction he turned in, he was greeted warmly by stars of film and television with congratulations being offered as if he had already won. Maddie appeared by his side and guided him to his first television interview with Ryan Seacrest for E! Entertainment News.

"Hey, good to see you man," Ryan said when Dan approached. "Congratulations on your nomination."

"Thanks," Dan smiled. "I'm still pinching myself. It doesn't feel real."

Ryan laughed. "Well it is real. Real huge! There's so much buzz around you, man. That's gotta give you confidence?"

"There are a lot of great actors in my category, all very deserving of the award. I'm honoured to be nominated alongside them, although admittedly I feel somewhat of an imposter."

"You deserve it man," Ryan slapped him on the back. "The girls in the studio wanna know who you're wearing."

"Damian de Landre," Dan replied as the camera zoomed in on his tuxedo. "And some very special cufflinks that I'm hoping will be my good luck charm."

Maddie grabbed his elbow to move him on to his next interview. "Looks like I'm wanted elsewhere," he said to Ryan.

"Have a great night.' Ryan was already onto his next interview.

Dan slowly moved down the red-carpet waving and smiling, pausing for interviews with broadcasters from around the world.

He posed for photographs with Cara and their director, edging ever close to the theatre entrance. He had instructed Maddie to make sure the BBC got an interview with him.

"BBC now," she said. "And you'll never guess who's doing it."

CHAPTER 78

Georgiana was waiting on the red carpet for Hollywood's elite to begin their ascent towards her into the Dolby Theatre for the biggest awards ceremony in the movie calendar. The air was charged with an excitement that was infused with the oppressive heat and humidity of Los Angeles in the grip of an unseasonal heat wave.

She had selected a vintage Versace dress in a shimmering silver silk fabric that poured over her skin like an ethereal waterfall, with some equally exquisite towering heels from Jimmy Choo. Her jewellery was simple and understated – the diamond and platinum heart-shaped locket that Dan had given her, some diamond studs in her ears, and a matching bracelet. Her hair was loose in waves down her back. The overall effect was stunning. She could outshine most of the world's best actresses, but her mind was only on one thing – Dan.

This was the first time she would see him since they had split up, and since his letter that she received just a few days ago. She was a bundle of nerves. She still missed him and definitely still loved him, but she hadn't yet been able to forgive him. Sebastian had told her that he believed Dan's story, but she needed proof and as yet, none had surfaced.

After her successful stint in Australia and at the Winter Olympics she was once again the shining light of the BBC, which is why they had sent her to LA to cover the Academy Awards. She had wrestled with the idea for a few days before agreeing to do it, and now here she was, about to see and interview her Oscar-nominated ex fiancée – who she absolutely was still in love with - and she was petrified.

"Right, this is it guys," the producer, Jen Pearson, announced in her ear. "They're starting to arrive."

Georgiana took a deep breath and gulped back her fear. She suddenly felt desperately out of her depth. She was a sports reporter – what did she know about entertainment?

She closed her eyes and breathed slowly in and out, and when she opened them Tom Cruise was standing in front of her. She sprang into action.

"Tom, thank you for talking to us, you're live with the BBC. How excited are you for your nomination tonight?" Tom had been nominated alongside Dan in the best actor category – direct competition. She talked to him for two more minutes before he was whisked away to another interview.

The guests came thick and fast after that. Dame Helen Mirren stopped by to say hello, Russell Crowe and Nicole Kidman threw her a few decent sound bites, and Jennifer Lawrence was happy to chat about her third best actress nomination. She interviewed Kate Winslet – nominated for yet another Oscar in a best supporting actress role, Ben Affleck – up for a producer gong, Matt Damon – because they had met at the boxing and got on well, Tom Hanks, Hugh Jackman and a host of other stars. She was exhausted.

The studio back in the UK was running some Oscar film clips, giving Georgiana a break. She bent down to take a sip of water and gasped as she saw Kylie Harrison sashaying up to her, bold as brass, expecting to be interviewed. Georgiana was about to refuse when her mobile phone bleeped. She glanced at it and saw there was a message from Sebastian, the beginning of which was displayed on the home screen.

READ THIS NOW!!!!!

She ignored Kylie pouting at her and opened the message. It had a video attachment. She clicked on it and her eyes almost popped out of her head. She watched for a few more seconds and then looked up at Kylie with a wry smile.

She turned the screen to show Kylie the contents of the video.

"Would you like to be interviewed now?" Georgiana smirked.

Kylie was speechless. Georgiana had shown her a clip – a second rate pornographic film from her early days in Hollywood that she thought she had buried. It had taken Sebastian's security team months to unearth it.

"I'm just going to get this out to a few major news outlets," Georgiana smirked at her again. "I'd disappear pretty sharpish if I were you. It ain't going to be pretty."

"You wouldn't dare, you little bitch," Kylie hissed.

"You tried to ruin my life." Georgiana accessed her contacts and attached the clip to an email. She held her phone in front of Kylie and pressed send.

Kylie shrieked in horror and bolted back down the red carpet away from the theatre.

Georgiana giggled. Sebastian's timing couldn't have been better.

Another text came through from him.

I have proof. Forgive him.

Suddenly an explosion of noise heralded the arrival of yet another major star. Georgiana peered through the throng of celebrities and her stomach flipped when she saw it was Dan. She had prepared for this moment, readying herself for the pain she would feel, but now, seeing him, all she could think about was being in his arms again.

It took forever for him to reach her. He was being steered to interviews by Maddie every which way, and stopping to chat to fellow actors and former co-stars. He looked dazzling in his tuxedo and was brimming with excitement. She could see how animated and keyed up he was. Maddie whispered something in his ear and he swung round in shock.

He lunged towards Georgiana and brushed his lips on the corner of her mouth. A gesture so intimate she had to grasp his arm for support.

"Why are you here?" He whispered in her ear, aware that almost every camera in the vicinity had trained their lenses on them.

"We're live," she spluttered. "Got to interview you."

"Can we talk after?" Dan pleaded with her.

She nodded her head in agreement. It was so good to see him. Her feelings had not diminished in any way - in fact they were stronger than ever.

She turned to the camera and composed herself. "We've just managed to grab the man of the moment, our very own Dan Flowers who's almost a dead cert for taking home the best actor gong." She smiled at him. "So, how are you feeling?"

"Much better now I'm with you." He beamed into the camera.

"I meant about your nomination," she giggled.

"I know," he smiled. "But this has just eclipsed any award I could ever win."

Her producer groaned. She had been warned about Georgiana's propensity to go off script and that she was a potential liability, but the bosses loved her anyway. She growled into Georgiana's ear. "Interview. NOW."

She shook herself into action. "How about you tell the Great British public what's going through your mind. You're about to step inside the Oscars. THE OSCARS!"

"I don't think it would be appropriate to tell everyone back home what's going on in my head right now." He grinned, never taking his eyes off her.

She was melting inside and fighting to retain her professionalism. "Your performance in Jigsaw Kids was gripping. The intensity of emotion you brought to your character was so deep I almost drowned watching it."

"You watched it?" He was surprised.

"I did. You were awesome," she breathed.

"Would you stop making eyes at him and do a proper bloody interview." Jen grumbled into her ear again.

"I wouldn't have done it if it you hadn't encouraged me. If I win tonight it will be because of you." Dan was serious.

"Oh," she squeaked. Her face flushed. "I hardly think so," she spluttered.

"You look beautiful, by the way." Dan looked her up and down slowly.

"Oh," she repeated. "So, do you."

"I'm not sure I could be described as beautiful, but thanks," Dan laughed.

Georgiana didn't know where to look.

Maddie indicated it was time to move on. The ceremony was about to begin and he needed to be in his seat.

He kissed her cheek again and she melted against him. He brushed his hand against hers and her knees almost buckled. "Promise you'll see me after?"

"Er, yes of course," she stuttered. "Thank you for stopping to talk to the BBC. Everyone back home is rooting for you tonight."

"And what about you?" he chuckled.

"Especially me," she smiled and blew him a kiss.

Dan walked towards the entrance of the theatre shaking his head. He couldn't believe what had just happened. Firstly, he had not expected Georgiana to be there – she was a sports reporter – and when she had greeted him so warmly he was stunned. He glanced over his shoulder to make sure he hadn't imagined her and saw her waving her mobile at him.

He reached into his pocket and pulled out his phone to find a series of texts she had just sent. The first told him to watch the video. The second said she was truly sorry and the third spelt out three little words.

I love you x

He stopped dead in his tracks, clearly watching the clip she had sent him. He turned and ran back towards her and threw his arms around her.

"Seriously?" he cried.

"Yes. Seriously," she giggled. "Put me down and go and win your Oscar."

He grabbed her hand. "You're coming with me."

"I can't." She pointed at the camera. "I'm working."

Dan looked around and raised his eyebrows. The red carpet was practically empty. He had been one of the last to arrive and the ceremony was imminent. The show's producer was frantically trying to get Dan inside before it started.

"Seems there's no one left to interview. No excuses, babe." He led her inside the theatre with the producer running ahead screaming into his walkie talkie for someone to rearrange the seating to accommodate Georgiana.

"Sorry Jen," Georgiana told her producer as she removed her microphone pack. "I have to be with him."

"You better bloody well get an exclusive if he wins or I'll string you up," she replied.

They made it into their seats with seconds to spare. She giggled when she realised she was sitting next to Brad Pitt and his mother.

"This is really weird," she whispered to Dan.

"What's going on? Where did the video come from?" He spoke in a low voice.

"Sebastian," she replied. "I'm so sorry I didn't believe you."

"You're sorry?" He was incredulous.

"Yeah. Now shut up and let's enjoy this. We'll talk later." She squeezed his hand.

"Kiss me and I'll say no more." He bent his head towards her.

Georgiana reached up and lightly kissed his lips. "I love you," she said. "I never stopped loving you."

"Sod the Oscars," Dan hissed. "Let's go."

"No way!" she exclaimed. "This is the biggest night of your career. It's exciting."

"So are you," he groaned.

The ceremony dragged on for what seemed like an eternity. All Georgiana wanted was to be alone with Dan, and she knew he felt the same, but they couldn't leave yet. It was almost time for his category. Last year's best actress, Emma Stone, stepped onto the stage and introduced each actor in the running for the award.

When it was Dan's turn, Georgiana gripped his hand and murmured words of encouragement under her breath. They watched a clip from his film and he smiled broadly when he was applauded for his performance.

A hush descended on the theatre when Emma Stone held up the envelope to announce the winner. Georgiana closed her eyes and held her breath. Dan's hand felt clammy around hers and he was shaking.

"And the Oscar goes to…"

CHAPTER 79

"*O*oh, doesn't he look handsome?" Dee Dee exclaimed when Dan appeared on screen.

"This is going to be interesting," Will muttered as he watched Dan step forward to greet Georgiana on the red carpet.

The residents of Appleton Vale were crammed into the pub to watch the red-carpet coverage and all eyes were fixated on the screen, captivated by Georgiana and Dan's interview.

"She's so getting laid later," Jem shouted. Josh and Freddie fell about laughing.

"I think it's lovely," Andrea sighed. "Those two are meant to be together."

"Look at her dress," Marjorie Rose gazed at the screen. "She's beautiful."

"Hush," Jane shouted. "I can't hear."

Tom turned up the volume and they watched as Georgiana and Dan flirted their way through the interview. They were proud of their girl and of the man they had taken into their hearts in the short time he had been in Appleton Vale.

"That's it folks," Tom shouted. "Anyone who wants to stay up and watch the actual ceremony is welcome up at the Manor. Sebastian has set up a giant screen in the barn and I'm fairly sure you won't go short of a drink there."

They whooped and cheered and began to file out into the night to make their way up to the Manor. No one was going to miss the moment when Dan won the Oscar - if he won.

By the time the ceremony started, the barn was packed full of expectant villagers settling in for a long night – it would be four o'clock in the morning before Dan's award was announced. Hattie had prepared a colossal buffet that could feed an army, and there was beer, wine, and dozens of bottles of champagne chilling in anticipation of victory.

Enormous beanbags and cushions littered the floor ready to welcome weary guests, and scores of lanterns hung from the rafters, casting a warm glow around the barn. Sebastian had erected a giant screen for the occasion and installed surround-sound for the full effect.

A few of the major awards were handed out earlier on in the ceremony and they cheered as Kate Winslet won for best supporting actress, and again for a handful of British people they had never heard of for wardrobe, lighting, cinematography and foreign language awards.

"Looks like the Brits are cleaning up," Peter shouted and raised his glass. "A good omen?"

"Ooh, I hope so," Marjorie Rose squeaked.

Around three o'clock Sebastian went back to the Manor to wake Olivia. She didn't want to miss Dan's award but had been too exhausted to stay up all night.

There were more cheers when Cara won the best actress award, and they all agreed it must mean that Dan would win too. And then it was time. The barn fell silent and all eyes fixed expectantly at the screen. Sebastian made sure everyone had a glass of champagne ready to toast Dan if he scooped the award.

"This is it," he shouted.

Emma Stone held up the envelope. "And the Oscar goes to…"

CHAPTER 80

"Oh my God," Georgiana screamed. She jumped out of her seat with the rest of the audience and hopped up and down with excitement. She pulled Dan to his feet and threw her arms around his neck and kissed him.

"You did it!" she squeaked. "You did it."

"Wow." Dan was stunned. He was rooted to the spot.

"Go on!" Georgiana pushed him towards the stage. Brad slapped him on the back as he passed, and he was congratulated by a host of other stars including Cara, who was clutching her Oscar. The applause was deafening. It was universally accepted that Dan's performance had been extraordinary and his award was well deserved.

He reached the podium and received his statuette from Emma Stone. He stepped towards the microphone and held his Oscar triumphantly in the air, waiting for the applause to die down.

"Wow." He shook his head and looked at the Oscar in his hand. "I honestly didn't expect to win this. My money was on Tom – if ever a man deserved an Oscar, it's him." He grinned down at the front row where Tom was sitting. "His performance was incredible, as well as those of the other outstanding actors in this category – Jimmy, Javier, Chris, Brian – you guys rock.

"I have so many people to thank for this award. I know we all say it, but this really was a team effort. We had a tiny budget, small cast and very little backing to speak of, but it was a story we all believed in. Jason Paine and Rollo Baxter – you guys put your hearts and souls into the script and gave my character so much depth, I'm glad I could do him justice." He sought out their faces in the crowd and saluted them both.

"Thanks also to Sandy Crane, Pebo Tolesta, Mick Jones, Jerry Goldstein, Chuck Masters, and the guys at MGM for taking our little film and giving it the blockbuster treatment once they knew how good it was. Mary Lewis, Gigi Ramirez, Brad Wood and Randy Krantz – couldn't have done it without you."

He continued. "My delightful co-star Cara Keating was a revelation, and her extraordinary acting made mine better. I'm so happy that she has been recognised tonight for her incredible talent. Thanks, babe." He blew her a kiss. "Thanks also to my team - Vinnie Manolo, Maddie Mitchell, Coby McBride, and especially the long-suffering Ken Kennedy. You've had a tough job over the years keeping me on the straight and narrow, so I hope this is a good enough pay back."

"My Mum and Dad are hopefully watching in London – I love you. Thank you for believing in me and encouraging me to pursue my dreams. Lastly, and most importantly, I want to thank the most beautiful, loving and generous woman I've ever had the good fortune to meet. She read the script for Jigsaw Kids and convinced me I could do it. Without her, I would not be standing here." He looked at Georgiana squirming in her seat and addressed her directly.

"This is for you sweetheart. I love you and I still desperately want to marry you if you'll have me?"

Georgiana nodded her head in agreement and Dan whooped with joy.

In Appleton Vale, the party was in full swing. The moment Dan's name was announced a joyous roar echoed around the barn.

"He did it!' Dee Dee cried.

"Oh, how wonderful," Marjorie Rose squeaked.

Sebastian jumped up on the hay bales and held his glass aloft. "To Dan!" he shouted. "Or should I say my incredibly talented, soon-to-be brother in law."

His phone burst into life. "It's Georgiana," he announced. The room went quiet again and Sebastian put her on speakerphone.

"You're on with the whole village," Sebastian laughed down the phone. "Congrats sis. How's Dan? Still in shock?"

"It was totally awesome," Georgiana cried. "Did you see it?"

"Of course we did," everyone shouted at the phone.

"Dan and I are back on," she squealed excitedly.

"We know," everyone shouted again. Georgiana laughed.

"Can't stop," she shouted. "It's totally mad here. I'll call you tomorrow."

Dan's victory had injected a second wind into the villagers and the party continued until the sun began to rise from behind the vale.

CHAPTER 81

"**Y**ou asshole," Kylie screamed down the phone. "I'm ruined."

"You knew the risks babe," replied the voice from the other end.

"How did I know they'd find it? You said you dealt with it," she growled. "What am I gonna do?"

"That's your issue."

"What about us?" Kylie was stunned.

"There is no us. Don't call me again."

The phone went dead and when she redialled she found her number blocked. The next call that came through was from her publicist.

"What the fuck?" she screamed at Kylie.

"Deal with it," Kylie bellowed down the phone and hung up. She quickly switched it off, knowing it would be ringing off the hook now her sordid sex tape was out in the open.

She buried her face in her hands and cried. Not only was she caught up in a sex scandal, but also the truth about what she had done to Dan was about to come out. Her career was over and her reputation in tatters, and the man she had done it for had just rejected her in the most cruel and callous way.

Wyatt was furious. He hurled his glass against the wall and watched it smash into tiny pieces. He had just suffered a call with his investor who had been enraged that their plan hadn't worked.

He turned up the volume on the television. The post-Oscars coverage was in full flow and Dan and Georgiana were getting the lions' share of media attention. Dan was being pulled from one interview to the next and Georgiana was by his side basking in his glory. He mentioned her time and time again until Wyatt could listen no more.

He sat back down at his desk and stared out onto the Manhattan skyline. His life had suddenly become complicated and he wasn't used to feeling out of control. His investor was turning the pressure screws, Ashley was refusing to go quietly – or at all, and The Riverside development was stalling at every hurdle. He'd also failed to trap Georgiana in his web and it was starting to send him a little crazy.

CHAPTER 82

*G*eorgiana and Dan attended the Governor's Ball for less than an hour. It was in the same building as the theatre and it was expected that every winner be present. Finally, they had twenty minutes alone together in the back of the limo on the way to the Vanity Fair party.

She reached for his hand. "I should have believed you. I'm sorry."

"You're sorry?" Dan spluttered. "You have nothing to be sorry for. I broke your heart. You're allowed to hate me."

"But you didn't do anything wrong. I could never hate you, and you didn't quite break it," she said. "Just a fracture. It's well on the way to being mended."

"Seriously?" Dan grinned.

"Yes, if you're very careful with me," she smiled.

"I'm so bloody sorry," he gushed. "I'll never let anything like that happen again. I'll get a bodyguard if I have to."

Georgiana laughed. "That might be a wise idea."

"And you're sure you still want to marry me?" He could hardly contain his joy.

"If you can put up with a neurotic lunatic like me, then yes, of course. Ask me again."

"Marry me?" He kissed her hand.

"Love to," she replied. "Now let's party!"

"I'd rather take you to bed." Dan nuzzled her neck. "This really is a beautiful dress." He ran his hands across the fabric and stroked the outline of her breasts. Georgiana gasped and arched towards him.

"Glad I still have the ability to make you squirm," he laughed. "We've got five minutes. Come here and kiss me."

Georgiana leant into him and melted when his lips met hers. They were still locked together when they finally pulled up outside the party, having been waved through a dozen checkpoints. Everyone knew who Dan Flowers was.

They climbed out of the car and ascended the steps of The Wallis where a lively mariachi band was playing for the guests. They were ushered through a metal detector before entering the world's best party, where A-list guests were bumping elbows and stepping on couture gowns as they hugged and greeted each other.

There was a roar of approval when Dan and Georgiana were spotted, and they spent the next hour receiving congratulations on both his award and their re-engagement. Steven Spielberg, Reese Witherspoon, Meryl Streep, Mick Jagger, Christian Bale, Orlando Bloom and James Cordon were amongst the first to offer their best wishes – Dan was the man of the moment and everyone wanted a piece of him.

"Interesting to see how long it will last," he whispered to

Georgiana. He was used to adulation from the film-watching public, but this was a new experience. He was finally being taken seriously as an actor and had now joined the upper echelons of Oscar-winning Hollywood stars. It was an elite group.

They made their way over to a corner booth and were joined by Leo and his date for the evening, along with Cara and Tammy, Kate Winslet and husband Ned, and the film's producer and director with their wives. Every thirty seconds another celebrity floated past offering their congratulations and the champagne flowed long into the night.

At two o'clock they left to head to Madonna's bash at Guy Oseary's estate. Georgiana was exhausted and more than a little tipsy.

"Know what you need?" he said as she leaned against him in the back of the limo.

"You?" she murmured.

"Food. In 'n' Out please," he instructed the driver to take them to the legendary burger joint on Sunset Boulevard - a favourite for post-award-ceremony refuelling. Dan jumped out of the car and walked up to the counter clutching his Oscar and ordered two double-doubles and animal fries. He posed for photographs with the staff and then rushed back to Georgiana who was sneaking a power nap in the back of the car.

She felt better after eating her burger and was revived enough to make an appearance for the queen of pop. "Can we go home after this?" she yawned as they got out of the car.

"That's the plan." Dan slung his arm around her shoulder. "I can't wait much longer to get you naked."

"Are you sure you don't want to stay and celebrate with your friends?"

"No way!" he cried. "I want to take you to bed."

Georgiana grinned sleepily. "Can't wait!"

"Let's go." He dragged her inside. "Sooner we do the rounds the sooner we can get out of here."

The sun was beginning to rise by the time Georgiana and Dan eventually got home. They had been unable to escape Madonna's clutches for several hours, and although they were both dog-tired they were desperate to reaffirm their love for one another. Georgiana kicked off her shoes and slipped out of her dress as soon as they were inside the front door.

She breathed out with relief. "God that was tight."

"Sexy though," Dan grinned. He scooped her up into his arms, carried her upstairs and deposited her on the bed before stripping off his own clothes.

He lay next to her and ran his hands over her skin. "I've missed you so much," he groaned.

"Which bits?" Georgiana teased.

"This bit," Dan kissed her neck. "And this bit." He teased her nipples with his tongue. "And most definitely this bit." He slipped his hand between her legs.

Georgiana moaned. His touch reignited her blazing desire for him and she was instantly lost. Dan took his time, savouring every inch of her. His touch was gentle, his kisses were soft, and when he finally entered her she cried out and clung to him as she rode the waves of desire that swept through her body.

Afterwards she fell asleep instantly. Dan, still buzzing from his Oscar win, held her in his arms and watched her. He picked up the Oscar from the bedside table and looked at it in awe. It wasn't a mistake, it wasn't a dream – although it felt like it with

Georgiana in his arms – he had got her back and he was an Academy Award winner - it felt damn good.

CHAPTER 83

*T*wo days after the Oscars, Dan and Georgiana flew home to lend their support to The Riverside development fight. Peppy had set up one full-on media day at the club as she had finally managed to co-ordinate everyone's schedules.

Sebastian was in the billiards room talking to The Times. "It's a nationwide issue that's entirely down to the councils hitting their housing targets and not caring how they do it. Two hundred and fifty new homes in a village with a current population of seventy-five is ludicrous." He leaned forward and showed the plans to the journalist.

He continued: "Why are our green field sites under attack? Is it because the developers know people will pay a premium for a pretty view? Use brown field sites near towns and cities that give people the opportunity to live where they work. Leave our countryside as it is. One has to wonder who's being paid off?"

In the next room Georgiana was giving an interview to the Daily Mail. "Of course it's something we feel passionately about. This is our home. This is a small, close-knit community in a tiny village in the middle of nowhere. One has to wonder who's being paid off?"

Dan was in the club lounge talking to BBC's Countryfile. They had jumped at the chance to have an Oscar winning mega-star championing the countryside on the most-watched show in the UK, and Peppy was keen to capitalise on his win as much as possible.

"I may be a Londoner but I love the countryside. I've made Appleton Vale my base when I'm in the UK and there's a reason for that, apart from the obvious." He referred to Georgiana. "It is stunningly beautiful and peaceful. It inspires me. It can't change, it would be a travesty. I own a piece of The Riverside and I'm determined to make sure it stays exactly as it is. One has to wonder who's being paid off."

Peppy had given them all key words and phrases to repeat in each interview. She wanted a strong, clear message to be imparted to the press to ensure cohesion for the campaign.

All the major newspapers and news channels were lined up for interviews with the three stars. Peppy's massive publicity push was also accompanied by full page advertisements in every daily newspaper in the country.

After her interview with the Daily Mail was over, Georgiana was ushered into the club lounge to do a pre-recorded piece with Dan for The One Show. She touched up her make-up, smoothed her hair down and hopped onto a stool next to Dan.

Anita Rani – doubling up in her role for Countryfile and The One Show - was asking the questions which Georgiana and Dan answered with authority and precision. They were well rehearsed.

"Isn't this a case of NIMBY?" Anita asked Georgiana.

She laughed. "Not in my back yard? Well of course there has to be an element of that with any development that's opposed by residents anywhere in the country, but you have to follow all the evidence and see where it takes us."

Dan took over. "And we've done exhaustive research into the environmental impact the development will have. That's really our major concern here."

"It's a bold move to engage in such a huge campaign." Anita said to Dan. "But lending your Oscar-winning celebrity to the cause can't do it any harm."

"It's the only move we had in our favour," Dan laughed. "We're in the fortunate position of having a voice loud enough to be heard. Using my celebrity for a good cause kind of makes me feel gooey."

Anita laughed and Georgiana snorted.

"You'll have to forgive him." Georgiana patted Dan's arm. "He's been in America for far too long."

By the end of the day the three of them were exhausted. They had talked non-stop and pleaded their case passionately.

"You guys were awesome." Peppy was grinning from ear to ear. "Makes such a nice change to work with professionals. They're still looking for a photo of you and Olivia with Alexander," she told Sebastian.

"Absolutely not!" He shook his head.

Peppy held her hands up. "Ok, ok. I get it. But you do realise the more you refuse, the more they're going to hound you for it? You've been lucky so far. They've only got some long lens shots that are really grainy."

"No," Sebastian repeated. "We've talked about this a hundred times and I won't change my mind. I don't understand this national obsession with my son."

"Goes with the territory. You know that," Peppy replied. "Once these two pop out a kid you'll pale into insignificance." She pointed at Georgiana and Dan.

Georgiana spat her drink out. "Not happening any time soon," she spluttered. "We're going home." She took Dan's hand. "Been a very long few days."

"A whole week of nothing," Dan sighed in contentment, looking forward to the week ahead.

"Well not entirely nothing," Georgiana replied. "There's the little matter of a wedding to organise."

CHAPTER 84

"*Y*ou need to get down here," Will told Sebastian.

"I'm on my way to the airport," Sebastian told him. "What's up?"

"You're never going to believe it, but I came in this morning to find Thelma Graystock, the Lavenham twins and my bloody brother chained to some of the trees that are due to be torn down."

Sebastian chuckled. "Now there's a stroke of genius."

"What do you want me to do?" Will asked him.

"Call Peppy, she'll get some media down to cover the story," he replied. "Then call Olivia and she'll rally the troops, maybe one or two more of our gang will join the protest. She'll also get Hattie to make a fabulous lunch for them all."

"This is a good thing?" Will asked.

"Too bloody right it is," Sebastian replied. "Go and get some photos and text them to me. I need to see it with my own eyes."

"On it," Will said. "Where are you off to anyway?"

"Tokyo, only for a few days. Keep me updated." He rang off and Will galvanised himself into action.

"You're a bloody idiot," Will shouted as he walked towards Freddie. His brother was chained to a giant oak and sitting directly in the path of the diggers.

"We lost but we're not going down without a fight," he grinned. "It was Thelma's idea."

"Was it really?" Will turned to Thelma who had positioned herself half way up the adjacent tree. "How the hell did you get up there?"

"The twins gave me a leg up," she shouted down to him. "I can see for miles up here."

"Well just be careful." He turned back to Freddie. "What's your plan?"

"Dunno," Freddie shrugged his shoulders. "But we're not leaving."

"Yeah!" Josh and Jem bellowed their agreement.

"William, be a darling and get the thermos will you?" Thelma called down to him.

"You sure that's a good idea Mrs G," Jem snorted. "What happens when you need the loo?"

"Got that covered." Thelma dug something out of her pocket and waved it around. "It's a She Wee," she announced. "Never used one before, but needs must."

"Oh God," Will shook his head. "I didn't need to know that."

"Don't be so churlish William," Thelma yelled. "I take it you'll be joining us?"

"Do I have a choice?" Will grinned.

"Not if you want to stay in my good books." Dee Dee tapped him on the shoulder. She was standing with Jane holding dozens of home-made placards with a variety of painted slogans.

More of the villagers began to arrive as word spread. Each was handed a placard and they were received with laughter.

Mary-Jane Lavenham hooted at her sign that read *'Quite miffed really'*.

"Only you could be so polite, Dee Dee," she said.

"I love an acronym," Peter snorted as held up a board that read *'Peeved. Irritated. Shocked. Surprised. Offended. Frustrated. Furious'*.

Susie bent down and rifled through the placards until she found one she liked. "*Ruly Mob*," she chuckled. "That'll do."

"Let me have that one," Marjorie Rose pointed at a white sign with writing in thick red paint that read *'Get lost Athos. You're nothing without Porthos and Aramis'*.

"This is awesome," Peppy exclaimed when she regarded Dee Dee and Jane's efforts. "Only in Appleton Vale could a protest be so charming. You guys crack me up. The press will love this."

Half an hour later, the local BBC and ITV news teams arrived along with the FAB Chronicle and a freelance journalist from the Daily Mail who lived nearby. Peppy had instructed Clive at the gatehouse to let them in, along with any additional media that would certainly arrive once word spread.

Dan and Georgiana were still around and Peppy was fairly sure they would happily join the protest - perhaps minus the chains - but they were the aces in her pack, regardless. Their presence would guarantee international coverage.

The building contractor, Chester Addington, was standing in the distance gesticulating with his hands and screaming into his mobile phone. He had been assured that everything was above board, that the permission had been fully passed, and that there would be no interference from the villagers. The first part of the development was the housing and the RFC members were protesting right in the middle of the plot.

He finished his phone call and was immediately pounced upon by the BBC reporter looking to get his side of the story. He glared at her and walked in the opposite direction whilst signalling to the foreman to send the workforce home for the day.

It was the middle of the night in New York when the message came through to Bobby Garnett about the situation in Appleton Vale. He made a series of phone calls to Athos' legal team in London demanding action and went back to bed. He had no need to be unduly worried – the villagers were staging an illegal protest and Athos was well within its rights to throw the weight of the law at them.

An hour later a blacked-out Mercedes flew in through the gates of the club and pulled up in front of the demonstration. A Savile Row-suited, grey haired gentleman stepped out and surveyed the scene in front of them.

"Can we help you?" Tom glared at him.

The lawyer handed him a document that demanded the demonstrators 'cease and desist', hastily issued and signed by a judge in Bath.

"You're staging an illegal demonstration on private land. You have half an hour to clear the site before we call in the police to remove you." The lawyer sneered and narrowed his eyes.

"Not a chance,' Tom spat back at him. "You'll be removing us by force and that's not going to play out all that well for your client on national television, is it?"

"We are well within our rights," the lawyer threatened. "As I've already stated, this is private land."

"Well you can rip up that document right away." Georgiana was standing behind the lawyer with her hands on her hips. "It's only trespassing if they don't have permission from the land owner."

"Which they don't," the lawyer scoffed.

"I take it you don't know who I am?" Georgiana mocked. "I own twenty percent of this land and these are my invited guests, so I suggest you take your court order and shove it where the sun don't shine."

Realising he was beaten, however temporarily, the lawyer glared at Georgiana and walked back to the car. "This isn't over Miss Bloom," he shouted. "We'll be back."

As the car sped off the villagers whooped and hollered at their small victory.

"They'll be back tomorrow with something else up their sleeves," Peter sighed. "But for now, I think we can call our little protest a success."

"Can I come down now?" Thelma shouted from the tree.

"If you can get down," Josh snickered.

"It's not funny Joshua," Jane admonished. "Go and help her before she breaks something."

"Let's call it a day, everyone." Tom addressed the group. "Great work from you all. We may just stop this thing yet."

The protest made it onto the six o'clock news that night. The entire village tuned in and listened as Fiona Bruce ended the programme with their story.

"And finally," she said. "In a story of lies, deceit and corruption, sprinkled with a little Hollywood magic, the picturesque village of Appleton Vale in West Chesterton put itself on the map today in a bid to halt what residents are calling an outrageous and illegal development. In an area famed for its outstanding natural beauty surrounded by hundreds of miles of greenbelt land, an American consortium has been granted permission to build a massive housing and recreational estate right on the edge of the village.

"But this isn't any old village. It's home to three well-known faces that are leading the fight to appeal the decision. World number one golfer Sebastian Bloom has lived in Appleton Vale all his life. His sister, Georgiana, is one of our own sports presenters, and her fiancée is none other than Oscar winner Dan Flowers. Earlier our reporter spoke to them and here's what they had to say."

The television picture switched to the site of the protest at The Riverside and the BBC news reporter talking to the camera. "The residents of this charming village have fought this development every inch of the way. But even with the backing of HRH The Prince of Wales, Natural England, the National Trust, RSPB, English Heritage and every other major association, they still lost. The diggers were set to roll in at nine o'clock this morning and this is what they found."

The camera panned across the protest site, catching a glimpse of Thelma in the tree and Freddie chained to the giant oak. It zoomed in on the demonstrators' placards, and the next shot was of Dan and Georgiana talking to the reporter about the protest.

The reporter turned to the camera. "Is this really just a high-profile case of NIMBY or could it be - as the residents tell me - a blatant act of land grabbing by outrageously wealthy Americans who care only about profit, and corruption at the grass roots of local government? This is Jemima Pinkham in Appleton Vale for the BBC."

Peppy slammed her drink on the bar in satisfaction. "Well that's certainly put the cat amongst the proverbial pigeons."

"What's the next move?" Tom asked her.

"They need a court order to end the protest, and that could take a week or so if we fight it. We still need to pray for a miracle though," she sighed.

"Sebastian is convinced Edward would have protected the land in some way. He was no fool and he loved this village." Susie refilled Peppy's glass.

"Well, if he did, we're yet to find it." Tom rolled his eyes.

"Like I said," Peppy grimaced. "Pray for a miracle."

$\mathcal{G}$eorgiana and Dan spent a week in Appleton Vale organising decorators, buying new furniture for Edward's house, and making wedding plans.

"Wow," Dan grinned when they drove through the gates of their new home for the first time.

Built in 1619, Avalon House was a brick neo-classical mansion that was perfectly symmetrical, with windows on either side of a columned portico with a triangular pediment. There was also a lodge and a gatehouse, positioned at either end of the one-thousand-acre estate, and the Capability Brown-designed gardens – added in 1745 - were the envy of the county.

"I can't believe it's mine," Georgiana exclaimed. "Ours," she corrected when Dan raised an eyebrow.

He insisted on carrying her – giggling - over the threshold, and they explored each room hand-in-hand whilst Lady tore around inspecting her new home.

"There's a bit of decorating to do, but Edward did a lot of updating and remodelling over the last few years so most of it is state-of-the-art." Georgiana grinned. "He had pretty good taste for an old dude. The kitchen is amazing."

They made their way up the central oak staircase that swept away to the right of the vast entrance hall and stuck their heads in various bedrooms and bathrooms before they got to the master suite.

Georgiana pushed open the double doors and took Dan into a sitting room that in turn led to the bedroom. There was also a huge dressing room and two bathrooms – one in masculine grey tones with a mammoth walk-in shower and separate sauna, the other in muted shades of pink with a free-standing bath positioned in front of a floor-to-ceiling window that overlooked the gardens.

"This will do very nicely," Dan sighed with contentment. "We should put the bed over there and then we can watch the sunrise every morning."

Georgiana walked over to where Dan had indicated and laid down on the floor. She lifted herself up onto her elbows and looked out of the window.

"Couldn't agree more," she smiled and laid back down. "Come here." She patted the floor next to her.

Dan dropped to his knees and bent to kiss her. "We've got a hell of a lot of rooms to christen." His eyes flashed with desire. "Better start now."

"Exactly what I was thinking," Georgiana giggled.

"$\mathcal{E}$m, it's me." Olivia finally plucked up the courage to call Emily. The longer she left it, the harder it had become. Emily had sent a card and present to the Manor when Alexander had been born, and Olivia had sent a polite a thank-you note in return, but they had not spoken since the argument.

"It's so good to hear your voice," Emily squeaked. "I was literally about to call you."

"Really? Weird," Olivia laughed.

"I've got something to show you," Emily said. "It's important."

"Why don't you come down?" said Olivia. "We can talk properly and you can meet Alexander."

"Really?" Emily exclaimed. "Where's Sebastian?"

"He's in Tokyo," Olivia replied. "Why does this feel awkward?"

Emily laughed nervously. "Because it is."

"Well it doesn't have to be. I've missed you, Em," Olivia sighed.

"Me too. When can I come?" Emily replied.

"Whenever suits. I'm not going anywhere," Olivia said. "Why the rush?"

"I can't talk about it on the phone." Emily finished the call and sat back in her seat. She took a deep breath and stuck the memory stick into the side of her laptop, and dragged the files onto it. She waited impatiently while the information uploaded and contemplated her next move.

Something had been off about the whole Athos deal right from the start, but she had been so keen to impress JJ and Wyatt that she had ignored her gut instincts. When she had found out what Wyatt had done to Georgiana, how he had treated her so heartlessly and ruthlessly, she had felt sick. She felt responsible for Georgiana's pain, for the breakdown of her friendship with Olivia, and for the mess they were all in right now. Possibly, just possibly, she had found something that may help fix everything.

She grabbed the memory stick and walked away from her desk. It was only nine thirty in the morning, and as she passed JJ's office he checked his watch and called her in.

"Where are you going?" he asked.

"Out," she replied.

"Out where, exactly?" JJ walked across the room and closed the door. He turned and faced Emily. "What's going on?"

"Nothing," she shrugged her shoulders. "I'm taking a few days off."

"It's customary to have holiday time signed off by your boss," he said, miffed. "Where are you going and with whom?"

"None of your business." Emily turned to leave, but JJ stopped her, trapping her between the closed door and his body.

"It is my business," he growled and pressed himself against her. "We haven't fucked for ages and it displeases me greatly." He put his hand up her skirt and pulled her pants to one side.

"Not here," she hissed and tried to push him away.

"Why not?" He leaned across her and locked the door. "I want you." His fingers continued to probe and Emily couldn't help but moan with pleasure.

"That's it. Don't tell me you don't like it," JJ growled as he stroked her with a quickening pace.

"Don't," she spluttered. "I mean it. Get off me."

"Don't what?" JJ muttered. "Don't make you come? I'd say you don't have much choice in the matter." He caught her wrists and pinned them above her head with one hand, using the other to unzip his trousers. He nudged her legs apart with his knee and was about to enter her when she screamed in his face.

"Get off me," she yelled.

JJ smirked. "You don't really mean that." He forced her back against the wall.

"I fucking do," Emily spat, and kneed him in the groin. JJ collapsed onto the floor, writhing around in agony. "That's the last time you'll ever touch me," she snarled.

"You bitch," he screamed. "What did you do that for?"

Emily rounded on him. "Because you deserve it. Don't ever try to force me to do anything again. I've been a complete fool. You'll never leave your poor wife – God, I feel sorry for her."

"If you walk out of here now you can kiss your job goodbye," JJ hissed, still unable to stand up.

"Fine," she sneered. "Take this as my resignation with immediate effect."

"What?" JJ spluttered. "You can't."

"I just did," Emily grinned. "And now I'm leaving." She picked up her bag, unlocked the door and walked out of Caleris Global for the last time.

CHAPTER 87

*W*hen Emily arrived at Appleton Manor, Olivia was waiting for her on the steps with Alexander in her arms.

"Hey," Emily smiled as she got out of her car.

"Hi," Olivia replied warmly. "Come and meet Alexander."

Emily rushed towards Olivia and embraced them both. "I'm so bloody sorry," she cried.

"Me too," Olivia replied. "We've been really stupid."

"The longer we went without speaking the harder it was to pick up the phone. And I knew you would be busy with this little one." Emily touched Alexander's tiny hand.

"Well you're here now," Olivia grinned and handed Alexander to her. "Don't worry, he won't bite," she laughed as a look of horror crossed Emily's face.

"Say hello to your auntie Emily," Olivia smiled. Emily was surprised.

"Really? You still want me to get to know him?"

"Of course I do you stupid cow," Olivia laughed. "And so does Sebastian, before you ask."

"Well I doubt that," Emily sighed. "We didn't really leave things on a good note. He must be furious he didn't get the club."

"He's fine, honestly,' Olivia reassured her. "He's so besotted with Alexander that no-one could upset him right now."

"He's beautiful," Emily smiled at Alexander. "Can you have him back now?"

Olivia burst out laughing and scooped him out of Emily's arms. "You'll need to become a bit more child-friendly. I'm pregnant again. Twins."

"Already?" Emily was shocked. "Twins?"

"I know," Olivia made a face. "It wasn't planned. My boobs will be on the floor if we carry on like this. Do you want a drink?"

They walked into the kitchen and Olivia reached into the fridge for a bottle of wine.

"Are you drinking?" Emily was surprised.

"Of course not," she laughed. "But since when did you say no to a glass of wine?"

"I need it. I've had a shitty few days. Wait till I show you what I've found out," Emily frowned. "It's not good."

"What did you say to JJ to get away from work?" Olivia asked.

"I resigned," Emily said. "And I kicked him in the bollocks for good measure so I've most definitely burnt that bridge. I have no idea what I ever saw in him."

"Blimey," Olivia laughed. "I'm guessing he didn't take it well?"

Emily shrugged her shoulders. "You could say that. What was I thinking? He was never going to leave his wife and he just showed me his true colours."

"I did tell you that time and time again, but you chose to ignore me," Olivia replied.

"And when have we ever really taken each other's advice?" Emily sighed.

"Maybe it's time?" Olivia reached out and grabbed Emily's hand. "Let's not let anything come between us again. I've missed you so much."

"I'll drink to that," Emily clinked her glass against Olivia's sparkling water.

"So? Are you going to tell me? Don't keep me in suspense." Olivia was itching to find out what Emily knew.

Emily pulled her laptop out and opened it on the kitchen table. She took the memory stick from an envelope inside her handbag and slid it into the side of the computer. She clicked on the folder and it opened to reveal a number of documents, photographs, and other files that all related to the sale of The Riverside.

She scrolled through one of the documents and turned the laptop to face Olivia.

She tapped on the screen as a list of names appeared. "Holy crap!" Olivia cried. "This is a list of the council members who have been paid off."

"I know," Emily exclaimed. "Can you believe it? And there's more." She clicked open several other documents. "All the files were encrypted with a code that even the FBI would struggle to crack. Luckily, I know a man who can. I think the Feds have been trying to employ him for a while," she laughed. "You'll never guess who the major investor behind this development is."

Olivia looked at the name she was pointing at and gasped in

horror. "This really is personal." she whispered. "Sebastian's going to go nuts."

Emily raised an eyebrow. "My thoughts exactly."

"Surely the council bribery is all we need?" Olivia was hopeful.

"Well that might be a moot point." Emily enlarged a photograph on her screen. "It's really hard to see, and I had to get it translated, but this is going to throw a massive spanner in the works for both sides."

"Both? Why?" Olivia was intrigued.

"Because it affects everyone," Emily replied. "But you don't have to use it if you don't want to. Athos is clearly trying to bury it."

"What does it say?" Olivia squinted at the screen.

"It's ancient, really ancient. Lots of fifteenth century mumbo jumbo, but the basis of it is that the land has got some kind of Royal covenant attached to it."

"What?" Olivia cried. "Why?"

"Apparently, it dates back to a feudal tax dispute in 1483. Seems Edward's ancestors weren't quite as upstanding as he would have had you believe," she grinned. "They didn't pay the tax they owed, the land reverted back to the Monarchy and then a covenant was attached. According to the files, the covenant was in an addendum to the document but that's not here so it must have been lost. Shame as it could have been useful in shedding some light on all of this."

"Wow," Olivia breathed. "That's incredible. How did no-one know this?"

"Because it's bloody ridiculous that's why. They abolished Feudalism at the end of the fifteenth century. The land has been in Edward's family for generations so there was never any reason to look for any documentation. God knows how Athos found it, but it must have been sitting in the British Museum or National Archives for hundreds of years. Weird huh?" Emily raised her eyebrow.

"What does it mean and what do we do about it?" Olivia replied.

"You need to find a shit hot barrister and blow the lid off this whole thing. It's really the only way to kill it dead forever. The opposition have got deep pockets and big egos, and they want to get their own way. I think that's apparent from the level of research they've done." Emily took a gulp of wine. "It certainly means they can't move forward until it's sorted out, so that's a good thing at least."

"This is crazy," Olivia frowned. "Are you going to get into trouble for this?"

"Probably, but I'm hoping that JJ cared enough about me at some point or another to let it go," Emily shrugged her shoulders. "He knew all about this – his dirty fingerprints are all over it - so I'm sure we can work out a mutually beneficial solution to the problem. He won't want to sully his own reputation, that's for sure."

"I've got to tell Sebastian," Olivia said. "He won't believe this."

"I'm sorry. I should have dug around a long time ago. It didn't feel right from the beginning, and I was fully aware of Wyatt Clayton's reputation for getting his own way at any cost," Emily said.

"It's not your fault," Olivia reassured her. She picked up her phone and Face Timed Sebastian.

"Hi gorgeous," he answered on the second ring. "What's up?"

"Did I wake you? You look a bit groggy."

"Yes, but it's the next best thing to waking up beside you. I miss you. I'm so bloody horny, you'd be getting a good seeing to right now if you were here," he grinned.

Olivia burst out laughing and turned her screen so Emily was in view. "I should have said. Emily's here."

Sebastian chuckled, unabashed. "I can see that now. Hey, Ems."

"Hi," she replied, trying not to laugh. "I won't ask how you are."

"You two have finally made up then?" Sebastian said. "About bloody time."

"And she's resigned from Caleris," Olivia told him.

"That's a bold move Ms Delevigne," Sebastian raised an eyebrow. "What brought that on?"

"I'm about to tell you," Emily grinned. "Good news and bad." Emily talked through what she had found, leaving the biggest bombshell for Olivia to tell Sebastian at the end.

"Wow," he exclaimed when Emily showed him the photograph of the Feudal document. "I didn't see that coming. Do you think Edward knew about it?"

"There's something else." Olivia cringed. "We've found out who Wyatt has been working with and you're not going to like it."

Sebastian sat bolt upright in bed. "Who?"

"Please don't go mad," Olivia begged.

"Tell me!" Sebastian demanded.

"Troy McLoud." She cringed just saying his name.

"Fuck," Sebastian replied. "I didn't see that coming either."

CHAPTER 88

*R*obin Hartford QC reviewed the documents that had arrived by special courier direct from Appleton Vale. It was an interesting and high-profile case, the kind that he relished and had built his career on.

After a lengthy telephone call with Olivia the previous day, he immediately instructed his team of lawyers, researchers and investigators to build a watertight case.

He was particularly intrigued by the land covenant documents and was convinced the missing text held the key. That would be the focus of the investigation and they had little time to unearth it before the court case.

The Riverside development had come to a grinding halt when the RFC had disclosed the documentation to the media on Robin's advice. Two days after the initial protest, Athos' lawyers had once again arrived at the club waving legal papers in their faces but it was an empty threat. They couldn't really do anything if Georgiana wouldn't back down.

The planning appeal had been fast-tracked through the County

Court and the judge had ruled in favour of Athos, but now they had the ancient document, Robin could take it to the High Court.

"This really does change everything Mrs Bloom," he told Olivia over the phone. "And once a case has been heard in County Court, the next stop is the High Court, so things have actually worked out in our favour."

"Really?" Olivia asked. "How so?"

"We have time to prepare our case, ramp up the publicity and search for the missing document now," Robin replied. "We just need to prove precedence and we could win this thing. The judges are top notch, as you would imagine, and they're sticklers for tradition. All good things for us."

"That's brilliant," Olivia cried. "What can I tell Sebastian?"

"To get his people digging around – we need all the help we can get - and that I look forward to meeting him on his return from Tokyo."

CHAPTER 89

"You said you had this under control," Troy McLoud snarled into his mobile phone.

"I do," Wyatt replied.

"Doesn't look like it from where I'm standing," Troy growled. "If the press links me to this I'll hunt you down and finish you off."

"Making empty threats isn't gonna change anything," Wyatt snarled. "Just leave it to me. I'll be in touch."

Troy hung up the call and returned to hitting balls on the range in the blistering heat of his South Carolina home. Once the darling of American golf – he had two Major titles to his name, as well as countless other tournament victories around the world - he had suffered a spectacular fall from grace at the hands of Sebastian.

He hated Sebastian. He was his arch nemesis, but it was much more than professional jealousy. It was personal, and they had clashed time and time again over their careers. They had met on the international junior golf circuit almost two decades ago and had been bitter rivals ever since. Sebastian was the better golfer, naturally talented with the determination to succeed. Troy was a great golfer but he would never be as good as his enemy. His success had only come when Sebastian had dramatically lost form in the two years after the death of Ellie, his first wife.

Even though Sebastian's treatment of him was deserved, Troy blindly refused to accept the blame and held his adversary entirely responsible for him becoming persona non-grata.

His affair with Ellie was the catalyst that eventually led to her death along with her daughter Lizzie. Troy had not attended her funeral – he hadn't even admitted the affair, nor Lizzie's parentage to anyone.

He tormented Sebastian for almost two years at golf tournaments and events around the world. Finally, Sebastian exposed the truth about Troy on national television during The Open Championship, and that's when things started to unravel.

Almost overnight he was universally loathed for his callous and cold behaviour. His actions had shocked the public and he had been booed off the golf course at the most important Major of the year.

The last eighteen months had been hell. His game was all but gone, he was still jeered at wherever he went, and to make matters worse Sebastian was back as world number one, having bagged another two Majors in that time. He had married Olivia, had a baby and was happier than ever.

Troy had watched resentfully from a distance and plotted to ruin Sebastian's life. He knew The Riverside was very special to him and it would hurt like hell if he took it from him, and bought misery to the village and Sebastian's friends at the same time.

It was Troy who had alerted Wyatt to the club and he had instructed him, as the major investor, to secure it 'no matter what'. Wyatt owed Troy for helping him out many years ago and was only too happy to oblige, especially considering it was exactly the kind of project he had been looking to get involved with.

Kylie had been all Troy's idea. She had been on his booty call speed dial list for years and always obliged him when they were in the same city.

He pulled out his phone again and sent a text to his manager.

> *Dump the shares. Got a feeling this thing is going to go bad.*
> *Don't want my name involved.*

CHAPTER 90

$\mathcal{T}$he rain was lashing down and an unusually squally wind was buffeting the estate as Georgiana scurried from the stables to the Manor. She burst through the kitchen door and fell over Ace, landing in a wet and muddy heap on the flagstone floor.

Sebastian looked up from his newspaper and laughed.

"Don't bloody laugh at me." She picked herself up and glared at him. "Ouch, that hurt." She rubbed her hip and looked around for a towel to dry her hair and hands.

"Wet outside, is it?" He smirked and threw her a tea towel.

"Guess what arrived in the post this morning?" she grinned.

"Your Royal wedding invitation?" he laughed. "We got ours too."

"It's so exciting," she squeaked. "Almost more exciting than my own!"

"Don't let Dan hear you say that," Sebastian raised an eyebrow. "I thought you were going to London today."

"I was supposed to go and look at dresses, but then I had a better idea." She slipped her boots and coat off and sat down at the table. "Would you mind if I wore Mum's wedding dress?"

He looked at her in surprise. "Why would I mind? She always said she was keeping it for you."

"I was looking at the photos of her and Dad's wedding last night and she looked so beautiful. Where is it?"

"I think it's boxed up in one of the attic rooms," Sebastian replied. "She'd be happy if you wore it. You're so like her."

Georgiana jumped up from the table. "I'll go and wash this mud off, and then I'll have a rummage around and see what I can dig out. Don't tell Dan, I want it to be a surprise."

She found the enormous, silk-lined box in the wardrobe where Sebastian had said it would be. She held her breath as she lifted the lid and gently peeled back the delicate tissue paper.

She carefully drew it out of the box and held it up in front of her. It was a little creased but still in perfect condition. Slipping out of her clothes she stepped into the dress and stood in front of the mirror, admiring its simple beauty.

"I thought I was looking at your mother for a moment." Hattie was standing in the doorway.

"Sebastian said he didn't mind if I wore it. I wanted to see if it would fit." Georgiana twirled around in front of the mirror. "Will you do the buttons up for me?"

Hattie sniffed. "Sabrina would have been so proud of you. I'm sad for you that she won't see you get married."

"Aww, Hatts," Georgiana grinned. "Don't be sad. If I wear the dress I'll feel like she's with me every step of the way."

"If?" Hattie cried. "Look at you. Of course you're going to wear it."

Georgiana looked at the floor and giggled. "We're going to have to have it taken up a bit. Mum was taller than me. Do you know where the veil is?"

"In the trunk over there." Hattie pointed to a huge wooden trunk next to the wardrobe. "She wore it with your great grandmother's tiara which is in the vault at the bank. Sebastian offered it to Olivia for their wedding, but she flatly refused, saying only you should wear it."

"Do you think it's a bit full-on to go down the tiara and train route?" Georgiana stood still whilst Hattie did up the buttons and attached the veil to the back of her head.

"Don't be silly." Hattie turned her around to face the mirror again. "See."

"Oh," she gasped. "It's perfect."

The dress was made from ivory and white, ultra-smooth satin gazar with a bodice narrowed at the hips. Its long sleeves had been delicately designed from rose point lace that also covered the bodice and two-metre train. The veil had also been lovingly handcrafted using the same rose point lace. There were two petticoats that fitted under the full skirt to give it volume. It was very reminiscent of Grace Kelly's dress when she married Prince Albert of Monaco.

"Why are you crying?" Georgiana asked Hattie.

"You look lovely," she wiped her eyes with a tissue. "I just can't believe this day has come. It only seems like yesterday you were running around in nappies."

"Believe it, sister," Georgiana grinned. "This thing is happening."

Thank God I don't have to worry about what I'm going to wear now."

"We need to get it adjusted. It's too loose around the back as well as being too long." Hattie pulled the material together. "I reckon an inch off the bodice but my rudimentary sewing skills won't cut it. We need a professional to come and fit it properly."

"Do you really think it's ok?" Georgiana needed reassurance.

"It's perfect." Hattie smiled. "Dan is going to be knocked off his feet."

"Well, that was easy." Georgiana twirled around in front of the mirror again and sighed with satisfaction.

CHAPTER 91

$\mathcal{T}$he press speculation was at fever pitch, and the Royal wedding was, for once, pushed off the front pages by the impending nuptials of Georgiana and Dan. The whole world knew they were getting married, but the question on everyone's lips was, when? The Daily Mail and several other newspapers and paparazzi were camped out in Appleton Vale knowing it was imminent, and their tenacity was rewarded when on the third Wednesday in April, trucks began to roll into the sleepy village and through the gates of the Manor.

The Sun newspaper also had photographers on stand-by at Heathrow, and at the private airports in Farnborough and Bath to catch the arrival of Hollywood's elite and the many sporting superstars that were on the guest list.

In the ten weeks since Dan had won his Oscar, Georgiana had attempted to organise their wedding on her own - a small, intimate affair with just their close friends and family in attendance.

Since they had drawn up the first guest list, it had grown exponentially day-by-day and was soon over a hundred and fifty people. Whilst Dan had been flying back and forth to America for work commitments, she had covered two events for the BBC that had taken her focus off the wedding preparations.

Hattie and Olivia had taken things out of Georgiana's hands. They could see she was overwhelmed by the sheer enormity of the task ahead and had called in an exclusive wedding planning company from London to run the show.

"It's totally out of control," Georgiana exclaimed when Hattie found her in the library hiding from the planners. "I can't cope."

"That's why we hired them to take care of everything," Hattie replied. "Come on now, you can't stay in here forever. Not unless you want Sebastian choosing your centre pieces."

Georgiana sighed. "We didn't want a big wedding and now look at it."

"Well you can't un-invite people, especially seeing as most are coming from all over the world to celebrate with you."

"It's bloody Dan's fault," she moaned. "First he invited Leo – which is fine – and then we started to have the 'well if we invite Leo we have to invite so and so' conversation."

"Well it's his day, too." Hattie turned to leave. "Are you coming?"

"Do I have a choice?' She stood up and followed Hattie back towards the drawing room where the planners were waiting for her to agree the decorations, flowers and centre pieces. They had asked Chef Bernard to create the wedding breakfast and cake – why go elsewhere when a Michelin starred chef lives on the doorstep?

"That's it, we're done," Georgiana said with relief after the planners had left for the final time before the big day. "Remind me not to do this again, ever."

Hattie raised an eyebrow.

"I'm kidding," she laughed. "We're going to go the distance, don't worry Hatts."

"I have no qualms whatsoever about you marrying Dan. He's a lovely man and fully deserving of you." Hattie patted her arm. "Now get out from under my feet and take these dogs with you."

"All right I'm going." Georgiana rolled her eyes. "I said I'd meet Will for a quick lunch anyway. Come on you lot." She pulled on her coat and trundled out of the back door with the three dogs at her heels.

The sun was hanging brightly in the sky but offered no real warmth, and there was a bitter wind cutting through the air as Georgiana walked briskly into the village. Will was already sitting at a table in the corner of the bar with his nose buried in the latest issue of Country Life when she arrived.

"I like looking at the expensive houses for sale," he laughed when Georgiana giggled at his reading material.

"I've had a traumatic morning and am in desperate need of a large glass of wine and some sustenance," Georgiana said as she leaned across the table and picked up the menu. "What are you having?"

"Ham and cheese toastie and a pint please," Will replied. "Why traumatic?"

"Just wedding stuff," she waved her hand dismissively. "But whilst we're on the subject I've got something to ask you."

Will looked at her with interest. "Ask away."

"We were originally only going to have a tiny wedding and it has since grown into an untamed beast. I hadn't planned on any bridesmaids - just Lady who will be ring-bearer if I can train her

441

in time – but now I'd really like someone by my side and I'd like it to be you."

"Bridesmaid?" Will snorted.

Georgiana laughed. "Well no, not a bridesmaid. You'd look shocking in a dress. I want you to be my wing-man, so to speak."

Will was dumbstruck. "Is that even allowed?"

"Of course it is, you idiot." She rolled her eyes. "I can do anything I want. It's my wedding."

"Well, in that case, I accept." Will grinned. "Just don't make me wear pink."

"I know it's last minute, but that's just the way I roll." She grabbed his hand. "I need you. You're my best friend in the whole world and you know me better than anyone. You'll keep me sane."

Will squeezed her hand. "And you've got me. I said yes, didn't I? Now can we eat?"

Georgiana went to the bar and placed their lunch order. She took a huge gulp of white wine as soon as Tom placed it in front of her. "Ahh that's much better. This wedding is turning me into a raging alcoholic."

"It's all anyone is talking about," Tom joked. "The wedding, not your alcoholism."

"Tell me about it." She rolled her eyes. "God only knows how bonkers it's going to get when Hollywood descends."

CHAPTER 92

The RFC's date with the High Court was set for three days after the wedding. Georgiana and Dan would be away on their honeymoon, but Sebastian and the rest of the village were in full battle mode and ready to take down Athos once and for all.

They had stopped the development of The Riverside – at least for the time being – by using the Feudal document that Emily had procured. It had, as predicted, left them in a state of limbo, but they had had no choice. The only way to stall for more time was to continue the search for the missing addendum to their ancient record.

Sebastian had been in touch with Edward's daughter Camilla, urging her to search through any documentation she had. Camilla had been unusually helpful, but as Sebastian had pointed out 'she couldn't afford not to be.' Camilla knew it would have financial implications for her if they couldn't resolve this issue, and she had already promised the bulk of her fortune to a charlatan witch doctor deep in the heart of The Congo.

Camilla's desperate search through her father's old records

443

turned up nothing that was even remotely linked to the Club. She had sent Sebastian a telegram:

Nothing here. Stop. You'd better find it. Stop. Keep me in the loop. Stop.

Robin Hartford QC had wiped the floor with Athos' team of world-class lawyers when he had issued a summons for them to explain their actions in trying to bury the document. The judge had taken a strong view on upholding the law – no matter how ancient – and his verdict had stopped the development in its tracks.

"We're almost out of time." Robin and Sebastian were meeting for the final time before the court case. "We need that missing document."

"Don't you think I know that?" Sebastian was just as tetchy as Robin. They both knew that it was a vital piece of evidence that could swing the verdict their way.

"There's no precedent. It's an unusual case. Right now, I can't tell you which way this is going to go. We need that document." He banged his fists on the table. Robin Hartford was not used to losing his cases, especially not ones as high profile as this.

"We have just a few days left to find it or we're screwed. Is that what you're saying?" Sebastian was frustrated. He had thrown a vast amount of money at the investigators, and although they had dug up dirt on Troy, Wyatt and all of the council planning committee, they had so far failed to find the elusive document.

Robin nodded. "That's exactly what I'm saying."

Sebastian stood up to leave. "I'm going back home this afternoon and I'll have a full report from the investigators by the morning. Let's talk again then."

He had one more job to do before he left London. His driver pulled up outside the Hatton Garden Safe Deposit Company where Sebastian met the duty manager. They went through a series of security and ID checks before he was led downstairs into a client room where a heavy metal box was sitting on the table.

"It only requires the key Mr Bloom," he told Sebastian. "Mr Hampton left us explicit instructions that only you or your sister would have access after his death. Such a loss," he sighed. "I'll leave you alone now." He backed out of the room and closed the door, leaving Sebastian to unlock the box.

He lifted out a red leather box and opened the lid. "Wow," he muttered. The Diadora diamonds that Georgiana had inherited from Edward were dazzling. The centrepiece of the necklace was a white pear-shaped diamond weighing in at twenty-five carats. It hung on a delicate, simple chain of white gold. The set-up only emphasised the significant size of the jewel.

In a second box were the matching bracelet and pear drop diamond earrings, each as stunningly beautiful as the necklace. Sebastian unfastened the ribbon that was securing the final box and whistled when he saw the enormous ring that was undoubtedly flawless and utterly spectacular.

He carefully placed all three boxes in the titanium briefcase he had been given to transport the jewellery back to Appleton Vale and walked out of the room.

"Did you find everything to your satisfaction Mr Bloom?" The manager was hovering by the exit.

"Yes, thank you. And you've arranged for them to be picked up immediately after the wedding?" Sebastian didn't want anything that valuable in his home for very long. The wedding was high profile and the media would speculate about Georgiana's dress and jewellery, and then the whole world would know about the Diadora diamonds. It was enough to give him nightmares.

He was on high alert as he was escorted back to his car by a discreet security guard. He locked the doors the instant he was inside and leaned back, clutching the briefcase in his arms.

"Let's go," he instructed his driver.

Two hours later he arrived at the Manor and breathed a sigh of relief.

"Hey," Olivia greeted him with a kiss. "Let me see."

Sebastian opened the briefcase and lifted out the boxes. "Now don't be jealous, darling," he grinned.

"Oh my God." Olivia opened the lid of the first box and gasped at the sheer beauty of the necklace.

"That's what I said." He handed her the other boxes and watched as her expression went from shock to awe. "Wow."

"Puts my gifts to shame eh?" He glanced at the ring he had given Olivia after Alexander's birth.

"No!" she exclaimed. "I love every single thing you've given me. I couldn't wear this. It's spectacular but way too much for me."

"Georgie is going to be blown away. I can't recall ever seeing these, even when Edward's wife was alive." Sebastian picked up the boxes and walked towards his study. "These are going in the safe immediately."

CHAPTER 93

$\mathcal{F}$or the first time in his adult life, Wyatt was out of control. He was consumed with The Riverside project and with each passing day he could feel it slipping away from him. He had no idea how they had found the documents, and now he had a high court battle hanging over his head.

To add to his misery, his ex, Ashley, was almost full term and about to present him with a child he did not want. She had resolutely refused to disappear, and had made it her mission to inform the world that she had ensnared one of the richest and most eligible bachelors in the northern hemisphere. She had used her considerable charms to convince the public that she was the wounded party and, as a result, Wyatt's reputation had taken a serious nose-dive. That, in combination with his part in the attempt by Kylie to split Georgiana and Dan up, was turning him into persona non-grata. Kylie had made damn sure that his name was linked with the sordid tale.

His main investor, Troy McLoud, was on his way to pulling his millions out of the project and the other shareholders were beginning to distance themselves from Wyatt. Every time he turned on the television, read a newspaper or scanned the internet he was faced with speculation about Georgiana and Dan's wedding – when would it happen? What would the bride wear? Who was on the guest list? It compounded his anger. His ego wouldn't allow him to understand why he hadn't been able to ensnare Georgiana for himself.

He opened the latest email from Lucinda.

Dear Wyatt,

There's still no sign of any additional documentation. They know it's vital to their case and they're worried. I don't think you have anything to be concerned about darling…other than where you're taking me for dinner next week. I've told Godfrey I'll be away for the entire night.

L x

Wyatt shuddered at the thought of spending any time at all with Lucinda, let alone in the bedroom. She hadn't produced anything substantial despite promising to do just that, so continuing the charade with her was pointless. He typed his response.

Lucinda,

We have nothing more to discuss and our arrangement has come to an end. You will be remunerated accordingly. I don't expect to hear from you again.

W. Clayton.

He pressed 'Send' and closed his laptop.

Lucinda shrieked when she read Wyatt's email. Its tone was cold and unforgiving. "You utter bastard," she yelled at the computer.

"What's happened darling?" Godfrey was standing in the doorway, watching his wife.

Lucinda jumped when his voice rang out. "Oh. Nothing for you to worry about." She smiled at him through gritted teeth. "Jean-Paul has double booked and there's no way he can get over here before the wedding."

"Your hairdresser?" Godfrey raised an eyebrow. "I hardly think that's the end of the world. The way you were going on I thought someone had died."

"Oh, shut up Godfrey," she snapped.

"And besides," he continued. "We're not even invited to the wedding. You haven't exactly ingratiated yourself with the Blooms. Your snobbery and jealousy know no bounds, my dear."

Lucinda gasped. Godfrey had never spoken out before now - he had been happily ensconced as the doormat in their relationship, or so she thought. He had the money and she had the glamour and connections, or at least that had been the assumption when they met and married – both for the second time. Godfrey liked Lucinda dominating him in every aspect of their lives and Lucinda loved his money.

She quickly ran over to him and placed her hand firmly on his groin, pressing against it until Godfrey took a sharp breath and started to harden under her touch.

"Oh Godfrey," she purred. "You may think I'm a piece of work but you'll never let me go. You've invested far too much in our marriage to walk away from it." She unzipped his pants and wrapped her hand around his erection.

Godfrey groaned. "I've no intention of letting you go. It would cost me far too much money and you're not worth it."

Lucinda tightened her grasp and he moaned further. "Don't underestimate me, Lucinda." He reached for his mobile phone and turned the screen to face her. "I received this little film a while ago."

She shrieked as the video of her and Will began to play.

"I was humiliated at the time but now, well, now it's just ammunition to keep you in line. Wouldn't want it falling into the wrong hands, would we?" He smirked at the shock on Lucinda's face.

He continued, "I don't believe this is the only time you've cheated on me, but I will allow you to stay."

"Keep me in line? Allow me to stay?" She was indignant. "How dare you."

He pulled her towards him and pushed her down, so she was on her knees in front of him. "Show me how much you want to stay married to me."

Lucinda was so completely flabbergasted by Godfrey's sudden showing of domination that she did as she was told. It was only afterwards, as she sat alone in her kitchen, that she realised she had played all her cards - and lost.

CHAPTER 94

"Oh my God," Dee Dee shrieked. "That's what's his name." She pointed at the car cruising past the Tea Room on its way to the Manor. "Georgiana said a few guests would be coming early."

"And there's the paparazzi chasing him down," Jane replied. "It's sickening."

"I can't remember his name. Wasn't he in that film with Dan?" Dee Dee was wracking her brains.

Jane laughed. "Oh yes, what's his name from that film with Dan."

Marjorie Rose burst through the back door making them both jump. "Did you see?" she squeaked. "Was that Ryan Gosling in the car with Dan?"

"That's his name!" Dee Dee exclaimed.

"We did see." Jane patted Marjorie Rose's arm. "It's rather exciting."

"Where on earth will they all stay?" Marjorie Rose asked Jane.

"The Four Seasons the other side of Bears Bridge is posh enough," Jane replied.

"Do you think Georgiana needs anything?" Dee Dee asked.

Jane smiled. "She needs you to stay away and stop being so nosey."

"I'm not being nosey." Dee Dee was miffed.

"Yes, you are," Jane laughed. "You're desperate to go up to the Manor to see what's going on, and engineer a meeting with some movie stars at the same time."

"I AM NOT," Dee Dee cried.

"Whatever you say." Jane stroked her cheek. "This time tomorrow we'll be in the thick of it and you can swoon as much as you like. Just don't get your head turned by Ellen Degeneres."

"Oh no," Dee Dee exclaimed. "She's definitely not my type."

"And thank God for that." Jane shuffled back into the kitchen leaving Dee Dee and Marjorie Rose on 'celebrity-watch' at the window.

"Lady. Sit!" Georgiana was attempting to tie an ivory bow around the whippet's neck and she was wriggling out of her grasp with every turn. "How are you supposed to be ring-bearer when you won't even wear it?"

She was at home waiting for Dan. She hadn't seen him for over a week and her wedding jitters had increased daily in his absence. She had spent the last two days hiding from the wedding planners again as they exquisitely realised her dream, and had complained that it was all too much when Olivia had tracked her down.

"I just want to get married," she moaned. "Do we really need all of this?" She threw her arms towards the giant glass marquee, and at the fifty or so trucks that were delivering various furnishings, decorations, food and drink and other essential items that the planners had deemed 'crucial' to the success of the wedding.

"I'm afraid you do sweetie." Olivia was treading carefully with Georgiana. She was so jumpy that she was liable to disappear entirely if she was pushed any further. "Dan's on his way. You'll feel so much better when you see him."

"Did you feel like this when you married Sebastian?" Georgiana was looking for reassurance.

"Of course I did," Olivia laughed. "Every bride gets pre-wedding nerves, it's only natural. Mine were just on a less grand scale."

"And that makes me feel so much better," she replied with sarcasm. "Don't you think it's all a bit much?"

"Not really, no." Olivia replied. "I think it's going to be beautiful and classy, just like you." She hugged her. "Have you looked at the diamonds yet?"

Georgiana shook her head. "Too scared. They might just tip me over the edge."

"They're rather stunning," Olivia said dreamily. "If you don't want them I'm sure I could find a home for them."

"I've asked Sebastian to bring them to me just before the ceremony," she replied. "If I see them now I might just do a runner."

"Do I need to talk you down from the ledge?" Olivia was a little concerned.

Georgiana shot her a weak smile. "No, don't be silly. I'm just being an idiot. Once Dan gets here I'll be fine."

"When did he land?" Olivia looked at her watch.

"About an hour ago. They'll be here soon." She couldn't wait.

"They?" Olivia asked.

"Yeah. Ryan Gosling and his partner Eva Mendes hitched a lift." Georgiana laughed. "How ridiculous does that sound?"

Olivia grinned. "It's not ridiculous, just a bit surreal."

"They're staying at the Four Seasons but are dropping Dan off on the way past," Georgiana said.

"We have room for them here if you like?" Olivia said. "I've moved my parents and erstwhile grandmother to Edward's house – sorry, your house – and José and Angelica decided to leave the kids in London, so we've clawed back another three bedrooms there. Emily isn't coming until tomorrow and Dan's parents are due any time now. I've put them in the Iris suite so they'll be nicely tucked away from the madness. Both sets of grandparents are in the Astraea and Gaia suites, Richie and Gillian are already here but they've gone into Fiddlebury – they're in the Maia suite - and Hattie is generously allowing Aiden to stay in the lodge with her – God help her."

"They'll be just fine in the hotel. Thank you for helping so much. I couldn't have done it without you." Georgiana hugged Olivia. "In fact, I probably wouldn't have done it without you," she grinned. "Are you sure your parents will be ok at our house? There's still a bit of work to finish before we move in properly."

"They'll be fine. I think they're a bit put out at being moved out of the Manor in favour of Dan's family, but they'll have to suck it up. They should think themselves lucky they got an invitation at all. And when is the best man arriving?" Olivia wanted everything to be perfect for Georgiana.

"Dan said he'd be here by supper time. He's really nice. You'll like him." Georgiana had met Matthew, Dan's best friend from school, several times and had found him to be a lot of fun, and endearingly loyal to his oldest friend.

"Ok, good. I can tick that one off my list," Olivia said. "But there's still two little things to finalise. The first is where you're going to stay. You can't be with Dan in the cottage."

"Why not?" Georgiana pouted.

"Because it's bad luck you idiot," Olivia rolled her eyes. "And Matthew is staying there."

"What a load of crap. I don't believe in that, but if it makes you feel better I'd like to stay in my old room."

Olivia smiled. "That's what I was hoping you'd say. It will be nice to have you to ourselves one last time."

"And what's the other thing?" Georgiana raised an eyebrow.

"Your father," Olivia replied.

"He can bugger off," Georgiana glowered. "Why are you even bringing him up?"

Olivia held up her hands. "Because this came today." She handed her an envelope with a foreign postmark.

"Nothing like leaving it till the last minute." Georgiana ripped open the envelope and read the short letter out loud.

"'My darling daughter'. Yeah, right," she snorted. "'It has come to my attention that you are to be married'." Georgiana laughed. "He sounds like someone from the eighteenth century. 'I thought it would please you if I were to attend. I fear I may be unwelcome therefore I would appreciate your response by return. Your loving father, William'."

Olivia shook her head. "What a nerve. How long has it been?"

455

"Ten years. TEN. And he expects me to welcome him back with open arms on the most important day of my life?" Georgiana was incredulous. "Not a bloody chance. Not now. Not ever."

Olivia sighed. "Do you really want to get married without him there?"

"I hadn't even thought about it until you gave me the letter, so it can't be that important to me, can it?" She scowled at Olivia.

"At least send a response?" Olivia urged.

"Oh, he'll get a response all right," Georgiana muttered.

"Well I'll leave it up to you. I need to go and organise the caterers for tonight." Olivia looked at her watch. "And I'm late."

"It's just family tonight, isn't it?"

"If you count Will, José, Angelica, Richie, Gillian and Aiden as family – which I know you do - then yes." Olivia looked at her watch again. "I've really got to go."

She hurried away from the cottage in the direction of the Manor, leaving Georgiana to stew over what to do about responding to her father. She thought about it for a second and then dismissed him from her mind.

"Right then," she looked at Lady. "We're getting this stupid ring thing on you if it's the last thing I do."

Lady squeaked and bolted after Olivia.

CHAPTER 95

"You're here!" Georgiana squealed. She ran towards Dan and threw herself into his arms.

Dan laughed and bent to kiss her. "Hi, gorgeous." He held her tightly and breathed in her scent. "Boy, are you a sight for sore eyes. Let's go to bed."

He picked Georgiana up and carried her upstairs. He deposited her on the bed and stripped naked in seconds.

"You're keen," she giggled.

"Get 'em off." Dan reached forward and unbuttoned her jeans and pulled them down, revealing a tiny pair of black lacy pants. "Those too!" he grinned lustily.

She wriggled out of her remaining clothes and Dan pounced on her like a man possessed. He ran his hands the length of her body and kissed every inch of her naked flesh. "I can't wait, babe," he groaned.

"Who said you have to?" she chuckled.

Dan didn't need telling twice. He parted her legs with his knee and thrust into her, making her gasp with desire. She wrapped her legs around him and rocked back and forth as he drove his hunger inside her.

"Oh God," he moaned moments later. "I'm coming."

Georgiana threw her head back and cried, "Me too."

It was over as quickly as it had begun, and they began to laugh as they caught their breath.

"Nothing like wham, bam, thank you ma'am," Georgiana snickered.

"Sorry, couldn't wait. I was thinking about that the whole flight home." Dan propped himself up on his elbow and looked at Georgiana. "So?" he asked.

"So, what?" she replied. She knew what was coming. She had told Dan about the letter in a text.

"Have you spoken to your father yet?" Dan's eyes were filled with concern.

"Nope. Not going to either," she pouted.

Dan brushed a tendril of hair away from her face. "I think you should."

"What?" She was shocked. "I thought you'd be on my side?"

"Babe," he smiled. "I'm always on your side, but he's your dad. Why not give him five minutes at least?"

She leaned across Dan and picked up her phone. "Fine. If it'll shut you up I'll email him." She furiously tapped a brief email to William.

> *William. Thank you for your letter, although why you couldn't send an email is beyond me. This is the most important day of my life and I don't want you here. You*

didn't come back for Sebastian's wedding, nor when your grandson was born. You haven't given a toss about us for a decade and the feeling is entirely mutual. You are not welcome. Georgiana.

She showed Dan.

"Wow." He was taken aback. "That's a bit harsh."

"Stuff him," she pouted. "This is about you and me and I don't want anything to ruin it. I don't need him in my life."

She pressed 'Send', chucked the phone on the floor and rolled on top of Dan. "I've done what you wanted. Are you satisfied now?"

Dan grinned. "When it comes to you, I'm never satisfied."

"We're getting married on Saturday," Georgiana giggled. "Weird, huh?"

"Not weird at all. It's awesome. I'm a very lucky man." Dan pulled Georgiana towards him and kissed her passionately.

"As much as I'd love to stay here, we need to get a move on or we're going to be late." Georgiana kissed Dan's nose and jumped out of bed. "Shower?" She winked and ran towards the bathroom.

Everyone was gathered in the drawing room at the Manor when Dan and Georgiana ran in, more than twenty minutes late.

"Sorry, lost track of time." Dan grinned and Georgiana blushed.

"Well you're here now." Dan's mother Claudia walked over and hugged him. "You look well," she smiled and turned to Georgiana. "Darling! We're so excited. You must be a bundle of nerves."

Georgiana kissed her. "Oh, you know. I'm just about coping.

Although if Dan hadn't come back when he did I might have disappeared into the night."

"Hello, son." Dan's father greeted him with a handshake and kissed Georgiana on the cheek. "Not long now, eh?"

Sebastian cleared his throat and addressed the room. "Has everyone got a drink?"

Hattie thrust champagne at Dan and Georgiana.

Sebastian continued. "There will be plenty of speeches on Saturday, so I'll keep this brief. This is a very special night and we're so pleased that you're all here to share it with us. Tonight is all about family, and spending some quality time together before the madness ensues."

He looked at Dan's parents and two sets of grandparents and smiled. "It's a pleasure to welcome you to the family. Dan has made my sister incredibly happy, and he's a credit to you all."

He paused and raised his glass in the air. "Georgie. Dan. Love and happiness."

"Love and happiness!" the rest of them repeated in union.

The dining room was incredibly atmospheric. The huge mahogany table that dominated the space was decorated with gleaming silver candelabra holding smooth white candles. The place settings were beautiful in their simplicity and the chef had gone all out to create a menu that was full of Georgiana and Dan's favourite dishes.

Sebastian sat at the head of the table, with Dan's father taking the same position at the other end. Georgiana and Dan were sitting directly opposite each other in the centre with his grandparents either side of them.

Olivia, and Dan's mother Claudia were placed on Sebastian's left and right respectively whilst Angelica and José, Richie and

Gillian, Olivia's parents and grandmother, the best man Matthew, Will, Hattie and Aiden were seated in boy-girl formation.

The temporary waiting staff fussed around them, offering red or white wine to accompany the first course - a parsnip and apple soup with roasted hazelnuts and truffled honey. There was much laughter as they chatted to each other and recalled stories from Georgiana and Dan's youth.

"She was a bit of a handful at times," Sebastian laughed. "Especially when Will was involved."

"Hey," Will shouted. "Don't blame it all on me. She was a willing participant."

"I don't want to hear about that," Dan joked.

"You've got nothing to fear from me, dude. She's only got eyes for you." Will chuckled and raised his glass to Georgiana. She blew him a kiss.

"I'm so excited to see your dress," Angelica said to Georgiana. "Olivia said it was your mother's?"

"We can't discuss the dress," Hattie hissed. "It's bad luck."

"You and your bad luck nonsense," Georgiana laughed at Hattie. "We're not discussing it because I want it to be a surprise for Dan." She smiled at him across the table. "Not because it's unlucky."

"You English have so many superstitions," José said. "I don't understand it."

"Don't even try," Will spluttered. "We're an odd bunch."

"Have you got the baby monitor on, Olivia?" Constance addressed her daughter.

"For God's sake mother, of course I have. Relax and enjoy yourself, please." Olivia bristled.

Sebastian put his hand on her arm and she took a deep breath to calm herself.

"Ignore her," he whispered.

"I'm trying," Olivia muttered. The baby monitor crackled and Alexander began to cry. "See what you've done now?" She glared at Constance.

"I'll go," Hattie said.

"No. I'll go." Olivia pushed her chair back and walked towards the door. "Carry on without me. He's been a bit grizzly so I may be some time."

They moved onto the second course of venison carpaccio with sweet onion, pickled mushrooms and a parsnip crisp. They had almost finished when Georgiana realised Olivia had not yet returned to the table.

She stood up and announced: "I'm just going to see if Liv is ok. She's been gone ages."

She ran up the stairs and found Olivia in the nursery rocking Alexander in her arms. Olivia saw her and put her finger to her lips telling her to be quiet. She carefully placed him back in his cot and walked out of the room, closing the door behind her.

"I thought he'd never go down," she sighed. "How's it going down there?"

"It's lovely. Thank you for organising it." Georgiana hugged her. "And ignore Constance. You're a brilliant mother, anyone can see that."

"She was appalled when I told her I was pregnant again," Olivia was glum. "She said I could hardly cope with one baby let alone another. I haven't dared tell her it's twins!"

"Don't listen to her," Georgiana exclaimed. "You'll be fine, and it's not like you can't afford to get some help, is it?"

"I don't want any help," Olivia pouted. "I'd just be happy if she could support me rather than finding fault in everything I do."

"Are we moving the party up here?" Sebastian was standing at the top of the staircase.

"Sorry," Olivia said. "We're coming now."

Sebastian walked over to her. "What's up?" He put his thumb underneath her chin and tilted her head towards his.

"Nothing." Olivia looked away.

"It's not nothing. Tell me," Sebastian urged.

"I'd better go back before they think we're being picked off one by one by some lunatic lurking in the house." Georgiana ran back downstairs.

"Well?" Sebastian said.

"She thinks I'm a terrible mother. I can't do anything right in her eyes." Olivia's eyes filled with tears.

"Tell her to bugger off." Sebastian wrapped his arms around her and kissed her head.

"You tell her," Olivia blurted into his chest.

Sebastian laughed. "Where's my feisty wife disappeared to? You've never let her bother you this much before."

"I think I'm a bit unhinged. It's the hormones." Olivia put his hand on her belly.

Sebastian smiled and kissed her again. "Don't listen to a word she says. Both she and your Dad are besotted with Alexander and they will be with these two as well."

"Doesn't stop her picking on me though." Olivia wiped her eyes and put her hand inside Sebastian's. "Better get back down there. It won't do for the hosts to disappear all night."

By the time they got back to the dining room the main course had been served – roasted rib of beef with crispy seasonal vegetables and Hasselback potatoes in a rich red wine reduction.

"This is really delicious," Richie said as he held out his glass to be refilled.

"Mmmm," Will agreed with his mouth full.

"Stunning," Matthew concurred.

"Wait till Saturday," Dan laughed. "Chef Bernard has really gone to town on the wedding breakfast. I actually think most people are coming for the food rather than the ceremony."

Georgiana nodded her head. "That's true."

"I can only imagine the gifts you're going to get. Wealth at its most extreme I should imagine." Nicolas wrinkled his nose in distaste.

"Dad!" Olivia growled. "That's enough. They've asked for charitable donations instead of gifts if you must know. If you can't be nice, then you should go."

"Olivia Carmichael, don't you dare talk to your father like that," Constance admonished.

"Olivia Bloom, Constance," Sebastian grumbled. "And I think we all need to remember that this is Georgiana and Dan's night."

Georgiana, tipsy from the champagne and wine, burst out laughing. Dan looked at her quizzically.

"Sorry," she muttered when she pulled herself together. "I was just imagining if Dad was here and the fireworks that would be going off." She looked at Nicolas and Constance. "You're a pair of teddy bears compared to him." Olivia's parents looked suitably ashamed.

"I think we need more wine," Aiden chipped in. The staff quickly responded to his request and glasses we refilled in an instant.

The rest of the meal passed without incident and at midnight Georgiana and Dan got up to leave.

"I don't suppose you have a spare room tonight?" Matthew asked Sebastian.

"Don't fancy listening to those two making up for lost time then?" he laughed. "I'm sure we can squeeze you in."

"I'm staying here," he shouted after Dan.

"What a good idea!" Dan grinned and winked at Georgiana. "See you in the morning."

CHAPTER 96

The day before the wedding the village was teeming with reporters and news crews desperate for a glimpse of Georgiana and Dan and their celebrity guests.

No-one knew exactly who would be turning up in Appleton Vale but several names had been touted in the morning newspapers: José de Silva, Gregor Balatov, Ory Hazzard and a handful of other big names from the golfing world; Georgiana's BBC colleagues Clare Balding, Sue Barker, Ed Leigh, Graham Bell and Gabby Logan, and Dan's Hollywood friends Leonardo DiCaprio, Ryan Gosling, Jack Black, and Emily Blunt. It was even suggested that Prince Harry and Meghan would attend ahead of their own big day. It was pure speculation.

When Georgiana arrived at the manor after breakfast, Chef Bernard was screaming profanities at his staff and throwing lettuce across the high-tech pop-up kitchen. He paused when he saw her, smiled and waved, and then went back to berating his sous chef.

She slipped in the back door and found Hattie alone in the

kitchen. "Chef Bernard is losing it out there," she snickered. "Where is everyone?"

"No idea. They all scattered in different directions after breakfast." Hattie poured Georgiana a coffee. "Olivia is upstairs with Alexander, that's all I know."

"Well, I know that Sebastian has dragged Dan out for a bloody four-ball with José and Matthew. Neither he nor Dan have ever played golf in their lives," she laughed. "I don't know what to do with myself. I can't sit still but there's nothing for me to do. Can I help you with anything?"

Hattie smiled. "Just relax. It's all in hand. Why don't you go for a ride?"

Georgiana pouted. "Because I promised Dan I wouldn't. He said I'd probably fall off and break my legs and not be able to marry him."

Hattie laughed. "Well, I suppose that makes sense. Go and play with your nephew then. Liv will probably be grateful for five minutes to herself. She's put a lot of effort into this wedding so make sure you thank her properly."

Georgiana picked up her coffee and went in search of Olivia. She found her in the attic rooms delving through dozens of open trunks.

"What are you doing?" She laughed as Alexander appeared from underneath a box.

"Christ, you scared me. Don't sneak up on people like that." Olivia got up from the floor and handed Georgiana a blue silk pouch.

"What is it?" she asked.

"Open it and see for yourself," Olivia urged.

She undid the bow, slipped her hand inside and pulled out an exquisite pale blue lace garter.

"Something old, borrowed and blue all wrapped up in one package," Olivia grinned. "It was your mum's, of course. Sebastian only mentioned it yesterday, so I've been frantically searching the house ever since. Will you wear it?"

Georgiana fingered the lace and sighed with pleasure. "This is perfect. It's the last thing I needed to sort out and you've done it for me." She threw her arms around Olivia. "Thank you so much, for everything. You're the best sister-in-law ever."

"Don't," Olivia sniffed. "You'll make me cry and there's going to be plenty of that tomorrow. Oh, and my dress came back this morning. It was so beautiful and now it's more like a tent."

Georgiana giggled. "Don't be silly, you'll look awesome like you always do."

"I'm bloody huge!" She pointed at her belly. "Look at me. It's gross. And I'm only five months pregnant."

"You've got two of the little blighters in there, what do you expect?" She looked at Olivia and realised she was crying.

"What now?" she laughed.

"I'm just so happy for you," she stroked Georgiana's face. "If anyone deserves a great love it's you. He's a good man."

She grabbed Olivia's hands and danced around the room. "And this time tomorrow he'll be my husband."

CHAPTER 97

"There you go," Hattie said, and turned Georgiana to face the mirror. "You look exquisite. I agree that the tiara was too much though."

"I've never seen you looking so lovely," Olivia's eyes welled up. "Bloody hormones," she muttered and pulled out a tissue.

Georgiana was ready to get married. She stood in the centre of her old bedroom at the Manor and looked at Hattie and Olivia gawping at her. "What?" she said.

"Nothing," they both laughed.

Georgiana rolled her eyes. "What time is it?"

"Eleven thirty-five," Hattie replied. "Plenty of time. Shall we have a little glass of champagne?"

"Make mine a large one," she laughed nervously. "I need it."

She glanced out of the window and gulped at the sheer enormity of her wedding. There were people everywhere. It was a stunningly beautiful spring day with bulbs and blossoms raising up to meet the warmth of the sun. There wasn't a cloud in the sky and the temperature was a balmy eighteen degrees. Olivia had been right about the weather in April.

She took the proffered drink and downed it in one gulp. "Ah. That's better."

There was a knock at the door and Sebastian poked his head inside the room. "Are we ready?"

"Almost," she replied. "Come in."

He walked inside carrying the three red leather boxes and placed them on the dressing table.

"Would you mind if I had five minutes alone with Georgie?" he asked Hattie and Olivia.

When they had left he walked over to Georgiana and kissed her cheek. "Wow sis, you look ravishing. Mum would love that you're wearing her dress. It really suits you. You're the spitting image of her."

"Aww, thanks," she grinned. "You don't look so bad yourself."

Sebastian was wearing a bespoke Damian de Landre black suit, and a tie in the exact shade of pink of the roses Georgiana had chosen for her bouquet.

"Time to see these sparklers, then." She picked up the smallest of the three boxes and undid the ribbon. "Oh," she gasped as she picked out the ring.

"Put it on," Sebastian urged.

She slid it onto the third finger of her right hand and it was a perfect fit. She held her hand up to the window and watched with joy as the sunshine bounced off the smooth edges of the diamond.

She gasped again when she saw the matching bracelet and held her arm out for Sebastian to fasten the clasp. She added the earrings to her outfit before Sebastian handed her the final box.

"Are you ready?" he asked.

"As I'll ever be," she replied. Having seen the other jewels, she was now desperate to look at the necklace. He opened the lid and passed her the box. She was shaking so much that it tumbled out of her hands and hit the wooden floor.

"Oh no," she cried. "Have I broken it?"

Sebastian bent down and scooped up the necklace and box. "No damage here," he fingered the huge diamond. "Can't say the same for the box."

He placed the damaged box on the table and walked around Georgiana until he was standing behind her. He fastened the necklace and pointed her towards the mirror.

"Holy crap!" she laughed. "That's one big mother." She fingered the pear-drop diamond and twirled around with glee. "Edward had such good taste."

"Can we talk for a minute?" Sebastian said. "Don't look at me like that, it's all good."

"Shoot," she said, continuing to admire the necklace in the mirror.

"I don't know if I'll get another chance today. Once we walk out of this room you'll be in demand so I want to say this now." He reached for her hand. "I'm so bloody proud of you. Dan's a fantastic bloke and I know he'll treat you like a princess. I have to take some credit for you turning out the way you have, although at times I wasn't the best role model. Georgiana? Are you even listening to me?"

Georgiana was looking at the broken box with interest. "What's that?" she pointed at a piece of paper sticking out from under the padded cloth the necklace had been sitting on.

"Probably the receipt, knowing Edward." Sebastian leaned forward and picked up the box. He lifted out the display cushion and carefully unfolded the document that had been buried underneath.

His face lit up. "I bloody knew it," he shouted. "I knew Edward wouldn't have left any loose ends."

"What is it?" Georgiana was dying to know.

Sebastian held up the document for her to see. It was in excellent condition for its age. It was the addendum to the Feudal document that they had been desperately searching for.

"Oh my God," she squeaked. "What does it say?"

"Well my sixteenth century Latin isn't up to scratch, but I'm rather hoping it says the land was handed back to Edward's ancestors." Sebastian was flabbergasted. "I can't believe it."

"What does it mean?" Georgiana squeaked again.

"Not a clue, but I'm sending it up to Robin Hartford immediately." Sebastian punched a number into his phone and barked orders to the person on the other end of the call.

Two minutes later he handed the precious document to his head of security – on hand to police the wedding paparazzi - to take directly to Robin's office. "Call him on the way and tell him you're coming," he said as he closed the door.

"Right then," he turned back to Georgiana and held out his arm. "Shall we?"

"Err, are we not going to discuss it? Tell everyone?" Georgiana was confused.

"For once, the RFC can wait. This is your day. Can we go now?

You're already well past the fashionably-late stage." Sebastian held out his arm again.

She nodded and lifted her dress to walk forward. She was wearing a towering pair of bespoke Jimmy Choo sandals and was terrified she was going to trip up. Sebastian led her out into the galleried landing and they descended the sweeping staircase.

Waiting for them at the bottom were Olivia with Alexander in her arms, Will with Georgiana's bouquet, and Hattie with a box of tissues.

"Hold it right there," the official photographer shouted from her place in the hallway. "That's beautiful, really stunning." She snapped away for a moment and then stepped back. "And you're good to go."

Hattie kissed her on the cheek. "I did a double take when you walked down the stairs. I thought you were your mother. You look beautiful, my darling."

Sebastian took her arm and linked it through his, leading her out to the gardens where Dan and their guests were waiting.

Olivia and Hattie rushed past her to take their seats at the front and Will walked behind, still clutching Georgiana's bouquet. They soon reached the giant oak framed pergola that had been erected especially for the wedding.

Every post and beam was entwined with delicate white roses and studded with tiny crystals that glimmered in the sunlight. The chair backs were decorated with yet more white roses, and petals were scattered on the perfectly-manicured grass all around. It was breath-taking.

Will straightened Georgiana's train and veil, and passed her the hand-tied bouquet of white and pink roses. "Good luck, Porg," he whispered.

Sebastian nodded at the pianist – a friend of Dan's who had written the score for Jigsaw Kids. He played the first notes of Georgiana's favourite song and was joined by a voice she recognised.

"Norah Jones?" She was stunned.

"A gift from Dan," Sebastian whispered. "Let's go."

> *'Come away with me and we'll kiss*
> *on a mountain top*
> *Come away with me*
> *and I'll never stop loving you'*

Georgiana took a deep breath and looked down the aisle. She locked eyes with Dan and allowed Sebastian to guide her towards the man she would love for the rest of her life.

There were audible gasps from many of the guests as she glided past. Her dress and the Diadora diamonds were simply stunning. Dan was smiling inanely and pointing at Lady who was patiently waiting by his side, white satin bow firmly in place.

He held out his hand as she reached the top of the aisle, Sebastian placed Georgiana's in it and took his seat.

"Wow," Dan whispered. "You look incredible."

"So do you," she whispered back. He was wearing a custom dark navy Hugo Boss suit with a white rose in the buttonhole. "Norah Jones? Seriously?"

"Cool, huh?" Dan grinned.

"You're crazy. She must have cost a fortune." Georgiana was stunned at the gesture.

"So what? We've got her for the whole day, so it's quite

economical really," Dan chuckled. He loved that he had managed to keep it a secret.

"When you two have finished catching up," Judge Conrad Masters smiled. He was an old friend of the family who had only been too delighted to marry Georgiana and Dan. They both giggled at him.

"What a beautiful day we have been blessed with for the union of this wonderful couple," he began. "I've known Georgiana since she was a child and it gives me great pleasure to perform this ceremony today. Let us begin."

The next ten minutes went by in a blur for both Georgiana and Dan. Olivia gave a reading and then it was time for their vows. Dan had insisted they write their own, and he stood proudly in front of her and read his aloud.

"I will be yours in plenty and in want, in failure and in triumph. I will dream with you, celebrate with you and walk beside you hand-in-hand. I will always have your back because there is nothing we cannot face if we stand together. I promise to take care of you, even when you've over-indulged the night before – you're such a cute drunk – and I won't ever let us lose our spark. There is still a part of me today that cannot believe that I'm the one who gets to marry you. I will try in every way to be worthy of your love."

Georgiana gulped back her tears. Dan's vows had touched her soul and his eyes told her he meant every single word. Olivia and Hattie were weeping openly, and the rustling of tissue packets in the congregation permeated the otherwise respectful silence.

"Did he say she was drunk?" Dee Dee hissed.

"No dear," Jane patted her hand. "He said she was a cute drunk. What lovely words and beautifully delivered."

"That's the actor coming through," Susie whispered from the seat behind.

"Hush," Tom interjected. "It's Georgiana's turn."

Georgiana took a deep breath and faced Dan.

"I feel truly blessed to have found you. I get to laugh with you and cry with you; care for you and share with you. I promise above all else to live in truth with you and to communicate fully and fearlessly. I will be your greatest fan, your toughest adversary and your ally in conflict. I will encourage your dreams because through them your soul shines the brightest. I will pick you up when you are down, soar through the skies with you when you are flying high, and I faithfully promise not to spend all our money on horses and dogs – or at least try not to. You are my person, today and always. I love you."

Dan was speechless. He squeezed Georgiana's hand and fought to maintain his composure.

"Do we have the rings?" Judge Masters looked pointedly at Matthew who scooped Lady into his arms and stepped forward.

Dan and Georgiana giggled as Matthew struggled to undo the bow that was holding the rings in place around Lady's neck. She was wriggling uncontrollably in his arms and a second later she jumped out of his grasp and bolted down the aisle.

Georgiana shrieked and Dan burst out laughing. "I told you it was a bad idea."

Their guests were double over laughing and pointing at Lady as she sprinted away from the wedding with Will in hot pursuit.

"Good job it's the dog and not the bride," Tom guffawed.

"Sorry," Georgiana apologised to Judge Masters. "We'll get her back in a minute."

"We have all the time in the world my dear," he smiled.

There was a ripple of applause when Will returned a few moments later with Lady in his arms and the rings in his hand. He gave them to Matthew who handed them to Judge Masters and they were ready to resume.

He addressed the guests. "Daniel and Georgiana have made their vows and will cement those promises with the giving and receiving of rings...Daniel?"

Dan picked up the ring – a diamond-encrusted platinum band – and slid it onto Georgiana's finger.

"I give you this ring to wear with love and joy. I choose you to be my wife, today and forever."

Dan's own ring was a simple platinum band. Georgiana was shaking as she guided onto his finger.

"With this ring, I join my life to yours. I choose you to be my husband, today and forever."

Dan and Georgiana stepped away to sign the register in the presence of Judge Masters whilst Norah sang 'The nearness of you.'

"I love this song," Andrea clutched Peter's hand. "It's so romantic."

"I'm guessing they have to get their money's worth out of her," Peter laughed. "Oh, how the other half lives eh?"

Andrea reached over and kissed him. "I like how we live, thank you very much."

"Me, too. Although if you want to start saving up for my fiftieth I wouldn't mind ELO playing at my party."

Norah came to the end of her song and the guests turned their attention back to Georgiana and Dan.

Judge Masters cleared his throat. "Daniel and Georgiana have made their vows and exchanged rings with you as their witness." He looked at them both and beamed. "It gives me undeniable pleasure to announce they are husband and wife."

Dan didn't need to be told that it was time to seal the deal with a kiss. He bent Georgiana back in his arms and placed his lips on hers. There was an explosion of delight from the guests, whooping and cheering at the newly-weds.

They held hands and slowly walked down the aisle, grinning from ear to ear, greeting their guests as they passed each row. Their joy was infectious.

"We did it," he whispered to her. "And for the record, I told you Lady would do a runner."

Georgiana laughed. "She likes to be the centre of attention."

"So, what now Mrs Flowers?" Dan asked.

"Photographs." She rolled her eyes.

"Do we have a few minutes?" Dan saw the photographer bearing down on them.

"Sure," Georgiana nodded. "It's our day, we can do what we like."

Dan grinned and led her towards the Manor. "I just want five minutes alone with you."

"Oh, yeah?" Georgiana giggled. "It'll take longer than that to get inside this dress."

He guided her through the open French doors of Sebastian's study and pulled her into his arms. "Mrs Flowers. May I be so bold as to kiss you?

"Thought you'd never ask," Georgiana laughed and melted into his arms.

CHAPTER 98

"Oh my God." Dee Dee's hand flew to her mouth. Look who we're sitting with." She pointed at the seating plan for the wedding breakfast.

Jane squinted at the board and was stunned. "How exciting!"

Susie and Tom were equally thrilled with their dining partners. "I can't believe it," Susie gasped. "I thought Georgiana was joking when she said she was going to mix things up a bit."

"A bit?" Tom snorted when he realised who he would be sitting next to. "Always fancied her."

"Who?" Andrea asked.

"Kate Winslet." Tom smoothed his hair down and puffed out his chest.

"Hey!" Susie cried. "I'm keeping my eye on you tonight. God only knows what will happen if you drink too much."

"We've got Ryan Gosling and James Corden and their partners as well as Gerry – he's one of Georgiana's producers - and Dan's manager Ken, and his agent Vinnie with his wife." Angelica peered at the seating plan. "And you're with us too, Emily."

"At least they didn't stick me on the singles' table," Emily laughed. "We're going to have fun with that lot."

"Who's that?" Susie pointed across the room. "I know him, but I can't remember his name."

"Kit Harrington," Tom replied. "Game of Thrones. He went to school with Dan and Matthew."

Sebastian appeared in the doorway. "How's everyone getting on?"

"It's very exciting and a bit strange." Dee Dee looked around wide-eyed.

"Mingle. Have fun. They won't bite," he laughed. "Ease yourself in with Clare Balding. She's lovely." He turned Dee Dee towards the bar and pointed at Clare. "Off you go."

A selection of exquisite-looking canapés on large silver platters were being offered to the guests, and waiters discreetly glided around the room topping up champagne glasses.

"I see our lot have got stuck in." Olivia appeared at Sebastian's side a few minutes later. "Dee Dee looks like she's in heaven."

"She loves all this show biz stuff," Sebastian laughed. "Look at her holding court with Clare and Sue."

"Where are my parents?" She looked around the room. "I bloody hope they're behaving themselves. Dad always says we're extravagant, so God only knows what he'll be thinking now."

Sebastian pointed to a group in the corner that included Norah Jones, Dan's PA Coby, his publicist Maddie and Vinnie's wife Marianne. "Over there. Your Mum looks a bit giddy."

"She's probably had one too many already. And I'm not even

going to ask where Diana is." Olivia's grandmother was a law unto herself.

"Are they nearly done?" Sebastian was eager to get the party started.

"Just finishing up. A few final snaps with the wayward ring-bearing dog and they'll be here." Olivia had just come from the house where the official photographs were being taken.

The late afternoon sunshine was disappearing behind the vale when Georgiana and Dan entered the glass marquee to rapturous applause and cheering from their guests. It was time to delight in Chef Barnard's exquisite menu, followed by the traditional cutting of the wedding cake and speeches.

The vast room was beautifully decorated with white rose flower balls entwined with branches and dazzling fairy lights hanging from the ceiling. The front of the marquee was set up as the dining area where dozens of round tables were assembled, each featuring silver candelabra and gleaming, silver-plated domed bowls brimming with white roses. The effect was effortless and breath-taking.

At the opposite end there was a bar, stage and dance floor. Thousands of fairy lights were interwoven inside vintage birdcages, and glass lanterns containing candles hung dramatically overhead.

Georgiana and Dan took their seats at the top table, along with Sebastian, Olivia, Hattie, Dan's parents and Matthew, the best man.

"Happy, babe?" Dan nuzzled her neck.

She reached up and stroked his face. "Never been happier. Bloody starving though."

"And as if by magic." Dan laughed as the first course was placed in front of them.

Chef Bernard had gone all out to create a wedding breakfast fit for royalty, never mind Hollywood. He was still smarting from his brother being chosen to cater the Riverside annual ball and had a point to prove. He had carefully selected the best ingredients from around the world and produced a menu that was drawing gasps of admiration from their guests.

Will picked up the menu and whistled his appreciation. "Now that's a feast if I ever saw one." He read it aloud.

The Wedding Breakfast of Dan and Georgiana Flowers
21ˢᵗ April 2018

Starters
Marinated Iberico pork, mooli and fermented chilli purée
Seared Yellowfin tuna, avocado purée, cucumber and coriander
Pea Royale, seasonal vegetables and truffle

Main Courses
Beef Wellington, Perigord Truffle and Wild Mushrooms
Steamed Aromatic Lobster, Carrot, Fennel and Angelica
Homemade Tagliatelle, Girolles, Parsnip, Basil Pesto and Parmesan

Desserts
Amedei Chocolate Cremeux, Oranges and Speculoos
Grand Marnier Soufflé with Crème Chantilly
Selection of British Cheese

Wine
Raveneau Chablis Grand Cru 'Clos' 2012
Château Margaux 2009
Taylor Fladgate Scion Vintage Port
Champagne Krug Vintage Brut 1988

"Sounds yummy." Peppy licked her lips as she slipped into the seat next to Will and ran her hand up and down his thigh. "Let's have some fun tonight," she purred in his ear.

He grabbed her hand and rested it on his crotch. "You're on," he laughed.

For the next two hours' the wedding party indulged their taste buds and devoured Chef Barnard's creations with vigour. The wine and champagne had been carefully selected by Dan and Sebastian, with Chef's input, and it was the best of the best.

As the dessert plates were taken away, Sebastian stood up and tapped a knife on the side of his glass. The marquee fell silent and all eyes were on him, in expectation of a first-rate speech.

"I've been waiting for this day to come for twenty-three years. That's how long I've been trying to give my little sister away, and today I finally nailed it." Laughter rang around the room.

He looked at Georgiana. "I'm supposed to use this speech to give your guests some hilarious anecdotes from your childhood of which there are many, or to embarrass you for our amusement, but you managed that yourself on board Leo's yacht last year." Georgiana feigned shock and threw her napkin at Sebastian. Leo stood up and took a bow.

He lovingly reminisced for about his sister for a further two minutes before his toast. "So, as your friends and family surround you, remember your promises to each other, and keep them with all of your heart." He raised his glass to the room. "Ladies and gentlemen, the bride and groom."

Matthew was next up with his best man's speech. He regaled the guests with tales of Dan's misspent youth and cracked some impeccably-timed jokes that had the guests doubled over with laughter. "As Dan's best man I'm supposed to reveal any skeletons he has in his closet but I'm afraid to say the paparazzi got there before me. I'm fairly certain there's nothing the world doesn't know about Dan – apart from maybe that time when we pretended to fight crime as Spiderman and the Hulk. Utterly convinced of his superhero abilities, he leapt off the garage roof and broke both legs when the organic webbing unsurprisingly failed to shoot from his wrists and break his fall."

Georgiana giggled and turned to Dan. "You never told me that."

"One of life's great embarrassments," he chuckled.

Matthew was on the home straight. "Georgiana and Dan, this is just the beginning. The best is yet to come." He raised his glass, "Mr and Mrs Flowers, may your marriage be long and happy."

The room erupted and Matthew sat down, looking relieved that his time in the spotlight was over. Finally, it was time for Dan's speech. He stood up and held Georgiana's hand to his lips. "Here goes nothing," he whispered.

"The day I met this gorgeous woman was the day my life changed. All it took was one smile and a transatlantic flight for her to steal my heart. But enough about my wife," he grinned.

"I want to thank you all for being here today to celebrate our union. Many of you have come a long way and we both appreciate it so much. It has made our day all the more special to know we have our closest friends here. To Sebastian and Hattie – you have done a remarkable job raising Georgiana, and it is credit to you that she has become such an incredible person. I promise you that I will never stop loving her, and will never let her down."

Hattie sniffed and reached for a handkerchief.

"And now to the star of this show. My beautiful wife. I feel so blessed to have found you, and continue to be flabbergasted every single day when I wake up next to you and realise that it's not a dream. You really did sit next to me on that plane. You really did give me your heart, and you absolutely did say 'yes' just a few hours ago. Lucky, lucky me." Dan reached down and stroked her cheek.

"You look extraordinary today, utterly stunning, and the absolute image of your mother, at least from the photographs I have seen. I would love to have met her, but from what everyone tells me I already have because she shines through you." He paused to give Georgiana a moment to compose herself and wipe away her tears.

"Georgiana, you have made me the happiest man on earth today. I love you. Now and forever."

Olivia and Hattie were openly weeping when everyone jumped up and gave Dan a standing ovation.

Sebastian clinked his knife on his glass again to refocus the guests. "We have a few messages from friends and family who sadly couldn't be here today." He sifted through a pile of paper. "We couldn't have done this on an iPad?" he joked.

"First up we have a proper, old-fashioned telegram from Georgie's doubles partner."

'I wish I could have been with you today but I'm actually in China covering your ass while you swan around getting married. Congratulations to you both. I know you'll make each other very happy. We can definitely call this a game, set and love match. John and Patty x'

"This one's from Dan's work wife," Sebastian grinned.

Dan and Georgiana. I'm so happy for you and sorry for not being there to celebrate your wedding. I'm on location in Botswana of all places. We'll party when we all get back to LA. I love you both. Cara x

"And it would seem we have the royal seal of approval," Sebastian chuckled.

Georgiana and Dan. Congratulations on your wedding day. We would love to have been there, but things are a little crazy right now! We both wish you all the happiness in the world.
Harry and Meghan x

He read several more messages aloud before coming to the last one, hidden in a silk envelope. He removed the letter from its pouch, turned to face Georgiana and began to read.

"To my beautiful daughter," he said.

Georgiana gasped and gripped Dan's hand. "Oh my God, it's from Mum."

Sebastian continued. "When I knew I wasn't going to be around to share this very special day with you, I realised that I needed to write this letter and instruct that it be given to you when you marry your one true love.

"You brought me so much happiness in the short time we had together. I hate that you have had to grow up without my love or guidance, and I want you to know that I do love you, so very much.

"As I write this letter, I am hopeful that you will have found someone worthy of your love. A good man. A man who will love you forever. So, my darling girl, be happy. Live your life with joy and laughter. Be the best person you can be, and never be afraid to show your husband how much he means to you. I love you. Mummy."

There wasn't a dry eye in the marquee. Georgiana was desperately gulping back her tears and Sebastian choked on the last few sentences before succumbing to his own emotions.

"That's it folks," Sebastian announced with a strained voice. "The bar is fully stocked, champagne is flowing freely, so let's get stuck in and celebrate these gorgeous people in style."

Several minutes later Norah Jones took to the stage to sing the Ella Fitzgerald song – 'Turn me on' - that Georgiana and Dan had chosen as their first dance. Hand in hand they walked to the centre of the dance floor as their guests surrounded them eager for a closer look. As the first bars of the song were played, Dan wrapped his arms around Georgiana and began moving her around the floor.

> *Like a flower waiting to bloom*
> *Like a light bulb in a dark room*
> *I'm just sitting here waiting for you*
> *To come on home and turn me on*

"Happy?" Dan whispered into her ear.

"Ecstatic," she sighed. "I love you."

CHAPTER 99

"What court are we in?" Dee Dee asked Jane, as they stood outside the imposing, Gothic-style building that housed the Royal Courts of Justice.

"Sebastian said it was number three," Jane replied. "Is everyone here?" She surveyed their group and did a head count. "Where is Emily?"

"Sebastian said she's running a bit late," Peppy said.

"Do you think we should go in?" Susie looked at her watch. "We've got about twenty-five minutes."

"And we want to get the best seats," Dee Dee agreed.

They had hired a minibus and driven up to London from the village early that morning in a show of support for Robin Hartford QC, who was heading up their case. He had done a marvellous job thus far and they were confident he would be able to swing the result in their favour now he was in possession of the missing document.

Robin had been both relieved and overjoyed when Sebastian informed him of the latest developments. Once the priceless piece of paper was in his hands, he was able to instruct his investigators to unearth supporting evidence that would give them the edge.

Robin had the document translated from Latin to English and informed Sebastian of its contents in another phone call.

"In layman's terms, what is says is that the land was returned to the Hampton family when the tax dispute was settled almost two years after the original writ. The addendum clearly states that it is forbidden to develop anywhere on the land without – and I quote – 'absolute consent of the Crown, other than a home and sporting estate of magnificent proportions befitting a noble and loyal subject'."

"Well that's that, then." Sebastian was jubilant.

"Whilst it is fantastic news it's not that straight forward I'm afraid," Robin replied. "The County Court judge ruled in Athos' favour on land ownership and, if you recall, he dismissed any notion that the original documentation was protected by any current or ancient law."

"But surely this changes everything?" Sebastian wasn't going down without a fight.

"I've got my team trawling through the archives as we speak," Robin informed him. "If there's a paradigm we can use as precedent they'll find it. It's quite often the case that covenants such as these, however ancient, are treated differently from land ownership disputes. Any supporting documentation we can get our hands on will be crucial."

Sebastian had updated the RFC on Robin's findings, and Dee Dee immediately organised a daytrip to London. Twelve villagers had made the journey, and they were now seated in the viewing gallery of court number three waiting for proceedings to begin.

At precisely ten o'clock, the judge entered from his chambers and the room fell silent. Bobby Garnett was sitting with his team of lawyers across from Robin and Sebastian, and he exuded an air of confidence that unnerved the RFC supporters.

"He looks pretty confident to me," Tom whispered.

"He's American," Peppy replied. "It's in their DNA."

"They can't win," Marjorie Rose cried. "It will be a travesty."

"Hush. I can't concentrate with you lot hissing behind me." Dee Dee was perched right at the front of the gallery, transfixed on the proceedings.

Over the next few hours expert witnesses were paraded by both parties – English Heritage, the RSPB and Natural England for the RFC - and every piece of evidence that had been gathered by Robin and the Athos team was scrutinised and contested.

Robin and the lead barrister for Athos slugged it out, cross-examining witnesses and rebutting testimony shown to be false or contradictory.

"I cite the case of Longridge versus The Crown." Robin slapped a dossier in front of Athos' legal team, and another copy was passed to the judge. It was a case dating back to the mid-eighteenth century in which a covenant was attached to a parcel of land owned by the Crown. In this instance, the private citizen – Longridge - held the right to enjoy occupation as an estate 'in land owner' but with an almost identical covenant to that of The Riverside. It forbade any changes without absolute consent of The Crown. Longridge sought to overturn the covenant and lost.

"May I bring it to the court's attention that The Crown declares absolute ownership of the entire country dating back to the Norman Invasions – a Land and Chattel law that technically still exists, however archaic it may seem." Robin addressed the judge. "When the feudal obligations of Mr

Hampton's ancestors had been fulfilled, as the owners of the freehold they 'held the land of The Crown in free and common socage'."

"What on earth does that mean?" Dee Dee whispered to Tom.

"Not a clue," he shrugged his shoulders. "But I think we're about to find out."

Robin continued. "The idea that the Queen will demand socage in this day and age is merely a notional one, of course. But the consensual part of the covenant is still very much law and must be adhered to for the credibility of our judicial system."

Athos' barrister was on his feet. "That's a draconian law that simply cannot resonate in the twenty-first century."

"Of course," Robin continued with a wry smile. "If Athos wants to seek permission from The Crown we won't object."

"Can we do that?" Bobby Garnett hissed at his legal team.

"No Mr Garnett, we can't," one of the bespectacled, grey-haired men replied. "It's a ridiculous concept."

Bobby jumped out of his chair. "This is crazy," he shouted at the judge. "You can't possibly be taking this seriously?"

"Sit down Mr Garnett, before I hold you in contempt." The judge glared at him and turned back to Robin. "Do you have anything else to add?"

"No, your honour. Thank you," he replied and sat down next to Sebastian.

"And you?" the judge looked at Athos' barrister.

The barrister shook his head. "What the fuck are you doing?" Bobby growled. "Get up there and find a way to buy us some time."

"Please be quiet Mr Garnett," the barrister hissed. "Do you want to spend the night in jail?"

The judge addressed the court room. "I shall review the evidence and return my verdict within the hour." He stood up and disappeared into his chambers.

"Is that it?" Andrea asked Tom.

"Seems to be," he replied. "I think the judge is leaning towards us."

"What makes you say that?" Susie asked. "Athos put up a pretty good fight and they do have a point about draconian laws."

"Well let's just keep our fingers crossed. I think it went well." Emily had slipped into the gallery half-way through the proceedings.

"I'm a rather good judge of character and he seems like an upstanding man who holds the law in the highest regard," Peter said.

"Do we have time for a cuppa?" Andrea checked her watch. "I'm parched."

"He said he'd be back within the hour, so I think we should stay close by." Peppy headed towards the exit. "Let's locate Sebastian."

Robin and Sebastian were deep in conversation when they found them outside the courtroom.

"Any idea which way this is going to go?" Peter asked Robin.

"Judge Branscombe is fairly traditional but it really could go either way," Robin replied. "Longridge versus The Crown was a bit of a stretch, but I'm hoping it gives him the ammunition he needs to rule in our favour."

"Fingers crossed he goes our way," Marjorie Rose squeaked.

"It's mayhem outside. There are TV crews everywhere," Emily said. "Had to fight my way through."

"Do you think that's for us?" Jane asked Sebastian.

He nodded. 'Let's hope we can give them some good news."

They found a drinks machine on the second floor and were passing round insipid coffee and tea when the call came for them to return to the courtroom. The judge had come to a decision. Dee Dee led the charge back to the viewing gallery and they slipped into their seats as the judge took his.

An expectant silence fell as all eyes were trained on him. He glanced at both parties and began to speak.

"I have heard and reviewed all of the evidence and have come to a decision. Clearly there is a need to ensure we follow the letter of the law, however ancient or ridiculous. There is also a need to ensure justice and have finality in respect of the proceedings generally. It has, I confess, been an interesting case and one that has captivated the nation, partly in thanks to the personalities involved and the historical aspect, but mainly due to the backlash from the general public against blatant land-grabbing for profit. I must admit, Mr Hartford, that you surprised me with Longridge versus The Crown, and I thank you for bringing it to my attention. It has made my decision straightforward."

He cleared his throat. "It is the view of this court that the addendum letter will take precedent over the Feudal dispute documentation and, as such, will be upheld by all current and any future landowners of The Riverside from now and in perpetuity. In addition to this, all pre-existing buildings and uses – which I am informed were in situ prior to nineteen forty-eight – are protected by the Town and Country Planning Act of 1947 and therefore will be granted permission in retrospect. There are no further grounds for appeal."

The satisfying thwack of the judge's gavel against the sound block echoed around the courtroom. Sebastian jumped up and hugged Robin. The villagers were on their feet in the gallery, whooping and clapping their approval.

"We did it," Dee Dee screamed and threw her arms around Jane.

"Oh my God," Susie squeaked. "We've won." She did a jig on the spot.

"I'm so relieved," Marjorie Rose breathed. "Didn't they do a wonderful job?"

"I dread to think how much our QC cost but whatever it was, he's worth every penny." Tom was impressed by what he had seen.

"Let's celebrate!" Emily laughed. "There's a great bar just down the road."

"Sounds perfect," Andrea replied. "We've got a lot to be thankful for."

"Wow," Peppy sighed with relief. "My work here is done," she laughed.

They rushed down to the foyer and congratulated Sebastian and Robin on a case well-fought and well won.

"We may have won but Athos still owns the land," Sebastian told them. "Although after this I'm pretty sure they'll be wanting to cut their losses."

"Who cares?" Dee Dee exclaimed. "We won. Let's tell the world."

Robin led the group outside and they were immediately surrounded by the media. Sebastian stopped and addressed them.

"This wasn't just a fight for our village. Today's ruling will have a lasting legacy that will protect our rural lands for many years to come. I have a message for any wannabe developers – especially our American friends – 'leave our countryside alone!' It is beautiful and diverse, and it's ours to wake up to every morning and watch the sun set over every evening. This man on my left has been nothing short of astounding and we have him to thank for winning our case. We're not taking any questions now, but Ms Grainger will be only too happy to furnish you with whatever information you require. Thank you all for your support. WE DID IT!" he punched the air and an explosion of flash bulbs went off in his face.

"Oh my God we won," Georgiana scrambled off the sun lounger and ran inside the villa. They were three days into their honeymoon, enjoying the luxury and privacy of Necker Island, courtesy of Sir Richard Branson - a friend of Sebastian.

She thrust her mobile in front of Dan's face and danced around the room. "Get off the phone you idiot, we need to celebrate."

Dan grinned and wound up his call. "Do it," he spoke softly into his mobile. "Buy them all."

Georgiana flung herself into his arms. "We did it, we did it. We beat him."

Dan laughed and kissed her. "Yes, we did. It's bloody awesome."

"Who were you on the phone to?" she asked.

"Never you mind," he chuckled. "It's a surprise."

CHAPTER 100

"*A*re you fucking kidding me?" Wyatt screamed down the phone. Bobby had just given him the verdict and he was furious. "How the hell did you let this happen?"

"They only presented the document two days before the case and we didn't have enough time to counter it," Bobby replied. "Where does this leave us?"

"In the shit," Wyatt growled. "I'm gonna have to call a board meeting to explain myself and you need to get your ass back here to do the same. I don't give a shit what they say. This is my company and we're keeping The Riverside. I'll run the place into the ground if I have to."

"You're being irrational," Bobby snapped. "Let's just dump it and move on. Sometimes a deal goes bad, that's life."

"I don't lose," Wyatt replied menacingly.

He hung up the call with Bobby and immediately set in motion a call for the board to meet at its earliest convenience. He wouldn't be beaten. One way or another he would wrestle control back from his investors and the board, and make the residents of Appleton Vale regret their actions.

His phone rang. "What?" he barked into the receiver.

"Wyatt this is Ashley's mother. She's gone into labour. You're needed."

"That's all I fucking need," he snapped.

"You got yourself into this by letting your cock rule your head," Ashley's mother spat. "It's up to you whether or not you want to be seen as the hero or the villain. It can go either way."

"You're as much a piece of work as your daughter is," Wyatt replied.

"And you were too stupid to see it," she sneered. "I'll let her know you'll be coming then."

Wyatt didn't reply. He slammed down the phone and picked up the bottle of scotch on his desk. He poured himself a large one and gulped it down in one go.

He was reeling, and in serious danger of losing control all together.

CHAPTER 101

"*W*hy are we leaving early?" Georgiana pouted. "It's our honeymoon."

"Because something has come up," Dan replied. "Trust me." He dropped a kiss on her head.

"I do trust you," Georgiana sighed. "I just hate surprises."

"What?" Dan laughed. "You hate it here, do you?"

"Oh no," she grinned. "This was a good surprise."

"Then you have to trust me this time as well." He sat on the edge of her sun lounger and stroked her back. "We still have a bit of time though."

Georgiana wriggled towards him. "What did you have in mind?"

Dan pulled the string that was holding her bikini top in place. "Come here," he growled. He lifted her so she was straddling him and buried his head in her breasts.

She gasped as he kissed each of her nipples in turn and pressed herself against him, slipping her hand inside his shorts.

"Be careful, Mrs Flowers," Dan groaned. "I won't be able to control myself if you keep doing that."

Georgiana giggled and continued to stroke him until he flipped her over and lay on top of her, pinning her arms above her head.

"The things you do to me," he whispered and thrust inside her.

"It's entirely mutual," she moaned and wrapped her legs around him.

They made love slowly and deliberately, knowing it was for the last time in their honeymoon paradise. An hour later they boarded the sea plane and said goodbye to their nirvana. Within twenty-five minutes they arrived on Virgin Tortola where the jet was waiting for them.

"At least Lady will be pleased we're coming back early," Georgiana sighed as she leaned back in the sumptuous leather chair.

"We're not going home just yet." Dan sat down next to her and fastened his seatbelt.

"Oh." Georgiana was puzzled. "So where are we going?"

"New York," he replied.

"Right," she grinned. "Why?"

"Never you mind." He put his arm around her and she melted into his chest.

"Ok, whatever." She didn't push him any further. She loved New York and the energy she felt coursing through her bones whenever she was there.

Dan tightened his arms around her. "And that's just another thing I love about you Mrs Flowers. You just go with the flow."

"I go where you go," she muttered. "Think I need a snooze.

You've not let me have much sleep the last ten days." She closed her eyes and drifted off in his arms.

Five hours later they touched down in New York and were whisked off to the Plaza where Dan had booked the palatial Royal suite. It was filled with roses and a bottle of champagne was chilling in a bucket.

"You're such a romantic," Georgiana reached up and kissed him.

"Time for our New York minute," Dan grinned and threw open the French doors leading onto the balcony. He expertly opened the champagne, poured two glasses and they stood side-by-side breathing in the charged atmosphere for a minute.

"What do you want to do this afternoon?" Dan asked.

"You're the one who dragged me kicking and screaming to New York," Georgiana poked him in the ribs. "You tell me."

"I'd hardly call it kicking and screaming," Dan laughed. "What happened to 'I go where you go'?"

"Precisely my point," she grinned. "You know why we're here, so you lead and I'll follow."

"Shopping and dinner. How does that sound?" Dan was attempting to be as vague as possible.

"And that's supposed to make up for taking me away from paradise?" She narrowed her eyes. "What are you up to Daniel?"

"Daniel eh? Must be serious," he snorted. He pulled her into his arms and kissed her passionately.

"Don't try to distract me," she giggled.

"Really?" Dan murmured into her neck.

"You're incorrigible." Georgiana prised herself out of his grasp and pretended to swat him away. "Take me shopping then, but don't be surprised if I clean out your bank account as my revenge."

"Says the girl who's happiest in filthy jeans and ancient jodhpurs." Dan stroked her cheek.

Georgiana laughed. "Good point. Perhaps I should buy some new breeches."

"Only if I can watch you squeezing your perfect little bottom into them." Dan's eyes glinted with lust.

"See. Incorrigible." She finished her champagne and picked up her bag. "Come on then." Georgiana sashayed out of the suite with Dan hot on her heels.

When they were in the elevator Dan donned a cap and sunglasses by way of disguise.

"Still looks like you." Georgiana rolled her eyes. "Don't know why you bother."

"Because I want to spend the afternoon with my wife without being photographed or having to sign autographs. Here." He handed her a pair of Chanel sunglasses.

"Like that's going to make a difference," she snorted. "Everyone thinks we're on honeymoon somewhere tropical. No one is looking for us here."

The lift door opened into the foyer and they stepped into an explosion of flashbulbs.

"For Christ's sake." Dan was livid. He pushed through the paparazzi and guided Georgiana outside. He was accosted by the duty manager on the steps.

"I'm so sorry Mr Flowers, Mrs Flowers. I don't know how they knew you were here, or how they got inside. Please accept my apologies and rest assured that the remainder of your stay will be uninterrupted."

"I should bloody well hope so," Dan growled. He opened the car door and followed Georgiana inside.

"I told you it was a crap disguise," she laughed. "Don't be so moody."

"I just want you to myself and to be left alone for five sodding minutes," Dan grumbled.

"Then we should have stayed on Necker." Georgiana held his hand. "Did you really think you could come to New York and carry on as if no one knows you?"

"Yeah." Dan muttered.

"Idiot!" she grinned. "I don't care. We're having a nice afternoon out together doing what normal people do. If someone wants to take a photo then let them."

Dan sighed. "I just want to protect you. I'm used to it, but I don't want you to have to deal with this crap, day in day out."

"You're one of the biggest movie stars in the world. That's the price you pay, and I knew that when I married you. So, buck up and let's have some fun."

"Where to sir?' The driver asked.

"Manhattan Saddlery please," Dan replied. "We're starting with the breeches, I need cheering up after that."

CHAPTER 102

"Where are we going for dinner?" Georgiana shouted from the bathroom.

"It's a surprise." Dan appeared in the doorway and whistled at Georgiana standing in front of the mirror in the tiniest black silky pants and bra. "You look gorgeous."

She rolled her eyes. "That may be so, but I kind of need to know what to wear."

"Something beautiful." Dan shot her a cheeky grin.

"I didn't pack for a posh night out. All I have are bikinis and sundresses."

"And that's why I got you this." Dan handed her a gift box with the Dolce and Gabbana logo on the side. "And these," he produced a Christian Louboutin box from behind his back.

Georgiana squealed and undid the gold bow of the gift box. Inside was a luxurious Italian silk and cotton blend black cocktail dress constructed from sheer lace with a silk inner lining.

"Oh, it's gorgeous, thank you." She kissed Dan and turned her attentions to the shoe box. She lifted the lid and gasped, "wow!"

She took out the shoes and held them in her hands. "Beautiful," she muttered.

"Limited edition," Dan replied, proud of his efforts.

The four-inch sandals were exquisitely adorned with handmade floral detailing at the toe and an elegant sari fabric ankle strap, accentuated by mirror-like gold specchio leather cross straps and a covered buckle.

She stepped into the dress and pulled her hair out of the way. "Can you do me up?"

Dan stood behind her at the mirror, slowly zipped the dress up and kissed her neck. "Perfect," he nodded.

She held onto the towel rail whilst Dan put her shoes on and did up the buckles. "There," he said. "You look awesome, babe."

Georgiana twirled around in front of the mirror. "You have particularly good taste Mr Flowers."

"I should have thought that was perfectly obvious when I married you," he laughed. "Come on, we're going to be late."

The driver pulled up outside Eleven Madison Park and Georgiana turned to Dan, wide-eyed. "Now, this is a good surprise."

"And for once I used my considerable charm and influence to get a reservation. They're booked up months in advance. Even Coby couldn't crack it." He helped Georgiana out of the car and into the very grand, art-deco building overlooking Madison Square Park that housed the world's best restaurant.

"Mr and Mrs Flowers. What a delight that you could dine with us this evening." The Maître d' welcomed them graciously. "Your guest has already arrived. Please, follow me."

"Guest?" Georgiana elbowed Dan in the ribs. "What guest? What are you up to?"

Dan said nothing and took her hand. They were guided through the restaurant, passing tables of customers gawking at them, delighted they would have a story to dine out on for months to come. They headed towards the back of the restaurant and into a private skybox that overlooked the dazzling city.

"What are you doing here?" Georgiana squeaked as she walked inside.

"Couldn't turn down a free meal in the best restaurant in the world now, could I?" Sebastian hugged Georgiana and shook Dan's hand.

"Where's Liv?" She asked.

"It's literally a flying visit so she stayed at home. She sends her love though and can't wait to hear all about the honeymoon."

"Seriously though," she frowned. "Why are you here? Why are we all here? I was perfectly content on my little Caribbean island."

Sebastian handed her a glass of champagne. "Sit down. We've got some news."

Georgiana slipped into the seat that Dan had pulled out for her. "We? Are you two in cahoots?"

Dan nodded and shrugged his shoulders. "Keeping it in the family, so to speak."

"Tell me," she demanded.

"Here." Sebastian slid a small black box across the table. "Open it."

She whipped the lid off and was puzzled by its contents. "A key? What for?"

"We're now officially the majority shareholders of The Riverside." Dan blurted out. He couldn't contain his excitement any longer. "You've no idea how hard its been keeping it a secret."

"I don't understand." She looked to Sebastian for answers.

"God, you can be so dense sometimes," he joked. "We knew that Athos shareholders would be dumping stock if the court case went our way, so Dan and I bought it. All of it."

"What? How?" Georgiana was flabbergasted.

"Remember Cecil Rossiter? The ancient board member who bid to play with me at St Andrews?" Sebastian asked. "Well, inadvertently he alerted me to the possibility of some shares coming up from another guy on the board who had run into some financial issues and needed cash fast. That's why I went to Tokyo. I had to be there in order to register F&B Corp."

"What the hell is F&B Corp?" Georgiana was totally perplexed.

"Flowers and Bloom," Dan informed her. "A dummy company, if you will."

"I needed the backing of Akio and Hiro and it made sense to do it there. We're now a subsidiary of Gijutsu." Sebastian referred to the Iwakura brothers who were his corporate sponsor. They owned one of the world's most successful gaming companies and were passionate about golf.

"They were only too happy to stump up some cash, and they had their financial guys do the work in return for a small piece of the club. We secured the first five percent through Cecil's mistake," Sebastian smirked.

Dan took over from Sebastian. "And then it was just a waiting game. Although it required precise timing to make the plan work."

Georgiana was stunned. She took a gulp of champagne and listened as Dan brought her up to speed.

"Everyone was on tenterhooks about the court case. Wyatt Clayton was so far up his own arse he never saw it coming." Dan's eyes glinted with triumph. "The second the judge declared in our favour, Sebastian sent a text to the team in Tokyo and they went share-buying crazy. Everyone wanted out and was dumping stock. It had turned into a nightmare investment for them and no one wanted to be associated with Clayton or Athos after such a humiliating and public loss. By the time Clayton had called an emergency board meeting it was too late."

"So how much did you get?" Georgiana was fizzing with excitement.

"Thirty-five percent," Sebastian replied.

"In total?" she asked.

Dan shook his head. "As well as. We already had twenty percent."

Georgiana's mouth dropped open. "Fifty-five percent?"

Dan and Sebastian nodded their heads.

"There's more," Sebastian said. "While we were at it we thought we may as well buy up as much spare Athos stock as possible. Just enough to get a seat or three on the board."

"Holy crap," Georgiana muttered.

"Aren't you pleased?" Dan was eager to celebrate.

She threw her arms around him. "Of course I am. I'm just a little stunned. Thank you. Both of you." She leaned over the table and kissed Sebastian.

"It still doesn't explain why we're here." She raised an eyebrow.

"That emergency board meeting Clayton called. It's tomorrow." Sebastian picked up his drink and held it in front of him. "He's about to meet his three new board members and the new major shareholders of The Riverside. Cheers."

CHAPTER 103

The Athos board of directors was made up of twenty men and women who had invested a great deal of time and plenty of money in making Athos the global force that it was. Wyatt brought the total to twenty-one and was the major shareholder.

Wyatt had been dreading this meeting. He had let his emotions rule his head and seriously taken his eye off the ball. Not being able to have Georgiana, and allowing himself to be strong-armed by Troy, had been the catalyst for his ego to take over and he had made poor choices from that moment on. His desire to own her had turned to hatred.

"Fucking bitch," he muttered over and over again as he made his way to the boardroom. He flung open the doors and met a wall of faces regarding him in utter disgust and contempt. He walked over to his chair at the head of the table and sat down.

"Let's get on with this," he barked.

"We're not all here yet," said one of the board members, indicating to three empty seats.

"Lassiter, Duggan and Wood. Should've known they'd be dragging their heels," Wyatt snarled.

"I think you'll find it's Flowers, Flowers and Bloom." Sebastian walked through the doors, followed by Georgiana and Dan.

"Sorry we're a little late," Georgiana smirked. "Traffic was awful." She looked at Wyatt and felt empowered. With Dan by her side she was stronger than ever.

"What the fuck?" Wyatt exploded. "Get out of my board room."

"I don't think he understands," Dan said to Sebastian. "Why don't you enlighten him."

"F&B Corp ring any bells?" Sebastian sneered.

"That's you?" Wyatt was dumbfounded. He looked around the table and immediately knew that the rest of them had been informed prior to the meeting.

"You snivelling bunch of bastards," he bellowed. "I've made you all rich, given you status far beyond what any of you deserve, and this is the fucking thanks I get." He shot an evil look at Bobby Garnett.

Sebastian pulled out a chair and sat down at the table, with Georgiana and Dan occupying the seats on his left. "I believe we have an emergency meeting. What's the emergency?"

Georgiana elbowed him. "Stop gloating," she muttered.

Bobby got to his feet. He glanced at Wyatt and took a deep breath, clutching the table to steady his nerves. "Firstly, I'd like to welcome our new board members. It has been a while since we had some fresh blood to shake things up a little."

Wyatt was incensed. His face had turned a putrid shade of green and he was shaking with anger. "You fucker," he screamed at Bobby.

Bobby ignored him and continued. "We all know why we've been summoned here today." He looked at Wyatt again. "You've done some underhand deals in your time and we've always supported you, me more than most, and it was for the good of the company, for all of us. This is different. You had your own agenda from the day you met Georgiana and you took your eye off the ball. This company has a certain reputation to uphold and you broke the code of conduct. You fucked up, man."

There was a collective sharp intake of breath from the rest of the board members. Georgiana shifted in her seat and fiddled with her engagement ring. Dan scowled at Wyatt, and Sebastian leaned back in his chair, enjoying the show.

Bobby looked around the room for support. The final nail in Wyatt's coffin needed to be knocked into place, but the board members were terrified of the consequences should they not succeed. Silence descended as Bobby sat down.

"Too fucking scared to take me on?" Wyatt sneered. He stood up to leave. "This meeting is over. I'll expect your resignations and transfer of shares on my desk before the end of the day."

"Sit down, Wyatt." Georgiana stood up and addressed him directly. "Whatever dodgy business dealings you've done in the past are of no concern to me. What you did to me also doesn't matter anymore. But what you did to Dan, setting him up like that, deliberately sabotaging our relationship, is unforgiveable. You deserve every crappy thing that's coming your way."

She looked at each member of the board knowingly, one by one, and turned back to Wyatt. "I move to a vote of no confidence."

'What?" Wyatt roared. "You can't. This is my fucking company."

"Oh, I think you'll find I can," she replied sweetly. "You'll retain your shares and take dividends each year, but your days at the helm are over. Athos is yours in name only. All in favour of removing Mr Clayton as president of Athos?"

Nineteen hands shot up in the air. Georgiana counted them slowly for maximum effect and turned to Wyatt. "That's twenty including my vote. I'd call that a full house. Consider yourself booted out."

"I'm staying fucking put," he screamed. "This is my company. I built it out of nothing. You can't take it away from me."

"I think you'll find we just did." Dan flashed his most brilliant smile at Wyatt. "Do we need to call security or can you make your own way out of the building in an orderly fashion?"

"This isn't fucking over," Wyatt bellowed. He stormed out of the board room and was immediately accosted by Sebastian's security team, who man-handled him into the elevator and out of Athos Towers for the final time.

"Well that was fun," Sebastian beamed. "I assume you'll be helping steady the ship?" he said to Bobby. "I don't trust you, especially seeing as you just stabbed your boss in the back to save your own arse, but we need your knowledge."

Bobby nodded. "I'm not putting myself forward to take over. Mitsy Grissinger is the obvious choice for president. She's been with us from the beginning and it's not too big a step up from chief financial officer."

"All those in favour of Mitsy please raise your hands." Bobby raised his own hand first. "Well that's settled, then."

Mitsy left her seat and walked to the head of the table. "Thank you all for your vote of confidence in me. This company is going to see some big changes now Wyatt's gone. I suggest we take a few weeks to get a handle on things and then reconvene at the end of the month."

"We won't be back," Sebastian replied. "Our interests here will be represented by Ms Emily Delevigne."

"Ooh, that's a good idea," Georgiana exclaimed.

"Just came to me a minute ago," Sebastian grinned. "That should make up for putting herself on the line for us and losing her job in the process."

Mitsy nodded at Sebastian in agreement. "Let's bring this meeting to a close. Thank you for your timely intervention," she said to him.

"It's my absolute pleasure," he replied. He looked at Georgiana and Dan. 'Let's go. Our work here is done."

They just made it to the elevator before Georgiana and Dan had a fit of the giggles.

"That was awesome," she cried. "Did you see his face? I thought he was going to have a heart attack."

"You were incredible." Dan hugged Georgiana. "You're so sexy when you take charge like that."

"Well someone had to do it," she grinned. 'And it felt bloody brilliant."

"That's him finished," Sebastian chuckled. "He really should have known better than to pick a fight with the Blooms."

"Flowers," Dan corrected him.

"Whatever," Georgiana laughed. "Can we go home now?"

CHAPTER 104

*T*hey arrived back in the village the next morning to a heroes' welcome. Sebastian had called Olivia immediately after the board meeting and she passed the news onto Dee Dee, knowing it would get around the village in double-quick time.

They congregated outside the pub and began clapping and cheering when the car came into view. Sebastian jumped out first and punched the air. "No-one messes with Appleton Vale and gets away with it," he cried.

Georgiana and Dan followed him out of the car and Susie thrust champagne in their hands.

"Bloody well done." Peter slapped Sebastian's back.

"Very, very sneaky," Tom grinned and shook Dan's hand. "How long were you planning that for?"

"Since the day I met my beautiful wife," he laughed. "I wanted to give Georgiana the club, but it was Sebastian's idea to get on the board of Athos, he just needed my money."

"Genius," Will exclaimed. "Does this mean I have a job for life?"

"That all depends on your future conduct." Georgiana winked.

"I'm a reformed man." Will grinned. "Pep has captured my heart."

"I knew it!" she cried. "Friends with benefits my arse. I knew you and Peppy liked each other more than you were letting on. Where is she anyway?"

Will flushed pink and averted his eyes from Georgiana's gaze.

"Oh my God. You really do like her." She was incredulous. "I'm so glad. She's awesome."

"Yeah, she is." A dreamy look crossed his face. "She's in London, back tonight."

"Just in time for the party," Andrea said.

"Another party?" Sebastian asked. "We're still getting over the wedding."

"We have to celebrate and we're doing it at the club tonight," Tom replied. "A few drinks, some nibbles and a whole lot of self-congratulating. Should be fun."

"Sounds like a plan.' Sebastian walked back to the car. "I'm going home to see my wife and son. Are you two coming? I'll drop you off on the way."

"Yes," they both said a little too enthusiastically.

A few minutes later they swept in through the gates of Avalon House and pulled up outside the entrance.

"Home sweet home,' Sebastian grinned. "The decorators finished two days ago so there won't be any interruptions."

"We're technically still on honeymoon." Dan's smile broadened. He grabbed Georgiana's hand and pulled her out of the car.

Before she could say a word, he scooped her up in his arms and walked towards the door.

"Absolutely have to carry you across the threshold, Mrs Flowers," he said. Georgiana was giggling uncontrollably.

"I'll see you tonight, if you can tear yourselves away from each other," Sebastian said.

They barely managed to close the front door before Dan started peeling Georgiana's clothes off. "Right then. Let's start as we mean to go on." He slapped her bottom and pointed her towards the stairs. "Upstairs NOW."

Georgiana shrieked as Dan started to chase her up the stairs. She was impeded by her jeans falling around her ankles and collapsed half way up in a fit of giggles.

"I'm stuck," she laughed and held out her arms.

Dan bent down and bundled her into his arms. He carried her towards their bedroom and kicked open the double doors with his foot before depositing her on the enormous bed. He yanked her jeans off and threw them on the floor. "Can't have you harming yourself now, can we?"

"Well it did hurt a bit when I fell." She batted her eyelashes. "It's a little tender just here." She pointed to the inside of her thigh.

"Oh, really?" Dan grinned. He pressed his lips against the spot she had indicated. "Better?"

Georgiana groaned. "Much. But you'd better check me all over, just in case there are any other injuries."

Dan quickly stripped naked and laughed. "It's a horrible job but someone has to do it."

"Do you really have to go away?" Georgiana said. "Can't we just stay like this forever?"

"It's only one night, babe. You won't even notice I'm gone. I just feel like I have to do it now we're back. It's for a good cause." He tightened his arms around her. "I'll miss you like crazy, though."

Georgiana sighed contentedly. "I'm so happy right now. Nothing could burst my bubble."

The next morning her bubble had burst. "I feel horrible," Georgiana moaned as she lay in bed watching Dan get dressed.

"I stand by what I said in my vows – you're a really cute drunk." He sat on the side of the bed and stroked her hair. "It was that last glass of champagne that tipped you over the edge."

"It was a good party though." She yawned and snuggled back under the duvet. "I'm staying in bed with this little one." She lifted the covers and revealed Lady fast asleep in Dan's recently vacated space.

"You've no idea how jealous I am of that dog right now." He looked at his watch and quickly pulled on his shoes. "I love you Mrs Flowers. Do you think you can behave for one night in my absence?"

Georgiana giggled. "I'm planning on cuddling up on the sofa with Lady, watching a movie and stuffing my face with chocolate."

"Sounds like heaven." He kissed her. "I'll see you tomorrow afternoon."

CHAPTER 105

*G*eorgiana slept until lunchtime and woke feeling revived. Her hangover had all but disappeared. She leaned over and picked up her mobile to scroll through her messages. There was one from Dan telling her he loved her and that he hoped she was feeling better, and another from Olivia inviting her to the manor for lunch.

She jumped out of bed, had a quick shower and was on her way to the manor within twenty minutes.

She walked in the back door and was hit with a delicious aroma. "Bloody hell, that smells amazing. I'm starving."

"Feeling a bit jaded?" Olivia laughed.

Georgiana nodded and gulped down a glass of orange juice. "Where's Sebastian?"

"At the club. Here." Olivia passed Alexander to Georgiana. "Give your nephew a cuddle."

"Hi, cutie," Georgiana murmured. She bounced him in her arms and laughed as he gurgled his welcome.

"What's for lunch?" She walked over to the Aga and started to lift the pan lids.

"Get away from my cooker." Hattie swatted her out of the way with a tea towel. "You only need to look at something and it burns."

"Come on!" she exclaimed. "I'm not that bad a cook."

"You are," Olivia laughed.

Georgiana stuck her tongue out at them and sat down at the table. "We can't all be good at everything you know? I don't have the patience to cook anyway."

"We know," they agreed.

"What time did Dan go to London?" Olivia started to lay the table.

"About six o'clock I think. To be fair, I was half asleep and totally hungover, so I can't be sure." She shrugged her shoulders and poured another glass of orange juice.

"Do you want to come over tonight?" Olivia asked.

"Nope. I'm having a night to myself. I fancy some alone time and I've still got a bit of jet-lag so I'll probably be asleep on the sofa by nine." Georgiana leaned over and slid Alexander into his high chair.

"Well you know where we are if you change your mind," Olivia replied. "Can you pass me one of the baby spoons please? This little man needs some lunch."

"Here you go." Hattie put a huge casserole dish on the table and removed the lid to reveal chicken cassoulet. The second bowl was brimming with steaming rice and there also a fresh green salad.

"Bloody delicious," Georgiana mumbled through a full mouth.

"Tell me about the wedding. What happened after we left? Have you got any photos?"

She and Dan had left the party early and spent their wedding night in the cottage before flying out to Necker at dawn the next morning. She was eager to discuss how wonderful the wedding had been.

"Here." Olivia slid the iPad across the table. "These are the ones Will and Sebastian took. The official ones are due tomorrow. Aren't they great?"

Georgiana scrolled through the photos and laughed. "Look at Richie. Who knew he could throw shapes like that on the dance floor? Oh, that's a nice one of you. Doesn't Hattie look gorgeous?" She looked at each one in turn whilst Olivia filled her in on the rest of the evening.

"It was the perfect wedding." Georgiana hugged Olivia after they finished lunch. "Thank you so much for organising it all."

"I really enjoyed doing it," she replied. "It took my mind off being eternally pregnant."

"That's your own fault," Georgiana laughed. "You should be more careful next time."

"Oh, don't you worry about that. I'm not taking any more chances. I'd like to get my body back before it goes completely to pot." Olivia rubbed her belly. "Can you believe there's two of them in there?"

"Three kids under the age of two." Georgiana giggled. "I can't wait to see how you both handle that."

"Cheeky cow," Olivia laughed. "And no, I'm still not employing a nanny before you ask."

"I wasn't going to! You can have that battle with your husband, but you do realise he'll win in the end. Always does."

"I'll cross that bridge when we come to it." Olivia rolled her eyes. "What are you doing this afternoon?"

"Going for a ride and then crashing out at home." She stood up to leave.

"Are you still ok to have Alexander tomorrow morning?" Olivia asked. "Hattie is out and I've got the dentist."

"Yep. I'll be over by eight-thirty." She kissed Alexander, who was busy spitting his puréed vegetables all over the floor. "See you tomorrow."

She went for a ride across the estate, made a quick pit-stop at Church Farm Food Barn to stock up on the essentials, and was home and in her pyjamas by five o'clock. She filled a tray with cheese, bread, popcorn, chocolate and coke and settled back on the sofa to watch a movie. Lady curled up next to her and sighed contentedly. Picking up her phone she sent Dan a text.

It's weird without you here. Lady and I are pigging out on the sofa having a girls' night. Good luck tonight, you'll be awesome.
Love you and can't wait to see you tomorrow xx

Having cut the honeymoon short Dan was happy to make an appearance on a live charity fundraising show along with Ewan McGregor and Benedict Cumberbatch. They had filmed a comedy sketch earlier in the year and it was getting its first airing that evening, followed by an impassioned plea from the movie stars for the public to donate generously to the very worthy cause.

He replied quickly.

Madness here. I'll try to call you later but might not be able to.
Love you too Mrs F. xx

Georgiana smiled and chucked her phone onto the table before scrolling through Netflix. "Perfect," she muttered, and pressed play. As the credits of *Dirty Dancing* rolled across the screen she sighed with satisfaction. "Everything is just perfect," she told Lady, who opened one eye and nodded her head in agreement.

CHAPTER 106

$\mathcal{G}$eorgiana sat bolt upright in bed and reached for the bedside light. Next to her she could feel Lady shaking. She gasped when she heard a noise from downstairs and was rooted to the spot.

She had watched Dan on television just before she had gone to bed and there was no way he could have got back from London so quickly. She checked her watch. It was two o'clock – the middle of the night.

Another noise came from outside the bedroom door and she froze. Panic washed over her and she scrabbled around frantically for her mobile phone. "Shit," she whispered. She had left it downstairs and the phone in the bedroom was yet to be unpacked from its box.

Lady began to growl as the door handle was pressed down. Georgiana looked around for a makeshift weapon to protect herself with but came up short. She barely dared to breathe. Her only option was to lock herself in the bathroom. She scooped Lady into her arms, ran across the room and quietly closed and bolted the bathroom door behind her.

Sitting in the dark, shivering and frightened, she began to fear for her life. The bathroom door handle rattled as the intruder continued to violate her home, seeking his target.

A moment later there was an almighty crash against the door and Georgiana screamed. She looked at the flimsy lock and knew that it wouldn't hold for long. She clutched Lady close to her chest, closed her eyes and whispered. "It's ok, we're ok, we'll be fine, it's just a bad dream."

The intruder threw his full weight against the door and the lock gave way. Georgiana cowered in the corner.

"You never could look me in the eye," a voice growled from the darkness.

She shrieked as she recognised the voice. "Get out of my house. Leave us alone. The police are on their way."

"I doubt that very much." He threw her phone across the floor and she saw it had been destroyed. "You screwed me over you little bitch, and now you're gonna pay for it."

Georgiana slowly rose to her feet, still clutching Lady, and faced her intruder. It took every ounce of courage she possessed to address him calmly. "What are you doing Wyatt?"

"You took the only fucking thing I ever cared about away from me – my business. I've got nothing left to lose." His voice was menacing and Georgiana immediately felt threatened again. She could smell stale scotch on his breath and clothing, and it made her nauseous. Her eyes had grown accustomed to the dark and she could now see his face more clearly. He looked completely crazed and was clearly unhinged.

"Don't you think it would be better to sit down and talk this through?" she asked. "You don't want to do this Wyatt, trust me." She squinted past his huge frame looking for an escape route.

"This is ending tonight," he sneered. "You've ruined me. I'm gonna fuck you up so bad." He produced a gun from behind his back and wielded it inches from her face.

Sensing Georgiana's fear, Lady leapt out of her arms and stuck her teeth into Wyatt's leg. He yelled in pain and then kicked her with such force that she bounced off the wall and fell into a heap on the floor. She wasn't moving.

Georgiana screamed and tried to get to Lady but Wyatt held her back. "You've killed her," she choked.

Wyatt laughed maniacally. "That's for starters." He walked towards Georgiana, backing her into the corner of the bathroom. "Your turn."

He grabbed her by the arm and forced her back into the bedroom and onto the bed.

"Wyatt. Don't. Please." She begged him to stop, terrified he was going to force himself on her. Tears ran down her cheeks and she was shaking uncontrollably. She glanced back to the bathroom where Lady was still splayed across the floor and felt her heart shatter into a million pieces.

"Hands. NOW." Wyatt shouted. She held out her hands and he tied them with some coarse rope. He pulled her to her feet and stood behind her as he covered her mouth with a gag, which he tied tightly at the back of her head.

"Move," he snarled and pushed her towards the door. She turned her head and took one last look at her beloved dog before allowing Wyatt to man-handle her out of the bedroom and down the stairs. She was too shocked to put up a fight and scared of antagonising him into using the gun.

He bundled her through the front door into a beaten-up white transit van, and smashed the barrel of the gun against the side of her head, knocking her unconscious. He slid behind the wheel and sped away from the house.

CHAPTER 107

When Georgiana didn't turn up at the manor for babysitting duties in the morning, Olivia presumed she had overslept and left her a voicemail telling her to get a move on. An hour later when she tried again, she began to worry. She called Sebastian at the club.

"Thought you were at the dentist," he said when he answered.

"I'm still at home. Georgiana hasn't turned up and it's not like her to forget. I can't get hold of her and her mobile keeps going to voicemail." Olivia was growing more concerned by the minute. "Can you go over? Alexander is asleep and I don't want to wake him."

"I'll cancel the meeting." He was welcoming his sponsors, Akio and Hiro Iwakura, who had flown in from Tokyo overnight to visit their new investment. As part owners of the Riverside they were keen to see what all the fuss was about.

"No, don't do that. Alexander will be awake soon and we'll go over," she replied.

Twenty minutes later, she couldn't stand it any longer. She ran upstairs, woke her son and bundled him into the car. She drove the short distance to Avalon House, let herself in through the electric gates, swept up the long driveway and parked outside the entrance.

"Georgie," she shouted as she opened the door with her keys. "Get out of bed you lazy cow. You've made me miss my appointment."

When there was no answer she wandered through the house moving from room to room looking for Georgiana. The instant she walked into the bedroom she knew something was wrong. She could hear whimpering and found Lady hiding under the bed.

"Oh my God." She set Alexander on the floor and kneeled next to the bed to coax Lady to come out. She refused to move. Olivia reached in and began stroking her head and making soothing noises. She pulled out her phone. Her hands were shaking as she dialled Sebastian.

"She's not here," she shrieked. "Something awful has happened. I found Lady crying under the bed and the bathroom door has been kicked in."

"What?" Sebastian was confused. "What did you say?"

"Get here NOW," Olivia screamed into the phone.

She dialled 999. "Police," she croaked when her call was answered. "My sister-in-law is missing. Her dog is badly injured, the bathroom door has been forced open, and her phone is smashed to pieces."

When Olivia was reassured that help was on its way, she turned her attention back to Lady. She could see that she was in a great deal of pain but didn't know if she should move her.

Less than five minutes later, she heard a car screech to a halt and the front door crashed open. Sebastian took the stairs two at a time and burst into the bedroom to find Olivia sobbing and Alexander screaming.

He took a moment to assess the scene before him, then picked Alexander up and comforted him in his arms.

"She's been kidnapped." Olivia choked on her tears.

"We don't know that, darling." Sebastian bent down and helped her stand up. He put his arms around her and waited until her tears subsided.

The sound of police sirens broke through her despair. "They're here," she whispered. "We need to open the gates."

Sebastian took her hand, led her downstairs and sat her down in the kitchen. "Call Devon," he instructed. He walked out into the hall, buzzed the gate and waited for the police on the doorstep.

Two squad cars and a Range Rover sped down the drive, followed a few minutes later by Devon who had instantly responded to Olivia's call for him to help Lady.

"Mr Bloom. I'm Detective Inspector Paul Hawkins." He shook his hand. "Tell me what you know."

Sebastian led Hawkins and three of the sergeants up to Georgiana and Dan's bedroom and gave them all the information he had, which wasn't much.

"May I move the dog?" he asked. "We didn't want to disturb anything."

Hawkins nodded but indicated that one of his men should do it. When Lady was placed in Sebastian's arms, he rushed downstairs and laid her on the kitchen table where Devon was waiting to examine her.

"What the hell happened?" Devon asked. "Why are the police

here? Where's Georgiana and Dan?" He immediately got to work on Lady.

"Oh my God," Olivia cried. "Dan! You've got to call him," she told Sebastian.

Sebastian grimaced. "What do I say? Your wife has been kidnapped. Come home."

"She's what?" gasped Devon.

"I don't care what you say, Sebastian. He needs to know right now." She started to cry again.

"Darling, take Alexander home. Please?" he begged her. "This is no place for him, and you being this upset isn't good for the babies. You need to call Hattie as well."

"But…" Olivia protested.

"But nothing." He was firm. "We're in the way here."

"Badly broken leg, a very nasty knock on the head and plenty of bruising." Devon fixed a splint to Lady's leg and picked her up in his arms. "I need to get her into surgery."

Olivia sobbed: "Please don't let her die. Georgie will be heartbroken."

"I've no intention of letting that happen," Devon replied gently. "She's going to be ok Liv, try not to worry."

"Mr Bloom." Hawkins entered the kitchen. "Can you escort me around the estate? There's no sign of forced entry at the main gates nor the house. We need to find the entry and exit points."

"Yes, of course. I just need to get hold of my brother-in-law. Can you give me five minutes?" Sebastian walked out of the kitchen and dialled Dan.

"I was just about to call you," Dan said when he answered the phone. "I can't get hold of Georgiana. Her phone keeps going to voicemail."

"You need to come home." Sebastian's voice was shaky. "She's gone missing."

"Missing? What do you mean? I was going to ask you to go and get her out of bed." Dan didn't quite understand what Sebastian was telling him.

"The police are here," Sebastian told him.

"What?" Dan cried. "What's going on?"

"We don't know anything mate, I'm so sorry. Olivia came over when Georgie didn't turn up to look after Alexander this morning and found Lady injured. There were signs of some kind of struggle, but that's as far as we've got."

"Lady? Is she okay?" Dan choked on his words. "I'm on my way. I'll get a chopper."

Sebastian walked back into the kitchen, grim-faced.

"What did he say?" Olivia asked.

"What do you think he said?" Sebastian snapped at her and instantly regretted it when he saw her face. He put his arms around her. "It's going to be ok. They'll find her."

"Mr Bloom. Now, please." Hawkins was keen to move the investigation forward.

"Go home, darling. Call Hattie, she'll know what to do." Sebastian kissed Olivia and followed Hawkins outside.

They jumped into the Range Rover and headed out across the fields closest to the house. They inspected every possible access point until they came to the gate at the very edge of the thousand-acre property. It had been forced open.

"I told them to get that fixed," Sebastian muttered. "It needed replacing," he told Hawkins.

"We checked the CCTV in the house and it doesn't appear to be working." Hawkins shook his head. "Why is that?"

"They've only just moved in." Sebastian put his head in his hands. "And if there was no sign of forced entry into the house then that's probably because my sister is too damn trusting. We've lived here our whole lives and it's always been safe, so I doubt she'll have checked all the doors and windows."

Hawkins barked instructions into his radio. "Send a team out to our location." He looked at Sebastian. "Forensics will find evidence, if there is any."

Sebastian nodded. His emotions were on the verge of taking over and he was unable to speak.

"Where was your sister's husband last night?" Hawkins asked.

Sebastian looked at him, wide-eyed. "Why? You can't possibly think he had anything to do with this?"

"We can't rule out anyone just yet." Hawkins stared at him, looking for an answer.

"For fuck's sake," Sebastian snarled. "He was on live television and there's about ten million people who can confirm that."

"Would he have any reason to hurt her?" Hawkins probed deeper.

"They've just got married. I've never seen two people more in love. That's a fucking ridiculous thing to ask," he growled.

"Where is he now?" Hawkins was making notes on his pad.

"On his way. He said he was going to get a chopper back from London, so he'll be here within the hour."

"We need to see him straight away, but right now I'd like to know if there's anyone who is holding a grudge against Mrs Flowers, or her husband. You even?" Hawkins asked. "It doesn't matter how insignificant, we just need to know. It will help with the investigation."

It suddenly hit him. He looked at Hawkins, pale-faced. "Wyatt Clayton."

"The American property billionaire?" Hawkins was surprised.

"He and my sister had a fling a while back, before she met Dan. He was also behind the development of my club." Sebastian shook his head. "I should have known straight away. He's definitely capable of something like this."

"I sense there's more to this story. Go on," Hawkins urged.

"We won our court case against him, bought a load of shares in his company and ousted him from the board three days ago. Georgiana was the one who called for a vote of no confidence."

"That's what they call motive, Mr Bloom. Thank you. I'll drop you back at the house, and I suggest you wait for Mr Flowers to arrive and bring him straight to me."

"Sure," Sebastian mumbled. His desperation was growing with every passing second.

Back at the house the forensic team was investigating every inch of every room, looking for clues, fingerprints, and anything else that would indicate what had happened.

Sebastian sat down in the kitchen and called Olivia. "Are you ok?"

"No," she mumbled. "Hattie's just got home. She's in shock. What's going on there?'

"The gates at the Bears Bridge road entrance were forced open. I bloody told Dan to get them fixed a hundred times."

"Oh my God," Olivia gasped. "What about CCTV?"

"Either not working or disabled," he replied. "Look darling, I've got to go. Dan should be arriving any minute. I'll call you as soon as I know more."

Sebastian heard the chopper overhead and ran outside to meet it as it landed on the front lawn. Dan opened the door and sprinted towards him.

"Well?' he said as he reached Sebastian.

"Nothing new I'm afraid." He hugged Dan. "We'll find her, I promise."

Dan was desperate. "I can't lose her. I just can't."

"She's going to be ok," Sebastian repeated.

"You don't know that," Dan choked.

"Hawkins, the DI in charge, wants to see you. Let's talk to him and then go back to the manor. We're in the way here." Sebastian led Dan over to where Hawkins was deep in conversation with his team.

"Ah, Mr Flowers." He stepped forward to shake Dan's hand. "Tell me what you know about Wyatt Clayton."

Dan looked at Sebastian in shock. "What? You think this was him?"

"It's a strong line of enquiry Mr Flowers. We've checked with the Home Office and it would appear that he entered the country yesterday on a private flight."

"I'll fucking kill him," Dan yelled. "If he lays a hand on her, I'll fucking take him apart."

Sebastian held him back. "Calm down. This isn't helping."

"Don't tell me to calm down." Dan shrugged Sebastian's hand off his shoulder. "I doubt you'd be very calm if it was Liv."

Sebastian sighed. "You're right, of course. But let's let them do their job, eh?"

"Where's Lady?" he asked shakily.

"Devon is operating on her leg," Sebastian said. "Don't worry. He said she'll be fine and I trust him."

"Thank God for that at least." Dan knew that losing Lady would break Georgiana's heart, and he was relieved that it was one less thing to worry about.

"Can we go?" Sebastian asked Hawkins.

"Yes. But stay close. We may need more information from you. We're going to start the door to door investigation in the next half an hour. It's possible someone saw something." Hawkins phone rang and he stepped away to answer it.

"Let's go." Sebastian bundled Dan into his car and drove back to the manor where Olivia and Hattie were desperately waiting for news.

Olivia hugged Dan as soon as he got out of the car. "Are you ok?" she asked.

"No," he croaked. "What if we don't find her?"

"We will," Hattie said sharply.

Sebastian put a calming hand on her arm. "Let's go inside and I'll fill you in on the latest. We're of no use anywhere else. It's just a waiting game now."

They followed him inside to begin the long, excruciatingly painful wait for news of Georgiana.

CHAPTER 108

The shocking news of Georgiana's suspected kidnapping was all over the village, even before the police started going door to door. Devon had quickly filled Patrick in when he got back from Avalon House with Lady.

Patrick immediately sent Dee Dee a text, and she replied saying that she was completely shocked and had wondered what all the police cars were for.

Dee Dee told Susie and Tom, who in turn alerted Peter, Andrea, Will and Peppy. None of them could fully comprehend what had happened to Georgiana and they were impatient to help.

"Can we do anything?" Tom asked as they gathered outside the pub.

"I doubt it," Peter replied. "Not unless anyone saw anything unusual."

"There was a rusty transit van parked on the green yesterday for a while,' Dee Dee replied. "I think I remember some of the number plate. Do you think that's got anything to do with it?"

"You need to tell the police straight away," Tom replied. "It could be significant."

"Poor girl," Jane choked. "Poor Dan."

"That family has had enough tragedy already," Patrick shook his head. "It's so unfair."

"We don't know anything yet," Susie patted his arm. "Let's not presume the worst."

"She's a little fighter, she'll be ok." Will didn't sound convinced.

"The police are at your door," Tom said to Dee Dee. "Better get over there and tell them about the van. Let's reconvene here this afternoon and see if there's anything we can do. They may want to organise a search party."

They all nodded in agreement and dispersed to await their turn to be questioned by the police, whose numbers were increasing by the hour.

By ten o'clock that evening there was still no word. Sebastian turned on BBC news and listened as Fiona Bruce broke the story.

"There's a nationwide hunt on this evening as police investigate the disappearance of Georgiana Flowers. The BBC sports presenter was reported missing earlier today after signs of a struggle at the home she shares with her husband, Oscar winning actor Dan Flowers, in Appleton Vale, West Chesterton. The police are appealing for any witnesses who may have seen a white transit van in the vicinity of the village or surrounding areas in the last twenty-four hours."

The footage cut to Detective Inspector Hawkins. "We're investigating the disappearance of Georgiana Flowers and are appealing for anyone with even the smallest piece of information to come forward. We're searching for a white transit van with a partial number plate KY02 that was seen in the village yesterday.

Please call the number at the bottom of the screen if you have any information that may help our investigation."

A recent photograph of Georgiana flashed up on the screen and Olivia started to cry again. A thick fog of despair had descended on the manor as the day had worn on. Not having anything new to go on was killing them all.

Will had turned up on the doorstep at three o'clock and Dan's parents, Claudia and Francis, arrived an hour later. By nine o'clock the media had set up camp outside both Appleton Manor and Avalon House, and were crawling all over the village looking for residents to interview. As usual, the tight-knit community clammed up and sent the paparazzi packing.

At nine thirty, Hawkins arrived at the manor to update the family. "We really don't have much in the way of leads right now. As you know, Mr Clayton entered the country yesterday morning but we're still trying to trace his movements once he left the airport. We've got a team working on that right now and we're using every available resource to aid the investigation."

"Every available resource? What the hell does that mean?" Dan growled.

"We're fully engaged in the investigation Mr Flowers. We're doing everything we can to get your wife back," Hawkins replied.

"Are you sure it's him?" Sebastian asked. "What if you're missing something? What if it's not him? Why haven't we had a ransom demand?"

"That's precisely why we do think Mr Clayton is involved. There hasn't been any sort of ransom demand, and we would have definitely received one by now had that been the case," Hawkins told him.

"So, what now?" Dan said wearily.

"I'll be back with another update as soon as we get something," Hawkins replied. "For now, just hang tight."

"Hang tight?" Hattie cried. "My baby girl is in danger and you're telling us to hang tight?"

Will rushed to her side and put his arms around her. "It's just an expression. I've been in enough scrapes with Porg over the years to know that she can fight her way out of anything. She can hold her own."

"Not if she's bound and gagged she can't," Dan muttered. He walked across the room and poured himself a large scotch. "Anyone else?"

"Drinking isn't going to help, Daniel." Claudia put her hand on his arm to stop him.

He slammed his glass down on the table. "Oh Mum, what am I going to do without her?"

"She's not dead," Sebastian bellowed. "I've got my men on the case as well, and they have access to all sorts of resources. Give it time."

"Time is one thing she doesn't have on her side," Dan snapped. "The longer this goes on, the more likely it is that she'll never come home."

"This isn't a fucking movie script, Dan," Sebastian snarled. "Have a little faith."

"That's not what he meant, darling," Olivia told Sebastian. "Let's not fall out amongst ourselves. We need each other more than ever now."

"Sorry, mate." Sebastian was contrite. "We all want her back as much as you do." He looked at Olivia. "Why don't you go to bed, Liv? You look washed out and the doctor said you have to rest."

"How can I sleep when I know Georgie's in danger?" Olivia replied.

"At least try. Don't make me worry about you as well, please?" Sebastian begged.

"Ok," she replied. "Can you come up with me?"

Sebastian took Olivia up to bed and stayed with her until she fell into an exhausted sleep. When he went back downstairs, he found Dan pacing the hallway.

"I'm so sorry," he told Sebastian. "I should have been there."

"It was one night. Don't beat yourself up about it. None of us knew he was capable of this." Sebastian put his arm around Dan's shoulder.

"Why didn't she lock up or use the alarm? I keep telling her to be more careful when she's on her own." Dan blamed himself for not pushing her harder. "And it's my fault the CCTV isn't working. I'm upgrading it, so it was offline."

"This is not your fault. Nor anyone else's for that matter," Sebastian reassured him. "Let's go and have that drink. Christ knows I could do with one as well."

They re-joined Hattie, Will and Dan's parents in the sitting room and sat in silence waiting for news. It was a minute past three o'clock in the morning when it finally came.

CHAPTER 109

Georgiana woke up on the floor in the pitch dark. She was groggy and in pain, and it took her a moment to work out that she was locked in a cellar and still very much in danger. Panic washed over her again - Wyatt had stashed her away in some remote location from which she would never return.

She had seen the deranged look in his eyes. He had crossed the line that separated ruthless from downright psychopathic. She tried to stand up but found her legs and arms still bound together. Wyatt had removed the gag, clearly confident that any sound she might make wouldn't be heard, but he didn't trust that she wouldn't try to escape.

"Pull yourself together," she muttered over and over again. She wriggled across the floor until she reached the far wall and used it to help stand up. When she was upright she felt around for anything that could aid in her bid to escape.

"You're not bloody killing me," she muttered.

She ran her hands along the length of the wall and came across a sharp piece of metal sticking out. It was old and rusting, but good enough for Georgiana to use to try and remove her hand ties. She rubbed the rope against the metal shard over and over again, desperately ignoring the excruciating pain of her skin being ripped into. Once her hands were free she bent down and undid the rope around her legs. As her eyes slowly adjusted to the dark, she worked out where the door was and quickly ran over to try it.

It was locked from the outside and could not offer her any escape. There didn't seem to be a window but it was so dark and dingy that she could hardly make anything out. She noticed a large wooden object in the middle of the back wall and went over to investigate. When she peered behind it she realised there was a tiny window – an escape route.

"Oh, thank God," she muttered. She reached for the latch and found that it was painted shut. She climbed up and started to kick it until it sprang open in front of her.

She stuck her head through the open window and wriggled. It was a very tight squeeze and painstakingly slow.

A door slammed above her, and she froze as the sound of footsteps echoed overhead and then down the stairs to where she was being held. Wyatt walked in just as her legs disappeared through the window.

"Fuck," she heard him scream. "You little bitch. You can't get away from me."

Georgiana, unaware of the ditch outside the window, hit the ground with a thud and felt her leg buckle beneath her. She gasped as a shooting pain ripped through her but she ignored it, instead letting her adrenalin take over. She hardly felt a thing as she stumbled away from the house where she was held captive. She could just about make out a line of trees in the distance through the black of the night. She had no idea where they were or if there were any roads nearby, and decided her best bet was to head for cover.

"You can run but you can't hide," Wyatt screamed. "There's nowhere for you to go, so you might as well give up."

Georgiana froze. She didn't want to make a sound and give away her location to Wyatt. She waited five minutes, shaking uncontrollably behind a fallen log, before Wyatt's threats faded into the distance. Assuming he was searching for her in another part of the property she made a run for it.

She had taken only three steps when he jumped out in front of her and knocked her on to the ground with a direct punch to her face. She yelled out in agony and put her hands up to protect herself from the next blow. He pinned her down and fastened her hands behind her back and threw her over his shoulder.

Georgiana screamed for help over and over again as Wyatt carried her back into the house.

"No-one can hear you," he laughed. "It's just you and me babe. That's how it should have been right from the start. Why did you have to reject me like that? This is your own fault. If you had just agreed to be mine we wouldn't be in this mess."

"I'd never agree to be with you," she hissed. "I fucking hate you."

"You weren't saying that when you were letting me screw you like a whore," he snarled. "You loved it."

"I was a fucking idiot," she spat. "The thought of sleeping with you now makes me sick to my stomach."

Wyatt crashed through the back door of the house and headed for the cellar. "Yeah? Let's see if you're still saying that in a minute."

"No!" she shrieked. "Don't you fucking dare touch me." She

lifted her head just enough to reach the back of his neck and bit into it with every ounce of strength she had left in her.

Wyatt screamed in pain and dropped her on the kitchen floor. "You're fucking crazy," he snarled. He looked at her in a heap at his feet and laughed again before repeatedly kicking her in the stomach. She closed her eyes and blacked out.

CHAPTER 110

*A*t three o'clock in the morning Detective Inspector Hawkins returned to the manor with the news they had been waiting for.

"We've arrested the owner of the van, and he happens to be in the employ of Mr Clayton. We're now certain he has Mrs Flowers. We've recovered some CCTV from outside the Riverside Club, time-stamped approximately half past two in the morning. It clearly shows the van speeding away from the village in the direction of Bears Bridge. We've gone as far as we can with the footage, it's fairly remote around here and we don't expect to get anything else on that front."

"Is that it?" Sebastian demanded.

"At the moment sir, yes," Hawkins replied. "We're doing everything we can."

"So you keep saying," Dan grumbled.

Sebastian's phone rang. "Yes?" he snapped. "Right. Send me the information now. Good work."

He looked at Hawkins. "My guys have found something."

"What?" Dan jumped to his feet. "Do they know where she is?"

Sebastian looked at his phone and opened the email his chief of security had sent.

"They've found documents linking Clayton to that crumbling farmhouse on the other side of Bears Bridge." He showed Hawkins the email and watched as he barked orders into his radio.

"Must have bought it the same time he got the club," Sebastian said. "Do you think she's there?"

"We'll know soon enough," Hawkins replied. "Stay here, please. The last thing we need is you interfering. I'm leaving one of my men here to keep you in the loop."

Hawkins ran out of the manor and jumped into the waiting car. Dan followed him before Sebastian caught up with him at the front door.

"Don't." Sebastian put his hand on his shoulder. "Let them do their job. We don't need you getting into trouble. She's going to need you by her side."

"She needs me now," he cried. "She must be terrified. What if he's hurt her, or worse?"

"Georgie's a tough cookie. She'll fight back." Sebastian reassured him.

"That's my worry." Dan choked on his emotions. "She may push him over the edge."

They waited another half-an-hour, both of them glaring at the policeman Hawkins had left at the Manor, willing him to give them some news.

"Oh my God," Hattie wailed from the sitting room. They ran inside to see her pointing at the television.

"This is Sky News. And our breaking story this hour is a major development in the kidnapping of Georgiana Flowers. As you can see from these images, there's an armed siege underway at what we're told is a farmhouse in West Chesterton, just a few miles from Appleton Vale where Georgiana lives with her Oscar-winning husband, Dan Flowers."

The images that flashed up on the screen showed a huge police presence surrounding a remote, run-down building. Firearms were trained on the house, and a police helicopter was hovering overhead with its searchlight fixed firmly on the scene below.

"Oh my God," Hattie cried again.

They were all rooted to the spot, watching in astonishment as the siege played out in front of their eyes.

"Fucking hell," Will muttered.

"Jesus Christ," Francis groaned.

"Oh my God," Hattie repeated.

Dan sat in shocked silence. He couldn't help but think the worst. How could she get out of this alive? There were guns involved. He was convinced he was going to lose the only woman he would ever love.

CHAPTER 111

When Georgiana came round she found she was back in the cellar, bound and gagged. She couldn't move, her leg was agony and her face was stinging from the recent battering. Her hands were sticky with blood and searing with pain. She turned her head to the side and saw Wyatt sitting in the corner.

"And here we are," he smirked. "You, me, a gun and nothing to live for."

Georgiana gulped. Terror ripped through her veins. She knew he was more than capable of shooting her, if it came to it.

"It won't be long now," Wyatt said. He had a distant look in his eyes.

She closed her eyes again and tried desperately to compose herself. Suddenly she heard the unmistakable sound of a helicopter in the distance, and the screaming of sirens drawing ever closer.

Every bone in her body cried out in pain, but her mind was still strong and willed her to hang on just a little while longer. She wanted to close her eyes and drift away, to free herself from the agony of her broken limbs, but she fought to stay awake.

"Wyatt Clayton." A voice crackled through a loud speaker. "We know you're in there. We just want to talk."

Wyatt snapped out of his reverie and stood up. He walked over to Georgiana and undid the rope around her legs. "Get up," he snarled.

She shook her head.

"Get up," he bellowed and reached down to remove the gag from her mouth.

"I can't," she croaked. "My leg is broken."

He stooped down, lifted her over his shoulder and walked up the stairs into the kitchen. He sat her on a chair, and as she looked around she realised he had blacked out the windows and barricaded the door.

"What are you doing?" she whispered. "Don't throw it all away."

"Too late for that babe," he drawled. "There's only one way out of here for me."

"You're crazy. You don't want to die," she choked. "And neither do I."

"If I go, you go." He started to pace up and down, running his fingers through his hair and muttering unintelligible words.

Georgiana stared at him and wondered how she could ever have thought she was in love with a man like him. She was totally and utterly terrified of him and of what he would do to her. She glanced at the gun in his hand, and any morsel of hope she had faded away.

"Wyatt Clayton," the voice repeated through the tannoy. "Come out with your hands above your head. You are surrounded. There's no way out of here."

"Time to go," he snarled at Georgiana. He pulled her up and supported her with one arm, dragged her to the front door, and opened it to find thirty guns trained on his chest.

He pushed Georgiana in front of him and held the gun to her head. "I'd back away if I were you," he snarled. "I said back off," he screamed.

Georgiana felt his grip on her loosen and seized her opportunity. She swung around, grabbed his hands and bit into his arm. Wyatt yelped but didn't let go of the gun. She stared up at him and saw the laughter in his eyes. The next thing she heard was the crack of a gunshot, followed by a searing pain in her stomach.

CHAPTER 112

"Get out of my way," Dan screamed. "Fucking move."

Reporters and television cameras were blocking the entrance and jostling for position as Dan and Sebastian arrived at the hospital. They were met by a police liaison officer who took them directly to a private room where they waited for news on Georgiana's condition.

Dan had spoken to the surgeon on the telephone before they had taken her into the operating theatre, but they still didn't know the true extent of the damage, or even if she would survive. He had described her injuries as life-threatening.

They had watched in horror as the siege played out in front of their eyes on television. When Wyatt appeared at the door with a gun to Georgiana's head, Dan had feared the worst, and when she tackled him for the gun he believed she had been killed.

Dan and Sebastian raced to the farmhouse and found Georgiana was already on her way to hospital in the air ambulance. Wyatt was being treated at the scene – his wounds were superficial, thanks to the expert marksmen in the TACT team who had no intention of letting him take the easy way out.

Dan had wanted to murder Wyatt with his bare hands, but Sebastian dragged him away, bundled him into the car, and headed to the hospital with a police escort. They had a long wait.

"How much longer?" Dan was desperate. Georgiana had been in surgery for almost twelve hours and he was wearing out the carpet with his incessant pacing.

"They said they'd give us an update as soon as they could." Sebastian looked up from replying to text messages. "I've told Hattie there's no point in her and Liv coming here until we know more."

They both jumped as the door opened and the surgeon walked in, straight from the operating theatre. He looked exhausted. "I'm David Peace and I operated on Georgiana. It was touch and go for a short time and the next twenty-four hours will be critical, but she's hanging on in there. She's definitely got some fight in her."

"Is she going to be ok, though?" Dan croaked. Tears were running down his face. The mere thought of losing Georgiana had almost destroyed him.

"I'm hoping so, yes," he nodded his head.

"Thank you so much." Sebastian shook Doctor Peace's hand. "When can we see her?"

"She's in recovery now and we'll be moving her to the intensive care unit shortly," Doctor Peace replied. "Once she's settled, you can see her for a short time. She was very lucky. The bullet lacerated her liver and that took the most time to repair. A millimetre or two to the right and it would have been a different story. She also has a badly broken leg that we needed to pin, four fractured ribs, deep lacerations on her hands and severe bruising to her face and chest."

"Was she awake when she came in? Did she say anything?" Dan was desperate to know everything.

"She was in and out of consciousness, but she did repeat the same few words several times before we got her into surgery," he told Dan. "'It sounded like she was saying 'New York minute.' Does that mean anything to you?"

A ghost of a smile crossed Dan's face. Sebastian looked at him quizzically.

"Somebody's going to emergency, somebody's going to jail." Dan said the line from a verse of the Don Henley song that had inspired his own New York minute.

"Oh, right." Doctor Peace nodded. "I need to get back but one of the nurses will be along soon to take you to see Georgiana. She's had a very lucky escape and is going to need a lot of care. I would also recommend she talks to a therapist. The mental scars from this kind of trauma tend to run very deep, as you can imagine."

Dan walked over and hugged Doctor Peace. "I can't tell you how grateful I am. Thank you so much."

As soon as they were alone he broke down. It had been the longest twenty-four hours of his life, and he had experienced a desperate range of emotions that he never wanted to feel again.

Sebastian dialled the manor. Olivia answered immediately, and he put her on speakerphone so Dan could hear the conversation.

"She's ok." He gulped back his tears. "Critical, but alive."

"Oh, thank God," Olivia cried. Hattie was still wailing in the background.

"The bullet damaged her liver, but they repaired it. She's got a badly broken leg and four fractured ribs, and a host of cuts and bruises," he informed her.

"Have you seen her?" Olivia asked.

"Not yet. Soon, hopefully." He turned around as the door opened. "The nurse is here, hang on."

"Mr Flowers. Mr Bloom. Can you come with me?" the nurse said.

"Got to go, Liv. I'll call you after we've seen her." He ended the call and rushed off after Dan and the nurse to see Georgiana.

"I have to warn you," the nurse said gently. "She doesn't look great, but it's mostly bruising and swelling. It will go away."

Dan gulped as they reached the door to Georgiana's room. He paused for a moment to compose himself and followed the nurse inside. She was hooked up to several machines, with tubes and wires that seemed to entwine her entire body.

He sat down by the side of the bed and reached across to touch her face. She was almost unrecognisable such was the extent of the bruising, but she was alive and would recover in time.

"I'm so sorry," he whispered over and over again. "I love you so much. You can do this. There's no way you're dying on me."

He sat with her for five minutes before the nurse ushered him out. "You can come back later," she told him. "She needs to rest."

"Can I have a minute please?" Sebastian asked her.

She nodded. "One minute. That's your lot."

Sebastian was shocked at Georgiana's appearance. Even though he knew it was superficial it was still hard to take in. He stroked her head. "Don't give up now sweetheart," he muttered. "We need you."

They left Georgiana and walked back to the waiting room together.

"You should go home and check on Liv," Dan told him. "I'm staying here."

Sebastian nodded. "I'll bring you a change of clothes when I come back. I'll only be a few hours. If anything changes, call me immediately." He walked towards the door. "Are you going to be ok on your own? Do you want me to let Hattie loose on the hospital?" Sebastian could afford a joke now the tension had lifted slightly.

"I'll be fine. I'd rather be alone to be honest. At least for a while," Dan replied.

Sebastian nodded. "My security team has two guys posted outside her room, and several others at the entry and exit points. She's safe here."

When Sebastian had gone, Dan sat back down and switched on the television. He wanted to see the news and find out what was being reported. He changed channel to the BBC and found Doctor Peace issuing a short statement to the press outside the hospital.

"In the early hours of this morning we treated a young woman with a serious gunshot wound to her abdomen. We repaired the damage in a twelve-hour surgery, which I am pleased to say went according to plan. She is currently in a critical but stable condition, and our hopes are that she will make a full recovery. There are a number of additional injuries, none of which are life-threatening. That's all we can tell you at this time."

The news report switched back to the studio where Fiona Bruce continued the story. "The American property billionaire, Wyatt Clayton, whose company was recently engaged in a very public battle with The Riverside Club, has been charged with the kidnap and attempted murder of Georgiana Flowers following an armed siege at a derelict farmhouse in Bears Bridge in the early hours of this morning. His motives are still unconfirmed, but it is thought that it was the loss of his company that was the catalyst for such a violent and enraged attack on an innocent woman. We'll bring you more on this story as it develops."

He sat alone for two hours, silently praying that Georgiana would make it through the night and promising that he would protect her forever. Finally, he was told he could sit with her for a while and he rushed upstairs to be by her side.

He brushed a tendril of hair away and kissed her forehead – it was the only part of her face that wasn't bruised.

"We're going to get you better," he whispered. "And I'm never letting you out of my sight again. Please wake up. I need you."

Dan stayed with her for the rest of the night. Doctor Peace checked on her twice, and there were several different nurses monitoring Georgiana's vital signs every half hour.

"She'll be awake soon, you mark my words," the nurse told him. "She's a fighter, this one."

"Hope so." He choked back his tears. She wasn't out of the woods just yet.

Dan was standing at the window watching the sunrise when Georgiana finally came back to him. He heard her moan and turned around to see her trying to open her swollen eyes.

"Oh, thank God." He ran over to the bed. "Hey, gorgeous. Welcome back," he smiled.

She was groggy and disorientated, and kept murmuring unintelligible words. Dan put his ear closer to her mouth. "Say that again, darling."

"Dead?" Georgiana whispered.

"You're not dead. Almost, but not quite." He pressed the call button and waited for the nurse to arrive.

"Lady," Georgiana mumbled. "Dead?"

She struggled to focus on him. Wyatt's vicious attack had broken her cheekbone, and both of her eyes were almost completely closed with the swelling.

Dan smiled and stroked her hair. "She's fine. I promise. Devon saved her."

Doctor Peace strode into the room. "Ah," he smiled. "I see you're back with us, Georgiana." He checked her chart and was satisfied with her progress. "We're off the critical list."

"Seriously?" Dan gasped.

"She's going to have to stay for a while, but yes, I believe we're heading in the right direction," he beamed. He spoke to Georgiana. "I'm David Peace. I operated on your bullet wound and fixed a few other bits while I was at it. You need to rest. I'll be back to see you in a few hours."

The nurses fussed around Georgiana for a few minutes and then left them alone again.

"Hurts," Georgiana whispered.

"I know darling. If I could take the pain away from you I would. Go back to sleep. I'll be here when you wake up." He kissed her head.

"Don't go," she murmured. "Don't want to be alone."

"I'm going nowhere, Mrs Flowers," Dan smiled. "And I'm never leaving you alone again."

Georgiana was asleep in seconds. Dan picked up his phone and sent Sebastian a text message.

She's out of the woods! She woke up briefly and asked about Lady. Doc says she'll hopefully be out of intensive care this afternoon. I'm so bloody relieved. I'll call you when she's more lucid. You'll be able to see her later.

He put his phone away and stared at Georgiana as she slept, thanking God for bringing her back to him. He laid his head on the bed next to her bandaged hand and closed his eyes. He had been awake for almost three full days and had finally run out of steam.

CHAPTER 113

Georgiana had woken up on and off that first day. She was for the most part incoherent, but she seemed to be aware that Dan was by her side. She kept asking about Lady, not quite understanding that she was alive and recovering well.

"She's hard as nails, just like her mum," Dan told her.

The next morning, she was moved out of intensive care and allowed short visits from family members. Sebastian, Olivia and Hattie arrived just after lunchtime and took it in turns to spend a few minutes with her.

Hattie went in first and came out sobbing. "My poor girl. Look at her, she's broken."

"And she'll mend." Olivia hugged her. She went in next.

"Hi sweetheart," she smiled at Georgiana. "You were so brave."

"Stupid," she whispered.

"Well, maybe a little, but that's just how you roll," Olivia laughed. "Dan hasn't left your side. He's devastated about not being there."

"Stupid," she mumbled again. "Not his fault."

Sebastian tapped on the window and pointed at the nurse who was looking stern.

Olivia kissed her head. "You can talk to me when you're ready. I've been where you are, and I promise you'll get over it. Sebastian's here now."

Olivia backed out of the room and Sebastian hovered over Georgiana. "Well, you gave us quite a scare."

"Sorry," she croaked.

"You've nothing to be sorry for. Don't be silly," he replied.

"Wyatt?" She was lucid enough to ask about her captor.

"In jail, where he belongs," Sebastian growled. "But try to forget him for now and concentrate on getting better. I know it's hard, but he can't get to you ever again. I'll make damn sure of that."

"Where's Dan?" she asked.

"Right outside the door. He really needs to come home and get some sleep, but he's refusing to leave you." Sebastian glanced at the door and saw the nurse tapping her watch and glaring at him.

"I'm being turfed out. I'll be back tomorrow. Get some sleep, sweetheart." He kissed her and strode out of the room before the nurse had the opportunity to man-handle him.

Three days later, Georgiana was well enough to be moved to a private clinic near Appleton Vale. An ambulance pulled up outside the service entrance, and unbeknown to the media, she was transferred to the exclusive facility without fuss or intrusion.

Dan employed round-the-clock security and spent every moment he was allowed with his wife. She was sitting up in bed now and was only attached to a drip and heart monitor. She was still finding it difficult to talk with the swelling and fractured cheekbone, but she was completely coherent and managed to give the police a short statement.

"Go home," she urged Dan. "You look terrible."

Dan laughed. "I'm faring a little better than you babe. I don't want to leave you."

"Then send Will over for the night. He'll look after me. You really need to have a decent sleep or you'll be no good to me at all."

Dan finally relented and sent Will a text.

G needs you tonight. Can you come over?

Will replied instantly.

Tell Porg I'm on my way!

Will had seen her twice in the last few days. After his first visit, he had raged to Dan at her stupidity and said he wanted to murder Wyatt for putting her through so much pain.

He arrived at the hospital an hour later, and Dan finally went home. It was a hive of activity at Avalon House when he arrived. Sebastian's security team was busy turning the place into Fort Knox. Door and window locks had been replaced with fingerprint access pads, CCTV covered every inch of the estate, and the whole system was set to back-up on a generator. Footage would also be streamed to an external server, and the state-of-the-art alarm system connected to both the private security team and the police directly.

The entire property's boundaries were reinforced, and the gate that Wyatt had used to get in was now completely closed off with a ten-foot brick wall in its stead.

"I've got them upgrading the Manor as well," Sebastian said. "We've all been a bit lapse."

"I'm never leaving her on her own again. Ever," Dan muttered. "I'm going to the cottage." He desperately needed to sleep, and there was just too much noise for him to do that at the house.

He woke in a start when the sunlight seeped through the window early the next morning. He had passed out on the bed as soon as he got back to the cottage and slept all night. He reached over and picked up his mobile to check for any messages, and then sent Will a text.

Sorry mate. Really didn't mean to sleep that long. Tell G I'll be over in half an hour.

He quickly showered and downed some coffee before heading back to the clinic. As he pulled up to the gates, he was met with a throng of reporters and paparazzi. Maddie had put out a brief statement the day after Georgiana's surgery asking for privacy, but the request had clearly been ignored. It had taken a few days, but they had finally found out where Georgiana was.

He sped through the gates and immediately went in search of the general manager, Christopher Tate. He found him in his office.

"I want to take her home," Dan blurted out. "The press is on your doorstep and I want my wife to recuperate in peace."

"I would advise against that, Mr Flowers," Tate replied gently. "Georgiana needs round-the-clock care for at least another week. She's quite safe here. They can't get in, and your own security people are here as well."

"I don't care," Dan growled. "Tell me what we need and I'll get it sorted out today. Give me a list of equipment and find me a nursing team that we can have at home."

"I can't stop you. It's a private facility, you're free to go whenever you choose. I'm just saying that it is against our advice. Why don't you discuss it with your wife before you make any final decisions?" Tate urged Dan to reconsider, but he was adamant.

He left Tate and went back to the car to pick up a special package he knew would make Georgiana's day.

"Morning, gorgeous," he grinned as he entered the room. "Thanks for staying last night," he said to Will.

"We had a riot," Will laughed. "She got high on drugs and refused to share them with me. Then she slept, and I played Nintendo. Rock and roll!" He looked at his watch. "Got to go, see you tomorrow Porg. Love you."

"How are you feeling, babe?" Dan walked over and kissed her.

Georgiana looked miserable. "Ok," she mumbled.

"I have something that will cheer you up." He lifted the cover off the crate and opened the door. Lady squealed when she saw her mistress and scrabbled around to try to get to her. Dan gently lifted her out and put her on the bed next to Georgiana.

She touched Lady's head with her fingers. "Thank you," she whispered to Dan. Tears were pouring down her cheeks, but she managed a crooked smile.

"Devon didn't want me to bring her, but I did anyway. I wanted you to see for yourself that she's ok." Dan wiped away her tears. "Don't let the bloody nurse see, she'll go bonkers."

Georgiana stroked Lady's head, and the little dog sighed contentedly.

"How would you feel about coming home today?" Dan asked gently.

"Really?" She was surprised. "Am I allowed?"

"Technically speaking, no. But if we get the right gear and some shit-hot nursing staff there's no reason why we can't," Dan said. "What do you think?"

She nodded her head. "Yes, please."

"We can go to the manor if you aren't ready to be at home. Or the cottage?" Dan was conscious that she may be reticent to return to the scene of her assault so quickly.

"Home." She was defiant. "It's our house and I'm not going to let him ruin it for me."

Dan sighed with relief. He wanted her home more than anything. "That's my girl. I'll let Tate know and get it sorted. I'll have you home by supper time."

He stepped outside the room to make some calls and set the wheels in motion. Georgiana was thankful for the time alone. She stroked Lady and immediately felt more relaxed. "Thank you, little one," she murmured. "I'm so sorry you got hurt, but you were so brave. And I've got a broken leg too, so we're matching now."

Lady stuck out her tongue and licked Georgiana's fingers.

She was trying hard to be upbeat for Dan and the rest of her family, but it was beginning to take its toll. She was in agony, her mind was overrun with darkness and consumed with terror. She had hardly been alone since her attack, and her only solace was when she slept. The drugs helped dull her mind and took the edge off the pain, but nothing could stop the anxiety that coursed through her entire body.

Dan bounced back into the room a few minutes later with a

broad smile plastered across his face. "All sorted. You'll heal more quickly at home, and your bruises are fading already. You'll be back to your beautiful self in no time at all."

She didn't respond.

"Talk to me Georgiana. Please don't bottle it up." Dan pleaded with her.

"Would you mind leaving me alone for a while?" she whispered.

"Oh," Dan was surprised. "Don't you want me here?"

"Not right now, no." she mumbled. She reached for the button that controlled her pain relief and pressed it. She began to feel its effects almost immediately and closed her eyes, willing herself to sleep and block out the demons that invaded her every waking thought.

Dan's concern for her mental health was growing, and no matter how much of a front she put on he knew her too well to believe the charade.

He bent down, kissed her cheek and lifted Lady back into the crate. He spoke to the security guard outside the room. "Do not leave this room for even a second. No one comes in except family and the nursing staff." The guard nodded his agreement.

"And contact me immediately if anything changes at all." Dan walked away, his heart heavy with worry and desperation. He was determined to move heaven and earth to get Georgiana well again.

CHAPTER 114

"*A*re you sure you're ready?" Olivia was holding a mirror in her hands as she sat on the edge of Georgiana's bed. "It's not pretty, but you look a hell of a lot better than you did a few days ago."

Georgiana had been transferred to Avalon House under the cover of darkness to avoid the paparazzi getting wind of her movements. One of the ground floor sitting rooms had been turned into a state-of-the-art hospital bedroom, and she was greeted by a team of three nurses that would care for her and monitor her progress for the next week.

She had purposely avoided looking at her face until now. She nodded, and Olivia turned the mirror around.

"Shit," she gasped. "I look like I've gone ten rounds with Rocky Balboa."

"The swelling has gone down a lot already," Olivia told her.

Georgiana's bandages had been removed from her hands, and the stitches were now only covered with light dressings. She reached up and touched her face. "He really did a number on me, didn't he?"

"Don't think about that for now. Just concentrate on getting better." Olivia patted her hand and got up to leave. "Do you need anything before I go?'

Georgiana looked at Lady in the basket on the floor. "Can you put Lady on the bed? She wants to be with me."

Olivia lifted the little dog and placed her next to Georgiana, and watched as they both relaxed when they were together. They were all worried about her state of mind, but she refused to talk to anyone about what she had been through, despite their many attempts.

"I'm here if you want to talk," Olivia said gently. She was halfway through the door when she heard Georgiana croak her response. "How did you get through it?"

Olivia had suffered a similar fate at the hands of her ex-partner, who had beaten her in a drunken rage and left her for dead.

"In the beginning, I cried a lot and was so angry I wanted to kill him. I was also terrified he would come back and finish the job. That feeling took a long time to go away, even when he was in jail and I knew I was safe." Olivia sat back down on the bed. "I was like you. I didn't want or need help, or so I thought. But you can't keep it all inside. What he did to you was horrific and evil, but you of all people won't let him win. Just give it a little time." Olivia stroked her head. "This is a very good first step."

"Can we talk some more tomorrow?" Georgiana mumbled. "I'm tired."

"Of course. Any time you like sweetheart. Get some sleep and I'll see you later." Olivia left her alone and went in search of Dan. She found him in the kitchen sifting through hundreds of cards and unwrapping gorgeous bouquets of flowers that friends and well-wishers had been sending to Georgiana on a daily basis.

"These just came from Harry and Meghan." He pointed to a beautiful bouquet of white roses in a vase on the table. "They said they were devastated for Georgiana and sad that we would miss their wedding."

"That's lovely," Olivia smiled.

"People need to stop sending flowers now," Dan sighed. "Can we give these to the local nursing home or something? How did the great unveiling go?" He wanted to know how Georgiana had reacted to seeing herself in the mirror.

"Actually, not too badly considering," Olivia replied. "The good news is that I think she's ready to talk. She asked me a few questions about my own experiences and wants to chat again tomorrow, so fingers crossed, eh?"

Dan was relieved. "Seriously? That's great."

Olivia nodded. "I know you want her to talk to you, but she isn't ready yet. Give her a chance to reconcile it in her head. I'll do what I can, and if we think she needs some professional help we'll get it as and when the time comes."

Dan jumped up and hugged Olivia. "Thanks, Liv. I just want her to get better. I don't care how it happens."

After Olivia left, Dan went and watched Georgiana sleep for a few minutes. She was so distant and he couldn't help but think she was slipping away from him. Nothing he did or said made any difference to her frame of mind. He had no idea how to get through to her. He blamed himself for not being there to protect her when she needed him the most.

He had cancelled his entire schedule, pulled out of two films and refused to undertake any promotional work for the foreseeable future. Nothing would take him away from Georgiana.

Over the next few days Georgiana spent hours talking with Olivia and she was beginning to feel a little brighter. She still didn't want to talk to Dan, but she was grateful for the love and attention he was lavishing on her. He had been trying so hard and she had pushed him away for reasons not even she could fathom.

She was lying on a sun lounger in the garden with Olivia, enjoying the feeling of the warm sunshine on her skin. The bullet wound, stitches in her hands and broken leg had forced her into a wheelchair, but she was grateful she could move around the house. Lady was also taking advantage of the wheels as her leg mended, and spent most of her time on Georgiana's lap.

"I think I need a therapist," she sighed. "You've been brilliant, but there are feelings I can't explain that might be best dealt with by a professional."

"I think that's a wonderful idea. Sebastian has got a fantastic lady on stand-by. Lara the Latvian," Olivia replied.

Georgiana glared at her.

"Don't look at me like that," Olivia groaned. "He knew you'd come around eventually. He just wanted to be ready when you did."

"You'd better send her in then." Georgiana shrugged her shoulders. "I'm in danger of losing my husband if I don't sort myself out."

"Oh, don't be ridiculous," Olivia exclaimed. "He's bonkers about you. All he wants is for you to get better. He understands that you need time, so stop being so hard on yourself, and on him."

"I hate feeling like this," she sighed. "I just want everything to be normal again. This is supposed to be the happiest time of our lives and look what happened."

Olivia reached for Georgiana's hand. "Speak to the therapist and then find a way to talk to Dan. I've got to go, I'm afraid. We've got a scan at lunchtime and Sebastian's away from tomorrow, so it has to be today. Do you want me to pop back later?"

"No, I'll be fine." Georgiana squeezed Olivia's hand. "Thanks."

"Don't be silly," Olivia smiled. "Us Blooms look after each other. It's your turn right now, but in a few months I'm going to need all the help I can get when the babies are born, so you'd better buck up your ideas and get well quickly."

"Can you send Dan out, please?" Georgiana shouted as Olivia headed back into the house.

Dan appeared almost instantly. "You rang m'lady?" he grinned.

"Will you sit with me?" she asked.

Dan slid onto the sun lounger and propped himself up on one elbow. "Nothing would please me more."

"I've asked Liv to send the therapist over," she mumbled. "I'm sorry I can't talk it through with you but I want to get better, so it's worth a go."

Dan leaned over and kissed her on the cheek. "I'm so glad."

"I'm sorry I've been horrible to you." She was ashamed that she had pushed him away. "Can you forgive me?"

Dan snorted. "Forgive you? For what?"

"For being stupid. For not locking the doors. For not putting the alarm on. For thinking I was Wonder Woman and tackling him for the gun. For everything. I'm so sorry." She burst into tears.

Dan pulled her closer and wrapped his arms around her. "You'd look awesome in a Wonder Woman outfit."

Georgiana laughed through her tears. "Trust that to be your first thought."

"Always," he smirked. "Although I don't think you're quite up to it yet."

"You could kiss me though." She tilted her head towards him. "Properly."

"Are you sure it won't hurt?" Dan was concerned.

"There's nothing wrong with my lips." She put her hands on his face. "It's just the rest of me you need to be careful with."

Dan didn't need asking twice. He pressed his lips against Georgiana's and felt her respond tentatively.

"That's so much better," she mumbled into his chest. "I love you."

Dan would have jumped to his feet with joy had he not been holding her in his arms. It was the first time she had told him that she loved him since the attack.

"Thank you for loving me." She reached up and kissed him again.

"It's not a choice," he grinned. "My DNA is hardwired to love you forever."

CHAPTER 115

Over the next week Georgiana and Dan fell into a routine. She saw the therapist in the mornings, after Dan had helped her bathe and dress. They ate lunch, provided by Hattie's daily visits, after which she slept for a few hours, and they spent the afternoons reading on the sofa or in the gardens enjoying the early summer weather.

She was slowly improving with the help of Lara the Latvian. It hadn't been easy when she asked Georgiana to take her through the attack step by step, but ever since that session the fog was beginning to lift. But she still had bouts of tremendous darkness and couldn't yet find a way to reconnect properly with Dan.

"You ready?" Dan held the crutches in front of her.

"Try and stop me," she laughed. "Freedom!"

The stitches in her hands had been removed the previous day and Georgiana was desperate to regain a semblance of independence. The swelling and bruises on her face had all but disappeared, her leg no longer ached incessantly, and the stitches from the gunshot wound were due to be taken out later that day.

Her broken cheekbone was also mending well. The only thing that was holding her back was the pain from her ribs, but there was nothing she could do about that other than rest and beg Dan not to make her laugh.

"Just take it easy," he said gently.

"I'm a whizz on crutches," she grinned and hobbled around the room. "You forget how many bones I've broken riding. I'm a pro."

"Are you ready to face the world yet?" Dan was hopeful that she would want to see her friends soon. So far, she had refused to have visitors, but now her appearance was almost back to normal she was running out of excuses.

"No." She hobbled towards the door.

"Where are you going?" Dan started to follow her.

"For a stumble around the garden with Lady," she replied, already heading outside.

"Hang on, I'll come," Dan shouted after her.

"I'll be fine on my own." She shut him down.

"And there you go again," he muttered under his breath. "Pushing me away."

Whilst Georgiana was in the garden, Dan sat in the kitchen and opened the laptop to Skype his mother.

"Hi," he croaked when she appeared on the screen.

"How are you, darling?" Claudia's face was etched with concern. "How's Georgiana?"

Dan started to cry. "I don't know what to say to her or how to help her. What do I do Mum?"

"Oh darling," she cried. "I hate seeing you like this. Do you want me to come down? Maybe I can help out a bit and give you a break?"

"I don't want a break," he moaned. "I want my wife back."

Claudia sighed. "She loves you darling, anyone can see that. She'll come around in her own time, you just need to be there waiting with open arms when she does."

"What if she doesn't?" he whispered.

"Do you remember when I miscarried?" Claudia asked. "Probably not, you were only five, but it was a horrible time. I was very depressed and your father bore the brunt of it. But he was strong enough for the both of us. You need to be strong for Georgiana now. I know you're used to her being able to take care of herself, but this is different. She needs you more now than ever, even if she doesn't know it."

"Thanks, Mum," Dan smiled weakly. "And thanks for offering to come to stay but I don't think she's ready for house guests."

"I'm only a few hours away. I'll be there in a jiffy if you need me. Just promise me you're looking after yourself as well as Georgiana. You look shattered, darling."

"I'm fine, honestly. I just had a moment, but you've talked me off the ledge." Dan smiled again. "You always know exactly the right thing to say."

"Of course I do, I'm your mother," Claudia laughed.

"I'll call you in a day or so. Thanks again, Mum." Dan blew her a kiss and closed the laptop.

He looked out of the window and saw Georgiana in the middle of the garden staring blankly into space. His instinct was to rush out and hold her in his arms, but he was afraid she would push him away. He couldn't bear another rejection right now. Instead, he tormented himself by standing and watching his wife slip further away from him.

CHAPTER 116

"*A*re you sure you'll be ok on your own? I don't want to leave if it's going to be a problem." Dan was standing in the doorway of the kitchen.

"Yes," Georgiana replied. "I said I was fine, didn't I?"

"What you say and what you mean are two very different things," Dan muttered. He was fighting hard to not let Georgiana see how frustrated he was with her.

"It would be easier all round if they came here," he continued.

Georgiana slammed her mug down on the table. "No," she snapped. "No visitors. Just go. Hattie will be here soon anyway."

Dan turned around, closed his eyes and breathed in and out slowly before walking out of the kitchen. No matter how many times he told himself she wasn't angry with him, it still hurt like hell when she used him as a punching bag for her moods.

"I'll only be an hour or so," he shouted with forced cheeriness as he left the house.

When she didn't reply, he was tempted to rush back in and

shake her out of her reverie, but he fought the urge, got into the car and sped down the winding driveway.

He had received a text early that morning from Vinnie, saying that both he and Ken were at the Four Seasons in Bears Bridge and wanted to see him. His first thought had been that it gave him a genuine excuse to leave the house, and then he felt guilty for even thinking it.

He arrived at the hotel fifteen minutes later and passed unnoticed through reception into the lift that took him to the fifth-floor suite that Vinnie was occupying. He knocked on the door and it swung open immediately.

"Hey," he smiled wearily.

Ken gave him a hug before responding: "How you doing, man?"

"I've been better, but it's not about me. Why the hell have you both come over?" Dan walked across the room and hugged Vinnie.

"There was no way you were coming back Stateside, so here we are," Ken grinned. "We've got stuff on hold, decisions to make."

Dan sighed. "I'm not really in the right frame of mind to be making any big decisions."

"Which is why you pay us the big bucks, dude," Vinnie replied. "And yeah, before you ask, we could have done this on the phone, but we're on our way to Romania so figured why not drop in on you at the same time?"

Dan smiled at them both. "Thanks, guys. It's actually really great to see you. How long are you here for?"

"No time at all," Ken replied. "Leaving this afternoon."

"What's in Romania?" Dan asked.

"Your next Oscar," Vinnie grinned. "The writer is agoraphobic, so I suggested we go to him. There's no way anyone else is getting their hands on this script until we've seen it."

"I'm not ready to go back to work yet." Dan flopped down on the sofa.

Vinnie sat down next to him. "We know. But you're gonna to be away a lot longer than we first thought so we gotta make some calls."

Ken opened his iPad and clicked on some files.

"Pre-production starts on the next Orion film in a month," he said. "We're gonna push back on this. How does three months sound?"

Dan shrugged his shoulders. "I don't know. I can't put a time on Georgiana's recovery and I'm not leaving her until she's better." He was adamant. "They can't make the movie without Orion Powell, can they?"

Ken nodded. "You've got studio commitments next month in China and Australia. What are we telling them?"

"Indefinite leave of absence," Dan muttered. "Next."

"'Hidden Voices'," Ken said. "You signed the contract before the wedding and shooting starts in September back in LA."

"Christ" Dan held his head in his hands. "There's no way I'm going to be able to do that."

Vinnie continued. "And Dieter Bremmer is waiting for an answer on the lead for 'Deceptions'. No?"

"No," Dan mumbled. "Sorry, guys. It's just not the right time for anything."

Vinnie groaned. "This is exactly the time you should be making the most of the Oscar win."

"Getting Georgiana better is my priority right now," he replied. "You're just going to have to postpone or cancel whatever we have on the books."

"And what about the Romanian script?" Ken asked. "Will you at least read it if we can wrestle it out of his hands?"

"Sure," Dan nodded his head. "What else?"

Ken pulled out a handful of documents for him to sign and Vinnie spent the next forty-five minutes updating Dan on some contractual issues that had been resolved in his absence.

"You sure you don't want to stay for lunch?" Ken said as Dan checked his watch for the hundredth time. He was itching to get back to Georgiana.

"No, I've got to get back," Dan replied. "It was good to see you both but we really could have done this on the phone."

Vinnie was grave-faced. "We needed to see how you were. And you look like crap by the way."

Dan laughed. "Ever the charmer, Vin."

Ken grabbed his arm. "We're worried about you. Everyone is."

"I'm fine, honestly. But Georgiana has to come first right now." Dan was wretched. He hated letting people down and hoped they would understand his situation.

"We get it," Ken said. "Just try to look after yourself as well."

"Yes, sir." Dan mock saluted him and turned to leave. "And if that script is any good I'll look at it. I promise."

"You'd be mad not to," Vinnie grinned. "Thanks for stopping by, and give our best to Georgiana."

On the drive home Dan was overcome with emotion and pulled in on the side of the road. He stared into the distance with tears running down his face and allowed himself to indulge in a few moments of self-pity. He was having to be so strong for Georgiana, pushing his own feelings aside whilst she dealt with hers, and the effort was too much.

He realised he wasn't just desperately worried about Georgiana, but he was also incredibly angry. Angry at Wyatt; angry at Georgiana's recklessness and subsequent slip into severe depression; angry at himself for letting her down and not being with her when she needed him the most, and now he was angry that he was bemoaning his own misfortunes when Georgiana was going through absolute hell.

He didn't care about work. He was never in it for the fame, and had made more money than he could ever dream of – plenty enough for them to live in luxury for the rest of their lives. He wasn't happy about letting down the directors of two movies he had signed on to do, but he could live with it. What he couldn't live with was if the vivacious, fun-loving, delightful woman he had fallen head over heels in love with never came back to him.

Georgiana was alone for the first time since the attack. Completely alone. There was no one else in the house. She had been waiting for this moment since she was able to get around on crutches and now it had come she was terrified.

She had deliberately avoided going back into their bedroom after coming home from hospital, but she knew she had to face it at some point and she wanted to do it alone. She couldn't let Dan or anyone else see how frightened she still was.

She took the stairs slowly and carefully, each step an effort. She paused at the top and stared at the double doors in front of her in trepidation. She hobbled towards the bedroom and placed her fingertips against the new key pad that had been installed. She heard a lock click and she pressed down on the handle and swung open the door.

Once she stepped inside, she stopped and looked around. Nothing seemed different or out of place. There were no signs of any sort of struggle – it was as if it never happened. She faced the door to her bathroom and held her breath. This was where she thought she might die, where she imagined Lady had been murdered.

The only change in the room was the significant increase in security that included a deadlock and bolts on the back of the door which was so heavy she could only imagine it had been reinforced with steel.

In an instant, she was crippled with anxiety and began to relive the trauma of that night in her head. Her crutches dropped to the floor and Georgiana slumped down next to them and curled up in a ball in the corner, in exactly the spot where she had been when Wyatt had broken through and abducted her.

All she could see was his face and hear his tormenting words repeating over and over again in her head. She was overwhelmed with fear.

When she heard a noise downstairs she went into a blind panic and lurched across the floor to close and lock the door. She rocked back and forth muttering to herself to stay calm, but her imagination was running wild. All sense of reason had left her, and when she heard footsteps coming up the stairs she began to scream.

"Georgiana, it's me darling. Open the door." Dan knocked on the bathroom door. "Let me in. It's ok, you're safe, I promise."

He waited a few moments for her sobbing to subside and then he heard her moving around. She drew the bolts back and clicked the lock open.

Dan turned the handle and gently pushed open the door. The look of sheer terror on Georgiana's face almost broke his heart.

He dropped down on the floor and held her in his arms as she cried.

"It's ok, you're ok," he whispered over and over again. "I've got you, you're safe."

They sat like that for half an hour until Georgiana found her voice.

"I'm sorry. I thought I could do this on my own. I never for one minute thought it would affect me this much." She looked at Dan wide-eyed.

"I knew I shouldn't have left you," he replied. He was furious with himself.

"It's not your fault," she mumbled into his chest. "It just all came flooding back to me."

"Shall we get out of here and get you somewhere comfortable?" Dan was conscious of her fragility and the injuries that were yet to fully heal.

She nodded, and he helped her to her feet and then swept her up in his arms. Georgiana clung to him as he carried her downstairs and begged him not to leave her alone again.

"I won't, I promise," he reassured her. "What happened to Hattie?"

"She sent a text to say she'd been held up in Fiddlebury and I told her not to worry about coming over. Sorry." She looked contrite. "I knew you wouldn't go if you thought she wasn't coming."

"Did you want me out of your hair?" Dan was wounded.

She nodded and looked ashamed. "I don't know why. Please don't ask me to explain."

"Do you still love me?" Dan asked gently.

"Yes," she exclaimed. "More than anything."

Dan kissed her head and tightened his arms around her. "Well that's ok then, isn't it?"

"I'm sorry," she sniffed. "I thought I was strong but I feel so weak and feeble."

Dan smiled at her. "I'm strong enough for the both of us sweetheart."

She fell asleep in his arms and he watched her for a while before extracting himself without disturbing her. He went into the kitchen and sat at the table with his head in his hands. She wasn't getting better and this latest incident had proven she still needed help.

He sent a text to Lara the Latvian asking her advice. She responded almost immediately, saying she would visit that afternoon, and in the meantime Dan should take Georgiana around each room in the house pointing out the security measures that had been put in place. Lara said that Georgiana needed to know exactly how safe she was in order to control that part of her anxiety and fear.

Dan was thumbing through a script in the chair opposite Georgiana when she woke up. He smiled at her and was relieved to see that she was completely calm again.

"Can I show you something?" he asked.

"Sure," she nodded.

"Come with me." He handed her the crutches and turned her to face the windows in the sitting room. "Look." He pointed at the fingerprint pads. "All the doors and windows have them, and they've all been reinforced so no one can break in. You'd need a tank to get into this house."

They moved from room to room and Dan pointed out the high-tech security at each entry point. He guided her into the room where the CCTV and centre of operations had been set up.

"There are cameras covering every inch of this property. The alarm and panic buttons are linked directly to the police and to our guys, who incidentally are patrolling the perimeter at all times. See?" He pointed out the team on each of the screens. "Even if you were alone in the house, you were never really alone. Do you really think I'd go out and leave you without back-up?"

Georgiana hadn't uttered a word as Dan had taken her around the house. She looked at the screens and all of the equipment in front of her and sighed. "Thank you."

"What for?" Dan asked.

"For all of this." She waved her arms around. "It does make me feel safe. I was being totally irrational before, I know that now."

Dan smiled. "You are safe. One hundred percent safe, and we'll keep the security guys as long as we need to. Forever, if that's what it takes."

"I hope not," she croaked. "I don't want to feel like this anymore. I want to be me again."

"Lara the Latvian is coming over soon." Dan grimaced, waiting for Georgiana to moan that she didn't need Lara any more.

"I think that's a good idea," she smiled weakly.

"Oh, thank God," he muttered. "I love you to the ends of the earth and back, but I'm not equipped to deal with what I witnessed earlier. I will do everything in my power to help you, but Lara is the expert. Please promise me you'll tell her everything that happened today?"

Georgiana nodded. "I promise."

CHAPTER 117

$\mathcal{W}$ill arrived at the imposing gates of Avalon House and pressed the intercom button. He looked up at the CCTV and made faces at the camera as he waited for the gates to swing open.

Dan was waiting for him when he pulled up outside the front door.

"Hey," Will smiled as he got out of the car. "How is she today?"

"Not great." Dan shook his head in despair. "She's been in a pretty dark place for a few days. I can't get her to do anything or see anyone apart from Lara, you and the family."

"She'll be ok," Will replied unconvincingly.

"Will she?" Dan muttered. "She's in the kitchen. Yell if you need me."

Will nodded and walked past him in the direction of the kitchen. He hovered at the doorway and quietly watched as Georgiana stared blankly out of the window, unaware of his presence.

He cleared his throat. "Right, then," he said brightly. "What do you want to do today?"

Georgiana turned around and attempted to smile. "Hi."

Hi," Will replied gently. "How are you feeling?"

"The same as the last time you asked me," she snapped.

"Right," Will sighed. "Do you want to be on your own?"

Georgiana shook her head. "Sorry. I'm just tired." She hobbled across the room and perched on a stool next to him. "Do you think you could take me to see Wednesday?"

Will smiled. "Yes! I can definitely do that."

"She must think I've abandoned her," Georgiana sighed. "I really should have moved her over here, but events kind of got in the way."

"Would it be easier if we brought her to you?" Will didn't want to push Georgiana to do something she wasn't ready for.

She hadn't left the grounds of Avalon House since she had come home from hospital, and no amount of cajoling from Dan or anyone else would make her budge.

"No, it's fine. I want to go." Georgiana reached for her crutches. She was now able to walk using only one for support.

"Ok," Will grinned. "I'll go and tell Dan. Do you want him to come too?"

"No," Georgiana answered sharply. "Just you and me."

Will gulped. Each time he visited Georgiana he sensed a distance growing between her and Dan, and when he tried to bring the issue up with her he was immediately shot down.

He stuck his head into the library where Dan was engrossed in a new script from the same director as Jigsaw Kids. "She wants to go and see Wednesday," Will grinned. "Progress!"

"Seriously?" Dan threw the script down and jumped up to follow him outside.

"Err. No. Sorry." He looked at Dan with wide eyes, "She doesn't want you to come."

The look that crossed Dan's face said it all. "Try not to take it personally," Will said. "She's just trying to find a way to cope."

Dan sat back down and put his head in his hands. "It's hard not to take it personally. I'm living through this nightmare every single day."

"She does love you," Will offered. "She tells me that all the time."

"I know," Dan mumbled, struggling to maintain his composure.

"Let's see how this goes, and then maybe you should think about going on holiday?" Will suggested. "You cut your honeymoon short, so why not finish it somewhere else?"

Dan nodded. "Yeah, maybe. Tell Steve where you're going, please. I want one of the guys with you all the time."

There was absolutely no way Dan was letting Georgiana step one foot off the property without a security detail.

"Yeah, yeah," Will grinned. "They're already in the car waiting to tail me."

"Thanks, Will," his voice was choked. "You've been a really great friend. She's lucky to have you."

"Right back at ya," he laughed. "See you later."

Georgiana was already waiting in the car when Will stepped outside. She was wearing an oversized pair of dark glasses and a baseball cap, and had slid down in the seat as if trying to make herself invisible.

"You ready?" Will asked.

She nodded, and he pulled away from the house with the security team following in the car behind.

When they entered the village, Georgiana hid herself from view. She wasn't ready to face any of her friends or neighbours yet. She breathed a sigh of relief when the gates of the Manor closed behind them.

Will helped her out of the car and across the yard to the paddock where Wednesday was grazing alongside Bray Davis Junior and Kong.

"Jenny says they're inseparable," Will said when Georgiana looked surprised at the donkeys and Wednesday sharing a field.

"She doesn't normally like sharing," Georgiana muttered.

"Well, she seems happy enough to me." Will walked slowly next to her as she headed towards her beloved pony. Wednesday squealed in delight when she recognised her mistress hobbling towards the field. She cantered up to the gate and whickered when Georgiana reached out and stroked her muzzle.

"Hi sweetie," she whispered. "Sorry I've been gone so long."

Will stood back and watched as Georgiana cried into Wednesday's mane. The little pony for once didn't even attempt to bite her, and stood completely still as she clung onto her. After a few minutes, Georgiana stood up straight and wiped away her tears.

"Feel better?" Will asked.

"A bit," she sniffed. "It's nice to have a change of scenery."

"You'll be riding again in no time. I might even join you." Will joked. He had tried riding several times and much preferred to keep his feet firmly on the ground.

"I can't talk to Dan," Georgiana whispered. She looked at Will with tears welling up again.

Will held open his arms and she stepped into his embrace. "You'll be ok Porg. I promise."

"Hope so," she mumbled into his chest.

"He's not pushing you, is he?" Will asked. He was feeling even more protective of Georgiana than usual.

"No!" she cried. "He's being brilliant. He's so patient with me and that just makes me feel worse. I don't understand why I feel like this."

"Have you talked to Lara the Latvian about it?" Will wiped away her tears.

Georgiana nodded. "She said to give it time."

"Well then," Will smiled. "I'm sure Dan knows that too."

"Can you take me back now please? I'm tired." She hobbled back towards the car.

"Sure thing," Will sprinted ahead and opened the door for her.

He dropped her off at Avalon house and watched as she tried to be cheery when Dan greeted her. But Will knew better. She was struggling with an inner turmoil that was threatening to engulf her and he was scared for her.

He drove away with a heavy heart.

CHAPTER 118

"*Well?*" Sebastian asked Emily. "What do you think?"

They were sitting at the kitchen table in the Manor enjoying a magnificent Sunday roast. Emily had arrived earlier, and Sebastian had been itching to discuss Athos with her.

"Are you sure I'm the right person?" Emily asked. "Don't you want to find someone more experienced? I don't know enough about the other parts of the business."

"I told you she'd say that." Olivia smirked. "She's never believed how good she is at her job."

"She is sitting right here," Emily replied. "And Liv is right, but it's still a big move."

Sebastian topped up her wine and leaned back in his chair. "I have utter faith in you. We need someone we trust to represent us on the board of Athos and you need a job. Match made in heaven I'd say."

"I'd have to move to New York, wouldn't I?" Emily took a gulp of wine.

"That's the only down side," Olivia replied.

"Down side?" Emily laughed. "I can't think of anything better right now." She registered the disappointment on Olivia's face. "I'll miss you, of course I will, but I quite fancy a fresh start, work-wise, and I love New York."

Sebastian grinned. "Well that's settled, then. I'll get the paperwork started tomorrow and inform the Board of your appointment. Oh, and you can pretty much name your salary."

"Really?" Emily squeaked.

"Yes, really," Sebastian chuckled. "And the company owns a pretty swanky apartment on the Upper East Side which is yours to use until you find somewhere of your choice."

"And you'll be flying first class," Olivia added.

Emily grabbed both of their hands across the table. "Thank you. You don't know what this means to me."

Olivia laughed. "I think we should be thanking you. You put yourself on the line to help us, so it's only right we do the same in return. And I'll have somewhere to escape to when the kids are driving me potty."

"Girls' weekends in Manhattan. Think of the shopping we can do!" Emily clapped her hands together.

"Oh God," Sebastian groaned. "I've created a monster."

Emily laughed. "I've really got to get my shit together now. No more shagging the boss."

"I don't think you'll be short of admirers in New York." Olivia squeezed her hand. "You deserve to find someone amazing, so maybe this was meant to be. New city, new country, new life. Just don't forget about us when you're flying high over there."

"Never," Emily exclaimed. "I'll be visiting all the time. In fact, I might even rent out the London house and stay down here whenever I'm back. Would that be ok?"

"And this is coming from the woman who said she could never live somewhere this remote or quiet," Olivia grinned. "This village gets us all in the end. You can have Georgie's cottage if you like?"

"This is all a bit too good to be true," Emily frowned. "What's the catch?"

Sebastian snorted. "There's no catch. Take what's being offered with both hands and enjoy it. We love you and we want you to be happy."

Emily feigned shock. "You love me? Well who'd have thought that would ever happen?"

He threw his napkin at her and laughed. "You are part of the family and don't ever forget it. Plus, there's always one of us heading in that direction so you'll be inundated with visitors. Dan and Georgie spend quite a bit of time there for work."

"Speaking of Georgiana, how is she?" Emily hadn't seen her since the attack and she had refused all visitors."

Sebastian shrugged his shoulders. "No change really. She puts on a brave face and she thinks she's fooling us into thinking she's getting better, but she isn't really."

"Poor thing," Emily replied. "And poor Dan. How's he coping?"

"He's doing exactly the same," Olivia sighed. "Pretending he's ok when he must be dying inside. They were so happy and now, this."

"Lara the Latvian will sort her out. I'm sure of it." Sebastian was adamant that all Georgiana needed was to talk it through with a professional.

"It's not always that simple, darling," Olivia replied gently. "We just have to keep supporting her and loving her. That's all we can do. She'll get there in her own good time."

"It took you ages to get back to normal after that bastard tried to kill you," Emily said to Olivia. "It was painful to watch, but you made it back to the light eventually."

"With a lot of help from you. And a ton of booze as I recall." Olivia smiled at Emily. She had been the only person Olivia could bear to have around after her attack, and she knew she wouldn't have recovered without her support.

"I told Dan to take her away," Sebastian said. "They never finished their honeymoon. Maybe getting out of the house will help her."

"What did he say?" Olivia asked.

"He thought it was a good idea and muttered something about a house in the south of France." Sebastian poured himself and Emily some more wine.

"I think that's a brilliant idea," Olivia smiled. "Just what they need."

CHAPTER 119

"We're going away," Dan informed Georgiana as he dropped their suitcases at the front door.

"I don't want to go anywhere," she pouted.

"Well, you don't have a choice." He had been pussyfooting around her for weeks, never knowing what kind of mood she would be in from one day to the next. It was exhausting to watch her lurch from one emotion to another, and painful when she pushed him away. She had moved back into their bed but was distant, and she slept with her back to Dan most of the time.

"You told me that Lara the Latvian said you needed to break the cycle, so I'm doing it for you. We're going and that's that." He picked up the cases and walked out to the waiting car.

"I can't leave Lady." Georgiana had a last-ditch attempt at avoiding the trip.

"She's coming too. I'm not daft enough to try and separate you just yet. Get in the car, please." He held the door open and Georgiana begrudgingly slipped into the back seat.

"Where are we going?" she asked wearily. "I'm not well enough to travel."

Dan wanted to tell her to snap out of it but he held back, as he had been doing more and more often recently. He'd had a session with the therapist in a bid to understand what Georgiana was going through, and she had told him to be prepared to be her punching bag for a while longer. She hadn't been wrong. Georgiana had been taking every raw and angry emotion out on Dan for weeks as she boomeranged from one dark place to the next.

"You're fine to travel. I checked with Doctor Peace and there's no reason we can't go away." Dan reached over and fastened her seatbelt. She glared at him and spent the journey to the airport staring out of the window.

Thirty minutes later they boarded the private jet and flew to Saint-Jean-Cap-Ferret in the south of France. Dan had borrowed the home of an old friend who was slightly paranoid and therefore very hot on security. It was the perfect place for them to reconnect.

As their car drove through the gates of the estate, the brilliant sunshine, cobalt blue sky and tropical flora only served to enhance the beauty of their surroundings. High in the hills of Cap Ferret, the enormous white stone house was enclosed on three sides with high walls, and overlooked the sea at the back of the property. There was a very steep pathway that led directly to a private beach belonging to the house, and a magnificent terrace that was the perfect spot for watching the sun set over the Mediterranean.

Inside was beautifully decorated in soft, warm colours and had a surprisingly cosy atmosphere, given the vastness of the house. The master suite had a balcony facing the sea and an enormous bed positioned to give them the best possible view of the ocean.

"It's lovely." Georgiana wandered from room to room, taking in the exquisite furnishings and paintings. 'Who owns it?"

"Pierre LaConte," Dan replied.

"The director?" Georgiana had heard of the French film director but had no idea he was a friend of Dan's.

"The very same." Dan stepped out onto the terrace and breathed deeply. "Oh yes, this will do nicely."

"It's so pretty." Georgiana slipped her hand into Dan's and they stood in silence for a few moments taking in the view.

"Thank you," she whispered. "For making me come. I feel a bit better just being here."

Dan put his arm around her and kissed her head. "My pleasure. We're going to do absolutely nothing but lie in the sun, relax, eat well and love each other."

"Ok," she murmured. "I can do that."

"Yes, you can," Dan smiled. "Go and get a bikini on and let's have lunch by the pool." He turned her back towards the house.

By the time she returned, Dan had laid out the lunch that had been prepared for them by the housekeeper, Mathildé. He opened a bottle of Chablis and poured two glasses.

"I look awful," she muttered. "I'm like the bride of Frankenstein." She stood in front of him pointing out her scars.

"You look gorgeous to me." Dan kissed her hand.

"Liar," she snapped, and immediately regretted it when she saw the distress on Dan's face. "I'm sorry. I didn't mean that. I don't know what's wrong with me."

Dan wrapped his arms around her and held her close to his chest. "You can bite my head off as much as you like. I'm not going anywhere."

"I'm sick of feeling like this. I want to be me again." She sniffed and wiped her nose on his t-shirt.

"Charming," Dan laughed. "It's a good job I love you. No one else would put up with you blowing your nose on their clothing!"

They ate a lunch of cold meats, salads and freshly baked bread, and enjoyed the delicate and crisp taste of the chilled wine. Georgiana slept by the pool for a few hours after lunch and then disappeared into the garden with Lady. Dan didn't pursue her. He knew he had to let her find her own way, and if that mean shutting him out for hours on end then he could accept it, if he had to.

For the next week, every day was the same. Georgiana slept late and joined Dan for breakfast when she woke. They sat together in the sunshine and talked about inconsequential things that made conversation light and easy. After lunch, she walked around the estate with Lady, and she immersed herself in books in the evenings whilst Dan read through a pile of scripts that Vinnie had sent over.

"Anything good?" Georgiana looked up from her book when Dan flopped down on the sofa.

"Total rubbish." He still wasn't ready to go back to work and was lacking enthusiasm for any of the scripts he had been sent apart from the Romanian one and the second film from the Jigsaw Kids creator. "It'll have to be the best script in the world to take me away from you."

"I'm fine. Don't turn down work on my account." She stuck her nose back in her book.

Dan was exasperated. "You're not fine," he snapped. "In fact, you're far from it. Do you really want me to disappear off on location somewhere for months on end? Because if you do then all you have to do is say."

"It would be easier," she muttered.

"Easier for whom?" Dan exploded. "Certainly not me. I've done everything in my power to help you, yet you continue to act as if I'm an uncomfortable pebble in your shoe that you can't wait to get rid of." He walked towards the door. "I can't help you if you won't let me."

"You have no idea how I feel," she screamed, and launched her book across the room at him.

"That's because you won't fucking tell me," he growled, and ducked out of the way. "I love you Georgiana, but if you continue to push me away there's not much I can do about it. You've been through an evil and traumatic event that you may or may not ever fully get over, but you have a responsibility to me, to your family, and especially to yourself to find a way to cope with it. Right now, I'm the one that needs a break. From you."

He slammed out of the room leaving Georgiana agog. She was fuming at his rant and preferred to stew over it than go and find him to apologise. Dan hated arguing, they both did, but he was always the one to break the deadlock. He could never stay mad at her for more than half an hour, but as Georgiana watched the clock, and as the minutes and hours ticked by, she started to worry.

She went to look for him and found him sitting in the dark on the terrace with a half-drunk bottle of scotch on the table and a glass in his hand.

"I'm sorry," she croaked from behind him. He didn't turn around. She walked forward and put her hand on his shoulder, and he shrugged it off.

"Leave me alone," he said wearily.

Georgiana was shocked. Dan was reliable, dependable, always ready to catch her when she fell, and best of all, the most loving person she had ever met. The coldness in his voice and his demand for her to leave him alone set off a hundred alarm bells in her head. She retreated to the bedroom and spent the night awake and miserable, waiting for him join her. He never came.

When she went downstairs the next morning she asked Mathildé where Dan was. The housekeeper told her he had gone out early and she didn't know where, or when he would be back. Georgiana was distraught. It was her own fault he had gone.

She sat with her legs dangling in the pool, going over everything in her head. Up until this point her mind had been full of Wyatt and what he had done to her. She had no room for Dan. But now, faced with the fear of losing him, Wyatt suddenly seemed insignificant and small.

"Buggered that up, didn't I?" She stroked Lady's head. "Do you think he'll come back?"

"Did you really think I wouldn't?" Dan's accusing voice from behind made her jump. He looked wretched. "I went to the market. I know how much you love those little tartlet things, so I've got you some."

Georgiana stared at him wide-eyed. "I thought you'd finally had enough of me. I wouldn't blame you."

"Don't be ridiculous," he sighed. "Look, Georgiana. I can't say I'm finding any of this easy, but I love you and would never, ever walk out on you. If you don't know that by now, then God help us."

"I'm sorry." She reached for his hand. "Sit with me."

He sat down next to her and dipped his toes in the water. He stared straight ahead and waited for her to speak.

"I love you too," she said in a small voice. "You're the only thing that's kept me going. Please don't give up on me now."

Dan softened. He put his arm around her and she rested her head on his shoulder. "There's no way I'm giving up on you, you bloody idiot. You married me and now you're stuck with me."

"Best thing I ever did," she mumbled.

"What was that?" Dan raised an eyebrow.

"You heard," she smiled. "I'm glad I married you. And to be fair I did warn you that us Blooms are a little crazy at times."

"Is that you saying sorry?" Dan tilted her head towards his so he could look into her eyes.

She nodded, her eyes brimming with tears. "I'm trying really hard."

"I know you are, sweetheart." He brushed his lips against hers.

That afternoon Georgiana pulled on a sun dress and stood in front of Dan. "I think it's time we saw the beach."

"There's no way you're going down that path. It's crazy steep. You won't be able to manage it." He was happy that she had initiated an activity they could do together, but concerned for her wellbeing.

"That's why we have a car, you dick," she laughed. "Even I'm not that stupid."

Dan jumped up and kissed her. "Let's go then."

They spent a glorious afternoon basking in the sunshine on the beach that belonged to the house. It was a tiny stretch of white sand flanked by steep rocks on either side. The entrance from the road was hidden from view and it was the epitome of seclusion. After lunch, hastily prepared and packed by Mathilde, Dan slept and Georgiana, pretending to read her book, watched him.

He looked exhausted and had lost weight. Her attack had affected him more deeply than she could have ever imagined, and until now she hadn't been able to see that. She reached over and stroked his face. "I love you," she whispered.

He stirred and peered at her through one eye. "Are you watching me sleep?"

She nodded. "You look tired."

"But you chose to wake me anyway?" he chuckled. "Come here." He opened his arms and she laid her head on his chest. He drifted off again almost instantly. She could hear his heart beating rhythmically through his chest and was overcome with a surge of love for him. At that moment, she knew she was ready to let him in.

On their way back to the house, Dan could sense a shift in Georgiana's demeanour. She seemed at peace for the first time since her attack. He was reticent to question her newly-found tranquillity, and instead sat back and quietly watched the woman he loved slowly starting to reappear.

"Can we talk?" she said as they climbed out of the car.

"Sure," Dan replied. Inside his stomach was doing backflips. This was the breakthrough he had been waiting for.

They sat on a bench in the garden and she drew her breath, steadying her nerves before speaking.

"I really though he was going to kill me," she whispered. "And I was terrified he was going to rape me. I could handle the beating, but not that. I don't think I would have been able to get past that."

"But he didn't," Dan interrupted.

"No," she looked into his eyes. "He didn't. But he said terrible things about me, and the longer it went on the more inclined I was to believe it. He made me feel like I was nothing, and certainly not worthy of being loved by anyone. That's why I pushed you away. Deep down I thought you'd be better off without me."

Dan opened his mouth to speak.

She held up her hand. "No. Let me finish. There has never been a moment when I doubted your love for me. It was me I was doubting. I thought I was strong, but he managed to chip away just enough to get me wondering. When you're sitting in the dark as someone's prisoner it's easy to let your imagination run away with you.

"Thinking I'd lost Lady was enough to tip me over the edge. It was just me and her for such a long time before you came along and I let her down. But what happened last night made me see what's really important. When you finally snapped – which you had every right to do – I realised that it wasn't only me going through this. It has made your life unbearable as well and I'm so incredibly sorry for that. What happened to me suddenly seemed insignificant in relation to losing you."

"If I'd have known arguing with you would make the difference I'd have done it weeks ago," Dan laughed. His relief was evident.

"I'm not saying I'm over it, but I will get there, I promise." She squeezed his hand.

"I don't expect it to be instantaneous," Dan replied softly. "Thank you for telling me. It's been so hard not knowing what to do or say, or how to help you. Promise me you'll never stop talking to me?"

She reached up and touched his face tenderly. "I promise."

That evening they dined on the terrace overlooking the sea, surrounded by candlelight. A gentle breeze lifted the oppressive heat of the day and the air was heavy with the heady scent of honeysuckle.

Georgiana made an effort with her appearance for the first time since the attack, and she looked radiant. Her hair was glossy and tumbled loosely down her back, and she had applied the lightest make-up - just enough to accentuate her eyes and lips. She wore a simple shift dress and Dan's locket around her neck.

Finally, she took out her wedding and engagement rings and slipped them back onto her finger. She hadn't been able to wear them with the stitches and swelling in her hands, and for reasons unfathomable to her, she hadn't put them back on even when she was able.

They ate an exquisite meal delivered from Le Club Dauphin – one of the best restaurants in Cap Ferret - and they drank a very special bottle of Chateau Margaux that had been a wedding present. Their conversation was light and easy. They reminisced about the wedding and how wonderful it had been, and about their time on Necker Island.

"I wish we'd never left there," Georgiana said wistfully.

"We'll go back," Dan promised. "I owe it to you for dragging you away."

"You didn't drag me away. I go where you go. Remember when I first said that?" Georgiana stood up and held out her hand. "Come to bed."

"Seriously?" Dan was both shocked and delighted. "Are you sure?"

"I'm not quite ready to resume normal vigorous activities, but if you're very gentle with me I think I'll manage it." She touched his face. "It's ok. You won't break me."

He made love to her slowly and more tenderly than she had ever experienced. He was gentle and unselfish, and she cried when he brought her to the height of her climax. It was a moment so intimate and emotional that it touched her very soul. Finally, she had broken through the pain that had consumed her for so long and found her way back to the man she loved.

She woke the next morning feeling refreshed and full of energy. Dan wasn't there but he had left a note on the pillow.

Gone to get breakfast from that little place in the harbour xx

He was waiting for her on the terrace with fresh coffee, a selection of delicious pastries, and a broad smile. "Good morning, Mrs Flowers. Breakfast?"

Georgiana stretched her arms out and yawned. "I slept so well. Didn't wake up at all." She picked up her coffee. "I feel different today. Better. Happy."

"I can see that," he grinned. "Coming here was a good idea."

"Well, yes, that's helped. But it's you who's made me happy." She walked around the table and sat on his knee. "You've been patient and kind, and not once have you pushed me to do anything I wasn't ready for. I was in a very dark place for a while, but I knew you'd be waiting for me when the fog lifted. I'm going to spend the rest of my life showing you how much I love you." She wrapped her arms around his neck and kissed him until they were both breathless.

"Does the rest of your life start right now?" Dan's eyes flared with desire.

"This very second." She took his hand and led him back to bed.

THE END

EPILOGUE

"*R*eady?" Gerry asked Georgiana through her ear piece.

"As I'll ever be," she grinned at the camera.

"Time to dazzle, love," Gerry replied.

Georgiana gulped back her nerves and at looked at Dan for reassurance. He was standing behind one of the cameramen, smiling encouragingly. "You'll be brilliant," he whispered, and blew her a kiss.

She had returned from France revitalised and more in love with Dan than she had ever thought possible. His devotion, constant support, and encouragement had helped her move on from the attack, and she could now talk about it without feeling pain or being crippled with anxiety.

She no longer lived in fear of Wyatt. He was languishing in jail awaiting a trial date as the British government fought an extradition battle with the US Secretary of State. His charge of kidnap and attempted murder meant he would be incarcerated for many years to come, regardless of where he served his sentence.

As time moved forward, so did Georgiana. She felt more like her old self, but also had a new steely determination to live her life to the full – which meant getting back to the job she loved. And now, seven months' after her ordeal, she was finally ready to be in front of the camera again.

"You're cutting it a bit fine," she laughed as John slipped into the seat next to her in the studio.

"Yeah, yeah," he smirked. "It's great to see you."

"It's great to be seen," she beamed. "Let's do this."

Gerry gave the countdown, and then they were on air.

She took a deep breath and began. "The world's eight best players are ready to commence battle in the round-robins, and if I'm honest, I'm just a tiny bit over excited! Welcome to the ATP Tour Tennis Finals, live from the O2 arena in London." She looked directly into the lens and flashed a mega-watt smile. "And may I just take this opportunity to say how happy I am to be here, and to thank you all for your kind messages and good wishes over the last few months."

"Man am I glad to have you back," John joked as the camera panned to him. "You picked a great week too. I've seen some awesome tennis matches over the years', but this season has been outstanding. I don't think I could single out a winner."

"But surely that's why you're here?" Georgiana teased.

"I thought I was here to make you look good," John retorted.

Gerry groaned and put his head in his hands, "Here we go again."

Georgiana giggled and looked over at Dan. He was grinning from ear to ear. "That's my girl," he whispered.

Dear reader,

We hope you enjoyed reading *Flowers In Bloom*. Please take a moment to leave a review, even if it's a short one. Your opinion is important to us.

Discover more books by Anneli Lort at https://www.nextchapter.pub/authors/anneli-lort

Want to know when one of our books is free or discounted for Kindle? Join the newsletter at http://eepurl.com/bqqB3H

Best regards,

Anneli Lort and the Next Chapter Team

You might also like:
The Handfasters by Helen Susan Swift

To read the first chapter for free, head to:
https://www.nextchapter.pub/books/the-handfasters

ABOUT THE AUTHOR

Anneli Lort lived with a charming cast of characters in her head for a number of years before she found the time to sit down and bring them to life in the Appleton Vale series. Once she put pen to paper her imagination was free to create a character driven world of contemporary romance that is packed with drama, and that takes the reader on a rollercoaster ride of emotions from the first page to the last.

Her debut novel, *The Sweet Spot*, topped the Amazon charts in its category within a week of its release, and *Flowers in Bloom* is the much-anticipated follow up in the series.

In a public relations career that spanned more than two decades, Anneli had an access-all-areas pass to some of the greatest sports and entertainment events on the planet, where she saw for herself the tension, drama and emotions that were played out behind the scenes.

While TV audiences around the world watched the excitement unfold, she was there to witness first-hand what really happened before and afterwards – the untold stories the rest of the world never got to see. Using this unique insight into the tangled lives and loves of the A-list, Anneli developed the idea that eventually became *The Sweet Spot*, and has carried that through into *Flowers in Bloom*.

Anneli lives in a village much like her fictional creation - Appleton Vale - that is nestled against the foothills of the South

Downs. She spends her days working in brand communications, writing, walking her dog, riding her horses and rescuing her cats from their latest attempt to prove that they really do have nine lives.

She is currently writing the third book in the Appleton Vale series and is also working on a television drama series.